The
Good O

For millions of readers, John D. MacDonald
is the consummate storyteller of our time.
He is a writer who with his energetic prose,
his sense of character, his skill in describing
every sort of person...makes us keep turning the pages of his novels and short stories.
The thirteen stories in this collection demonstrate how good his best work was at the
very start of his career.

The
Good Old Stuff

Featuring a fascinating introduction detailing
the life and work of

JOHN D. MacDONALD

Fawcett Gold Medal Books
by John D. MacDonald:

ALL THESE CONDEMNED

APRIL EVIL

AREA OF SUSPICION

BALLROOM OF THE SKIES

THE BEACH GIRLS

A BULLET FOR CINDERELLA

CANCEL ALL OUR VOWS

CLEMMIE

CONDOMINIUM

CONTRARY PLEASURE

THE CROSSROADS

THE DAMNED

DEAD LOW TIDE

DEADLY WELCOME

DEATH TRAP

THE DECEIVERS

THE DROWNER

THE END OF THE NIGHT

END OF THE TIGER

THE EXECUTIONERS

THE GIRL, THE GOLD WATCH AND EVERYTHING

The Good Old Stuff

13 Early Stories

John D. MacDonald

**Edited by
Martin H. Greenberg,
Francis M. Nevins, Jr.
Walter and Jean Shine**

FAWCETT GOLD MEDAL • NEW YORK

To the memory of a lot of good men who wrote well for the pulp magazines but had less luck than I

CONTENTS

INTRODUCTION

Francis M. Nevins, Jr.

For millions of readers John D. MacDonald is *the* consummate storyteller of our time, a writer who, with his energetic prose, his vivid sense of character, his all but miraculous skill at describing every sort of person and setting and event with economy, elegance, and total credibility, makes us turn and turn his pages with our minds in awe and our hearts hovering around our Adam's apple. The thirteen stories in this collection demonstrate how fantastically good his best work was at the start of his career.

MacDonald was born in Sharon, Pennsylvania, on July 24, 1916. His father was a strong-willed workaholic who rose Horatio Alger-like from humble origins to become a top executive at a firearms company in Utica, New York. A near-fatal attack of mastoiditis and scarlet fever at age twelve confined young MacDonald to bed for a year, and lack of anything else to do in those days before radio and TV virtually forced him to read or have his mother read to him, huge quantities of books. As soon as he was back on his feet, he began haunting the public library, compulsively devouring every book on the shelves.

After graduating from the Utica Free Academy in 1933, MacDonald took some courses at the University of Pennsylvania's Wharton School of Finance, then transferred to Syracuse University where, in 1938, he received a B.S. in Business Administration. He married fellow Syracuse graduate Dorothy Prentiss the same year, and was awarded an M.B.A. from Harvard Business School in June 1939. After an assortment of jobs that he hated, he accepted a lieutenant's commission in the Army in June 1940, and was assigned to procurement work in Rochester, N.Y. until June 1943, when he was sent overseas to Staff Headquarters, New Delhi, India. A year later he was recruited by the Office of Strategic Services, the forerunner of the CIA, and served in Columbo, Ceylon as a branch commander of an Intelligence detachment, rising to the rank of Lieutenant Colonel.

During the idle times, instead of writing his wife letters that he knew would be heavily censored, MacDonald began writing and sending her short stories. One of these, "Interlude in India," Dorothy sold for $25 to Whit and Hallie Burnett's prestigious *Story Magazine*, in whose July-August 1946 issue it appeared. "I can't describe what it was like," MacDonald said recently, "when I found out that my words had actually sold.... I felt as if I were a fraud...as if I were trying to be something that I wasn't. Then I thought, my goodness, maybe I could actually be one."

At the end of the war MacDonald was entitled to four months of stateside terminal leave with pay before his official discharge. He spent the time behind the typewriter, working harder than ever before in his life, putting in 80 hours a week, cranking out 800,000 words worth of short stories, keeping 30 to 35 yarns in the mail at all times—and selling not a word. Finally, early in 1946, a few of the less-than-first-class pulp mystery magazines like *Detective Tales* and *Mammoth Mystery* began to buy from him, and by the end of the year he had earned about $6,000, enough to support himself and Dorothy and their seven-year-old son in modest style. For the next half-dozen years most of MacDonald's income was from magazines, primarily the great pulps like *Black Mask*, *Dime Detective*, *Doc Savage*, *The Shadow*, and *Mystery Book*, whose gaudy and lurid covers could still be seen on every newsstand in those immediate postwar years. Once in a while a MacDonald story would sell to a slick periodical like *Esquire*, *Liberty*, or *Cosmopolitan* that paid top dollar, but the vast majority of his tales of the late forties and early fifties went to the pulps, and his name became a fixture on those garish covers several times a month. He made so many pulp sales so quickly that some magazines would run two, three, or even four of his stories in a single issue, one under his own byline, and the rest under "house names."

MacDonald was the last great American mystery writer who honed his storytelling skills in the action-detective pulps as Hammett and Chandler and Gardner and Woolrich had done before him. During the half-dozen years after the war he produced more than two hundred pulp tales whose variety in length and content is astonishing. There were two Westerns,[1] at least

[1] One of these, a bizarre revenge story entitled "The Corpse Rides at Dawn" (*Ten-Story Western*, April 1948), was reprinted a few years ago in Damon Knight's anthology *Westerns of the 40s: Classics from the Great Pulps* (Bobbs-Merrill, 1977).

21 sports stories, well over 40 ventures into science fiction,[2] but most of MacDonald's energies during his formative years as a writer were concentrated in the crime-suspense genre, to which he contributed more than 160 stories between 1946 and the early 1950s.[3]

Gingerly turning the now brown-edged pages of those old pulps and tracing MacDonald's apprenticeship as a tale-spinner, we can watch him growing stronger in countless ways in record time. He was writing everything from straight detective stories like "The Simplest Poison" and biter-bit yarns like "Death Writes the Answer" to psychological suspense tales like "Miranda" or thrillers like "Trap for a Tigress." He was writing about disturbed war veterans, professional criminals and gamblers, city cops, country cops, and all sorts of private adventurers, including one or two recognizable prototypes of that perpetually disappointed boat bum and contemporary knight, Travis McGee. He was experimenting with mini-minis of under two thousand words and short novels the length of a Simenon and everything in between. The best of his stories are masterful and the worst marginal, but in grinding them out at breakneck speed he was evolving the uncanny instincts that shape his sixty-plus novels, from *The Brass Cupcake* (1950) to *Cinnamon Skin* (1982).

Several of MacDonald's earliest pulp crime stories were set in the China-Burma-India locales in which he'd spent the war. But magazine editor Babette Rosmond persuaded him to take off the pith helmet and start writing about the United States, and from then on the majority of his stories dealt with the postwar American scene. Indeed MacDonald portrayed more vividly and knowledgeably than any other crime writer the readjustment of American society in general and American business in particular from a war footing to a consumer-oriented peacetime economy, and the redemption and return to the real world of all sorts of warhaunted people on the verge of self-ruination by drink and detachment. Several stories of this sort, such as "They Let Me Live" and "She Cannot Die," are collected here, and even though MacDonald has eliminated or

[2]A selection of MacDonald's old and new science-fiction stories is available in his collection *Other Times, Other Worlds* (Gold Medal, 1978).

[3]The ultimate word in MacDonaldology, giving full publication data on every scrap of his that has appeared in print anywhere, is Walter and Jean Shine's *A Bibliography of the Published Works of John D. MacDonald* (Gainesville: Patrons of the University of Florida Libraries, 1980).

updated some of the topical references that he feels would be lost on today's reader, perhaps enough remains of the ambience of the late forties and early fifties to demonstrate how the best crime fiction of any period bears witness to later generations about the way we lived then.

In 1950 MacDonald had his first novel published, not in hardcover but as a Fawcett Gold Medal paperback original, and throughout that decade and most of the sixties he continued to write paperbacks so prolifically and well that he forced critics and intelligent readers to take notice of a new book-publishing medium that they might otherwise have dismissed as junk. With the debut of his series character Travis McGee in 1964, MacDonald's royalties and readership soared even higher, and in due course the author and his hero migrated to hardcover publication and to the best-seller lists.

What's the secret of his success? The values he admires most in others' fiction and embodies in his own have been best summarized by MacDonald himself. "First, there has to be a strong sense of story. I want to be intrigued by wondering what is going to happen next. I want the people that I read about to be in difficulties—emotional, moral, spiritual, whatever, and I want to live with them while they're finding their way out of these difficulties. Second, I want the writer to make me suspend my disbelief. . . . I want to be in some other place and scene of the writer's devising. Next, I want him to have a bit of magic in his prose style, a bit of unobtrusive poetry. I want to have words and phrases really sing. And I like an attitude of wryness, realism, the sense of inevitability. I think that writing—good writing—should be like listening to music, where you identify the themes, you see what the composer is doing with those themes, and then, just when you think you have him properly identified, and his methods identified, then he will put in a little quirk, a little twist, that will be so unexpected that you read it with a sense of glee, a sense of joy, because of its aptness, even though it may be a very dire and bloody part of the book. So I want story, wit, music, wryness, color, and a sense of reality in what I read, and I try to get it in what I write."

In these thirteen early tales MacDonald gets what he wants, and so will his millions of fans. This is the good old stuff indeed. Read, and be carried away.

AUTHOR'S FOREWORD

These stories have been selected from hundreds written and published during the five-year period from 1947 to 1952.

This was the process of selection: Martin H. Greenberg of the University of Wisconsin and Francis M. Nevins, Jr., both of them aficionados of the pulp mystery story, wrote me that it would be a useful project to make a collection of the best of the old pulp stories of mine. I was not transfixed with delight. Mildly flattered, yes. But apprehensive about the overall quality of such a collection.

With the invaluable aid of Jean and Walter Shine, they acquired copies of those stories they had not read, and between the four of them, they whittled the list down to thirty. The tear sheets of these stories were obtained from the archives at the University Libraries, the University of Florida in Gainesville, and Sam Gowan, the Assistant Director of Special Resources, sent them along. I had them all turned back into typed manuscript form before looking at them.

I brought the hefty stack of thirty stories up here to the Adirondacks and went through them with care. To my astonishment, I found only three which I felt did not merit republication. The twenty-seven remaining totaled a quarter million words, so I divided them into two lots of approximately equal length. This is the first.

I have made minor changes in *all* these stories, mostly in the area of changing references which could confuse the reader. Thirty years ago everyone understood the phrase "unless he threw the gun as far as Carnera could." But the Primo is largely forgotten, and I changed him to Superman.

I have updated some of the stories, but only where the plot line was not entangled with and dependent upon the particular era. Those that depend for their effect on the times, the period pieces ("Death Writes the Answer," "They Let Me Live"), were not updated.

Those stories which could happen at any time, such as "A Time for Dying," have been updated. I changed a live radio show to a live television show. And in others I changed pay scales, taxi fares, long-distance phoning procedures, beer prices, and so forth to keep from watering down the attention of the reader. This may offend the purists, but my original intention in writing these stories was to entertain. If I did not entertain first the editor and then the readers, I did not get paid. And if I did not get paid, I would have to go find honest work. So the intention is still to entertain, to bemuse, and even to indicate how little changed is our time from that time when these were written.

I was horribly tempted to make other changes, to edit patches of florid prose, substitute the right words for the almost right words, but that would have been cheating, because it would have made me look as if I were a better writer at that time than I was. I was learning the trade.

The fifth and sixth stories in this collection intrigued me because they dealt with the same hero, one Park Falkner, who in some aspects seems like a precursor of Travis McGee. And in other aspects he foreshadows the plots of a lot of bad television series which came along later.

I remember with a particular fondness those editors who gave honest and valuable advice during the early years: Babette Rosmond at Street & Smith; Mike Tilden, Harry Widmer, and Alden Norton at Popular Publications; Bob Lowndes at Columbia Publications.

I remember Mike Tilden saying, "John, for God's sake stop *telling* us about people. Stop saying, for example, 'She was a very clumsy woman.' Show her falling downstairs and ending up with her head in the fishbowl. Don't ever say, 'He was an evil man.' Show him doing an evil thing."

I remember Babette Rosmond saying to me, after I had sent her a couple of dozen stories which used my Ordnance and

OSS background in the China-Burma-India Theater, "John, now is the time to take off your pith helmet and come home."

These stories, with the hundreds of others, were written and rewritten at 1109 State Street, Utica, New York; at 8 Jacarandas, Cuernavaca, Morelos, Mexico; at rented houses on Gardenia Street, Clearwater Beach, Florida, and Bruce Avenue three blocks away during the next season; at a rented house on Casey Key, Florida; at Piseco, New York, where I have been editing this collection; and finally at 1430 Point Crisp Road, Sarasota, where we lived for eighteen good years.

I wrote stories in such dogged quantity that often, when I had more than one in a magazine, the second had to be published under a house name: Peter Reed, John Wade Farrell, Scott O'Hara. In this collection, "A Time for Dying" was published under the name of Peter Reed and "Check Out at Dawn" as by Scott O'Hara.

In 1946 I tried to keep at least thirty stories in the mail at all times. When I finished a story, I would make a list of the magazines which might be interested and then send it out again and again until either it was sold or the list was exhausted. There were lots of magazines then. There was an open market for short fiction. There were lots of readers. Bless them!

Assembling this collection was like walking into a room and finding there a lot of old and good friends you had thought dead. The stories are better than I expected them to be, and so in taking the occupational risk of having them published, I hope you will enjoy them as much as they were enjoyed the first time around.

John D. MacDonald

Piseco, New York
June 20, 1982

The Good Old Stuff

Murder for Money

Long ago he had given up trying to estimate what he would find in any house merely by looking at the outside of it. The interior of each house had a special flavor. It was not so much the result of the degree of tidiness, or lack of it, but rather the result of the emotional climate that had permeated the house. Anger, bitterness, despair—all left their subtle stains on even the most immaculate fabrics.

Darrigan parked the rented car by the curb and, for a long moment, looked at the house, at the iron fence, at the cypress shade. He sensed dignity, restraint, quietness. Yet he knew that the interior could destroy these impressions. He was in the habit of telling himself that his record of successful investigations was the result of the application of unemotional logic—yet his logic was often the result of sensing, somehow, the final answer and then retracing the careful steps to arrive once more at that same answer.

After a time, as the September sun of west-coast Florida began to turn the rented sedan into an oven, Darrigan pushed open the door, patted his pocket to be sure his notebook was in place, and walked toward the front door of the white house. There were two cars in the driveway, both of them with local licenses, both of them Cadillacs. It was perceptibly cooler under the trees that lined the walk.

Beyond the screen door the hallway was dim. A heavy woman came in answer to his second ring, staring at him with frank curiosity.

1

"I'd like to speak to Mrs. Davisson, please. Here's my card."

The woman opened the screen just enough for the card to be passed through, saying, with Midwest nasality, "Well, she's resting right now. . . . Oh, you're from the insurance?"

"Yes, I flew down from Hartford."

"Please come in and wait and I'll see if she's awake, Mr. Darrigan. I'm just a neighbor. I'm Mrs. Hoke. The poor dear has been so terribly upset."

"Yes, of course," Darrigan murmured, stepping into the hall. Mrs. Hoke walked heavily away. Darrigan could hear the mumble of other voices, a faint, slightly incongruous laugh. From the hall he could see into a living room, two steps lower than the hall itself. It was furnished in cool colors, with Florida furniture of cane and pale fabrics.

Mrs. Hoke came back and said reassuringly, "She was awake, Mr. Darrigan. She said you should wait in the study and she'll be out in a few minutes. The door is right back here. This is such a dreadful thing, not knowing what has happened to him. It's hard on her, the poor dear thing."

The study was not done in Florida fashion. Darrigan guessed that the furniture had been shipped down from the North. A walnut desk, a bit ornate, leather couch and chairs, two walls of books.

Mrs. Hoke stood in the doorway. "Now don't you upset her, you hear?" she said with elephantine coyness.

"I'll try not to."

Mrs. Hoke went away. This was Davisson's room, obviously. His books. A great number of technical works on the textile industry. Popularized texts for the layman in other fields. Astronomy, philosophy, physics. Quite a few biographies. Very little fiction. A man, then, with a serious turn of mind, dedicated to self-improvement, perhaps a bit humorless. And certainly very tidy.

Darrigan turned quickly as he heard the step in the hallway. She was a tall young woman, light on her feet. Her sunback dress was emerald green. Late twenties, he judged, or possibly very early thirties. Brown hair, sun-bleached on top. Quite a bit of tan. A fresh face, wide across the cheekbones, heavy-lipped, slightly Bergman in impact. The mouth faintly touched with strain.

"Mr. Darrigan?" He liked the voice. Low, controlled, poised.

"How do you do, Mrs. Davisson. Sorry to bother you like this."

"That's all right. I wasn't able to sleep. Won't you sit down, please?"

"If you don't mind, I'll sit at the desk, Mrs. Davisson. I'll have to make some notes."

She sat on the leather couch. He offered her a cigarette. "No, thank you, I've been smoking so much I have a sore throat. Mr. Darrigan, isn't this a bit... previous for the insurance company to send someone down here? I mean, as far as we know, he isn't—"

"We wouldn't do this in the case of a normal policyholder, Mrs. Davisson, but your husband carries policies with us totaling over nine hundred thousand dollars."

"Really! I knew Temple had quite a bit, but I didn't know it was that much!"

He showed her his best smile and said, "It makes it awkward for me, Mrs. Davisson, for them to send me out like some sort of bird of prey. You have presented no claim to the company, and you are perfectly within your rights to tell me to be on my merry way."

She answered his smile. "I wouldn't want to do that, Mr. Darrigan. But I don't quite understand why you're here."

"You could call me a sort of investigator. My actual title is Chief Adjuster for Guardsman Life and Casualty. I sincerely hope that we'll find a reasonable explanation for your husband's disappearance. He disappeared Thursday, didn't he?"

"He didn't come home Thursday night. I reported it to the police early Friday morning. And this is—"

"Tuesday."

He opened his notebook, took his time looking over the pages. It was a device, to give him a chance to gauge the degree of tension. She sat quite still, her hands resting in her lap, unmoving.

He leaned back. "It may sound presumptuous, Mrs. Davisson, but I intend to see if I can find out what happened to

3

your husband. I've had reasonable success in such cases in the past. I'll cooperate with the local police officials, of course. I hope you won't mind answering questions that may duplicate what the police have already asked you."

"I won't mind. The important thing is . . . to find out. This not knowing is . . ." Her voice caught a bit. She looked down at her hands.

"According to our records, Mrs. Davisson, his first wife, Anna Thorn Davisson, was principal beneficiary under his policies until her death in 1978. The death of the beneficiary was reported, but it was not necessary to change the policies at that time as the two children of his first marriage were secondary beneficiaries, sharing equally in the proceeds in case of death. In 1979, probably at the time of his marriage to you, we received instructions to make you the primary beneficiary under all policies, with the secondary beneficiaries, Temple C. Davisson, Junior, and Alicia Jean Davisson, unchanged. I have your name here as Dinah Pell Davisson. That is correct?"

"Yes, it is."

"Could you tell me about your husband? What sort of man is he?"

She gave him a small smile. "What should I say? He is a very kind man. Perhaps slightly autocratic, but kind. He owned a small knitting mill in Utica, New York. He sold it, I believe, in 1972. It was incorporated and he owned the controlling stock interest, and there was some sort of merger with a larger firm, where he received payment in the stock in the larger firm in return for his interest. He sold out because his wife had to live in a warmer climate. She had a serious kidney condition. They came down here to Clearwater and bought this house. Temple was too active to retire. He studied real estate conditions here for a full year and then began to invest money in all sorts of property. He has done very well."

"How did you meet him, Mrs. Davisson?"

"My husband was a sergeant in the Air Force. He was stationed at Drew Field. I followed him here. When he was sent overseas I had no special place to go, and we agreed I should wait for him here. The Davissons advertised for a companion for Mrs. Davisson. I applied and held the job from early 1974 until she died in 1978."

"And your husband?" –

"He was killed in a crash landing. When I received the wire, the Davissons were very kind and understanding. At that time my position in the household was more like a daughter receiving an allowance. My own parents died long ago. I have a married sister in Melbourne, Australia. We've never been close."

"What did you do between the time Mrs. Davisson died and you married Temple Davisson?"

"I left here, of course. Mrs. Davisson had money of her own. She left me five thousand dollars and left the rest to Temple, Junior, and Alicia. Mr. Davisson found me a job in a real estate office in Clearwater. I rented a small apartment. One night Mr. Davisson came to see me at the apartment. He was quite shy. It took him a long time to get to the reason he had come. He told me that he tried to keep the house going, but the people he had hired were undependable. He also said that he was lonely. He asked me to marry him. I told him that I had affection for him, as for a father. He told me that he did not love me that way either, that Anna had been the only woman in his life. Well, Jack had been the only man in my life, and life was pretty empty. The Davissons had filled a place in my life. I missed this house. But he is sixty-one, and that makes almost exactly thirty years difference in ages. It seemed a bit grotesque. He told me to think it over and give him my answer when I ws ready. It occurred to me that his children would resent me, and it also occurred to me that I cared very little what people thought. Four days later I told him I would marry him."

Darrigan realized that he was treading on most dangerous ground. "Has it been a good marriage?"

"Is that a question you're supposed to ask?"

"It sounds impertinent. I know that. But in a disappearance of this sort I must consider suicide. Unhappiness can come from ill health, money difficulties, or emotional difficulties. I should try to rule them out."

"I'll take one of those cigarettes now, Mr. Darrigan," she said. "I can use it."

He lit it for her, went back to the desk chair. She frowned, exhaled a cloud of smoke.

5

"It has not been a completely happy marriage, Mr. Darrigan."

"Can you explain that?"

"I'd rather not." He pursed his lips, let the silence grow. At last she said, "I suppose I can consider an insurance man to be as ethical as a doctor or a lawyer?"

"Of course."

"For several months it was a marriage in name only. I was content to have it go on being that way. But he is a vigorous man, and after a while I became aware that his attitude had changed and he had begun to . . . want me." She flushed.

"But you had no feeling for him in that way," he said, helping her.

"None. And we'd made no actual agreement, in so many words. But living here with him, I had no ethical basis for refusing him. After that, our marriage became different. He sensed, of course, that I was merely submitting. He began to . . . court me, I suppose you'd call it. Flowers and little things like that. He took off weight and began to dress much more youthfully. He tried to make himself younger, in his speech and in his habits. It was sort of pathetic, the way he tried."

"Would you relate that to . . . his disappearance?"

For a moment her face was twisted in the agony of self-reproach. "I don't know."

"I appreciate your frankness. I'll respect it, Mrs. Davisson. How did he act Thursday?"

"The same as always. We had a late breakfast. He had just sold some lots in the Lido section at Sarasota, and he was thinking of putting the money into a Gulf-front tract at Redington Beach. He asked me to go down there with him, but I had an eleven o'clock appointment with the hairdresser. His car was in the garage, so he took my convertible. He said he'd have lunch down that way and be back in the late afternoon. We were going to have some people in for cocktails. Well, the cocktail guests came and Temple didn't show up. I didn't worry. I thought he was delayed. We all went out to dinner and I left a note telling him that he could catch up with us at the Belmonte, on Clearwater Beach.

"After dinner the Deens brought me home. They live down

6

on the next street. I began to get really worried at ten o'clock. I thought of heart attacks and all sorts of things like that. Of accidents and so on. I phoned Morton Plant Hospital and asked if they knew anything. I phoned the police here and at Redington and at St. Petersburg. I fell asleep in a chair at about four o'clock and woke up at seven. That was when I officially reported him missing.

"They found my car parked outside a hotel apartment on Redington Beach, called Aqua Azul. They checked and found out he'd gone into the Aqua Azul cocktail lounge at eight-thirty, alone. He had one dry martini and phoned here, but of course I had left by that time and the house was empty. He had another drink and then left. But apparently he didn't get in the car and drive away. That's what I don't understand. And I keep thinking that the Aqua Azul is right on the Gulf."

"Have his children come down?"

"Temple, Junior, wired that he is coming. He's a lieutenant colonel of ordnance stationed at the Pentagon."

"How old is he?"

"Thirty-six, and Alicia is thirty-three. Temple, Junior, is married, but Alicia isn't. She's with a Boston advertising agency, and when I tried to phone her I found out she's on vacation, taking a motor trip in Canada. She may not even know about it."

"When is the son arriving?"

"Late today, the wire said."

"Were they at the wedding?"

"No. But I know them, of course. I met them before Mrs. Davisson died, many times. And only once since my marriage. There was quite a scene then. They think I'm some sort of dirty little opportunist. When they were down while Mrs. Davisson was alive, they had me firmly established in the servant category. I suppose they were right, but one never thinks of oneself as a servant. I'm afraid Colonel Davisson is going to be difficult."

"Do you think your husband might have had business worries?"

"None. He told me a few months ago, quite proudly, that when he liquidated the knitting-company stock he received five

7

hundred thousand dollars. In 1973 he started to buy land in this area. He said that the land he now owns could be sold off for an estimated million and a half dollars."

"Did he maintain an office?"

"This is his office. Mr. Darrigan, you used the past tense then. I find it disturbing."

"I'm sorry. It wasn't intentional." Yet it had been. He had wanted to see how easily she would slip into the past tense, showing that in her mind she considered him dead.

"Do you know the terms of his current will?"

"He discussed it with me a year ago. It sets up trust funds, one for me and one for each of the children. He insisted that it be set up so that we share equally. And yet, if I get all that insurance, it isn't going to seem very equal, is it? I'm sorry for snapping at you about using the past tense, Mr. Darrigan. I think he's dead."

"Why?"

"I know that amnesia is a very rare thing, genuine amnesia. And Temple had a very sound, stable mind. As I said before, he is kind. He wouldn't go away and leave me to this kind of worry."

"The newspaper picture was poor. Do you have a better one?"

"Quite a good one taken in July. Don't get up. I can get it. It's right in this desk drawer."

She sat lithely on her heels and opened the bottom desk drawer. Her perfume had a pleasant tang. Where her hair was parted he could see the ivory cleanness of her scalp. An attractive woman, with a quality of personal warmth held in reserve. Darrigan decided that the sergeant had been a most fortunate man. And he wondered if Davisson was perceptive enough to measure the true extent of his failure. He remembered an old story of a man held captive at the bottom of a dark, smooth-sided well. Whenever the light was turned on, for a brief interval, he could see that the circular wall was of glass, with exotic fruits banked behind it.

"This one," she said, taking out a 35-millimeter color transparency mounted in paperboard. She slipped it into a green

8

plastic viewer and handed it to him. "You better take it over to the window. Natural light is best."

Darrigan held the viewer up to his eye. A heavy bald man, tanned like a Tahitian, stood smiling into the camera. He stood on a beach in the sunlight, and he wore bathing trunks with a pattern of blue fish on a white background. There was a doggedness about his heavy jaw, a glint of shrewdness in his eyes. His position was faintly strained and Darrigan judged he was holding his belly in, arching his wide chest for the camera. He looked to be no fool.

"May I take this along?" Darrigan asked, turning to her.

"Not for keeps." The childish expression was touching.

"Not for keeps," he said, smiling, meaning his smile for the first time. "Thank you for your courtesy, Mrs. Davisson. I'll be in touch with you. If you want me for any reason, I'm registered at a place called Bon Villa on the beach. The owner will take a message for me."

Darrigan left police headquarters in Clearwater at three o'clock. They had been as cool as he had expected at first, but after he had clearly stated his intentions they had relaxed and informed him of progress to date. They were cooperating with the Pinellas County officials and with the police at Redington.

Temple Davisson had kept his appointment with the man who owned the plot of Gulf-front property that had interested him. The potential vendor was named Myron Drynfells, and Davisson had picked him up at eleven fifteen at the motel he owned at Madeira Beach. Drynfells reported that they had inspected the property but were unable to arrive at a figure acceptable to both of them. Davisson had driven him back to the Coral Tour Haven, depositing him there shortly after twelve thirty. Davisson had intimated that he was going farther down the line to take a look at some property near St. Petersburg Beach.

There was one unconfirmed report of a man answering Davisson's description seen walking along the shoulder of the highway up near the Bath Club accompanied by a dark-haired girl, some time shortly before nine o'clock on Thursday night.

The police had no objection to Darrigan's talking with Drynfells or making his own attempt to find the elusive dark-haired girl. They were reluctant to voice any theory that would account for the disappearance.

Following a map of the area, Darrigan had little difficulty in finding his way out South Fort Harrison Avenue to the turnoff to the Belleaire causeway. He drove through the village of Indian Rocks and down a straight road that paralleled the beach. The Aqua Azul was not hard to find. It was an ugly four-story building tinted pale chartreuse with corner balconies overlooking the Gulf. From the parking area one walked along a crushed-shell path to tile steps leading down into a pseudo-Mexican courtyard where shrubbery screened off the highway. The lobby door, of plate glass with a chrome push bar, opened off the other side of the patio. The fountain in the center of the patio was rimmed with small floodlights with blue-glass lenses. Darrigan guessed that the fountain would be fairly garish once the lights were turned on.

Beyond the glass door the lobby was frigidly air-conditioned. A brass sign on the blond desk announced that summer rates were in effect. The lobby walls were rough tan plaster. At the head of a short wide staircase was a mural of lumpy, coffee-colored, semi-naked women grinding corn and holding infants.

A black man was slowly sweeping the tile floor of the lobby. A girl behind the desk was carrying on a monosyllabic phone conversation. The place had a quietness, a hint of informality, that suggested it would be more pleasant now than during the height of the winter tourist season.

The bar lounge opened off the lobby. The west wall was entirely glass, facing the beach glare. A curtain had been drawn across the glass. It was sufficiently opaque to cut the glare, subdue the light in the room. Sand gritted underfoot as Darrigan walked to the bar. Three lean women in bathing suits sat at one table, complete with beach bags, tall drinks, and that special porcelainized facial expression of the middle forties trying, with monied success, to look like middle thirties.

Two heavy men in white suits hunched over a corner table, florid faces eight inches apart, muttering at each other. A young couple sat at the bar. They had a honeymoon flavor about them.

Darrigan sat down at the end of the bar, around the corner, and decided on a rum collins. The bartender was brisk, young, dark, and he mixed a good drink.

When he brought the change, Darrigan said, "Say, have they found that guy who wandered away and left his car here the other night?"

"I don't think so, sir," the bartender said with no show of interest.

"Were you on duty the night he came in?"

"Yes, sir."

"Regular customer?"

The bartender didn't answer.

Darrigan quickly leafed through a half dozen possible approaches. He selected one that seemed suited to the bartender's look of quick intelligence and smiled ingratiatingly. "They ought to make all cops take a sort of internship behind a bar. That's where you learn what makes people tick."

The slight wariness faded. "That's no joke."

"Teddy!" one of the three lean women called. "Another round, please."

"Coming right up, Mrs. Jerrold," Teddy said.

Darrigan waited with monumental patience. He had planted a seed, and he wanted to see if it would take root. He stared down at his drink, watching Teddy out of the corner of his eye. After the drinks had been taken to the three women, Teddy drifted slowly back toward Darrigan. Darrigan waited for Teddy to say the first word.

"I think that Davisson will show up."

Darrigan shrugged. "That's hard to say." It put the burden of proof on Teddy.

Teddy became confidential. "Like you said, sir, you see a lot when you're behind a bar. You learn to size them up. Now, you take that Davisson. I don't think he ever came in here before. I didn't make any connection until they showed me the picture. Then I remembered him. In the off season, you get time to size people up. He came in alone. I'd say he'd had a couple already. Husky old guy. Looked like money. Looked smart, too. That kind, they like service. He came in about eight thirty. A local guy. I could tell. I don't know how. You can always tell them from the tourists. One martini, he wants. Very dry. He gets it very dry. He asks me where he can phone. I told him about the phone in the lobby. He finished half his cocktail, then phoned. When he came back he looked satisfied about the phone call. A little more relaxed. You know what I mean. He sat right on that stool there, and one of the regulars, a Mrs. Kathy Marrick, is sitting alone at that table over there. That Davisson, he turns on the stool and starts giving Mrs. Marrick the eye. Not that you can blame him. She is something to look at. He orders another martini. I figure out the pitch then. That Davisson, he went and called his wife and then he was settling down to an evening of wolfing around. Some of those older guys, they give us more trouble than the college kids. And he had that look, you know what I mean.

"Well, from where he was sitting he couldn't even see first base, not with Mrs. Marrick, and I saw him figure that out for himself. He finished his second drink in a hurry, and away he went. I sort of decided he was going to look around and see where the hunting was a little better."

"And that makes you think he'll turn up?"

"Sure. I think the old guy just lost himself a big weekend, and he'll come crawling out of the woodwork with some crazy amnesia story or something."

"Then how do you figure the car being left here?"

"I think he found somebody with a car of her own. They saw him walking up the line not long after he left here, and he was with a girl, wasn't he? That makes sense to me."

"Where would he have gone to find that other girl?"

"I think he came out of here, and it was just beginning to get dark, and he looked from the parking lot and saw the lights of the Tide Table up the road, and it was just as easy to walk as drive."

Darrigan nodded. "That would make sense. Is it a nice place, that Tide Table?"

"A big bar and bathhouses and a dance floor and carhops to serve greasy hamburgers. It doesn't do this section of the beach much good."

"Was Davisson dressed right for that kind of a place?"

"I don't know. He had on a white mesh shirt with short

12

sleeves and tan slacks, I think. Maybe he had a coat in his car. He didn't wear it in here. The rules here say men have to wear coats in the bar and dining room after November first."

"That Mrs. Marrick wouldn't have met him outside, would she?"

"Not her. No, sir. She rents one of our cabañas here."

"Did she notice him?"

"I'd say she did. You can't fool Kathy Marrick."

Darrigan knew that Teddy could add nothing more. So Darrigan switched the conversation to other things. He made himself talk dully and at length so that when Teddy saw his chance, he eased away with almost obvious relief. Darrigan had learned to make himself boring, merely by relating complicated incidents which had no particular point. It served its purpose. He knew that Teddy was left with a mild contempt for Darrigan's intellectual resources. Later, should anyone suggest to Teddy that Darrigan was a uniquely shrewd investigator, Teddy would hoot with laughter, completely forgetting that Darrigan, with a minimum of words, had extracted every bit of information Teddy had possessed.

Darrigan went out to the desk and asked if he might see Mrs. Marrick. The girl went to the small switchboard and plugged one of the house phones into Mrs. Marrick's cabaña. After the phone rang five times a sleepy, soft-fibered voice answered.

He stated his name and his wish to speak with her. She agreed, sleepily. Following the desk girl's instructions, Darrigan walked out the beach door of the lobby and down a shell walk to the last cabaña to the south. A woman in a two-piece white terry-cloth sun suit lay on an uptilted Barwa chair in the hot sun. Her hair was wheat and silver, sun-parched. Her figure was rich, and her tan was coppery. She had the hollowed cheeks of a Dietrich and a wide, flat mouth.

She opened lazy sea-green eyes when he spoke her name. She looked at him for a long moment and then said, "Mr. Darrigan, you cast an unpleasantly black shadow on the sand. Are you one of the new ones with my husband's law firm? If so, the answer is still no, in spite of the fact that you're quite pretty."

"I never heard of you until ten minutes ago, Mrs. Marrick."

"That's refreshing, dear. Be a good boy and go in and build us some drinks. You'll find whatever you want, and I need a fresh gin and tonic. This glass will do for me. And bring out a pack of cigarettes from the carton on the bedroom dressing table."

She shut her eyes. Darrigan shrugged and went into the cabaña. It was clean but cluttered. He made himself a rum collins, took the two drinks out, handed her her drink and a pack of cigarettes. She shifted her weight forward and the chair tilted down.

"Now talk, dear," she said.

"Last Friday night at about eight thirty you were alone in the bar and a bald-headed man with a deep tan sat at the bar. He was interested in you."

"Mmm. The missing Mr. Davisson, eh? Let me see now. You can't be a local policeman. They all either look like fullbacks from the University of Florida or skippers of unsuccessful charter boats. Your complexion and clothes are definitely northern. That might make you FBI, but I don't think so somehow. Insurance, Mr. Darrigan?"

He sat on a canvas chair and looked at her with new respect. "Insurance, Mrs. Marrick."

"He's dead, I think."

"His wife thinks so too. Why do you?"

"I was alone. I'm a vain creature, and the older I get the more flattered I am by all little attentions. Your Mr. Davisson was a bit pathetic, my dear. He had a lost look. A . . . hollowness. Do you understand?"

"Not quite."

"A man of that age will either be totally uninterested in casual females or he will have an enormous amount of assurance about him. Mr. Davisson had neither. He looked at me like a little boy staring into the candy shop. I was almost tempted to help the poor dear, but he looked dreadfully dull. I said to myself, Kathy, there is a man who suddenly has decided to be a bit of a rake and does not know just how to go about it."

"Does that make him dead?"

"No, of course. It was something else. Looking into his eyes was like looking into the eyes of a photograph of someone who has recently died. It is a look of death. It cannot be described. It made me feel quite upset."

"How would I write that up in a report?"

"You wouldn't, my dear. You would go out and find out how he died. He was looking for adventure last Friday night. And I believe he found it."

"With a girl with dark hair?"

"Perhaps."

"It isn't much of a starting place, is it?" Darrigan said ruefully.

She finished her drink and tilted her chair back. "I understand that the wife is young."

"Comparatively speaking. Are you French?"

"I was once. You're quick, aren't you? I'm told there's no accent."

"No accent. A turn of phrase here and there. What if the wife is young?"

"Call it my French turn of mind. A lover of the wife could help your Mr. Davisson find . . . his adventure."

"The wife was with a group all evening."

"A very sensible precaution."

He stood up. "Thank you for talking to me."

"You see, you're not as quick as I thought, Mr. Darrigan. I wanted you to keep questioning me in a clever way, and then I should tell you that Mr. Davisson kept watching the door during his two drinks, as though he were expecting that someone had followed him. He was watching, not with worry, but with . . . annoyance."

Darrigan smiled. "I thought you had something else to tell. And it seemed the quickest way to get it out of you, to pretend to go."

She stared at him and then laughed. It was a good laugh, full-throated, rich. "We could be friends, my dear," she said, when she got her breath.

"So far I haven't filled in enough of his day. I know what he did up until very early afternoon. Then there is a gap. He comes into the Aqua Azul bar at eight thirty. He has had a few

15

drinks. I like the theory of someone following him, meeting him outside. That would account for his leaving his car at the lot."

"What will you do now?"

"See if I can fill in the blanks in his day."

"The blank before he arrived here, and the more important one afterward?"

"Yes."

"I'm well known up and down the Gulf beaches, Mr. Darrigan. Being with me would be protective coloration."

"And besides, you're bored."

"Utterly."

He smiled at her. "Then you'd better get dressed, don't you think?"

He waited outside while she changed. He knew that she would be useful for her knowledge of the area. Yet not sufficiently useful to warrant taking her along had she not been a mature, witty, perceptive woman.

She came out wearing sandals and a severely cut sand-colored linen sun dress, carrying a white purse. The end tendrils of the astonishing hair were damp-curled where they had protruded from her shower cap.

"Darrigan and Marrick," she said. "Investigations to order. This might be fun."

"And it might be dull."

"But we shan't be dull, Mr. Darrigan, shall we. What are you called?"

"Gil, usually."

"Ah, Gil, if this were a properly conceived plot, I would be the one who lured your Mr. Davisson to his death. Now I accompany the investigator to allay suspicion."

"No such luck, Kathy."

"No such luck." They walked along the shell path to the main building of the Aqua Azul. She led the way around the building toward a Cadillac convertible the shade of raspberry sherbet.

"More protective coloration?" Darrigan asked.

She smiled and handed him the keys from her purse. After he shut her door he went around and got behind the wheel.

The sun was far enough gone to warrant having the top down. She took a dark bandanna from the glove compartment and tied it around her hair.

"Now how do you go about this, Gil?" she asked.

"I head south and show a picture of Davisson in every bar until we find the one he was in. He could have called his wife earlier. I think he was the sort to remember that a cocktail party was scheduled for that evening. Something kept him from phoning his wife."

"Maybe he didn't want to phone her until it was too late."

"I'll grant that. First I want to talk to a man named Drynfells. For this you better stay in the car."

The Coral Tour Haven was a pink hotel with pink iron flamingoes stuck into the lawn and a profusion of whitewashed boulders marking the drive. Drynfells was a sour-looking man with a withered face, garish clothes, and a cheap Cuban cigar.

Darrigan had to follow Drynfells about as they talked. Drynfells ambled around, picking up scraps of cellophane, twigs, burned matches from his yard. He confirmed all that the Clearwater police had told Darrigan.

"You couldn't decide on a price, Mr. Drynfells?"

"I want one hundred and forty-five thousand for that piece. He offered one thirty-six, then one thirty-eight, and finally one forty. He said that was his top offer. I came down two thousand and told him that one forty-three was as low as I'd go."

"Did you quarrel?"

Drynfells gave him a sidelong glance. "We shouted a little. He was a shouter. Lot of men try to bull their way into a deal. He couldn't bulldoze me. No, sir."

They had walked around a corner of the motel. A pretty girl sat on a rubberized mattress at the side of a new wading pool. The ground was raw around the pool, freshly seeded, protected by stakes and string.

"What did you say your name was?" Drynfells asked.

"Darrigan."

"This here is my wife, Mr. Darrigan. Beth, this man is an insurance fellow asking about that Davisson."

Mrs. Drynfells was striking. She had a heavy strain of some Latin blood. Her dark eyes were liquid, expressive.

17

"He is the wan who is wanting to buy our beach, eh?"

"Yeah. That bald-headed man that the police were asking about," Drynfells said.

Mrs. Drynfells seemed to lose all interest in the situation. She lay back and shut her eyes. She wore a lemon-yellow swimsuit.

Drynfells wandered away and swooped on a scrap of paper, balling it up in his hand with the other debris he had collected.

"You have a nice place here," Darrigan said.

"Just got it open in time for last season. Did pretty good. We got a private beach over there across the highway. Reasonable rates, too."

"I guess things are pretty dead in the off season."

"Right now we only got one unit taken. Those folks came in yesterday. But it ought to pick up again soon."

"How big is that piece of land you want one hundred and forty-five thousand for?"

"It's one hundred and twenty feet of Gulf-front lot, six hundred feet deep, but it isn't for sale any more."

"Why not?"

"Changed my mind about it, Mr. Darrigan. Decided to hold onto it, maybe develop it a little. Nice property."

Darrigan went out to the car. They drove south, stopping at the obvious places. They were unable to pick up the trail of Mr. Davisson. Darrigan bought Kathy Marrick dinner. He drove her back to the Aqua Azul. They took a short walk on the beach and he thanked her, promised to keep in touch with her, and drove the rented sedan back to Clearwater Beach.

It was after eleven and the porch of the Bon Villa was dark. He parked, and as he headed toward his room a familiar voice spoke hesitantly from one of the dark chairs.

"Mr. Darrigan?"

"Oh! Hello, Mrs. Davisson. You startled me. I didn't see you there. Do you want to come in?"

"No, please. Sit down and tell me what you've learned."

He pulled one of the aluminum chairs over close to hers and sat down. A faint sea breeze rattled the palm fronds. Her face was a pale oval, barely visible.

"I didn't learn much, Mrs. Davisson. Not much at all."

"Forgive me for coming here like this. Colonel Davisson arrived. It was as unpleasant as I'd expected. I had to get out of the house."

"It makes a difficult emotional problem for both of you—when the children of the first marriage are older than the second wife."

"I don't really blame him too much, I suppose. It looks bad."

"What did he accuse you of?"

"Driving his father into some crazy act. Maybe I did."

"Don't think that way."

"I keep thinking that if we never find out what happened to Temple, his children will always blame me. I don't especially want to be friends with them, but I do want their . . . respect, I guess you'd say."

"Mrs. Davisson, do you have any male friends your own age?"

"How do you mean that?" she asked hotly.

"Is there any man you've been friendly enough with to cause talk?"

"N-no, I—"

"Who were you thinking of when you hesitated?"

"Brad Sharvis. He's a bit over thirty, and quite nice. It was his real estate agency that Temple sent me to for a job. He has worked with Temple the last few years. He's a bachelor. He has dinner with us quite often. We both like him."

"Could there be talk?"

"There could be, but it would be without basis, Mr. Darrigan," she said coldly.

"I don't care how angry you get at me, Mrs. Davisson, so long as you tell me the truth."

After a long silence she said, "I'm sorry. I believe that you want to help."

"I do."

She stood up. "I feel better now. I think I'll go home."

"Can I take you home?"

"I have my car, thanks."

He watched her go down the walk. Under the streetlight he saw her walking with a good long stride. He saw the headlights, saw her swing around the island in the center of Mandalay and head back for the causeway to Clearwater.

Darrigan went in, showered, and went to bed. He lay in the dark room and smoked a slow cigarette. Somewhere, hidden in the personality or in the habits of one Temple Davisson, was the reason for his death. Darrigan found that he was thinking in terms of death. He smiled in the darkness as he thought of Kathy Marrick. A most pleasant companion. So far in the investigation he had met four women. Of the four only Mrs. Hoke was unattractive.

He snubbed out the cigarette and composed himself for sleep. A case, like a score of other cases. He would leave his brief mark on the participants and go out of their lives. For a moment he felt the ache of self-imposed loneliness. The ache had been there since the day Doris had left him, long ago. He wondered sourly, on the verge of sleep, if it had made him a better investigator.

Brad Sharvis was a florid, freckled, overweight young man with carrot hair, blue eyes, and a salesman's unthinking affability. The small real estate office was clean and bright. A girl was typing a lease agreement for an elderly couple.

Brad took Darrigan back into his small private office. A window air conditioner hummed, chilling the moist September air.

"What sort of man was he, Mr. Sharvis?"

"Was he? Or is he? Shrewd, Mr. Darrigan. Shrewd and honest. And something else. Tough-minded isn't the expression I want."

"Ruthless?"

"That's it exactly. He started moving in on property down here soon after he arrived. You wouldn't know the place if you saw it back then. The last ten years down here would take your breath away."

"He knew what to buy, eh?"

"It took him a year to decide on policy. He had a very simple operating idea. He decided, after his year of looking around, that there was going to be a tremendous pressure for

20

waterfront land. At that time small building lots on Clearwater Beach, on the Gulf front, were going for as little as seventy-five hundred dollars. I remember that the first thing he did was pick up eight lots at that figure. He sold them in 1980 for fifty thousand apiece."

"Where did the ruthlessness come in, Mr. Sharvis?"

"You better call me Brad. That last name makes me feel too dignified."

"Okay. I'm Gil."

"I'll tell you, Gil. Suppose he got his eye on a piece he wanted. He'd go after it. Phone calls, letters, personal visits. He'd hound a man who had no idea of selling until, in some cases, I think they sold out just to get Temple Davisson off their back. And he'd fight for an hour to get forty dollars off the price of a twenty-thousand-dollar piece."

"Did he handle his deals through you?"

"No. He turned himself into a licensed agent and used this office for his deals. He pays toward the office expenses here, and I've been in with him on a few deals."

"Is he stingy?"

"Not a bit. Pretty free with his money, but a tight man in a deal. You know, he's told me a hundred times that everybody likes the look of nice fat batches of bills. He said that there's nothing exactly like counting out fifteen thousand dollars in bills onto a man's desk when the man wants to get seventeen thousand."

Darrigan felt a shiver of excitement run up his back. It was always that way when he found a bit of key information.

"Where did he bank?"

"Bank of Clearwater."

"Do you think he took money with him when he went after the Drynfells plot?"

Sharvis frowned. "I hardly think he'd take that much out there, but I'll wager he took a sizable payment against it."

"Twenty-five thousand?"

"Possibly. Probably more like fifty."

"I could check that at the bank, I suppose."

"I doubt it. He has a safe in his office at his house. A pretty good one, I think. He kept his cash there. He'd replenish the

21

supply in Tampa, picking up a certified check from the Bank of Clearwater whenever he needed more than they could comfortably give him."

"He was anxious to get the Drynfells land?"

"A very nice piece. And with a tentative purchaser all lined up for it. Temple would have unloaded it for one hundred and seventy thousand. He wanted to work fast so that there'd be no chance of his customer getting together with Drynfells. It only went on the market Wednesday, a week ago today."

"Drynfells held it a long time?"

"Several years. He paid fifty thousand for it."

"Would it violate any confidence to tell me who Davisson planned to sell it to?"

"I can't give you the name because I don't know it myself. It's some man who sold a chain of movie houses in Kansas and wants to build a motel down here, that's all I know."

Darrigan walked out into the morning sunlight. The death of Temple Davisson was beginning to emerge from the mists. Sometime after he had left the Coral Tour Haven and before he appeared at the Aqua Azul, he had entangled himself with someone who wanted that cash. Wanted it badly. They had not taken their first opportunity. So they had sought a second choice, had made the most of it.

He parked in the center of town, had a cup of coffee. At such times he felt far away from his immediate environment. Life moved brightly around him and left him in a dark place where he sat and thought. Thought at such a time was not the application of logic but an endless stirring at the edge of the mind, a restless groping for the fleeting impression.

Davisson had been a man whose self-esteem had taken an inadvertent blow at the hands of his young wife. To mend his self-esteem, he had been casting a speculative eye at the random female. And he had been spending the day trying to engineer a deal that would mean a most pleasant profit.

Darrigan and Kathy Marrick had been unable to find the place where Davisson had taken a few drinks before stopping at the Aqua Azul. Darrigan paid for his coffee and went out to the car, spread the road map on the wheel, and studied it. Granted that Davisson was on his way home when he stopped at the Aqua Azul, it limited the area where he could have been. Had he been more than three miles south of the Aqua Azul, he would not logically have headed home on the road that would take him through Indian Rocks and along Belleaire Beach. He would have cut over to Route 19. With a pencil Darrigan made a circle. Temple Davisson had taken his drinks somewhere in that area.

He frowned. He detested legwork, that dullest stepsister of investigation. Sharing it with Mrs. Marrick made it a bit more pleasant, at least. It took him forty-five minutes to drive out to the Aqua Azul. Her raspberry convertible was under shelter in the long carport. He parked in the sun and went in, found her in the lobby chattering with the girl at the desk.

She smiled at him. "It can't be Nero Wolfe. Not enough waistline."

"Buy you a drink?"

"Clever boy. The bar isn't open yet. Come down to the cabaña and make your own and listen to the record of a busy morning."

They went into the cypress-paneled living room of the beach cabaña. She made the drinks.

"We failed to find out where he'd been by looking for him, my dear. So this morning I was up bright and early and went on a hunt for somebody who might have seen the car. A nice baby-blue convertible. They're a dime a dozen around here, but it seemed sensible. Tan men with bald heads are a dime a dozen too. But the combination of tan bald head and baby-blue convertible is not so usual."

"Any time you'd like a job, Kathy."

"Flatterer! Now prepare yourself for the letdown. All I found out was something we already knew. That the baby-blue job was parked at that hideous Coral Tour Haven early in the afternoon."

Darrigan sipped his drink. "Parked there?"

"That's what the man said. He has a painful little store that sells things made out of shells, and sells shells to people who want to make things out of shells. Say that three times fast."

"Why did you stop there?"

"Just to see if anybody could remember the car and man if

they had seen them. He's across the street from that Coral Tour thing."

"I think I'd like to talk to him."

"Let's go, then. He's a foolish little sweetheart with a tic."

The man was small and nervous, and at unexpected intervals his entire face would twitch uncontrollably. "Like I told the lady, mister, I saw the car parked over to Drynfells's. You don't see many cars there. Myron doesn't do so good this time of year."

"And you saw the bald-headed man?"

"Sure. He went in with Drynfells, and then he came out after a while."

"After how long?"

"How would I know? Was I timing him? Maybe twenty minutes."

Darrigan showed him the picture. "This man?"

The little man squinted through the viewer. "Sure."

"You got a good look at him?"

"Just the first time."

"You mean when he went in?"

"No, I mean the first time he was there. The second time it was getting pretty late in the day, and the sun was gone."

"Did he stay long the second time?"

"I don't know. I closed up when he was still there."

"Thanks a lot."

The little man twitched and beamed. "A pleasure, certainly."

They went back out to Darrigan's car. When they got in Kathy said, "I feel a bit stupid, Gil."

"Don't think I suspected that. It came out by accident. One of those things. It happens sometimes. And I should have done some better guessing. I found out this morning that when Temple Davisson wanted a piece of property he didn't give up easily. He went back and tried again."

"And Mr. Drynfells didn't mention it."

"A matter which I find very interesting. I'm dropping you back at the Aqua Azul and then I'm going to tackle Drynfells."

"Who found the little man who sells shells? You are not leaving me out."

"It may turn out to be unpleasant, Kathy."

"So be it. I want to see how much of that tough look of yours is a pose, Mr. Darrigan."

"Let me handle it."

"I shall be a mouse, entirely."

He waited for two cars to go by and made a wide U-turn, then turned right into Drynfells's drive. The couple was out in back. Mrs. Drynfells was basking on her rubberized mattress, her eyes closed. She did not appear to have moved since the previous day. Myron Drynfells was over near the hedge having a bitter argument with a man who obviously belonged with the battered pickup parked in front.

Drynfells was saying, "I just got damn good and tired of waiting for you to come around and finish the job."

The man, a husky youngster in work clothes, flushed with anger, said, "Okay, okay. Just pay me off, then, if that's the way you feel. Fourteen hours' labor plus the bags and the pipe."

Drynfells turned and saw Darrigan and Kathy. "Hello," he said absently. "Be right back." He walked into the back door of the end unit with the husky young man.

Mrs. Drynfells opened her eyes. She looked speculatively at Kathy. "Allo," she said. Darrigan introduced the two women. He had done enough work on jewelry theft to know that the emerald in Mrs. Drynfells's ring was genuine. About three carats, he judged. A beauty.

Drynfells came out across the lawn, scowling. He wore chartreuse slacks and a dark blue seersucker sport shirt with a chartreuse flower pattern.

"Want anything done right," he said, "you got to do it yourself. What's on your mind, Mr. Darrigan?"

"Just checking, Mr. Drynfells. I got the impression from the police that Mr. Davisson merely dropped you off here after you'd looked at the land. I didn't know he'd come in with you."

"He's a persistent guy. I couldn't shake him off, could I, honey?"

"Talking, talking," Mrs. Drynfells said, with sunstruck sleepiness. "Too moch."

"He came in and yakked at me, and then when he left he

25

told me he could find better lots south of here. I told him to go right ahead."

"How long did he stay?"

Drynfells shrugged. "Fifteen minutes, maybe."

"Did he wave big bills at you?"

"Sure. Kid stuff. I had my price and he wouldn't meet it. Waving money in my face wasn't going to change my mind. No, sir."

"And that's the last you saw of him?" Darrigan asked casually.

"That's right."

"Then why was his car parked out in front of here at dusk on Friday?"

"In front of here?" Drynfells said, his eyes opening wide.

"In front of here."

"I don't know what you're talking about, mister. I wasn't even here, then. I was in Clearwater on a business matter."

Mrs. Drynfells sat up and put her hand over her mouth. "Ai, I forget! He did come back. Still talking, talking. I send him away, that talking wan."

Drynfells stomped over to her and glared down at her. "Why did you forget that? Damn it, that might make us look bad."

"I do not theenk."

Drynfells turned to Darrigan with a shrug. "Rattle-headed, that's what she is. Forget her head if it wasn't fastened on."

"I am sorree!"

"I think you better phone the police and tell them, Mr. Drynfells, just in case."

"Think I should?"

"The man is still missing."

Drynfells sighed. "Okay, I better do that."

The Aqua Azul bar was open. Kathy and Darrigan took a corner table, ordered pre-lunch cocktails. "You've gone off somewhere, Gil."

He smiled at her. "I am sorree!"

"What's bothering you?"

"I don't exactly know. Not yet. Excuse me. I want to make a call."

26

He left her and phoned Hartford from the lobby. He got his assistant on the line. "Robby, I don't know what source to use for this, but find me the names of any men who have sold chains of movie houses in Kansas during the past year."

Robby whistled softly. "Let me see. There ought to be a trade publication that would have that dope. Phone you?"

"I'll call back at five."

"How does it look?"

"It begins to have the smell of murder."

"By the beneficiary, we hope?"

"Nope. No such luck."

"So we'll get a statistic for the actuarial boys. Luck, Gil. I'll rush that dope."

"Thanks, Robby. 'Bye."

He had sandwiches in the bar with Kathy and then gave her her instructions for the afternoon. "Any kind of gossip, rumor, anything at all you can pick up on the Drynfellses. Financial condition. Emotional condition. Do they throw pots? Where did he find the cutie?"

"Cute, like a derringer."

"I think I know what you mean."

"Of course you do, Gil. No woman is going to fool you long, or twice."

"That's what I keep telling myself."

"I hope, wherever your lady fair might be, that she realizes by now what she missed."

"You get too close for comfort sometimes, Kathy."

"Just love to see people wince. All right. This afternoon I shall be the Jack Anderson of Madeira Beach and vicinity. When do I report?"

"When I meet you for cocktails. Sixish?"

On the way back to Clearwater Beach he looked in on Dinah Davisson. There were dark shadows under her eyes. Temple Davisson's daughter had been reached. She was flying south. Mrs. Hoke had brought over a cake. Darrigan told her he had a hunch he'd have some real information by midnight. After he left he wondered why he had put himself out on a limb.

* * *

At four thirty he grew impatient and phoned Robby. A James C. Brock had sold a nine-unit chain in central Kansas in July.

Darrigan thanked him. It seemed like a hopeless task to try to locate Brock in the limited time before he would have to leave for Redington Beach. He phoned Dinah Davisson and told her to see what she could do about finding James Brock. He told her to try all the places he might stop, starting at the most expensive and working her way down the list.

He told her that once she had located Mr. Brock she should sit tight and wait for a phone call from him.

Kathy was waiting at her cabaña. "Do I report right now, sir?"

"Right now, Operative Seventy-three."

"Classification one: financial. Pooie. That Coral Tour thing ran way over estimates. It staggers under a mortgage. And he got a loan on his beach property to help out. The dollie is no help in the financial department. She's of the gimme breed. A Cuban. Miami. Possibly nightclub training. Drynfells's first wife died several centuries ago. The local pitch is that he put that plot of land on the market to get the dough to cover some postdated checks that are floating around waiting to fall on him."

"Nice work, Kathy."

"I'm not through yet. Classification two: Emotional. Pooie again. His little item has him twisted around her pinkie. She throws pots. She raises merry hell. She has tantrums. He does the housekeeping chores. She has a glittering eye for a pair of shoulders, broad shoulders. Myron is very jealous of his lady."

"Any more?"

"Local opinion is that if he sells his land and lasts until the winter season is upon him, he may come out all right, provided he doesn't have to buy his little lady a brace of Mercedeses and minks to keep in good favor. He's not liked too well around here. Not a sociable sort, I'd judge. And naturally the wife doesn't mix too well with the standard-issue wives hereabouts."

"You did very well, Kathy."

"Now what do we do?"

"I buy you drinks. I buy you dinner. Reward for services rendered."

28

"Then what?"

"Then we ponder."

"We can ponder while we're working over the taste buds, can't we?"

"If you'd like to ponder."

They went up to the bar. Martinis came. Kathy said, "I ponder out loud. Davisson's offer was too low. But he waved his money about. They brooded over that money all day. He came back and waved it about some more. Mrs. Drynfells's acquisitive instincts were aroused. She followed him, met him outside of here, clunked him on the head, pitched him in the Gulf, and went home and hid the money under the bed."

"Nice, but I don't like it."

"Okay. You ponder."

"Like this. Drynfells lied from the beginning. He sold the land to Temple Davisson. They went back. Drynfells took the bundle of cash, possibly a check for the balance. Those twenty minutes inside was when some sort of document was being executed. Davisson mentions where he's going. In the afternoon Drynfells gets a better offer for the land. He stalls the buyer. He gets hold of Davisson and asks him to come back. Davisson does so. Drynfells wants to cancel the sale. Maybe he offers Davisson a bonus to tear up the document and take his money and check back. Davisson laughs at him. Drynfells asks for just a little bit of time. Davisson says he'll give him a little time. He'll be at the Aqua Azul for twenty minutes. From here he phones his wife. Can't get her. Makes eyes at you. Leaves. Drynfells, steered by his wife's instincts, has dropped her off and gone up the road a bit. She waits by Temple Davisson's car. He comes out. He is susceptible, as Mrs. Drynfells has guessed, to a little night walk with a very pretty young lady. She walks him up the road to where Drynfells is waiting. They bash him, tumble him into the Drynfells car, remove document of sale, dispose of body. That leaves them with the wad of cash, plus the money from the sale to the new customer Drynfells stalled. The weak point was the possibility of Davisson's car being seen at their place. That little scene we witnessed this morning had the flavor of being very well rehearsed."

Kathy snapped her fingers, eyes glowing. "It fits! Every

29

little bit of it fits. They couldn't do it there, when he came back, because that would have left them with the car. He had to be seen someplace else. Here."

"There's one fat flaw, Kathy."

"How could there be?"

"Just how do we go about proving it?"

She thought that over. Her face fell. "I see what you mean."

"I don't think that the dark-haired girl he was seen with could be identified as Mrs. Drynfells. Without evidence that the sale was consummated, we lack motive—except, of course, for the possible motive of murder for the money he carried."

Kathy sat with her chin propped on the backs of her fingers, studying him. "I wouldn't care to have you on my trail, Mr. Darrigan."

"How so?"

"You're very impressive, in your quiet little way, hiding behind that mask."

"A mask, yet."

"Of course. And behind it you sit, equipped with extra senses, catching the scent of murder, putting yourself neatly in the murderer's shoes, with all your reasoning based on emotions, not logic."

"I'm very logical. I plod. And I now plod out to the phone and see if logic has borne any fruit."

He went to the lobby and phoned Dinah Davisson.

"I found him, Mr. Darrigan. He's staying at the Kingfisher with his wife."

"Did you talk to him?"

"No. Just to the desk clerk."

"Thanks. You'll hear from me later, Mrs. Davisson."

He phoned the Kingfisher and had Mr. Brock called from the dining room to the phone. "Mr. Brock, my name is Darrigan. Mr. Temple Davisson told me you were interested in a plot of Gulf-front land."

"Has he been found?"

"No, he hasn't. I'm wondering if you're still in the market."

"Sorry, I'm not. I think I'm going to get the piece I want."

"At Redington Beach?"

Brock had a deep voice. "How did you know that?"

30

"Just a guess, Mr. Brock. Would you mind telling me who you're buying it from?"

"A Mr. Drynfells. He isn't an agent. It's his land."

"He contacted you last Friday, I suppose. In the afternoon?"

"You must have a crystal ball, Mr. Darrigan. Yes, he did. And he came in to see me late Friday night. We inspected the land Sunday. I suppose you even know what I'll be paying for it."

"Probably around one seventy-five."

"That's too close for comfort, Mr. Darrigan."

"Sorry to take you away from your dinner for no good reason. Thanks for being so frank with me."

"Quite all right."

Gilbert Darrigan walked slowly back into the bar. Kathy studied him. "Now you're even more impressive, Gil. Your eyes have gone cold."

"I feel cold. Right down into my bones. I feel this way when I've guessed a bit too accurately." She listened, eyes narrowed, as he told her the conversation.

"Mr. Drynfells had a busy Friday," she said.

"Now we have the matter of proof."

"How do you go about that? Psychological warfare, perhaps?"

"Not with that pair. They're careful. They're too selfish to have very much imagination. I believe we should consider the problem of the body."

She sipped her drink, stared over his head at the far wall. "The dramatic place, of course, would be under the concrete of that new pool, with the dark greedy wife sunbathing beside it, sleepy-eyed and callous."

He reached across the table and put his fingers hard around her wrist. "You are almost beyond price, Kathy. That is exactly where it is."

She looked faintly ill. "No," she said weakly. "I was only—"

"You thought you were inventing. But your subconscious mind knew, as mine did."

It was not too difficult to arrange. The call had to come from Clearwater. They drove there in Kathy's car, and Dar-

31

rigan, lowering his voice, said to Drynfells over the phone, "I've got my lawyer here and I'd like you to come in right now, Mr. Drynfells. Bring your wife with you. We'll make it business and pleasure both."

"I don't know as I—"

"I have to make some definite arrangement, Mr. Drynfells. If I can't complete the deal with you, I'll have to pick up a different plot."

"But you took an option, Mr. Brock!"

"I can forfeit that, Mr. Drynfells. How soon can I expect you?"

After a long pause Drynfells said, "We'll leave here in twenty minutes."

On the way back out to Madeira Beach, Darrigan drove as fast as he dared. Kathy refused to be dropped off at the Aqua Azul. The Coral Tour Haven was dark, the "No Vacancy" sign lighted.

They walked out to the dark back yard, Kathy carrying the flash, Darrigan carrying the borrowed pickaxe. He found the valve to empty the shallow pool, turned it. He stood by Kathy. She giggled nervously as the water level dropped.

"We'd better not be wrong," she said.

"We're not wrong," Darrigan murmured. The water took an infuriating time to drain out of the pool. He rolled up his pants legs, pulled off shoes and socks, stepped down in when there was a matter of inches left. The cement had set firmly. It took several minutes to break through to the soil underneath. Then, using the pick point as a lever, he broke a piece free. He got his hands on it and turned it over. The flashlight wavered. Only the soil underneath was visible. Again he inserted a curved side of the pick, leaned his weight against it, lifted it up slowly. The flashlight beam focused on the side of a muddy white shoe, a gray sock encasing a heavy ankle. The light went out and Kathy Marrick made a moaning sound, deep in her throat.

Darrigan lowered the broken slab back into position, quite gently. He climbed out of the pool.

"Are you all right?" he asked.

"I . . . think so."

He rolled down his pants legs, pulled socks on over wet feet, shoved his feet into the shoes, laced them neatly and tightly.

"How perfectly dreadful," Kathy said in a low tone.

"It always is. Natural death is enough to give us a sort of superstitious fear. But violent death always seems obscene. An assault against the dignity of every one of us. Now we do some phoning."

They waited, afterwards, in the dark car parked across the road. When the Drynfellses returned home, two heavy men advanced on their car from either side, guns drawn, flashlights steady. There was no fuss. No struggle. Just the sound of heavy voices in the night, and a woman's spiritless weeping.

At the Aqua Azul, Kathy put her hand in his. "I won't see you again," she said. It was statement, not question.

"I don't believe so, Kathy."

"Take care of yourself." The words had a special intonation. She made her real meaning clear: Gil, don't let too many of these things happen to you. Don't go too far away from life and from warmth. Don't go to that far place where you are conscious only of evil and the effects of evil.

"I'll try to," he said.

As he drove away from her, drove down the dark road that paralleled the beaches, he thought of her as another chance lost, as another milepost on a lonely road that ended at some unguessable destination. There was a shifting sourness in his mind, an unease that was familiar. He drove with his eyes steady, his face fashioned into its mask of tough unconcern. Each time, you bled a little. And each time the hard flutter of excitement ended in this sourness. Murder for money. It was seldom anything else. It was seldom particularly clever. It was invariably brutal.

Dinah Davisson's house was brightly lighted. The other houses on the street were dark. He had asked that he be permitted to inform her.

She was in the long pastel living room, a man and a woman with her. She had been crying, but she was undefeated. She carried her head high. Something hardened and tautened within

33

him when he saw the red stripes on her cheek, stripes that only fingers could have made, in anger.

"Mr. Darrigan, this is Miss Davisson and Colonel Davisson."

They were tall people. Temple had his father's hard jaw, shrewd eye. The woman was so much like him that it was almost ludicrous. Both of them were very cool, very formal, slightly patronizing.

"You are from Guardsman Life?" Colonel Davisson asked. "Bit unusual for you to be here, isn't it?"

"Not entirely. I'd like to speak to you alone, Mrs. Davisson."

"Anything you wish to say to her can be said in front of us," Alicia Davisson said acidly.

"I'd prefer to speak to her alone," Gil said, quite softly.

"It doesn't matter, Mr. Darrigan," the young widow said.

"The police have found your husband's body," he said bluntly, knowing that bluntness was more merciful than trying to cushion the blow with mealy half-truths.

Dinah closed her lovely eyes, kept them closed for long seconds. Her hand tightened on the arm of the chair and then relaxed. "How—"

"I knew a stupid marriage of this sort would end in some kind of disaster," Alicia said.

The cruelty of that statement took Darrigan's breath for a moment. Shock gave way to anger. The colonel walked to the dark windows, looked out into the night, hands locked behind him, head bowed.

Alicia rapped a cigarette briskly on her thumbnail, lighted it.

"Marriage had nothing to do with it," Darrigan said. "He was murdered for the sake of profit. He was murdered by a thoroughly unpleasant little man with a greedy wife."

"And our young friend here profits nicely," Alicia said.

Dinah stared at her. "How on earth can you say a thing like that when you've just found out? You're his daughter. It doesn't seem—"

"Kindly spare us the violin music," Alicia said.

34

"I don't want any of the insurance money," Dinah said. "I don't want any part of it. You two can have it. All of it."

The colonel wheeled slowly and stared at her. He wet his lips. "Do you mean that?"

Dinah lifted her chin. "I mean it."

The colonel said ingratiatingly, "You'll have the trust fund, of course, as it states in the will. That certainly will be enough to take care of you."

"I don't know as I want that, either."

"We can discuss that later," the colonel said soothingly. "This is a great shock to all of us. Darrigan, can you draw up some sort of document she can sign where she relinquishes her claim as principal beneficiary?" When he spoke to Darrigan, his voice had a Pentagon crispness.

Darrigan had seen this too many times before. Money had changed the faces of the children. A croupier would recognize that glitter in the eyes, that moistness of mouth. Darrigan looked at Dinah. Her face was proud, unchanged.

"I could, I suppose. But I won't," Darrigan said.

"Don't be impudent. If you can't, a lawyer can."

Darrigan spoke very slowly, very distinctly. "Possibly you don't understand, Colonel. The relationship between insurance company and policyholder is one of trust. A policyholder does not name his principal beneficiary through whim. We have accepted his money over a period of years. We intend to see that his wishes are carried out. The policy options state that his widow will have an excellent income during her lifetime. She does not receive a lump sum, except for a single payment of ten thousand. What she does with the income is her own business, once it is received. She can give it to you, if she wishes."

"I couldn't accept that sort of . . . charity," the colonel said stiffly. "You heard her state her wishes, man! She wants to give up all claims against the policies."

Darrigan allowed himself a smile. "She's only trying to dissociate herself from you two scavengers. She has a certain amount of pride. She is mourning her husband. Maybe you can't understand that."

"Throw him out, Tem," Alicia whispered.

The colonel had turned white. "I shall do exactly that," he said.

Dinah stood up slowly, her face white. "Leave my house," she said.

The colonel turned toward her. "What do—"

"Yes, the two of you. You and your sister. Leave my house at once."

The tension lasted for long seconds. Dinah's eyes didn't waver. Alicia shattered the moment by standing up and saying, in tones of infinite disgust, "Come on, Tem. The only thing to do with that little bitch is start dragging her through the courts."

They left silently, wrapped in dignity like stained cloaks.

Dinah came to Darrigan. She put her face against his chest, her brow hard against the angle of his jaw. The sobs were tiny spasms, tearing her, contorting her.

He cupped the back of her head in his hand, feeling a sense of wonder at the silk texture of her hair, at the tender outline of fragile bone underneath. Something more than forgotten welled up within him, stinging his eyes, husking his voice as he said, "They aren't worth . . . this."

"He . . . was worth . . . more than . . . this," she gasped.

The torment was gone as suddenly as it had come. She stepped back, rubbing at streaming eyes with the backs of her hands, the way a child does.

"I'm sorry," she said. She tried to smile. "You're not a wailing wall."

"Part of my official duties, sometimes."

"Can they turn this into . . . nastiness?"

"They have no basis. He was of sound mind when he made the provisions. They're getting enough. More than enough. Some people can never have enough."

"I'd like to sign it over."

"Your husband had good reasons for setting it up the way he did."

"Perhaps."

"Do you have anyone to help you?" he asked impulsively. He knew at once he had put too much of what he felt in his voice. He tried to cover by saying, "There'll be a lot of arrangements. I mean, it could be considered part of my job."

He detected the faintly startled look in her eyes. Awareness made them awkward. "Thank you very much, Mr. Darrigan. I think Brad will help."

"Can you get that woman over to stay with you tonight?"

"I'll be all right."

He left her and went back to the beach to his room. In the morning he would make whatever official statements were considered necessary. He lay in the darkness and thought of Dinah, of the way she was a promise of warmth, of integrity.

And, being what he was, he began to look for subterfuge in her attitude, for some evidence that her reactions had been part of a clever act. He ended by despising himself for having gone so far that he could instinctively trust no one.

In the morning he phoned the home office. He talked with Palmer, a vice-president. He said, "Mr. Palmer, I'm sending through the necessary reports approving payment on the claim."

"It's a bloody big one," Palmer said disconsolately.

"I know that, sir," Darrigan said. "No way out of it."

"Well, I suppose you'll be checking in then by, say, the day after tomorrow?"

"That should be about right."

Darrigan spent the rest of the day going through motions. He signed the lengthy statement for the police. The Drynfellses were claiming that in the scuffle for the paper, Davisson had fallen and hit his head on a bumper guard. In panic they had hidden the body. It was dubious as to whether premeditation could be proved.

He dictated his report for the company files to a public stenographer, sent it off airmail. He turned the car in, packed his bag. He sat on the edge of his bed for a long time, smoking cigarettes, looking at the far wall.

The thought of heading north gave him a monstrous sense of loss. He argued with himself. Fool, she's just a young, well-heeled widow. All that sort of thing was canceled out when Doris left you. What difference does it make that she should remind you of what you had once thought Doris was?

He looked into the future and saw a long string of hotel

rooms, one after the other, like a child's blocks aligned on a dark carpet.

If she doesn't laugh in your face, and if your daydream should turn out to be true, they'll nudge each other and talk about how Gil Darrigan fell into a soft spot.

She'll laugh in your face.

He phoned at quarter of five and caught Palmer. "I'd like to stay down here and do what I can for the beneficiary, Mr. Palmer. A couple of weeks, maybe."

"Isn't that a bit unusual?"

"I have a vacation overdue, if you'd rather I didn't do it on company time."

"Better make it vacation, then."

"Anything you say. Will you put it through for me?"

"Certainly, Gil."

At dusk she came down the hall, looked through the screen at him. She was wearing black.

He felt like a kid trying to make his first date. "I thought I could stay around a few days and . . . help out. I don't want you to think I—"

She swung the door open. "Somehow I knew you wouldn't leave," she said.

He stepped into the house, with a strange feeling of trumpets and banners. She hadn't laughed. And he knew in that moment that during the years ahead, the good years ahead of them, she would always know what was in his heart, even before he would know it. And one day, perhaps within the year, she would turn all that warmth suddenly toward him, and it would be like coming in out of a cold and rainy night.

Death Writes the Answer

He held the magazine up as though he were still reading it, but he watched her across the top of it, ready to drop his eyes to the story again should she look up.

For the moment the excitement, the carefully concealed anticipation, of the past month faded, and he wondered, quite blankly, why he was going to kill his wife. Myra had no major faults. In the eight years of their marriage, they had had no serious quarrels.

Peter Kallon looked across the small one-room apartment at her, and slowly the dislike and the determination built up again in equal quantity. It had started about six months before, and then it was only an intellectual game. How would a man kill his wife without fear of discovery? And, in the midst of the game, he had looked at Myra with the cold objectivity of a stranger and found that the eight years had changed her.

Eight years had thickened her figure, put a roll of soft tissue under her chin, but the years had done nothing to alter that basic untidiness which he had once found so charming.

Peter Kallon was a very tidy man. By day he entered neat columns of figures on pale yellow work sheets. His linen was always fresh, his razor in the exact same spot on the bathroom shelf, trees inserted in his shoes each night.

But Myra, even though childless, seemed to find it impossible to handle the housekeeping details of an efficiency apartment with its minuscule bath, cubbyhole kitchen, Murphy bed. Eight years of litter had worn away his quite impressive patience with the monotony of water dripping on sandstone.

The thought of being a widower was quite engaging. Peter Kallon had a passion for puzzles. Crosswords, cryptograms, contests. He attacked all with equal dry ardor. Murder became a puzzle.

And a month ago he had arrived at the final detailed answer.

He looked across at her. A strand of graying brown hair hung down her cheek. She sat with one leg tucked under her, an unlaced shoe on the swinging foot. She was reading a novel, and as she came to the end of each page she licked the middle finger of her right hand before turning the next page. That little habit annoyed him. Long ago he had given up trying to read any book Myra had finished.

It would be such a pity to have the answer and not put it into effect.

Lately he had been looking at the young girls on the street and in the office. There was the clean line of youth about them.

Myra set the book aside, smiled over to him, and scuffed her way into the kitchenette. He heard her fill a glass with water from the faucet, heard the small familiar sound she made in her throat as she drank. He knew that as she came back into the room she would be wiping her mouth with the back of her right hand. She was.

It would never do, he thought, to say, "Myra, I'm tired of being married." Poor Myra. She would never be able to support herself. That would mean quite a drain on him, supporting two establishments. No. Murder would be tidy. Myra could die without knowing that he had grown to hate her and her ways with all the dry passion of a careful, fastidious man.

She turned on the transistor radio, spun the dial to a station. Myra continued to read.

"You've got two stations there," he said.

She cocked her head on one side, listening. "But you can hardly hear that other one."

He came angrily across the room and reset the dial. She never did anything crisply and purposefully. Never on time, never able to move fast.

Most murders were too hasty. The motive was too clear. Their few friends would never suspect him of having a motive

40

to kill Myra. He knew that their friends considered them beautifully adjusted.

When murders weren't too hasty, they were too contrived, too full of details that the murderer was incapable of handling neatly.

The perfect murder, he had decided, could be quite detailed, if the details were handled by a man competent to do so. A man like Peter Kallon. He was the sort of man that no one had ever called Pete. Not even his mother or his sister.

He looked over at her again and saw that the book had sagged down onto her heavy thigh. Her head was tilted over onto her shoulder and she breathed audibly through her open mouth. Each night they stayed home it was the same. She would expect him to awaken her when he was ready to go to bed. Now there was no need to discipline his expression. While she slept he could look at her with all the naked, helpless fury at his command.

In that moment he made up his mind, finally and completely, with no possibility of changing it. Peter Kallon decided to make himself a widower and put into effect the plan he had worked out.

Friday he made her write the note.

He sat at the small desk, scribbling. He made frequent grunts of disgust, crumpling what he had written. She asked him what the trouble was.

"Nothing, nothing," he said impatiently.

He wrote for a long time, then said irritably, "The hell with it," crumpling what he had written.

"What is the trouble, darling?" she asked.

"Maybe you could help me. You see, I've got one account, a garage, that's giving me a bad time. The man won't keep the books the way I tell him to. We've quarreled about it. I'm trying to write a letter to him, but I can't seem to get it right. If I could dictate it to you and you wrote it down . . . I always think better on my feet somehow."

"Of course, darling," she said.

He laid out a fresh sheet of her notepaper and put his fountain pen beside it. She took his place at the small desk.

41

"What's his name?"

"Don't bother with that, Myra. I'll copy it over. Let me see now. First paragraph. 'You know how hard I've tried to make everything work out. But there is no use trying any more.' New paragraph. 'Please don't condemn me too much for taking this step. I am certain that you will be happier in the future because of it.' There! That ought to do it."

He leaned over her shoulder and read the words she had written in her childish scrawl. The words, as usual, slanted uphill to the right edge of the paper.

"Like that pen?" he asked casually. There was the coldness of sweat against his ribs.

"I like a heavier point," she said. "You know that."

"Just a habit. A fine point makes better-looking writing. Here, sign your name on that sheet. For my file."

She obediently wrote "Myra." He took the pen from her hand before she could write the last name. "Wait a minute," he said. "Let me look at this. I think you were bearing down too hard on it." He examined the point, holding it under the lamplight. "Get up a minute, dear. I want to try it."

He sat down and wrote on another sheet.

"No, I guess it's okay. Thanks, dear. I'll recopy this letter and send it to the man. I think it'll be all right."

"You're welcome," she said. For a long time he did not risk looking at her. When he did he saw that she was engrossed in the novel again, without suspicion. Just to be certain, he copied the letter, using the actual name of one of his clients, making the contents a bit more businesslike. He showed it to her. She said that she guessed it sounded all right.

After she had fallen asleep he read the note over. Fingerprints on it were quite all right. He would just make certain that he found the note first.

You know how hard I've tried to make everything work out. But there is no use trying any more.

Please don't condemn me too much for taking this step. But I am certain that you will be happier in the future because of it.

Myra

42

A bit stilted, perhaps, but the intent was unmistakable. It was on her gray monogrammed notepaper. He put it with his business papers, knowing that she never looked at them. He wanted to take a long walk to get the tension out of him. But that might look a bit odd, and his plan didn't call for it.

Instead he took out the manila folder containing the contest puzzles he was currently working on. Within fifteen minutes he was so deeply engrossed in the puzzle that he had actually forgotten his plan. The deadline of this one was near. It was a puzzle that assigned numerical values to letters of the alphabet, and the object was to fill out a grid with words in such a way that the highest possible total was reached.

At midnight he put his solution into the envelope and addressed it. Myra awakened by herself, yawned, and smiled sleepily at him. Trusting Myra! For a moment his resolve was weakened by pity. He thought of the envelope in his hand. The first prize was fifty thousand dollars. With fifty thousand dollars, life could be made bearable, even with Myra. Money would buy a certain amount of liberty from the married state.

But, as a winner of many very small prizes, he knew how remote his chances were.

He smiled back at her and they went to bed.

On Saturday afternoon he had, as he expected, an hour alone in the apartment. It was a ground floor apartment in the back of the building, the windows half shadowed by cedars. That was a necessary part of the plan. He took the fishline from the closet shelf, cut off a ten-foot length and tied a loop in the end, made a slipknot. The windows were of the sort with a permanent screen, and they could be opened or closed by inside cranks. Each movement had been planned. The handles on the small gas stove pointed straight down. They turned in the right direction for his purposes. He slipped the noose over one handle, pulled it tight, ran the other end of the string to the window, and poked it through one of the meshes of the screen. The window was open a few inches. Then, carrying a screwdriver for the sake of appearances, he went outside and around the building to the window. He found the end of the string, pulled it slowly and firmly. It gave slightly and then came free. He pulled it all the way out through the mesh, forcing the knot through, then pushed firmly against the window. As he had expected, the crank made a half turn and closed.

He hurried back into the apartment and found that the kitchenette was filled with the stink of gas. The burner, unlighted, was on full. He turned it off, opened the window to air the place.

The stove had four burners. He made three more lengths of string with slipknots at the end, knots that would slip off when the handles pointed directly at the window. He put the four lengths of string on the closet shelf.

When Myra returned from the store, he was working on a new puzzle which had just come out.

That was on Saturday. He gave himself Sunday as a breathing space and began the second part of the campaign. Myra was a person who needed a great deal of sleep. Peter decided to see that she would become starved for sleep.

Monday night he talked her into a late movie. After they got back to the apartment he talked long and animatedly about the picture they had seen, ignoring her yawns and sighs. They were in bed by two thirty. He set the alarm for seven and saw that she got up when he did. On Tuesday he phoned four times during the day, knowing from the drugged sound of her voice that he was awakening her each time. Tuesday night he took her out to dinner and then to another movie. He watched her in the movie and awakened her the two times she fell asleep. He insisted on seeing part of the picture over and afterward invented an excuse to call on friends.

They were in bed by midnight, but Peter lay in the darkness for a time and then awakened her to tell her that he was ill. Her concern for him kept her from getting very much sleep that night. And on Wednesday morning Peter phoned the office and said that he was not well. He demanded copious attention all through the day. Myra cared for him and dragged about with the drugged look of a sleepwalker.

It was hard for him to conceal his excitement and anticipation. At five o'clock he got up and dressed, declaring that he felt much better. In fact, he said, he was famished.

44

At seven o'clock, with the dishes washed, Myra sat across the room from him and fell asleep, making no attempt to read.

"Myra!" he said, quite loudly. "Myra!"

She didn't stir. Everything up to this point had been preparation. And now he realized that the actual commission of the deed required no particular call on his strength and determination. Actually it was as though she were already dead. He opened the kitchenette window several inches, took the four strings, fastened them to the handles, careful not to touch the handles with his fingers. Myra was snoring throatily.

He poked the strings through the screen knowing that she had no more reason to use the stove, knowing that in the semi-darkened kitchenette the dark strings would be invisible. He took his keys out of his pocket and put them on the desk. He took the note from among his business papers, folded it once and placed it on the desk, an ashtray on top of it, in a conspicuous spot. It was important that he be without keys and that the note be out in the open for anyone to find. It would be best if someone else should find it. Then he could snatch it away and handle it.

Everything was ready. He spoke to her sharply, went over and shook her.

"Myra!"

She smiled blearily up at him. "Gee, I'm so tired I could die!"

That startled him for a moment, and then he felt a deep ironic amusement at her choice of words.

"Honey, I feel guilty not working today. I'm going down to Benninger's drugstore. They're a client, and I can do a little checking. I'll be back in an hour or so."

"Maybe I'll go to bed."

"No. Don't do that. It's only a little after seven. You go to bed now and you'll wake up before dawn."

"Okay," she said dreamily. "I'll wait until you come back."

He opened the door, looked back at her, and said, "Goodbye, honey."

She yawned. "'Bye, Peter."

He shut the door, heard the latch click. Now came the period of most danger. The night was very dark. The apartment house was on a quiet street. When he was certain that he was unobserved, he went quickly along the dark line of cedars. He looked cautiously through the windows of the living room. He could see the back of the wing chair in which she sat, her hand slack on the arm of the chair, the edge of one shoe. She did not move. Every object in the room stood out with a strange clarity, as though he were seeing the room for the first time, and had been asked to memorize the contents and the position of each item.

Cedar brushed his cheek as he moved back to the kitchenette window. He found the four strands, conquering panic as, for a moment, it appeared that one had slipped back through the screen. He pulled slowly and steadily. The four strings pulled free and he yanked them through the screen, balled them in his hand. Then he pressed the window shut, walked out to the edge of the building, looked up and down the deserted sidewalk, then hurried across to the walk and went south with long strides to the Benninger drugstore.

The younger brother was behind the counter. Peter's lips felt stiff as he smiled. It seemed to him that in some secret place in his mind he could hear the whisper of escaping gas. A good thing the stove was a cheap one without a pilot light.

"Thought I'd stop by and see how the new register tape is working."

"It seems to be going okay, Mr. Kallon. It slowed us up the first week getting used to it, but now it's second nature. I like the way it keeps all the sales separated by department."

"Sure," Peter said. "It gives you a check on how you're doing."

"There's a couple of new books of crosswords in since you were here a couple days ago."

"Are there? Good." He went casually over to the rack, picked out the new ones, put them on the counter, and slid up onto a stool. "I'd like a root beer, please."

"Sure thing," Benninger said. Charged water hissed into the glass. It also sounded like gas escaping. "How's the missus?"

"What? Oh, she's fine. Say, you don't mind if I sit here and work one of these puzzles, do you?"

"Goodness, no! You go right ahead, Mr. Kallon."

46

The puzzle he picked was based on names of cities and states. He glanced at the clock as he took his pencil out of his pocket. Ten of eight. He started the puzzle, lettering neatly and quickly. The Christmas city. Ah, that would be Bethlehem, Pennsylvania. Number ten down bothered him. Six letters. The only all-rock town in the U.S. He worked on the surrounding words and finally the stubborn one turned out to be Ingram. He felt a glow of satisfaction as he filled it in.

But he couldn't quite forget the hollow feeling in his middle, the flutter that was partly excitement, partly worry. What was going on at the apartment? Had she been awakened by the smell?

He finished the puzzle and looked at the clock. Nine fifteen. Later than he had dared believe.

"Finished it off?" Benninger asked.

"I got it."

Benninger laughed. "You sure are one for the puzzles and contests. Remember that contest blank I give you and you won a fifty-dollar government bond with it?"

"Of course I remember it. Well, time to get home. I've been a little worried about Mrs. Kallon lately. She acts depressed."

"It's this changeable weather. Gets all of us down."

"Well, be sure you get those tapes and your check stubs down to the office on Friday, Harry. 'Night."

"Good night, Mr. Kallon. We'll have 'em there on time."

Peter let the door swing shut behind him. He felt that he had handled it exactly as planned. Nothing crude like calling attention to the time. His hand hadn't shaken as he'd picked up the change from his dollar. No, it had gone quite well. That's what came of understanding details and knowing how to handle them from a purely objective viewpoint.

He found himself walking too fast and forced himself to slow down. The night air was cool on his face. Breathable air. Fresh, life-giving air. His heels struck firmly and crisply and tidily against the sidewalk. He passed a neighborhood couple by a streetlight. He knew them by sight. That was lucky.

"Good evening," he said cheerfully.

"Hello, Kallon," the man said. Better and better. He hadn't realized that the neighbor knew his name.

He pushed the front door open and walked down the long corridor, past the elevators, down to the corner and then turned left and went to his own door. He took a deep breath, knocked, and called gaily, "Myra! Myra! Open up. I forgot to take my keys with me."

He could smell it then, the faint odor of gas. He waited to make certain that he actually smelled it before simulating panic. "Myra!" he yelled, hammering on the door. In a few moments now, other doors would open. "Myra!"

He was rattling the doorknob helplessly, kicking at the bottom of the door, calling to his dead wife when it happened. In the last fractional second of life that was left to him it was as though the door had curiously pulled loose in his hand. It smashed against him with a white-hot blasting flare, the heavy panel smashing him against the opposite wall of the corridor....

Because the girl was very upset and because she looked a little like his daughter, the police lieutenant was very gentle.

"You had no way of knowing," he said.

"I still don't understand how it happened."

He shrugged his heavy shoulders. "There was a heavy concentration of gas in the apartment. When a phone rings it makes a little spark inside it between the magnet and the arm on the clapper. So of course, after you dialed and got the connection, the line went dead at the first ring. You had no way of knowing."

There was a stricken look in her eyes. "I . . . I was so anxious to make that call. One of the other girls wanted to, but it had to be me. I thought it would be exciting telling somebody that they'd won a fifty-thousand-dollar prize."

The lieutenant reached over and clumsily patted the girl's shoulder as she buried her face in her hands. "You had no way of knowing," he said again. A nearby machine began to clack out a telegram, imprinting the words on the long paper tape. The lieutenant turned and walked stolidly out of the Western Union office.

48

Miranda

They put a plate in the back of my head and silver pins in the right thighbone. The arms were in traction longer than the legs. The eye, of course, was something they couldn't fix.

It was a big, busy place they had there. The way I had come in, I guess, was a sort of challenge to the doctors. A postgraduate course. See, gentlemen, this thing is alive—indubitably alive. Watch, now. We will paste it back together the way God made it. Or almost as good.

My friends came—for a while. For a few months. I wasn't too cordial. I didn't need them. It was the same thing every time. How terrible to be all strung with wires and weights! Aren't you going mad from boredom, George?

I wasn't going mad from boredom. I learned how to keep my face from laughing, how to laugh on the inside. As if I was sitting back there in my mind, hugging myself, shrieking with laughter, rocking from side to side, laughing and laughing. But nothing but silence on the outside. The faraway dignity of the very sick.

They brought me in and I was dead. That is, for all practical purposes. The heart had no right to keep beating.

But you see, I knew. When you know a thing like that, you can't die. When you know a thing like that, it is unfinished business.

Poor George. Poor old George.

And me all the time laughing away. It was a joke that I could understand, but nobody else would. The joke goes like this. I'll tell you and you can laugh with me too. We'll rock

and giggle together. Once upon a time there was a good-na-
tured, broad-shouldered slob named George A. Corliss who
lived in an eleven-thousand-dollar frame house in an orderly
little suburban community called Joanna Center. He lived at
88 April Lane. He made a hundred and thirty-eight fifty each
and every week in a New York publishing house, carried a
little more insurance than he should have, loved his dainty,
fragile-boned, gray-eyed, silver-blond little wife named Connie
very much indeed. In fact this slob had his happiest moments
when Connie would give him a speculative look and tell him
that he really did look a little like Van Johnson. This George
Corliss, he made replicas of early American furniture in a
basement workshop, bought a new Plymouth every time he
had the old one about paid for, conscientiously read "good
books" while commuting, and often brooded about the child-
lessness of the Corliss household, a thorn in his side.

He drove too fast, smoked too much, knocked off too many
cocktails. In all respects a very average guy. But what George
didn't know was that Connie, the little silver-blond wife,
feeling the thirties coming on, had acquired an itch for a Latin-
type twenty-two-year-old kid, a gas pumper at the local lubri-
torium, a pinch-waisted kid with melting eyes, muscles, and
a fast line of chatter. Since the kid obviously could not support
Connie in the style to which George had gradually accustomed
her, nothing seemed simpler than to find some nice safe way
of knocking George off and glomming onto the fifty-six thousand bucks his demise would bring in.

So one day when George had told Connie in advance that
he had to take a run up to a mountain town called Crane, New
York, to dicker with a recalcitrant author, Connie took the
Plymouth to the garage and the kid, Louie Palmer by name,
did a judicious job of diddling with the tie-rod ends with the
idea of their parting when a turn was taken at high speed.

So I took a turn at high speed. Rather, I tried to take it.
The steering wheel went loose and gummy in my hands. They
killed me, all right. They killed George, the slob, all right.

Funny, how it was. Take the moment the car started rolling.
I had maybe one second of consciousness left. And in that
second a lot of little things added up. I'd had the steering

50

checked in town that week. Connie always buying gas in one-dollar quantities. The funny way she'd said goodbye. At the last minute I wanted her to come along. She was emphatic about saying no. And there was the time I found the initialed cigarette case on the car floor. She took it and I forgot it until I saw that Louie Palmer using it. Then he got all red and bothered and said it had slipped out of his pocket while he was checking the car, maybe when he reached in to yank the gimmick that releases the hood.

And before things went out for me, in a blinding whiteness that reached across the world, I said to myself, almost calmly, "George, you're not going to let this kill you."

But it did kill the George I was talking to. The man who came out of the coma eight days later wasn't the old furniture builder, huckster, and loving husband.

No, he was the new George. The boy who could lie there and laugh inside at his joke. They tried to kill him and they did. And now he was going to kill them. Murder by a corpse. There's something you can get your teeth into and laugh at. But don't let it move the face muscles. It might pull out some of the deep stitches.

"You're the luckiest man in the world," the young doctor said. Young, with a nose like a bird's beak and no more hair than a stone.

"Sure," I said.

"I would have bet ten thousand to one against you."

"Good thing you didn't." I wanted him to go away. I wanted to think about Connie and Louie and just how I would do it to them.

He fingered the wasted arm muscles. "Doing those exercises?"

"Every day, Doc." I liked to see him wince when I called him Doc.

He clucked and muttered and prodded. "I warned you that you might not ever be able to walk again, the way those nerves were pinched. But the nurse told me you took a few steps today. I don't understand it."

I looked him in the eye, with the one I had left. "You see, Doc," I said, "I've got everything to live for."

The way I said it made him uneasy.

"Mr. Corliss, you're not going to be exactly as good as new. We can improve that face for you by hooking a plastic eye in those muscles so that the eye will turn in its socket, but the two big scars will still show. You'll limp for a few years and you will have to be very careful for the rest of your life, protecting that plate in your head from any sudden jars. No sports, you understand. Bridge is going to be your speed."

"You've said this before, Doc."

"I want to impress it on you. A man can't go through what you went through and expect—"

"Doc, I don't expect a thing. I was thrown through a shatter-proof windshield and then the car rolled across me."

He didn't like me as a person. He loved me as a case. I made his mouth water. He had showed me to every doctor within a ten-mile radius. He was writing me up for some kind of medical journal. The before-and-after pictures were going to go in his scrapbook. But we always parted with him looking as though he wished I was healthy enough to hit in the mouth.

Pain to the average person is just that. Pain. Nothing else. A mashed finger or a bad headache. But when you have it a long time something else happens to it. It turns into something else. You live with it and get to know it. With me, it was a color. Green. Green is supposed to be restful. I would see it behind my eyes. Eye, I should say. I'd wake up in the night and look at the color. Dull dark green. That was good. That was above standard. That was more than you could expect. But there were the nights in the beginning when it was a hot, bright, harsh green, pulsating like a crazy living plant. That was when the night nurse was always there. During the first weeks she used the needle when it was bad, and later it was pills, which never worked as fast or as well.

One time it was that new green that they say you can see for two miles on a clear day. It stayed that way, they told me later, for four days. Something about those pinched nerves.

And one day I searched and searched and could find no green at all, even the dark, almost pleasant kind. I missed it. Believe me, I missed it.

I didn't want them coming, and they sensed it and didn't

52

come any more. But I liked to have Connie come. I liked it when there was traction on the two arms and the leg and both legs felt dead and the bandages on my head covered all but my mouth and my right eye.

She came every day. She wept a little every time she came.

"Don't cry, Connie."

"I—I can't help it, George."

"I'm getting better, they keep telling me. So why are you crying?"

"It's so awful to see you there like this."

"Just think, Connie. I might be dead. Wouldn't that be worse, Connie? Wouldn't it? Or maybe you'd like that better."

"What do you mean? What do you mean?"

"Then there wouldn't be all this pain and suffering."

"Oh."

"What did you think I meant, Connie? What on earth could I have meant except that, dearest? I know that you love me very much. You've told me so often."

"It's hard to understand you, George, not seeing your face and all. Just your . . . eye. What you say just comes out . . . and it's hard to know what you mean sometimes." She always worked hard on that explanation. It meant a lot to her to get it right. Her knuckles always had a bone-white look while she talked to her loving husband.

Every time it was a lovely game. And I had all the time in between to plan the next visit.

"Connie, I hope you're taking good care of the car."

"But, George! It was a total loss."

"Sorry, dearest. I keep forgetting. We'll have to get a new one. But when we do you'll help me see that it's well taken care of."

"Of course, George."

There was a continuity about it. If I kept after her too hard she'd get suspicious. Then the fear would show in her eyes. I'd let her carry the fear around for a few visits and then I would drive it away.

"I'm so lucky to have a wife like you, Connie."

"Thank you, George."

"I know I've been acting strangely. But I haven't the courage

53

to do what I planned. I wanted to estrange you, to drive you away, so that you could find a new life with a whole man, not some smashed item like me."

"Is that what you were doing?"

"Of course!"

"Oh, George! Darling, I thought—" A very abrupt stop.

"What did you think?"

"Well, that maybe the accident had . . . well, hurt your head in some way so that you were beginning to think I was to blame for the accident." Then she laughed to show how silly that idea was. She flushed, too. I imagine she was considering her boldness to be the best defense, in addition to being rather fun because of the risk.

"You? Hey, I was alone in the car, remember?"

"You've always driven too fast."

"Never again."

At the end of the visiting period she would kiss me and go. Before the bandages came off my face she would press her lips to mine very sweetly. Loving little silver-blond Connie with those enormous gray eyes and that dainty figure.

After the bandages came off and there was just the patch on the eye she kissed hard, but not in passion. As though it was something she had to do hard and quick in order to do it at all.

After her fears had gone away and after, I guessed, she had told Louie that she had been wrong about thinking that I might have guessed, I would slowly bring her suspicions back to a boil.

I was giving Connie and Louie some exciting dates. Giving them something to talk about.

A good thing about carrying too much life insurance is that you sometimes have too much accident insurance along with it. And I had a lot. Complete coverage of all medical expenses plus thirty-five hundred consolation prize for the loss of the eye plus six hundred a month for complete disability until I could get back to my job. They said a full year from the time of discharge from the hospital.

To go home would give me more time for the game I was playing with them. But it was good in the hospital, too. I could lie there at night, and it was as if I had them fastened to a string, two puppets. When I yanked the string they jumped.

The books talk about having to live with guilt and how it can subtly change the relationship of lovers. But I was no body, firmly and safely planted away. I was between them. I wondered if she could taste my lips when she kissed Louie, and if he looked deep into her eyes and saw a hospital bed. . . .

The nurse was something else. A tall, gawky girl, almost grotesquely angular and yet full of a strange grace. Miranda. She charged at the bed looking capable of tripping and falling over it, yet always her hands were light as moths. Her eyes were deep-set, smallish, a brilliant and Technicolor blue. She knew.

I saw it in the strange, wry amusement in her eyes.

Once she told me she knew. She cranked the bed up a little to rest tired muscles. She stood and folded her arms. I heard the starched rustle of the material. Her hair was a soft dusty black under the cap. Her mouth was wide and quite heavy.

"Delirium," she said in her abrupt voice, "is usually dull." She had a trick of starting a sentence boldly and then letting it fall away.

"I was delirious, I expect."

"But not dull, George." That was the tip. Up until that point it had been a most discreet and proper Mr. Corliss.

"Like living out a soap opera, Miranda?"

She shrugged. It was typical of her to shrug too hard, hiking her wide, thin shoulders almost up to her ears. "But no part in it for me, I would think."

I watched her. There was nothing awkward in our silence.

"Delirium isn't much to go on, Miranda. Not when there's been a brain injury."

"Perhaps the delirium is partly due to her. So sweet. She's all tinkle and ice and teensy little gestures. Oh, she's a one, that one. What mothers want their daughters to grow up to be—on the outside."

"And the inside. Will you hazard a guess on the inside, Dr. Miranda?"

No more banter. She looked hard at me, and up through the

55

little blue eyes welled the fanatic light. "Rotten," she whispered. "Dead, soft rotten." She turned and walked out with her lunging stride, a whisper of starch.

It made the game better. A new piece on the board, allowing more permutations and combinations.

Later that day I had my arm around her as I walked. She looked as though her back and shoulders would feel hard, slatted. She was a softness and a warmth. I took five steps away from the bed and four back to the wheelchair. Her lip was caught under her teeth and her breath came hard as though it were she who was making the effort.

The next day, dozing on the sun porch, I felt someone staring at me. I looked over and saw Miranda in the doorway. We looked at each other for an impossible time, the white antiseptic walls and the neat floral arrangements tilting and spinning away until we looked across a bottomless void at each other and there was nothing alive in creation except the wild blue of her eyes. When she turned and left, without speaking, the time weave was ripped across with a sound I could almost hear.

The young doctor and the absentminded old one came in one morning and told me that this was the day I would go home, that an ambulance was being provided, that Connie had been informed, that arrangements had been made for Nurse Wysner to live in for a time until Connie became accustomed to the necessary work.

"In a couple of months you'll be ready for the eye work," the young doctor said.

"Yes, of course," I said. "We mustn't forget that."

He turned away, looking as though his mouth hurt him.

They didn't use the siren, and it awakened in me a childish disappointment. It would be fitting to arrive with siren, that sound which in our neat world has replaced the night cough of the unknown beast.

When they rolled me out onto the asphalt of the drive I lifted my head and looked at the house. This was where the big amiable clown who sometimes looked a little like V. Johnson had lived. All the details of it were sharp and it looked unreal, a house seen in a movie. I knew that all things would

56

now look that way. Two eyes give depth perception. One eye gives everything a two-dimensional flatness.

Miranda Wysner, blinding white in the sun, stood tall and straight, with a tiny smile at the corner of her mouth. A smile no one else could see.

Connie trotted delicately back and forth between the wheeled cart and the side door, telling everybody to be careful, please, don't bump him on anything, and her voice was like the mirrored wind chimes in a lost lake house of long ago.

Connie had moved into the guest room across the hall from the bedroom we had shared—or rather the bedroom she had shared with George A. Corliss, who died in such an unfortunate accident. They put me in the big double bed, and the Hollywood frame creaked in a well-remembered way and I was very tired and went to sleep almost immediately.

I dreamed I was laid out in that room with candles at head and feet and the smell of flowers and soft chanting. I awoke in the purple-gray dusk and there were flowers and a distant chanting but no candles. The chanting was a muted newscaster, his Airedale voice tamed by a half twist of the dial. There were the sharp yelps of neighborhood children at play, and for a moment I was a guy who had taken a nap. Just a nap. Get up, go down, kiss Connie, mix the drinks, check the stove to see what dinner might be.

But Miranda came in with her starchy rustle and bent over me and put her hand on my forehead. "Cool," she said. "Probably a little subnormal."

"We're living in a subnormal household. Where are you?"

"The next room. Beyond the bath. With both doors open, I'll hear you if you cry out in the night."

Connie smells sweet and dainty and feminine. Miranda had her special scent. Long illness makes the senses acute. Miranda smelled of medicinal alcohol, antiseptic, and, underneath, a deep perfume that throbbed. It was probably against regulations. It had a musky jungle beat.

"Maybe I'll just whimper."

"I'll hear that, too." There was just enough light so that I could see her teeth flash white. "I told her not to try to talk to you until tomorrow. Excitement, you know."

"Just like a county fair."

"I'll bring your tray."

When I awoke in the morning, a fat rain, oyster colored, viscid, was coming down in straight lines. I could see it bouncing off the roof peak across the street. The bedside clock said three minutes of six. Hospital habits. In three minutes Miranda came striding in with a basin of warm water, glass of cold, toothbrush, comb.

"I've put the coffee on," she said. I had finished breakfast and was shaving with an electric razor when Connie came in, her pink housecoat belted tightly around her child's waist, her face all cute and vacant with sleep.

"Goodness, you people get up early!"

Miranda turned from the window. "Good morning, Mrs. Corliss."

"Good morning, nurse. Welcome home, darling! Oh, welcome home!" She came over to the bed. Miranda watched stonily. Connie bent and gave me that quick, hard kiss. I got my hand around the back of her frail neck and prolonged it. When I released her she took a step backwards, her eyes wide, bringing her hand up as though to scrub her lips, not quite daring.

"Well!" she said unevenly.

At the end of the week, I made four full circuits of the room. At the end of two weeks I went downstairs, dressed for the first time. The clothes hung on me. The more independent I grew, the more coldness appeared in Connie's manner toward Miranda.

At the end of the second week she brought it to a head, in Miranda's presence.

"George, I think we can get along beautifully now without Nurse Wysner."

"I'll leave in the morning," Miranda said. "I'll pack tonight. That is, if you really feel you don't need me, Mr. Corliss."

I gave the words the proper emphasis. "I can handle everything myself," I said.

"You mustn't get too confident," Miranda said.

"I know my own limitations," I replied.

"You two talk as if I weren't here to help," Connie said with small-girl plaintiveness.

"I'm certain you'll be a great help, Mrs. Corliss," Miranda said, starting bluntly, sliding into her odd breathlessness at the end of the sentence.

"Then it's settled," Connie said brightly, clapping her hands once, a habit I had at one time found almost unbearably sweet. . . .

In the middle of the night Miranda's hand against my cheek awakened me. The bed stirred as she sat on it. The night was as black as a sealed coffin.

Her whisper had the same quality as her speaking voice. "You can't do it alone, you know."

"Do what?"

"Whatever it is that you've been planning, my darling."

"May I take this as a declaration of your great and undying passion?"

"See? You can't hurt me that way. You can't hurt me by trying to hurt me. That's a sort of secret we have. We've said more things with a look than we can ever say with words."

"I'm touched, deeply."

Her nearness was more vital than any caress. "You've got to let me help. You've got to let me share."

"Why?"

"Doing something and never having a sharing of it is bad. Then it's all on the inside. We can talk, you know. Afterward."

Nurse and patient, probing together a deep and desperate wound.

"But I have a way and you aren't in it."

"Then there must be a new way. Two can think better. You might forget something important."

"You're accepting the correctness of the decision, then?"

"Only because it's yours. I don't matter. I've never had any strong feelings about right and wrong."

"That's a lie, Miranda."

Hoarsely: "So it's a lie! When you've seen the evil I've seen—"

"I'll let you help on one condition, Miranda."

"Anything."

"We haven't used the words yet. I want you to say the words

59

we've been skirting so carefully. I want you to say them slowly. All the words. Now, what are you going to do?"

Her hands found my wrist and the moth touch was gone. Her nails dug in with a surprising force. "I am going to help you kill your wife and her lover."

"Why?"

"Because they hurt you so badly, and it's something you want to do."

"But more than that. The other reason."

"Because after it is done it will be something so strong between us that we'll never be apart again."

"Love, then?"

"No. Something stronger than that. Something more exciting."

"You want half a man?"

"I'm strong enough for two. I knew it would be this way. Ever since that night I kept you from dying. You gave up that night. I sat and whispered in your ear why you had to live. Over and over. And you did."

"It's settled, then. Go in the morning. Be patient. I'll come to you when I can."

She left quickly, plunging towards the doorway, miraculously finding it in the blackness.

Strength slowly came back. My clothes began to fit again. Tone came back to the mended muscles. Connie stayed in the guest room. For a long time she seemed to be waiting, and when she saw that there would be no demands on her uxorial capacities, there seemed to be a relief in her. Once, when she was out, I went over her personal checks against the small income from her father. I checked back far enough to find out when it had started. They had been a little careless several months before my accident. Instead of cashing two of the checks, she had turned them over to her friend. The endorsements were a scrawled *L. Palmer*, with a self-conscious flowery squiggle under the name. I took those two checks. They were both for twenty-five.

60

I didn't hate either of them. I was cold—cold as any self-respecting corpse should be.

With the proceeds of the collision insurance I bought a good used car. I wasn't cold about that. It frightened me. That was unexpected. I sat behind the wheel, and when I shut my eyes I could feel the car rolling, first sideways and then end over end. I opened my eyes quickly and the world returned to sanity. The first time I drove to the city, the sweat ran down from my armpits, soaking my shirt. I had the checks photostated on that first trip, front and back. I returned them to her file.

That night, at dinner, I put the next brick in the foundation. I looked across at Connie. "You're mine, you know," I said.

Little puzzled wrinkles appeared above the bridge of her nose. "Of course, dear. What brought that on?"

"I just was thinking. You know how you imagine things. I was imagining how I would react if you ever wanted to leave me. The answer is very simple. I'd never, never let you go."

She smothered the quick alarm. "Why think of such a thing, George? Such an impossible thing!"

I shrugged. "I don't know. Say, the new car holds sixteen gallons of gas."

The fork trembled in her hand. "What's that got to do with—"

"Nothing, Connie. Don't be so silly. I saw the conversation disturbed you, so in my own feeble way I was changing the subject."

"Oh!"

"The steering seems pretty sound. I had it checked at the station. That Palmer boy seems to know his business."

Vacant stare. "Palmer? Oh, Louie, the dark one."

She was getting better at it. That was really a good effort. I thought it was too bad I couldn't tell her just how good an effort it was. Then she spoiled it by being unable to finish the dinner she was eating with such appetite. That's one thing about her that always amazed me. A tiny girl, yet almost rapacious about her food. Red lips eager and white teeth tearing and champing. Once upon a time it had been cute. Funny how little you can learn about a woman in seven years of marriage.

I had to make her see Louie. I had to give her a reason.

Over coffee I said, "I've been asking around."

"About what, darling?" A shade too much casualness and disinterest.

"We could make a good deal on this house right now."

The petulance showed immediately. "But, George! I love this house and this neighborhood. I don't want to move."

"I stopped in at the office. I told Mallory how the docs recommend I keep out in the air as much as possible. He hinted that they might be able to give me a traveling job, based in California. I'd cover eleven Western states, part promotion work, part digging up new talent for the list. I'd also do some coordination work with the movie agents. I'm to let him know."

She looked as if somebody had hit her in the stomach. "But isn't the job you had a better one? I mean, we could see that you got plenty of fresh air."

"I don't know if I'm too anxious to pick up this commuting treadmill again. I'm going to give it a lot of thought. We'd make a profit on the house. In the new job my trips would be so long that you would travel with me, naturally."

"I do get a little carsick," she said, the dread showing.

I laughed. "Say, remember in the hospital when I told you I was going to drive slow from then on?"

"Yes, I do."

"Found out today I've got my nerve back. I kicked it up to seventy-five on Route Twenty-eight. The old reflexes seem pretty good."

I watched and saw the speculative look dawn. She covered it by getting up to bring more coffee. But when she poured it into my cup, she spilled some in the saucer and didn't seem to notice.

At a quarter to nine she said she was going for a walk. I knew that the station closed at nine. I yawned and said I might go to bed. She left. I waited five minutes and backed the car out. The station was six blocks away. I was curious to see how it was done. I took the parallel road, then turned left after six blocks and parked in the tree shadows. I could see the station. Connie walked by it, very slowly, silhouetted against the station floodlights. She continued on down the street. I turned around in a driveway, went back to the parallel road, sped down three blocks, and parked as before. Soon Connie went by, walking quickly now, high heels twinkling. I eased out after her.

Thirteen blocks from our house on April Lane she turned left. It was a cheap neighborhood. Midway in the second block was a green neon sign against a pale brick front: UNICORN—BAR AND GRILL. Beyond it was another sign, *Ladies' Entrance*. She darted in there, reluctant to linger under the harsh green light. I could remember the exact stage of pain that green light represented. Not the worst, but bad.

I went down the street, turned around, parked on the same side as the Unicorn, facing toward it. I was barely in time. A '40 Ford convertible parked across the street and Louie Palmer in jacket, open sports collar, hatless, walked across the street. He stopped in the full glare of green and lit a cigarette. He handled it in a thoroughly Bogart fashion, hand cupped completely around it, lowering it with calculated slowness after each drag. He looked up and down the street. He flipped it away, squared his shoulders, and went inside. After all, he was a desperate character. A real killer. The murder didn't quite pan out, but what the hell. The intent was there. Louie was a real sharp apple, all wound up in a capital A affair, just like out of James M. Cain.

It would be nice to tell him that he was a sniveling little grease monkey preening himself over a tramp wife, a hired banty rooster with grease in his hair. But that was a pleasure I would have to forego.

I was in bed when she got home an hour later. I heard her in the bathroom. I wondered how radiant she looked.

Miranda lived alone in an efficiency apartment crowded into what had apparently been one of the bedrooms of a vast old Victorian house. To the left of the house was the parking lot for a supermarket. The street had been widened until the bottom step of the porch was a yard from the sidewalk.

She came down the street from the bus stop, lean legs in the white cotton stockings scissoring below the hem of the cheap coat.

She watched the sidewalk ahead of her and suddenly looked

63

across the street directly into my eyes and stopped. It did not seem strange that she should have that utter awareness.

She waited and I walked across to her. The small blue eyes narrowed just a bit. Her heavy lips were laid evenly together. She wore no lipstick, and the strange thinness of the skin of her lips made them look peeled, raw.

We did not speak to each other until she had shut the apartment door behind us. "You should take stairs more slowly," she said.

"Showing off, I guess."

"You look better, George. Give me your coat."

The apartment was absolutely characterless at first glance. Then the signs of her presence intruded. An ashtray squared precisely to the edge of a table. Three birch logs, so perfect as to look artificial, stacked in the shallow, ashless fireplace. Shades all pulled to exactly the same level. She plunged back and forth through the room, physically threatening to derange all its neatness, but her touch on each object was light and precise. She pulled a glass-topped table closer to the armchair where I sat. From the kitchenette alcove she brought bottle, glass, small bowl of ice cubes, new bottle of soda. She set them down with evenly spaced clicks against the glass top. She made the drink deftly and said, "With you in a moment," and shut herself into the tiny bath.

She came out with her hair fluffed out of its rigid nurse's style, and she wore a turtle-necked gray sweater and a harsh tweed skirt in a discomfiting orange shade. No stockings. Ancient loafers. She fell toward a chair, sat lightly in it. The bones of her wrists and hips were sharp. She looked harsh, brittle, angular. I thought irrelevantly that she was a woman made for a blind man. To his touch she would have the remembered softness and warmth.

I put the drink down. "How do we start?"

"Tell me how we're going to do it." The sentence faded away. Each of her sentences brought silence after it, so that forever we spoke across silence more clearly than with words. Her eyes were dedicated blue flames.

"Not that fast. I want to know if you still insist on sharing this thing. Without knowing when or how we're to do it."

"I insist."

I studied her. "Have you ever wondered about your own sanity, Miranda?"

"Of course. Everyone does. They say that to wonder means that you are really quite all right."

"Odd that you're a nurse."

"Is it? People fighting, dying. I'm there. I can watch and decide about them. Oh, you don't have to do anything crude, like the wrong medicines. I like them caught between living and dying. Like you were. Then you can do it with words. You can decide, and it always comes out the way you say. It makes you strong to think about it."

I smiled, and my lips felt stiff. "Have you decided against anyone lately?"

"Oh, yes. This past week. An old man. They wanted him alive because, you see, he was a great-grandfather and in another month he'd be a great-great-grandfather and it was all a matter of pride with him and with them. To have all those generations living at once. He fought, that one, to keep living just for the sake of living, which is never any good. I whispered in his ear. 'Give up,' I said. 'Let it go. Stop fighting. Give up.' They say they can't hear you, but they can. They always can. He finally gave a great sigh and died. They couldn't understand why he died. But, of course, I couldn't tell them."

"You like doing that?"

"You kill the rotten ones and keep the good ones. Like sorting things. Like being neat about yourself."

"I'm one of the good ones?"

She shook her head, as though puzzled. "No, and yet I kept you. I keep wondering why."

My glass was empty. She sprang toward me, and had I not learned about her I would have flinched away. But she stopped in time and the new drink was made.

I caught her wrist and pulled her onto my lap. Oddly, she seemed lighter than Connie, though she was much heavier, I knew. The calm lips folded against mine. But there was nothing there. It was holding a senseless pose, like a charade that no one can guess. She went back to her chair.

"I expected anything but that," I said.

65

"Wait," she said. "Wait until afterwards. There isn't enough togetherness yet. Afterwards the thing shared will make it right."

"Maybe I died," I said. "Maybe this is a fancy-type hell, like the mythological one where the sinner is chained for eternity just out of reach of food and drink."

"Am I food and drink?" She showed, for the first time, a trace of coyness. Like a child's rattle placed atop a small white coffin.

"Maybe not that. But necessary. In an odd way. Essential."

"That's because I know more about these things. I'm like a guide. You're just learning."

"Is it a taste you can acquire?"

"That you can't help acquiring."

"But when there's no one left to kill?"

"Then we'll help each other find someone else. And do it in a better way than words."

I stood up. "I'll let you know."

"I'll be waiting."

On the way home I could feel the clear imprint of the plate inlaid in my skull, the perfect outline of it, as though gentle fingers were pressing it against the jelly of my brain.

I went into the cellar and fitted a length of soft white pine into the lathe. I let my hands work the way they wanted to work, without direction. The cutting tool ate away the wood, turning angles into curves. I took it off the lathe and turned on the sander. I held it one way, then another way, rounding it the way my hands said. It turned into the crude elongated torso of a woman, a woman as thin as Miranda. Then I put it back into the lathe and cut it down to a round rod, shaving away the woman form.

The pressure against the plate had turned into an ache, the beginning of green behind my eyes. I broke the rod over my knee.

I went up to Connie and said, "Rub the back of my neck."

I stretched out on the couch. She was awkward about it, lacking the skill of Miranda. I turned and held her close, telling myself she was precious. I kissed her. I saw surprise in her eyes and then a most patient resignation. I sat beside her on the couch and took the patch off the empty socket. She shut her eyes hard. Her small fists were clenched. I tiptoed away from her and up the stairs and shut myself in my room. I heard her go out. I lay in the livid green and the world was green neon and the outline of the plate changed slowly, forming letters, pressing the word UNICORN deep into the gray-green brain, deep into the softnesses in which forever a car rolled and leaped and bounded like a child's toy thrown aside in petty rage.

"You won't be needing the car, will you?" I asked Connie.

She gave me her prettiest frown. "Gosh, I don't think so. How long will you have it?"

"Overnight."

"Where on earth are you going?"

"I went in and talked to Mallory yesterday. We decided I'd start to take on a few odd jobs, just to get my hand in. That splendid creative artist up in Crane is yammering at his agent to arrange a switch of publishers again."

"But that is where you were going when—"

"Correct. Sort of like a movie. This is when I came in."

"When are you leaving?"

"He keeps crazy hours. Starts writing after a midnight breakfast. It's a two-and-a-half-hour drive. I'll leave tonight after dark, and after I see him I'll hole up somewhere and come back down tomorrow. No point in getting too tired at this stage of the game."

The upper surfaces of her rounded arms had the faint tan that she never seems to lose, even in the dead of winter. I held her by the shoulders and looked into her eyes. She was facing the light. I saw then, and for the first time, the slight yellowness of the whites of her eyes. Once they had been that bluey white that only children seem to have. The pores of her snub nose and on her rounded cheeks were faintly enlarged, and everywhere, eye corners, around her mouth, across her forehead, I could see the spreading inevitable network of wrinkles, cobwebby against the skin. Enlarge those wrinkles to the maximum, and she would have the face of a withered monkey, out of which the gray eyes would still stare, acquiring through that contrast the knowledge of evil which had always been there but which I had never been able to see or understand.

She moved uncomfortably in my grasp. "What are you staring at?"

"My fine true wife, my loyal little Connie. Darling, what did I do to deserve you?"

She had the grace to blush. "Oh, come now."

"It's the truth, isn't it? Why, any other woman would be scheming and planning how to get rid of me. But not you, Connie. Not you. Love is bigger than expediency, isn't it?"

"If you say so, George."

"Read any good books lately?"

"George, right now you seem . . . more like yourself. You've been so odd, you know."

"I'll be my very own true self very soon now."

"Are we going to move away from here?"

"I think so."

Her voice became wheedling. "Darling, before you make up your mind for sure, let's go up to the cabin for a long week. Just the two of us. There won't be anybody around at this time of year. We can walk in the woods. Oh, we'll have a wonderful time."

"Just the two of us?"

Her eyes grew as opaque as gray glass. "Call it a second honeymoon," she breathed.

That would be ideal for them. Not difficult to arrange at all. So many ways to do it up there. I could almost see Louie Palmer pushing me off the high front porch onto the lake-front rocks and then lighting a cigarette in his Bogart way, saying, "I'll run along. You drive out and make the phone call. Remember, he complained about feeling dizzy and you told him not to go near the steps."

There would be a deep satisfaction in that for them. An end of tension. It had failed the first time. Their frozen world would begin to revolve again.

"A second honeymoon," I said. . . .

In the late afternoon I took the car down to the station. Conner, the owner, was there as well as Louie Palmer. Louie was in his coveralls, his sleeves rolled up over muscular forearms, a smear of grease on his chin near the corner of his mouth, a lank end of black hair curling down across his forehead to the black eyebrow. He avoided meeting my eye.

"Taking a little trip," I said heartily to Conner. "First one since my accident. Have Louie check the tires, steering arms, kingpin, front wheel bushings, please."

"Put it on the rack, kid," Conner said in his husky, domineering voice. I wondered how much Conner's constant scorn was a factor in Louie's bold play for big money. I watched the coveralls tighten across Louie's broad shoulders as he ducked under the car. How had it started? A few sidelong glances? The realization that the Corliss woman was coming around oftener than strictly necessary? Then, probably, "I guess we better road-test it, Mrs. Corliss. Just move over and I'll take the wheel."

How does it start?

"Change the oil, sir?" Louie asked.

"No thanks, kid," I said. I rasped that "kid" across him, saw the color creep up the back of his neck.

I waited, and when he was through I tipped him a quarter. He looked as if he might throw it in my face. "Buy yourself a beer," I said. "Try the Unicorn. I hear that's a good bar."

His mouth sagged a little, and the color left him. I grinned into his face and turned away. Louie was jumpy.

"Take it easy, Mr. Corliss," Conner advised.

"I'll do that," I said. "Made myself a promise that I'll never drive over forty-five again, and I'm sticking to it."

Beyond Conner I saw a puzzled look on Louie's lean white face.

I went over right after dinner. Miranda was waiting for me. Her eyes seemed deeper in her head, their glow strong and steady. The wide lips were parted a faint fraction of an inch. It added to the breathlessness of her words. The spring within her was wound as tightly as the key could be turned. A deb waiting for the grand march. A horse player waiting for the sixth race. An animal watching, from a limb, the trail beneath.

She shut the door and leaned against it. "Tonight?"

"Yes, tonight."

69

She shut her eyes for a moment. With her eyes shut she had a corpse face.

"How? Tell me how. Quickly!"

"They think I'll be gone. They think I'll be gone overnight. We'll come back."

"They'll be together?"

"Why not? They have planning to do."

"But how?"

"Electricity."

She looked disappointed. "Is—is that a good way?"

"The best. Clean and quick and final."

She nodded slowly. "Yes, I can see a lot of ways how it could be. But I won't just watch, will I? I'll be part of it." You there, little girl! Get into that game of musical chairs with the other children.

"You'll be part of it. I promised."

"Do they have a good chance of catching us, blaming us?"

"Not a chance in the world."

"Oh, good! And later . . . we'll go away."

"Far away."

"How much time is there?"

"Three hours. Four."

"Long hours to wait, George."

"We'll take a ride. That'll kill time. Come along."

She had not sat beside me in a car before. She was unexpectedly feline, a part of her that I had not noticed. She sat with her legs curled up under her, partly facing me, and I knew that she watched, not the road, but my face, the glow of the dash lights against it, the pendulum swing of the streetlamps.

"Scared?" I asked.

"No. Something else. Like when you're a child. You wake up in the morning. Another day. Then you see the snow on the windowsill and it all comes with a great rush. The day after tomorrow is Christmas, you say. One more day gone. Yesterday it was the day after the day after tomorrow. Now it's getting so close it closes your throat. That's how I feel. Getting one at last that isn't a sick one."

She inched closer so that the hard ball of her knee dug against my thigh. The musky perfume was thick in the car.

Without turning to see, I knew how her eyes would look. "We've never had to say much, have we?" she asked.

"Not very much. We knew without saying. A look can say everything."

"Later we can talk. We can say all the words that ever were. Good words and bad words. I've said bad words when I'm alone. I've never said them out loud to anybody. And we can say the other words too, and it won't be like after reading a story."

"How do you mean?"

"Oh, murder. Death. Kill. Blood. Bodies. I kill, you kill, we kill. The way you had to learn the Latin words in school."

"Conjugations, you mean."

"That's what I was trying to think of. Miranda Wysner, conjugate the verb to kill. I kill, I shall kill, I killed, I had killed, I should have killed."

She laughed. Her fingers shut on my arm above the elbow. "Think about it, George. Like swinging a big shining white sword. You swing it at evil and you tell yourself that's why you do it, but all the time way down inside your heart you know that it isn't the reason for it, it's the act itself."

I was on the road north out of town. She looked out the windows.

"Where are we going?"

"We'll just go north out of town up into the hills and then swing around and come back."

She was silent. I drove ever more rapidly. The road climbed and then began to gather unto itself a series of gentle curves that later would grow hard, the shoulders popping and crackling as the car threw itself at them.

I knew the landmarks. At the crest I slowed down, my arms tired from the strain. I started down the other side. The rising whine of the wind grew louder. The needle climbed. Sixty-five, seventy, seventy-five.

"We're killing the two of them, you see," I yelled above the wind. "We can't make the curve coming up. You wanted a part of it. You've got it, baby. You've got it I left a letter with Mallory to open if I should die. It's all in there. They'll

71

never worm out of this one. Electricity will kill them, all right. Courtesy of the State of New York, baby."

I saw the white posts of the curve in the farthest reach of the headlights.

Her scream filled the car, filled my ears, drilled into my soul. "Faster, Georgie! Oh, faster!" Wild ecstasy, beyond the peak of human endurance.

I gave her one quick look. The dash lights hit the white-ridged bone structure of her face so that the shape of the skull was apparent. The mouth was wide-screaming, lip-spread. Her voice told me that she had known.

I came down hard on the brake. The car went into a long skid toward those posts. I let up on the brake, accelerated it straight, came down on the brake again. This time the skid was the other way so that the car headed toward the brink, still skidding sideways. I could hear only the scream of tortured rubber, then the jolting metallic scraping as tires were rolled right off the rims. I couldn't bring it out of the second skid. The front right wheel smacked the posts and the car spun so that I lost all sense of direction. For a moment it looked as though the car were spinning in one spot, like a top, completely ringed about with the white posts. Then it hit again and I was thrown toward Miranda. I tried to find her with my arms but I couldn't.

The crescendo of sound was fading. The car jolted, lurched, stood absolutely still in a world where there was no sound.

I got out. Other cars stopped. I looked for Miranda. I couldn't find her. The tow truck had a spotlight on it, and so did the trooper car. I made them shine the lights down and search down the slope. They looked and looked. After I told them a little more about her they stopped looking and they were most polite, and they took me to a doctor who gave me white powders.

I was in bed for ten days. I told Connie everything. She was very grave about it all and kept her eyes on my face as I answered every one of her questions.

By the time I was on my feet the car had been repaired. I didn't care what happened any more. I didn't protest when she took me to the gas station. Conner acted odd, and the questions seemed to embarrass him. He said, "Why, sure, a few times

Mrs. Corliss cashed checks with me, and I guess I turned some of them over to Louie as part of his pay." Louie came over and shuffled his feet. He looked younger than I'd remembered. He was smoking a cigarette and he didn't hold it in his Bogart way.

"Louie," she said, "have you and I ever had a date?"

He stared at her. "What the hell! What the hell, Miz Corliss!"

"Have we?"

He manufactured a pretty good leer. "Well, now you bring the subject up, if you want a date, I'd—"

"Shut up!" Conner rasped.

"Get behind the wheel, George," Connie said, "and take me to the Unicorn."

I found the street. It wasn't there. I tried two other streets and then went back to the first one. I parked and went in a cigar store and asked what had happened to it. The man told me he'd been there twelve years and there'd never been a place of that name in the neighborhood.

We went home. I sat on the living-room couch. She pulled a small footstool over and sat directly in front of me.

"George, listen to me. I've been checking everything. That address you gave me. It's a parking lot. There aren't any old Victorian houses on that street made over into apartments. There's no local record of a nurse named Miranda Wysner. I brought you home from the hospital and took care of you myself. They told me I should put you in a psychiatric nursing home. They thought I was in danger from you. You said some pretty wild things about me in the hospital. I took the risk. For the first two weeks you were home you called me Miranda as often as you called me Connie. It was, I thought, the name of some girl you knew before we were married. Then you stopped doing that and you seemed better. That's why I thought it was safe to let you drive again. You were almost rational. No, you *were* rational. If it had been just almost rational, if I had thought that you were in danger, I wouldn't have permitted it. The steering did break when you had your accident. That's because the garage you took the car to installed a defective part "

I said haltingly, "But . . . you. The way you acted towards

73

me. I know that I'm repulsive to you now. This eye and all—"

She left the room, came back quickly with a mirror. "Take off the patch, George." I did so. My two eyes, whole again, looked back at me. I touched the one that had been under the patch.

"I don't understand!" I cried out.

"You were convinced you had lost an eye. They gave up and decided to humor you when you demanded the patch. And as far as my turning away from you in disgust is concerned, that is precisely what you did, George. Not me."

I sat numbly. Her grave eyes watched me.

"I followed you that night," I said.

"I went for a walk. I didn't want you to see my cry again. I'd cried enough in front of you—until I thought that no more tears could come. But there are always more tears. Funny, isn't it? No matter how many already shed."

"Why have I done this to you?" I demanded.

"George, darling. You didn't do it. It wasn't you. It was the depressed fracture, the bone chips they pulled out of your brain, the plate they put in."

"Miranda," I whispered. "Who is Miranda? Who was Miranda?"

Connie tried to smile. Tears glistened in the gray eyes. "Miranda? Why, darling, she might have been an angel of death."

"When I nearly died, she was there. . . ."

"I was there," Connie said, with an upward lift of her chin. "I was there. And I held you and whispered to you how much you had to live for, how much I needed you."

"She said she whispered to all of them on that borderline."

"Maybe she does."

"Take me in your arms, George," Connie said.

I couldn't. I could only look at her. She waited a long time and then she went alone up the stairs. I heard her footsteps on the guest-room floor overhead.

We went to the cabin on the lake. I was sunk into the blackest depths of apathy. Once you have learned that no impression

74

can be trusted, no obvious truth forever real, you know an isolation from the world too deep to be shattered.

I remembered the thin pink skin of her wide lips, the lurch of her walk, the unexpected competence of her hands.

I do not know how many days went by. I ate and slept and watched the lake.

And one day I looked up and there was Connie. She stood with the sun behind her and she looked down at me.

The smile came then. I felt it on my lips. I felt it dissolving all the old restraints. I reached for her and pulled her into my arms. The great shuddering sighs of thanksgiving came from her. She was my wife again, and she was in my arms, and everything between us was mended, as shining and new as in the earliest days of our marriage.

She wept and talked and laughed, all at once.

That night a wind was blowing off the lake.

When she slept I left her side and went to the windows. They look out onto the porch.

The old rocking chair creaked. Back and forth. Back and forth.

It was no surprise to me to see her sitting there. In the rocker. There was a wide path of reflected moonlight across the black water, and her underlip was moist enough to pick up the smallest of highlights from the lake.

We smiled at each other the way old friends smile who have at last learned to understand each other.

You see, Miranda knows about the drop from the top steps to the lakeshore rocks.

I turned back to gather up my small and dainty wife in my arms.

They Let Me Live

The silly woman from the alphabetical agency kept trying to move in on me as I lay on top of the blue canvas of the hatch cover. The weary little ship chewed its way doggedly across the Pacific, and I thought I'd never be able to soak up enough sun. The doc in Calcutta had grinned like a well-fed cat when he told me that I had better just pretend that I had been dead for a year. There was a lot to think about, and the dumpy girl yawped at me until my head ached. I grunted at her for four days and finally told her that it was too bad she was a lady because that made it impossible for me to tell her what was wrong with me. She stiffened and then nearly went over the side trying to get off the boat deck.

It was queer. There was a war on and you were bustling around. They sent you on strange trips because you were a specialist. Then you crashed, and when they finally got you out of Tibet it was nineteen forty-six and the war was over and the big installations were deserted and the aircraft were gone and the East was drifting back into its usual dim variety of slow death.

I had lots of time to think on that slow trip back. They put me on a slow boat because they thought I'd mend better.

I soaked up the sun and remembered.

The crew chief had stuck his head through the door and told us to strap on the belts. It was the hump trip, early '45. I rubbed the glass clear, and it scared me to look at the ice growing on the wings of the old crate. It was one of the few night trips that the China National Airways Corporation ever made. Those

76

kids liked to take it on the bright days with just enough cloud to duck into one if necessary. The old Allergic to Combat had to fly it in any weather at any minute on the clock.

The motors had been churning away when we hit. I knew we hit, and that was all. A grinding continuing crash and I knew I was torn loose from the strap and was being hurled toward the opposite side of the plane. Then nothing.

When I came to, the sky was gray with dawn and the brown rocks stuck up out of the snow. The wind of the Himalayas needled the flying ice into my face. I hurt in a hundred places. The great plane lay silent and crumpled against the rocks. Snow had drifted high against the side of it. Bits of wing and tail surfaces were scattered around. I was cold. Almost too cold to stand. I tried to stand. My right ankle gave out, and I chipped my chin on a rock when I fell. I crawled around and felt the port motor. Cold. I crawled out of the wind and sat against the side of the ship and hugged my knees, waiting for it to get light enough to see.

They hadn't had any luck. The pilot and co-pilot sat rigid and frozen in their seats, their heads at the same strange angle. The other two passengers had crushed skulls. I found the crew chief thirty feet from the plane, his blood frozen to one of the brown rocks.

I tried to build a fire outside and couldn't. Then I tried to build it inside the plane. My hands were shaking too much. I spilled the little gas I had collected and the fire roared up. I had tried to haul the bodies out, but the fire was too fast and I was too weak. Besides, there was little point in it. I crawled through the hole in the side and sat in the snow and watched the whole thing blaze up. When it was half burned, the yellow sun climbed up and paled the flames. The sun was as cold as the snow.

I had warmed myself a little in the radiant heat of the burning plane. I had no food. I looked around at the weird wild hills. Blinding snow, though a hundred miles away white men were passing out from sunstroke. I imagined that it was some part of Tibet. That's all I knew. I was so cold that I knew I'd have to move. We had hit on the side of a mountain. Only one way to go. Down the hill.

I died before I hit the bottom. That's the way the doc told me to think about it. Stumbling and falling and rolling in the thin sharp air with my bare hands blue and my face numb. Feeling the slow, warming comfort, the driving desire for sleep, and remembering that you freeze to death that way. Crawling and rolling some more. The acid edges of the brown rock tearing my freezing flesh. I marveled stupidly at how little I bled. Then there wasn't any more. Not until '46.

A very solid little Britisher with a face like a wrinkled boot sat beside my hospital bed in Calcutta and told me how they got me out. That was before they found out who I was. News doesn't travel very fast in the wild villages of the hills. He estimated that I had traveled about twelve miles. They must have found me at the edge of one of their trails across the high passes. They must have marveled and loaded me like a sack of grain across one of their shaggy ponies. Eventually they had heard in the outside world that there was a sick white man in one of the far villages.

I lay in the sun and remembered the fatuous nurse who had stood by the bed and tried to distract me while the doc changed bandages.

"My! You certainly'll have a lot to tell about living in the wilds."

I hadn't bothered to argue with her. I could remember hot food being crammed into my mouth so I had to swallow it or strangle. I remembered the bitter smoke that hung in a small room and burned my eyes. Bulky people with wide heavy faces that grunted at me in strange tongues. Furs that stank. Somehow, they kept me alive.

Coming to life in the hospital was like being born again. My voice was dusty in my throat, and I couldn't fit my mouth and tongue over the words. The white sheet on the bed had been the most wonderful thing in the world. I remembered running my left hand across it and noticing something odd about my hand.

I stared at my own hand for a long time, and my mind wouldn't tell me what I had noticed. It didn't look like my hand. It was thin, with the cords and bones showing clearly. Then I knew that the fingers were wrong. Not enough of them.

The two on the end were gone, and the top of the middle one. But it wasn't important. It was only important to feel the crisp soft texture of the sheet under my fingers. I know that I didn't look to see how the other hand was.

It had been a time for sleeping. I know that I was mending then. Coming back from death. Growing into awareness and life. There was the day I realized that I was in a hospital.

I remembered the afternoon that the young doctor with the sharp face and the wise eyes sat beside the bed.

"Well, man from the hills, can you remember who you are yet?"

"Remember? Why not? Howard Garry. Captain. Engineers."

"I've been asking you that question for three weeks."

"I don't remember you asking."

"You seem pretty bright today, Garry. What was the date when you got lost in the hills?"

"Early April."

"What year?"

"This year. Nineteen forty-five."

"Sorry, Garry. This is nineteen forty-six. May. The war's over. Most of your people have gone home."

When I looked again, he was gone. I had to think it out. Thirteen months out of my life. The war was over. From that day on, I mended more rapidly.

I remember the nurse getting excited when I told her that there was nobody to notify. Just the War Department. No relatives, no wife, no children. I wanted to tell them to find Dan Christoff and tell him that I was okay. Then I realized that I could have more fun walking in on him.

They finally let me go in September. They loaded me on a boat. Howard Garry, back from the dead. Not quite all back. I usually run about one eighty. I was weighed out at one forty-two. Two and a fraction fingers missing. Top of the left ear gone. All the toes on the left foot gone. Fingers and toes were frozen. Slight limp. Big silver plate in my right ankle, replacing an area where infection had eaten away the bone. A big scar across my right cheek. And in each day there were long minutes when I couldn't grasp where I was or what I was doing. Seconds of mental blindness. They told me that when the spells happened, I stood rigid and expressionless, staring straight ahead of me. Then the world would float slowly back.

I wanted to get back to the States and find Dan Christoff. We've always been as close as two citizens can get. Worked together, got drunk together, and had some beautiful battles.

I realized that I was one year older. Thirty-three. Dan would be thirty-four. We both worked as construction engineers for Saggerty and Hartshaw before the war.. That's the outfit that blankets the Midwest and grabs off more road stuff and bridge stuff than any other two you can name. They don't do it so much by pressure as they do by sticking in very low bids on stiff penalty contracts. They have the equipment, and, as Dan and I always said, they hire the best brains.

Saggerty and Hartshaw realized that Dan and I could work well together. I'm tall, dark, lean, and nervous. I blow off the handle about once a week and ride the hell out of the guys who work for me and the guys I work for. I've always worked best under pressure. I used to be able to get along on four hours sleep and a dozen cups of coffee a day.

Dan is the other way. He's middle height, but heavy in the chest and shoulders. A blondish reddish guy with freckles and a good grin. He moves slow and talks slow, and it takes him about ten minutes to load the pipe he smokes all the time. He's smart—smarter than I am by a long way. He plays them close to the vest, but there's nothing devious or hypocritical about him. In the old days, we drove the men and drove the equipment and sweated over the plans. We built stuff and it stayed built. The firm made dough on us and paid us back a nice little fraction of it.

Dan's married. But when the board tapped us on the shoulder, we both got tapped at the same time. Same outfit for basic. Same group going through engineer's OCS. Oh, we were sharp kids with those little gold bars. Big shots.

We had managed to stay together. At one point I was his company commander, and that burned him down to the ground.

Then we got the assignment to C.B.I., and for some strange reason we got shoved into staff work in Delhi. There were some decent guys around, but it suffered from the usual dry rot of any theater headquarters in a relatively inactive theater. We each objected in our own way. I stomped and stormed and beat on the walls, wrote nasty little formal notes through channels.

Don't get the idea that we were being boy heroes, yearning for the sound of rockets and grenades. Far from it. We wanted to get away from the starched-shirt boys and go build something. That's a hard fever to explain. I will never be able to understand what sort of satisfaction there is in working at a desk. Any kind of a desk. But if you've thrown a stinking little bridge over a dry creek, you can go and look at it in one year or twenty, and it will be there. You can step on it and touch it. Spit on it and jump off of it. It's tangible. It exists.

Dan used his own system of objecting. He merely loaded his pipe and leaned on the wall in the colonel's outer office. Whenever he saw the colonel, he smiled. The colonel knew what Dan was thinking. After a time he got tired of having his wall held up. He got tired of the pipe.

We were both called in on the same day at the same time.

"Garry?"

"Yes, sir."

"Here's your orders. You fly over the hump to Chengdu and join a Major Castle. It's a little trip over a proposed route for the Trans-Iranian Highway into China. You come back with a complete report of all construction necessary."

"Yes, sir."

"And Christoff. You're going down to Ceylon and join Lord Louis Mountbatten's staff. He wants a man for a survey of local materials for floating dock construction for an amphib invasion he's cooking."

That seemed to be all. We grinned at each other and then pulled our faces back into the right lines. We highballed him and started out.

He said, "Wait a minute, gentlemen." We stopped and turned around. "I've got to consider the reputation of this office. Can't send out experts unless they look like experts. I've requested captaincies for both of you. Ought to clear this afternoon. Pick up your orders for promotion and travel in the A.G.'s office.

81

Get out of town tonight. You're both driving me nuts. Good luck."

We had joined hands in the hall and done a solemn circling dance. He slapped me on top of the head, and I nearly broke a knuckle on his shoulder. Outside of a quick beer in the room, that was the last I saw of him.

So I wanted to see him again, and we could drink beer and check on the year or so that had elapsed. I wouldn't have much to tell.

I rolled over onto my back on the hatch cover. The long gray-blue swells raced by the ship, and she bobbed her bow in stately dance. The sun blazed down on me. I lifted my head and looked down at my legs. They were the worst part. Wasted muscles. Coat of tan on sagging flesh. Emaciated.

It was a forty-six-day trip. We coasted down the long channel of L.A. Port with the factories on either side. October in the States. I saw a blond dish in an aqua convertible steaming down the road that bordered the channel. She looked good.

Carter, an ex-accountant from Philadelphia, one of the boys they left behind to clean up the property accounting, came up beside me where I leaned on the rail. We had gotten fairly friendly on the trip back. He didn't talk too much or try to ask questions or dish out the dripping sympathy.

"No bands out there for us, Garry. We're too damn late coming home."

"Band music gives me cramps."

"Cheery today, hah? What're you going to do now, go back to work? Build yourself a bridge or dig yourself a ditch someplace?"

"If the company wants me back. And you'll go add up two and two on Market Street."

"Nice clean work. By the way, are you in good enough shape so that they won't stick you back into a hospital for a while?"

"Better not try it. Twenty-five pushups in a row now. Twenty slow deep knee bends. Less of a limp. Hundred and sixty-three now, according to the infirmary scales. Only seventeen to go."

"You look good, Garry. I better get my stuff together. See you around."

He walked off down the deck, a round little man with a tremendous store of calm and satisfaction. I envied him. Somehow I felt restless, felt a sense of impending trouble. I didn't know what it could be. I judged that it was the aftereffects of a year of blackout. You can't stop using your mind for a year without some very queer things happening to it. You let a field lie fallow, and it picks up chemicals you need to grow plants. The brain lies fallow and it seems to pick up a store of doubt, uncertainty, indecision. You imagine black catastrophe at every turn, and when you try to pin it down you get noplace. My dreams were an indication of that. On the average of every third night I would wake up, the sheets damp with sweat. It wouldn't have been a specific dream, just a vague black nothingness that was about to close in on me or fall on me. Sometimes I would be on the edge of a sort of gray cliff. The path would get narrower as I stood still on it. A gray wall would move toward me, and I would know that it would force me off to fall blindly, tumbling, spinning in the moist air down and down into blackness. The little doc had been right. He had a trick of sticking the point of his pink tongue out and carefully wetting down the two halves of his thin black moustache. He told me that I had been dead for a year. I would have to think of it that way. Dead and in a cold hell where the furred demons grunted at me and forced food into my mouth.

The mechanics of discharge were a joke. The system was built for millions, and it was too unwieldy to use for hundreds. But they followed it. Each and every form, each and every lecture.

A bored sergeant counted out my fifty-eight hundred dollars' worth of back pay. They told me that they'd mail me my discharge. Then they sent me off on a three months' vacation with pay, which went under the alarming name of terminal leave. They gave me a life pension of fifty bucks a month. Money for cigarettes and beer. And a movie once in a while. I toyed with the idea of using the back pay to buy some place so far off in the woods that I could live on the fifty bucks. A year or two would give me a chance to heal. My body was healed, but inside my head it felt as though there were long open wounds which pulsed.

There was a little town of about two thousand named Bennetville only about five miles from the separation center in Ohio. It looked quiet and clean. I registered into the only hotel. Even with my baggage, they made me hand over a week in advance. That little town was used to the army. They must have learned the hard way.

Then I took a train down into the city. After four hours I had a meager wardrobe. I put one suit on and stuffed the monkey suit into a trash basket outside the dressing room. I held the little gold button with the eagle on it in my hand for a while and looked down at it. I wasn't being bitter. I wasn't being the hot novelist's idea of the cynical soldier. I just didn't want to wear the damn thing. I knew that they'd see the button and tie it up with the little limp and the missing fingers and the deep scar across my face. I didn't want to be a professional veteran. I tossed it into the trash can after the suit.

Then I hunted around in the used-car lots. I finally found a little '40 Plymouth convertible with a decent motor. I paid them their thousand and got it licensed. I got back to my hotel room in Bennetville by midnight. I was tired, but I felt like a civilian. I tossed out the rest of the brown clothes and went to bed. I didn't dream.

In the morning I placed a person-to-person call to Dan Christoff in Youngstown, Ohio. I sat and drank my breakfast coffee and felt the chill butterflies of excitement as I waited for the call to go through.

The phone rang and I picked it up. "Mr. Garry? This is the operator. Mr. Daniel Christoff isn't at that number, and they don't expect him back. What do you wish me to do?"

"Let me talk to his wife, Dorothy Christoff."

I waited a few seconds, and then the operator came on again. She sounded a little embarrassed. "I'm sorry, Mr. Garry, but Mrs. Christoff doesn't wish to speak to you."

"What the hell do you mean? This isn't a collect call."

"I know, sir, but she refuses to take the call."

"Okay, cancel it." I slammed the phone down onto the

cradle. I jumped up and paced the room. I drew a cigarette down until it scorched my fingers. I threw it out the window with a full arm swing. I couldn't understand it. It sounded as though Dan and Dorothy had broken up. That didn't make sense. They were made for each other. I remembered her as a tall, fair girl with dusky red hair and a face with a warm pallor like old ivory, gray-green eyes, and a quick wide grin like a boy's. It didn't make sense. We had always liked each other. I threw the stuff I'd need into the new bag I'd bought and went down to the desk. I gave them another week's rent and got into the car. I took the little automobile by the nape of the neck and yanked it out of town. It screamed in protest on the corners. It didn't make sense, for her to refuse to talk to me.

I drove two hundred miles before I cooled off. I had to keep the speed down, because, if I felt one of those blank spells coming on, I'd only have a few seconds to stop the car. I carefully went over every possible answer I could think of. None of them seemed to make any sense. It wasn't fair to me. I wanted to see her, and I wanted a look at Dan's kid. He'd been three when we left. Billy Christoff. Round and grave and sturdy.

I didn't stop for lunch. It was quarter after four when I rolled up in front of the small bungalow on the shaded street where Dan and I had thrown the party the week before we left for the Coast. I remembered the house as being larger. The paint had been whiter. The lawn had looked greener. A chill rain was falling as I walked to the steps and went up onto the porch.

I leaned on the bell and waited. After about thirty seconds, she opened the door. Her eyes widened a little when she saw me.

"I thought you'd come here, Howard, but I didn't want you to. I didn't expect you so soon. I suppose I better ask you in." She turned and walked ahead of me. She was as slim as ever but not as straight, somehow. I wanted to ask all sorts of questions, but I realized that it would be more comfortable for her if I let her handle it her own way.

She led me into the familiar living room. The furniture had been changed around, but the walls and windows were the same. There was a large picture of Dan on the mantel. He wasn't in uniform.

When she sat on the couch, the light from the windows fell harshly across her face. It shocked me. Her face had been thin. It looked gaunt. There was no life in her eyes. There were new lines across her neck, and puffy shadows under her eyes. She sat and examined her fingernails for a few seconds. Then she looked up at me.

"Dan's dead, you know."

I hadn't known. I hadn't even considered it. The guy had always seemed so indestructible. So durable, as though he and his pipe would be around forever. I glanced up at his picture and then I looked down at the pattern in the rug. I took out a cigarette and carefully examined the little pattern of brown grains of tobacco. The white paper had a small wrinkle near the end where the label was. I took out a packet of matches: WORT'S GARAGE. BODY AND FENDER WORK. Red and white and yellow. I struck one of the green-tipped matches on the scarred scratching surface and lit the cigarette. I drew the smoke deep into my lungs and exhaled it in a long gray column toward the far wall. It broke up in the still air. Dan was dead. You're a long time dead. What did friend Hemingway say? When you laugh, laugh like hell—you're a long time dead. Something like that. Dan dead. Alliteration. Both one-syllable words.

I had it under control. I looked over at her. Her eyes were still dead.

"Are you positive, Dorothy? Certain?"

"His body was recovered a few days later. Washed up on the beach."

"Combat?"

"No. Not even line of duty, according to the army. They marked it NLD. I suppose that means not line of duty. They were going to punish him for it if he hadn't been drowned by accident."

"That doesn't make much sense to me."

"I'll get you the letter." She stood up with a sigh and walked out of the room. I sat and waited. She was back in a few moments and handed it to me. Long stained envelope. Many times read. I opened it and pulled out the letter.

Dear Mrs. Christoff:

This is something not normally done, I believe, but I feel that you should have some information regarding the unfortunate death of your husband. You will undoubtedly ask other people who were with him at the time, and I feel that it is better for you to have a clear report from someone in authority, rather than a garbled account.

Your husband was placed in temporary command of the crew of a Quartermaster Crash Boat which was berthed in Colombo Harbor, Ceylon. He didn't have the knowledge to command the boat at sea, and it was only a temporary arrangement pending the arrival of a replacement for the original captain of the boat.

He not only took it to sea one night, exceeding his verbal instructions, but he took as passengers two civilians from Colombo. They ran into a monsoon squall, and he was washed overboard and drowned. His body was recovered and properly identified before burial.

Had he not been drowned, he would undoubtedly have faced courts-martial on his return to shore, as his breach of security regulations alone would have been sufficient to break him to his original officer rank. The combination of offenses might well have resulted in a dishonorable discharge from the army.

His death was rated NLD by the theater commander, and as such you will not receive one half of a year's base pay and allowances.

Please understand that it is a most unpleasant task for me to write this type of letter to you. Your husband had a superior rating as an officer up until the time of this incident. I thought you should like to know the facts in this matter.

Sincerely,
C. C. Argdeffer
Colonel, Infantry

I folded it up and placed it in the envelope. I walked over and threw it into her lap. "I don't believe it, Dorothy."

She shrugged. "Why would the man write it, then?"

"He's wrong. He's got to be wrong. Dan wasn't that type. Sure, he's taken on a load at times, but he never mixed pleasure with business, civilian or military. He was a very sober guy about his work. That was a stupid trick. He couldn't do it."

"I thought the way you did. So did his father. And then we got the other letters."

"More!"

"Not like that. Dan's father called the right people in Washington, and somehow he got hold of a list of names and addresses of the crew of the boat. He wrote to them all. Asked them all to come clean with him."

"What happened?"

"They were worse. A couple didn't answer. A few didn't want to talk about it. The rest said that Dan came onto the boat drunk at ten o'clock at night with a woman and a man, both civilians. They said that the next ranking officer tried to argue with Dan, but Dan wouldn't listen. He insisted that they go on a 'moonlight cruise.' They went, and he was drowned. Now what can I believe?"

I sat and thought it over. It didn't sound like Dan, but then again, you can't tell. Sometimes the soberest people pull the damnedest stunts. . . .

I smacked my fist into my left palm and said, "They're wrong, Dorothy. I know they're wrong. Dan couldn't do it. There's a mistake someplace. I'm going to find it."

I didn't feel quite as confident as I sounded. But the look in her eyes was worth it. She held her head high, and for a fraction of a second she was the girl I had known before. Her eyes were bright.

Then that slack mask seemed to slide down over her face. She smiled at me with immense politeness. "That's very nice of you, Howard. I'm certain Dan would have appreciated it. Now, if you'll excuse me, I've got some housework to do."

She walked me to the door. I stood uncertainly, one foot still in the hall and one down on the brick porch. She put her hand on my arm and looked at me. "I know it's hopeless, Howard, but I want you to try. For your sake. If you don't you'll always wish you had. But don't let it get you. Please. It isn't that I've lost faith in Dan. That isn't it. Anybody can make a mistake. I think he did. I just hate the whole stigma of the thing. How will Billy like reading that letter when he grows up? What kind of a background does it give the boy? You see how it is? I hate it all." She turned and leaned her face against the doorframe.

I didn't have the guts to say a word. I half ran out to the car and drove down the street. The soft rain hissed against the windshield. I seemed to see Dan's bulky, soaked body on a white sandy beach. The waves seemed to nudge and nibble at it as they rolled up against his shoulder. . . .

Mr. and Mrs. Christoff sat across from me in the booth in the hotel coffee shop in Cleveland. They both looked much older and more frail than I had remembered. Mrs. Christoff's eyes had a shadow of the same expression that Dorothy's had worn. But they had another boy. Mr. Christoff sucked noisily at his coffee and then clattered the cup down into the thick saucer.

"Damn it, Howard, what'll you get out of it? Why don't we forget it? Let's not tear the top of a cut that's beginning to scab over."

"I don't want to be stubborn. I told you before, Mr. Christoff. I don't believe it."

He turned to his wife and spread his hands with a mock helpless gesture. "Eight or nine letters we got, saying that Danny got drunk and took out a boat he wasn't supposed to. Eight or nine letters we got, and this fella doesn't believe any of them."

She stuck her small chin out and tilted her head up at his. "Now you leave him alone, Carl Christoff. He's trying to help. Sometimes in the night I wake up and wonder if all those letters are wrong. Maybe he was drugged. You can't tell. Give him that list of names and addresses. Let him try. He can't hurt anything." She turned to me and her voice softened. "What do you plan to do?"

"Go see all those fellows. Get a firsthand account. Then see if there's anything in any of the stories that doesn't add up. There'll be something out of line."

They sat and stared across the table at me, two seamed faces in which hope struggled with the habit of despair . . . and lost.

"There was a piece in the paper about it, you know," she said. "The Cleveland paper. People know about it. They still tell us they're sorry. And it was a year ago. They like to tell us they're sorry." She looked down into her coffee.

"I like you, Howard," the man said. "Always have. I'm glad to know you're loyal to Dan. But I don't want you wearing yourself out on this thing. You've had a bad time." He reached in his inside pocket and pulled out a list of names and addresses. It was a new typed list, clean and crisp. He slid it across the black marble top of the table. "Here's the names. Take some time before you do anything. Think it over. Maybe it'd be better for you to keep that little germ of doubt . . . maybe it'd be worse to find out that Dan made that kind of mistake. Think it over."

I didn't look at the list. I slipped it into my own pocket.

Mrs. Christoff turned to her husband. "Maybe you ought to give him the letters the boys wrote to you."

"Can't, Mary. Tore 'em up. Didn't want 'em around." He looked down at his thick, twisted hands. Then he looked up with a quick smile. "No need to make this a wake, Howard. Tell us about yourself."

We sat for an hour while I talked gently of the high wild mountains, the stinging cold of the Himalayas. It was the first time I spoke of it to anyone. I skipped the parts they wouldn't want to hear. As I spoke, I remembered a part I had forgotten. A small dark room with the shifting light of a fire. Two stocky men pawing at my hand and speaking in low tones to each other. A heavy block of wood and the flash of a knife. No pain as the rotted fingers were pared away. Then a bright needle of pain and the smell of burnt flesh as something that glowed red in the dusky light was touched against my hand.

I was conscious of a great stillness, and the booth and the two pale faces across from me faded off into a blackness. I was lost on a high plateau, and there was no way to turn to get my face out of the burning wind, the flakes of driving ice. I stood silently for a time, and then I heard a muttering. The two faces came out of the gloom at me, slowly growing until

I was again in the booth and the old man, his eyes wide and frightened, was fumbling with my rigid right hand, the hand that had closed down over the heavy tumbler of water, splintering the glass, the dark blood flowing out onto the black tabletop.

I was okay. We found a drugstore and the clerk bandaged the long slit in the palm of my hand. But they weren't at ease with me after that. I took them back to their apartment and left them at the door. I promised to tell them what I discovered, no matter how damning to Dan it might be.

I walked back out to the car and drove slowly through the broad streets of night. Red neon screamed at me: *Mick's Bar and Grill*. I stopped between two cars and went in. I sat at the bar and ordered brandy and water. I pulled the list out and looked at it. Rochester, Boston, Waterbury, Scranton, Harrisburg, Brooklyn, Jersey City, San Francisco, Seattle. Most of them in the East. Made it easier.

The bar was noisy. I sat and drank quietly, brushing off two drunks that tried to make conversation. As I sat there, the point of following it up seemed to fade away. Everybody makes a mistake sometime. Who was Dan to be different? Surely his family would have more faith in him than a friend. Blood is thick. They had been convinced. They were trying to forget, trying to readjust. I would be stirring up all the old pain. He was dead. Let it lie. Drop it. I ordered another brandy. I took the list out again. In a few motions I could tear it to ribbons and drop it into the spittoon underneath the red leather stool. I shoved it back into my pocket.

I drove back to Bennetville and checked out. The room clerk smiled in a superior fashion and said, "I'm very sorry, Mr. Garry, but we can't refund the nine days' rent you've paid. It's impossible."

I stood with both hands on the desk and looked at him. I stared at his small pale eyes, his gay necktie, his white hands. Slowly the smile faded.

"Surely you understand our position?"

Again I didn't answer. I continued to stare. Then he smiled again, but I noticed he moved back a little way, to where he was certain I couldn't reach him.

"I believe, Mr. Garry, that in this situation maybe we can make an adjustment. Maybe a return of one week's rent."

I nodded.

It bothered me. I wondered what there was in merely staring at him that had made him back down. I went into the men's room and looked into the mirror. I really saw myself for the first time. I hadn't wanted a refund particularly. I knew that I would be cheated. In the mirror I saw a long gaunt face with a scar that glowered in a reddish line across my cheek. My eyes looked sunken back into my head. They were dark and shadowed and much too bright. There were deep lines from my nostrils to the corners of my mouth. It was the face of a violent man. I stared at myself and understood. My face, in repose, carried the look of a man in whom slow anger is bubbling up, ready to break out in physical violence. I didn't like it. It bothered me.

I drove to Chicago. I made an appointment with Saggerty. He sat behind his desk and studied me for long minutes. I remembered that he used to make me uncomfortable. I realized that it was a technique with him. I stared back at his wispy figure, his mop of iron-gray hair, thinking that it was a technique with him, a means of feeding his own self-esteem. I grinned inside when I saw it was working in reverse. I was making him uneasy. He picked up a pencil and tapped his nose with the eraser end.

"So you want to come back to work, Garry. You look fit, but pretty thin."

"You looking for an engineer or a guy with a shovel?"

"Don't be huffy, son. We want you back. We've got a million highway jobs, all hot. I was just remembering how you and Christoff used to work together."

I didn't answer.

"Strange thing about Christoff. I heard about it. Always seemed like a solid boy. Guess he came a little unwrapped."

"If that's what you want to call it."

"You can report in the morning. I'll have Boon pick the job for you. See him. How about pay?"

"How about it? I'm three years older, nearer four. I'm that much smarter. I'll take what I had before, plus fifteen hundred."

"Too much."

I picked my hat off the corner of his desk and stood up. He stared up at me and I held his eye. I turned and walked toward the door. He didn't break until I had it open. He coughed.

"Okay, Garry. Your price. Tomorrow morning." I nodded and left.

Boon gave me an average one. Forty miles of two-lane concrete potholes to convert to four-lane divided blacktop. Grade elimination. Curve elimination. A big shortage of equipment and some very porky labor—guys who wanted the water brought in a sterling bucket and wanted a half hour to drink it. We had to clip off as much as we could before the blizzards shut us down. Then the rest of it could be handled in the spring.

For a couple of weeks I felt good. I spent every minute on the job and slept like sudden death. Then Dan came between me and the work. Something would come up, and I'd stand and look off toward the blue hills. How would Dan handle this? I'd see his blunt face and slow grin. Hear him say, "What makes Garry run? Slow down, kid. Relax. You got a chunk of hill over there you can use for fill. Save fifteen minutes on each truck." Then maybe I'd stomp on his foot and we'd roll over and over in the dust, growling at each other, while the men stood around and grinned at each other, delighted with the damn fool engineers.

That's the way it was. It happened oftener and oftener. I'd stand in the chill mornings and expect him to walk around the side of one of the cats. It wasn't that I needed the guy so badly. The job was going okay. It seemed almost as though he hadn't been buried, as though he couldn't rest. I owed him something, and I knew it. I knew what he would have done for me.

I went back to Chicago and talked to Boon. Then I went in and saw Saggerty. He started to get tough with me.

I held up my hand and stopped him. "Now look. I like the outfit. I like to work for you. Don't get me wrong. Let's not do a lot of fencing and trying to break each other down. I've got something I have to do. It's a favor for a friend. An obligation. I've tried to ignore it, but I can't. If it keeps on, I won't be any good to you. Let me go handle it. Give me a leave of absence. I'll be back. I've talked to Boon. The job's under control. He's got a new guy named Brent that he can assign to it. I'll help Brent for a few days and then shove off."

For a while his face was as sour as spoiled milk. Then he grinned and stuck out his hand. I was surprised. But when I thought it over, I realized that he'd have to have a few qualities like that to get where he was. You can't be petty all the way through and expect to hold anything but a petty job.

I got Brent established and gave him some advice about finishing it off. Then I went back to town. I packed my stuff and loaded it in the car. I sat and pulled the list out of my pocket. With a pencil, I marked the sequence.

The repair manager said, "Dosani? Yeah. You can talk to him. He's over in the far right corner of the shop."

I walked over. Dosani had a starter motor in the vise. He had just clipped one battery cable onto it. He started to hold the other against the housing. He saw me and waved me back with his hand. I stepped back. He was a tall slim boy with swarthy skin and black shining hair that fell down across his forehead. He held the other battery cable against the housing and the motor spun, throwing the fresh oil back in a fine mist. He unhooked the battery and then spun the heavy handle of the vise. He whistled. He laid the motor carefully on the bench and then turned to me.

"Which car is yours?"

"None of them. I want to talk about something else. The manager told me I could come back here and bother you."

"Look, mister. I'm not paying that bill until the damn radio works. Understand?"

"Not that either. I want to talk about that crash boat business in Ceylon, where the skipper was drowned."

He looked up at me, and he was angry. "I've given testimony on that thing till I'm blue in the face. I'm sick of it."

I waited a few seconds, then I said, "Look, Dosani. I'm not official. The guy was a friend of mine. My best friend. I just want to know what happened. Just what is a crash boat?"

He relaxed. "Oh, sure. If that's the way it is. A crash boat is a job with nearly a P. T. hull. Crew of thirteen. Two aircraft

94

motors. Uses hundred octane. Not much armament. Couple of Browning fifties, maybe a forty millimeter, and sometimes an eighty-millimeter mortar mounted on the stern. Used to dash in and pick wounded guys off the shore. Pretty fast job. Uses an army crew. Quartermaster."

"What did you do?"

"Down there nursing those damn motors. Seasick every minute we were out."

"What happened that night?"

"I don't know much about it. This Captain Christoff comes aboard about ten o'clock with these two people, a guy and a babe. We knew it wasn't right, but he was in charge of the boat. Quinn, the warrant, tried to argue with him, I heard, but no soap. We bust up a poker game and take her out. We went straight out of Colombo harbor, and then he opened her up. Quinn was handling her. I hear the three of them, Christoff and two passengers, went out on the bow. About ten miles out, Quinn turned her around and for a few seconds we were parallel to the ground swell. Just at that minute, according to the passengers, Christoff tried to get back to the bridge. You have to walk along a narrow spot near the low rail. He went over, and by the time the passengers got Quinn's attention, he was too far past the spot to find Christoff. We circled for a half hour or so. They say that Christoff was potted, and that he probably sank like a rock."

"Hear anything else from the other guys? Anything that struck you as funny?"

He rubbed the side of his face, leaving a streak of grease. Then he shook his head. "Not a thing. He just stepped out of line and got caught. He seemed like a good joe, a teek hai sahib. It was just a technicality that they put him in charge of *Betsy* for a few days until the regular replacement showed up. He wasn't supposed to take her out, because he didn't know anything about her. But I guess he got tight and that skinny British bitch went to work on him. Joy ride."

"What happened to the first skipper you had?"

"Silly damn thing. Went swimming outside of Trincomalee Harbor. He and another guy were fishing with plastic explosive. Fenner swam out just as the other guy tossed one in with a short fuse. He wasn't watching Fenner. The concussion under water collapsed his lungs. We didn't cry none when he got it. He was one of those guys with a rule book in each hand and a frosty look in his eye. Thought he was an admiral."

Nothing else of consequence was said. I noticed that he was impatient to get back to work. I thanked him and shook hands with him and left. I crossed his name off the list.

Stenwitz was sitting on his front porch in a T-shirt and khaki pants as I went up the walk. I'd gotten his description from the clerk at the corner grocery. He was a fat boy with white freckled arms and a puffy face. He scowled at me.

"You're Stenwitz, aren't you?"

"Yah."

"I'm Howard Garry, and I want to ask you a couple of questions about that time in Colombo when Captain Christoff was drowned."

"What's your angle?"

"I was a friend of Christoff's."

"Sure. You were a friend of Christoff's." He got up and walked to the railing. He spat down into the shrubbery. Then he turned toward the front door. "Write me a letter," he said. "I'm busy."

I took a quick step and caught him by the shoulder and spun him back just as he got inside the door. I grabbed his wrist and yanked hard. He came back out onto the porch and swung at me. I ducked it. He tried again, grunting as he swung. He missed again. He stood, breathing hard, his round head lowered, his eyes small in their puffs of flesh.

"Shove off, bud. I'll call the cops. This is private property."

I didn't move and he tried again, a roundhouse blow. I stepped inside of it and let it wind around the back of my neck. I sunk my right hand deep into his stomach. He doubled over, his face greenish. I lugged him to the chair and sat him in it. I sat on the railing and lit a cigarette. I waited while he got his breath back. He made strangled sounds in his throat which finally died away.

"Now, Stenwitz, we'll have a nice little talk. Okay?"

"I don't tell you a thing."

"You act like you must have been the guy who shoved Christoff overboard."

"You're nuts. The drunken jerk fell off."

"Then why are you so nasty about it?"

"I just don't like guys with questions. That's all. Now get off the porch."

"Not for a while. You talk nice or I'll drop another one into your stomach. I got nothing to lose, Stenwitz. Where were you when it happened?"

He looked at me sullenly. I slid off the rail and stood up. "Port, stern. Coiling line," he said quickly.

"Could you see Christoff and the two passengers up in the bow?"

"No. Couldn't see a thing. Not a damn thing. Too dark. Bridge in the way."

"When did you know Christoff was gone?"

"When Quinn brought her around and started whamming the bell."

"Where were the passengers then?"

"I don't know."

There was nothing he could add. There was nothing else I could think to ask. I tried some pointless questions and he gave sullen direct answers. At last I left. As I climbed into my car at the curb, I looked back toward the porch. He was still in the chair, and he was smiling. I couldn't read the smile.

Two days later I walked into a bar in Rochester, New York, and picked a spot at the end where I could lean my shoulder against the plaster wall.

I ordered a brandy and water, and when the thin pale bartender set it in front of me I said, "You're Stan Benjamin, aren't you? Cook on the *Betsy* when you were in Ceylon?"

The distant look faded, and he gave me a slow grin that turned him into a human being. "Yeah. But I don't know you. Were you there?"

"No, but my best friend was. Captain Christoff."

"Sure. I remember him. He was only with the boat a few days. Tough break for the guy. Did you look me up here?"

97

"If you can do it and still take care of the customers, I'd like to hear what happened."

"It's slow this time a day. I was sitting in on a poker game when your friend came aboard tight with a couple of guests, a thin British doll that he called Conny and a big red-faced guy named O'Dell. They come aboard by coming across the decks of some British boats that we were moored to. Quinn and Christoff had some kind of an argument that I didn't hear, and then Quinn came down the ladder and told the guys to get to their stations, that we were taking a run. He was sore as hell.

"There wasn't anything for me to do at first, and then Christoff and the two guests sat in the main cabin and they opened the door over the booth into the galley. Christoff slid a bottle of John Hague in and told me to fix up some drinks. That was against the rules too, but I got my orders so I did it. I took a little nip myself and fixed up three tall ones, using plain water. When I set them through the little door I could see that the babe and O'Dell were on one side of the booth and the captain was on the other side. He acted tight."

"What did they talk about?"

"I couldn't hear so good. They were talking about some club they'd just come from. Christoff had trouble talking straight. The other two didn't seem so bad. They seemed a little tense about being out in *Betsy*. As soon as we got outside the harbor, the groundswell rocked us around. I made another round, and then the gal said that she'd like to go topside and get a look at the moon on the ocean. Only by that time there were clouds over it. They went on up."

"Anything else?"

"You probably heard the rest. How we circled around for more than a half hour with the woman having hysterics. Couldn't find the guy. When I went back down, I saw the big guy with the red face draining the last of the bottle. I stopped and looked at him. He set it down, empty, wiped his mouth with the back of his hand, and glared at me. I went back into the galley. Then we went in, and there were investigations that lasted for weeks. I understand Quinn was in for promotion, and that little tea party sort of screwed him out of it."

He bought me my third brandy on the house and then I had the last one and bought him one. He ducked below the bar to polish it off. I liked the little guy. I made him take another one and he acted pretty jolly.

Then I said, "What'd you think of Stenwitz?"

"A moody jerk if there ever was one. Nobody liked him. He was the only guy on the weather deck when it happened. He didn't see a thing. Used to get sore as hell when we asked him why not. Strange guy. Didn't have a friend in the army. Not a one."

While I was eating dinner at the hotel I checked Benjamin's name off the list. Nothing yet. There didn't seem to be much point in going on. Only three covered out of the seven left in the country. Four to go: Baker, Ruggerio, Janson, and Quinn.

Two weeks later I stopped in a gas station just outside of Seattle. Only one left: Quinn. Wilmert L. Quinn.

I paid for the gas and kept the gas pedal down near the floor until I got into town at four o'clock. I went to the address I had been given and found that the Quinns had moved. The woman didn't know where they had moved to, but she thought that they were still in town. I stopped in a drugstore and tried the phone book. Then I called information and found that he had a new phone that had not been listed yet. She gave me the address. It was ten minutes to five when I pulled up in front of a new house on the edge of town. Standard stuff. White with a high peak to the roof. Green shutters and a tall red-brick chimney with a big Q in wrought iron fastened to it.

I rang the bell. A girl opened the door. She looked about eighteen. Average height, hair dyed the color of summer flax, wearing a cheap print dress that was too tight for her. Her mouth was moist and her eyes had the flat, automatic joy of a woman who steps out of a doorway at night on a dim street.

She giggled before I could open my mouth. "Whatever you got to sell, brother, maybe I could buy some."

"I'm not selling today. I want to see Mr. Quinn. You his wife?"

"Yeah. I'm a brand-new wife, practically a bride. Come on in." She stood aside, and as I stepped past her she swung her body so that I had to brush against her. I smelled the raw liquor on her breath.

The living room was small and perfectly square. The furniture was bright and ugly, the colors too raw, the lines without grace. I stood in the doorway and she minced past me, swinging her hips. She sat down on a green couch and patted the cushion beside her. "He ain't here yet. Tell me about it."

I crossed the room and sat in a gray chair with crimson buttons on the cushions. She gave me a mock pout and said, "Unfriendly, huh? I won't eat you, mister."

"When does he get home? Maybe I ought to go and then come back."

"Don't rush off. He'll be along in maybe a half hour. Want a drink?"

I nodded and she flounced out. She paused at the door and said, "Come and help me." I got up and followed her out to a cluttered kitchen. There was a tray of melting ice cubes on the enameled top of the table, along with a half bottle of cheap rye and four or five small bottles of ginger ale.

She jumped up onto the sink shelf and swung her legs. "Make your own, mister."

I stepped over to the table and mixed a light rye. I opened one of the bottles of ginger ale. It was warm. It foamed up over the top of the bottle. I stepped over to the sink and let it run down my hand. She slid over so that her knees were against my side. I looked up at her in protest just as she launched herself at me, both arms tight around my neck, her loose mouth clamped on mine.

I dropped the bottle into the sink and tried to pry her hands loose. She giggled through the kiss. She didn't smell clean. I got hold of her wrists and pulled her arms loose. She slid down to the floor and twisted her wrists away from me. She swung and slapped me so hard on the ear that my head buzzed. She stepped back and said, "Just who the hell do you think you are? What makes you think you can come in here and paw me?"

A tired voice behind me said, "Shut up, Janice. I saw more of that than you thought I saw."

I turned around. A middle-sized man with a tight, disciplined face stepped by me. He slapped her with the hard heel of his open hand. She slammed back into the door to the back hall. A trickle of blood ran down her chin.

"You got no right to hit me, Will," she gasped.

"All the right there is, baby. That's the last time I touch you. Pack your stuff and get out of here."

She opened her mouth to object. He stood and looked at her. She dashed by him and ran out of the kitchen. I heard the quick stomp of her heels as she went to the stairs.

He turned to me. I could see that he was about thirty, even though he looked nearer forty. "I'm sorry, friend. Always thought she was like that, but never had the proof before. A little tough on you, though. What'd you come here for, anyway?"

"This is a hell of a time to bother you with it, Quinn, but I wanted to get your story on the Captain Christoff drowning. He was my friend."

He looked hard at me, and I returned the stare with as much candor as I could manage. "Sure you aren't a slick customer trying to open it up again? I don't want to do any more testifying. That business knocked me out of a promotion I could have used."

"I understand it did. Sorry. But suppose I come back tomorrow when you aren't all upset?"

"Never mind that. I'm okay. Who else have you talked to about this?"

I told him whom I had seen. He led me into the living room. I could hear a low wailing noise coming from upstairs. He seemed to ignore it.

"Then I should tell you what the others wouldn't have had a chance to know, I suppose. Let's see now. Best place to start is where he came aboard. I was sitting with my legs hanging over the side smoking a pipe. The harbor was quiet. I could hear a hot poker game belowdecks. There were footsteps behind me, and Captain Christoff walked up. I jumped up. I could see two people behind him.

"He introduced me. Miss Constance Severence and a Mr. O'Dell. The girl was in evening dress. O'Dell was in a white jacket with a maroon bow tie. A big guy. She looked slim and cool like most of those British babes do when they're upper-class stuff.

"I knew that he wasn't supposed to bring strangers on board. I told him that I had something to tell him in private. I thought maybe he didn't know the rules. We went up forward, and the two visitors waited.

"I told him about the rule, and he said he wanted to take them out on a short trip. I told him that I was against it, and he said that I should trust him and take orders, that he knew what he was doing. I tried to argue, and after a while he made me stand at attention. Then he told me to shut up and prepare to cast off. There wasn't a thing I could do. I did like he told me."

"Did he act drunk?"

"Later, yes. Not when I talked to him."

"What happened then?"

"They went below with a bottle. About six miles out, they came on deck and went forward. They sat on some life rafts that are strapped down there. I could see them by standing on my toes. I was at the wheel. It began to get rough. He'd told me to go out ten miles. At ten miles I made a sharp hundred and eighty to starboard and headed back. A couple of minutes later, O'Dell bellowed at me. I couldn't catch it. He came up to the bridge and said that Christoff had gone overboard. I circled back, but we never found him."

"Do you think there was anything fishy about it?"

He waited a few minutes before he answered. He stared down at the vile brown rug, his forehead wrinkled. "I've wondered and wondered about that. Of course, the turn could have caught him off guard. He wasn't used to boats. I tried to tell the investigating officers that he didn't act like a guy who was disobeying rules, but then I had only known him a few days. I guess it was just like they decided. He had too many strikes on him. Visitors, an unauthorized trip, and liquor on board. If he hadn't drowned they'd have skinned him alive and broiled him."

"Any of the other guys in the crew figure that something was fishy?"

"Not a one. If one of them had, maybe I'd have stuck to my guns a little longer."

I waited, and he told the story again in more detail. But he kept glancing up at the ceiling as he spoke. When he started on it the third time, I interrupted him and told him that I had to be on my way, thank you very much, sorry about this trouble I caused, glad to hear your slant on it. . . .

He saw me to the door. I got into the car, and I had gone about eight or nine blocks when I remembered that I had wanted to ask about Stenwitz. No specific question. I had just wanted to start him talking about the kid. Something about Stenwitz had bothered me.

I turned around and headed back for his house. I parked in front and walked up onto the porch. I had my finger an inch from the bell when I heard it. A dull smacking sound, as though someone were beating a featherbed with a slat. Through the noise of pounding, I could hear tired screams of pain.

I turned around and walked back out to the car. Mrs. Quinn wouldn't be leaving home. She'd never leave home. She'd just hang around and collect an occasional beating for the next thirty years. I grinned as I drove off, my question forgotten.

It was a long jaunt back to Chicago. I didn't let myself think too much. I drove along with tires droning on the concrete, the motor singing heavily in my ears. Dan was dead and I had collected a blank. Not a complete blank, but so close to it that it might as well have been a blank. A little glimmer of doubt in Quinn's mind. Unexplained resistance by Stenwitz. Those two things plus the fact that the behavior pattern didn't sound like Dan Christoff. Not at all.

I drove straight to Chicago, barely stopping to eat and sleep a little. In Chicago I noticed a cheap hotel and took a bottle of brandy up to my room. I planned to sleep all day and get back to work the next morning. To be able to sleep after driving seven hundred miles at one stretch the last leg of my trip, I had to get a little tanked. I sat on the edge of the bed in my underwear and drank raw brandy out of the bathroom tumbler while I thought over the talks I had had with the crew members. I didn't blame Dan's parents and Dorothy for getting discouraged. I was discouraged. There didn't seem to be any crack I could get my fingers into and widen into a definite clue. Something wasn't right about it all. I shrugged and tossed off some more brandy. No skin off me. On the following day I could go back to work and forget it—or try to forget it.

I remembered the time that Dan and I had sat in a duck blind and ignored the ducks while we drank half the brandy in the world to keep off the chill. He had been a great guy. Suddenly I stopped moving, almost stopped breathing. I snapped my fingers softly.

I waited for about ten minutes after I placed the call to Dorothy. At last she came on the line, misty with sleep, a yawn in her voice.

"Hello, Howard. What's the matter?"

"Just thinking, Dorothy. Maybe I got something. I want to know something. You see Dan tight very often?"

"Couple of times. Why? You sound tight yourself, Howard."

"Maybe I am, a little. Look, Dorothy, what happens to him when he gets tight? Physically, I mean. How does he react?"

"He never shows it—I mean showed it. Why do you have to use the present tense, Howard? It hurts."

"How did he show it?"

"His legs just gave out on him. He'd sit looking as sober as a bishop, and the only thing would be that he couldn't get up, couldn't stand. Please tell me why you want to know."

"Did that happen every time?"

"Every time I know of. Why can't you forget it, Howard?"

"Not now, baby. I've got a lead and I'm going away and track it down, and look, Dorothy . . . uh . . . ."

"What is it?"

"Wish me luck."

"Good luck, Howard." Her voice was soft, and the phone clicked in my ear as she hung up. I drank the rest of the brandy and went to bed.

The passport problem was cleaned up in a week. I wired for reservations on the *Siam Express* from Los Angeles. She was due out in six days for a twenty-eight-day run to Rangoon.

That gave me time to get out to L.A. and sell the heap for fifty bucks more than I paid for it.

I loaded a big suitcase with clothes, brandy, cigarettes, and paperbacks. I walked up the gangplank in the morning and found my tourist-class stateroom. I met my roommate, a sly citizen named Duckwood, who claimed he was going to Rangoon to head a sales agency for one of the big motion picture studios. He had peppery hair, wattles under his thin chin, and a violent case of halitosis. I decided to leave him strictly alone for the rest of the trip. I bought a chair, forward and starboard, and settled down for twenty-eight days of boredom.

We hauled out in the afternoon. It took three days to settle into the routine of eating, sleeping, reading, and exercising. I didn't avoid people, but neither did I enter into any casual conversations of my own accord. Thus I was left pretty well alone. It was a good ship, with a slight tendency to corkscrew in choppy weather. The food was good, and I ate my share of it. There were four at my table, myself, Duckwood, and two well-stuffed schoolteachers from Kansas who had been penned up in the States for five years by the war. They were taking a year off. They both had the fetching trait of chewing with their mouths open. I loved them both, dearly. I never did catch their names.

At the end of ten days I was bored. At the end of twenty days I was too lethargic to even be bored. I tried to nap as much as possible.

On the twenty-fifth day, in the morning, I found that we were going to be late getting into Rangoon. We were going to make a stop at Trincomalee on the northeast shore of Ceylon. I went to see the purser. He was difficult. He said that it would be impossible.

I went to the cabin and packed my bag. At two in the afternoon we floated slowly into the great British naval base of Trincomalee. Wooded hills sloped steeply down to the blue harbor. A trail wound up from the dock buildings, and a dusty truck rocked down it. I carried my bag out onto the deck. I set it down near the passenger gangplank on B deck. The sailor manning the unlowered gangplank looked at me oddly. I carefully ignored him. I had to take a chance on their nuzzling the big ship up to a dock. They did.

When the gangplank was lowered, I brushed by the man on the deck and hurried down it. Men on the dock and on the ship stared at me stupidly. Someone shouted, "Stop that man!" I guessed that it was my friend, the purser.

I walked along the dock toward the shore. I heard steps hurrying along behind me. I stopped and turned. It was the purser and a fat sailor. They stopped, too.

"Now listen to me," I said, "I've got a visa for Ceylon, and if either of you monkeys lays a hand on me I'll sue the line for a hundred thousand and you'll both be out of a job."

I stepped onto land while the two of them were still screaming at each other. I looked back. The purser was waving his arm toward me and the sailor was waving his arm toward the ship. Their noses were a half inch apart.

There was no American consular representative in Trincomalee. I wired the notification of my presence on the island to the American consul in Colombo. The British were very pleasant about searching my baggage and changing some dollars into Ceylonese rupees. I thanked them and they thanked me and I thanked them again. Small bows and brief handshakes. All very pleasant. They smiled and asked me what I was doing on the island. I smiled and told them that I was a tourist who was thinking of writing a book. When they smiled and asked me the title, I smiled and said, "British Spheres of Influence, or, the Mailed Fist Around the World." They stopped smiling and bowing and I left.

I had to stay overnight in Trincomalee. It cost me a hundred rupees to hire a car to drive me to Kandy in the morning. It was a bone-shattering road, narrow, winding upward through the jungle. The asphalt was dotted with holes a foot wide and six inches deep. I sat on the leather back seat of the ancient touring car and bit my tongue by accident twice on the way down. The driver kept his bare brown foot on the gas and ignored the condition of the road. After every particularly bad bump, he would look around at me with a shy grin splitting his face. He wore a pale green European shirt and a flowered sarong. The road smoothed out just outside of Kandy. The driver let me off in front of the Queen's Hotel. I had a curry lunch and took a taxi to the station to catch the Colombo train.

Before arriving on the island, everything had seemed simple. All I wanted was to contact O'Dell and Constance Severence and find out what had actually happened. During the long days on the ship I had imagined how the interviews would go. In my imagination they all seemed to take place in discreet hotel rooms, with the other persons putting me on the track of an answer to why Dan had died.

On the island, it was different. I sat in my compartment and looked out at the towering mountains as the little train screeched around the downhill curves. I hadn't thought of the island and how it fitted into the picture. There was something warm and green and lush about the island that made intrigue and indirection a natural response. The clean-limbed natives were so different from the ones I had grown used to in India. It was an island of spice, gems, and color. My serious practical interviews with O'Dell and Severence faded out of my mind. I lost my certainty. All the old doubts came back. I wondered what I was doing back in the East.

I got into Colombo before the American consul's office closed. I went up in the creaking elevator and sat beside a desk while a blond young man looked over my passport. I stared out the window, across the big harbor. Rows of ships rode at anchor, and dozens of little craft moved lazily to and from the long docks. The air in the office was warm and sticky. Fans turned slowly overhead. The young vice-consul had a rash of prickly heat on the undersides of his tanned arms. Heavy traffic thundered in the street outside the open window.

At last he pushed the passport back into my hand. "How long do you plan to stay, Mr. Garry?"

"Indefinite. Maybe a week. Maybe a month."

"You have . . . ah . . . sufficient funds, I imagine."

"Plenty."

"There's a lot of theft here. Do you want us to hold some of it for you in the safe? Even traveler's checks aren't safe."

I counted out three thousand in cash on the corner of his desk. He entered it in a book and gave me a receipt. I asked him about hotels, and he recommended one called the Galle Face. I phoned from his office and got a room.

The Galle Face is located at one end of a mile expanse of white sand beach not far from the center of the city. A high wall borders the beach, and a promenade walk runs the length of the wall. Beyond the walk is a wide green expanse with the asphalt highway curving wide around it. The Colombo Club, refuge of the sedentary planter, sits majestically on the far side of the road, gazing out to sea.

My room was on the fourth floor on the seaward corner near the green. I could sit on the edge of the bed and stare up a mile of beach, watch the couples strolling along the promenade, follow the horses as they were galloped across the green.

My room boy introduced himself as Fernando. He promised to serve me faithfully and always run to me when I rang for him. I gave him a five-rupee note to clinch the bargain, and it would almost have been possible to tie his grin around the back of his neck like a bib.

After I stuck my things around in various drawers, I took a shower and changed to cooler clothes. I went down to the big lobby and wrestled with the telephone directory. It was alphabetical only in spots. It took me nearly ten minutes to find an O'Dell. The name was Clarence J. O'Dell, 31 Galle Road. I had a leisurely dinner in the vast dining room. The food was fair, and not plentiful.

When I was through eating, a small string group climbed solemnly onto a stand at the end of the dining room and started bravely on some sour Chopin. I walked out and stood for a moment on the front steps of the hotel. It was dusk, and the surf seemed to boom more loudly than it had during the day. The rickshaw bells tinkled with a better noise than the music inside. I waved the white-bearded doorman away when he asked me if I wanted a cab. I walked up to the corner and found that, as I had expected, the Galle Road ran right by the hotel.

I walked almost a block before I found two numbers: 18 and 20. I was headed in the right direction. It was a neighborhood of big bungalows set far back behind high hedges and green lawns. I crossed the road and found 31. The number was

108

set into the gatepost of the driveway. I walked up the drive, feeling tense and expectant. I hadn't imagined the O'Dell that I wanted to see in such luxurious surroundings. I threw away my cigarette, a red glow arching into the grass, exploding in a tiny fountain of sparks.

Ahead, golden oblongs shone out onto the grass from the wide windows. As I approached the porch, a man stepped from behind a pillar and stood waiting for me. I peered at him and saw that it was a Singhalese in a white uniform.

"What does the master wish to see?" he asked politely.

"O'Dell. Clarence O'Dell. I'm Howard Garry, and he doesn't know me."

"Who in the bloody hell're you mumbling at, Pereira?" a voice boomed so close to me that I jumped. A big man stood on the porch, silhouetted by one of the windows. He was enormous, a flabby giant of a man.

"I'm Howard Garry. I'd like to talk to you, Mr. O'Dell. If you're busy I can come back."

"Not busy," he roared. "Never busy. Come on in. Come in and sit. Have a drink. Pereira! Get this man what he wants. Scotch, rye, beer, anything."

I told the boy to get me some brandy and water. I stared at O'Dell. He was at least six five and I guessed his weight at about three hundred and a quarter. He was naked, except for a big blue turkish towel around his fat waist. His flesh sagged on him, but I could see that there were muscles left under the flab. His face and hands were burned red by the sun. The rest of him was dead white. His wide deep chest was hairless.

There was something odd about his face. I stared at him rudely until I had figured it out. He merely didn't have the coarseness of feature that you would expect with a man of that size. His nose was surprisingly delicate, and his lips were molded like a woman's. I guessed that the loud voice and gruff manner were his way of proving to himself that he was a man.

"What's your business, boy. Come on! Let's get it over with."

"Are you alone here, Mr. O'Dell?"

"Completely, except for four or five servants. Never can

keep track of them. Wife and daughters're in South Africa. Wretched place to be. Rather be here, eh?"

"I want to talk to you about something that happened well over a year ago. You went on a pleasure ride on an American boat. A small one. A Captain Christoff went overboard and was drowned. I'd like your story of what happened."

"Good Lord, boy, I've told that a dozen times to your officers. Told 'em all about it. Blasted nuisance, you coming here like this. Clumsy beggar caused me enough trouble. What do you care? Whom do you represent?"

"Nobody. Just myself. I was his friend."

"Suppose I told you that I'd give my story again to somebody with an official interest, but not to any bloody Nosey Parker?"

"I'd say you were being rude and unpleasant. I'd ask you what you'd have to lose by telling me about it. You don't look busy."

He threw his head back and laughed, great resounding yelps that rattled the walls. He wiped his eyes and rubbed the spilled liquor off his thigh. "Direct chap, aren't you? Don't you know that retired planters never look busy? We retired so we wouldn't have to look busy. What do you want me to do, tell the whole thing in detail?"

I relaxed as the boy handed me a thick brandy and water. I sipped it. It was light on the water. "Just run through it once and hit the high spots. If I have any questions, I'll stop you."

He drained his drink, and Pereira scurried over and took the glass on a silver tray. "I had a bridge date with Constance Severence at the January Club. She happened to know Christoff. He was there. I—"

"Wait a minute. Who is Constance Severence?"

"A girl who lives here. Does some kind of clerk work in the Royal Navy. Good family. She lives at the Princess Hotel."

"What's the January Club?"

"Bridge and tennis. A half mile away. Nice place. As I was saying, we met Christoff, and we all had a few drinks. Then he wanted to take us on the ride. I wasn't too keen about going, but Conny liked the idea. I went along. Had a few drinks on the boat and then went up forward. The spray felt good. Hot night. Sat on some roundish yellow things up there.

110

"Christoff was pretty intoxicated. He started toward the stern just as the man at the wheel made a big turn to go back. Constance thought she heard something, ran over to where he had gone around the edge of the main superstructure. No sign of him. She ran back to me, and I shouted to the man at the wheel. Boat was too noisy. He couldn't make out what I shouted. Then I had to go up and yell in the beggar's ear. He turned again and ordered the boat searched. No sign of the captain. Circled forever and couldn't find him. Went back in and spent two weeks answering bloody silly questions."

"Where was Miss Severence when you went back to the bridge?"

"She followed along. Stayed down on the deck as I climbed up the few steps to where I could yell in the chap's ear. Quinn, I think his name was."

I had run out of questions. I sat silently, nursing the lost feeling of a man who has run down a dark alley and crashed into a blank wall.

He held up his drink and squinted through it. He was a great white monolith of a man. He spoke in a surprisingly gentle voice. "The bloody war is long gone, Yank, and you're raking around in the ashes. Why not forget the whole thing. I'm guessing that you're trying to clear him—trying to find some mysterious reason for someone to shove him into the water. It won't wash. He got drunk and he drowned. As simple as that. Why not forget it? You'll only wear yourself out. Remember, I was there. If anything odd had happened, I'd have seen it and raised a stink. I like to make a fuss. The people here expect it of me. I've been creating disturbances for over thirty years in this city."

I sat for an hour, sipping brandies while he rambled on about his spotted career in Colombo. I gathered that he had, at one time or another, been thrown out of every club in the city. He talked and I sat and sulked. It seemed to be the end of the trail. Finally he began to yawn and mumble his words. His huge head fell forward, his chin on his hairless chest. I stood up and tiptoed out. I didn't see the servant. I walked back down the Galle Road to my hotel, weary and dispirited.

I didn't sleep well. In the morning I felt tired and dull. I phoned the Royal Naval Headquarters after breakfast and eventually located a Miss Constance Severence. I told her that I was an acquaintance of O'Dell's and made an appointment for cocktails at five thirty at her hotel, the Princess.

She was late. I was on my second stinger when she walked into the small lounge. She was a tall woman, and from a distance she looked fragile and delicate. I jumped up and she noticed me and smiled. She walked over and I pulled the small table out for her. She looked cool and fresh, but not fragile. Her hair was silvery blond, very fine, her eyes pale gray and her skin faintly sallow. I guessed her age at about thirty-two. She was built well but wore clothes more designed to conceal the fact than to reveal it. There was a strange look of hidden coarseness, hidden sensuality, about her. It was caused by a few small things about her that didn't match the rest of her appearance. Her cheekbones were too high and too wide, her fingers too plump and spatulate, her thin mouth too moist. I noticed, as I held the table out, that though her feet were rather short they were far too broad. I didn't like her.

She asked for a sling, and I ordered it from the boy. When he left to get it, she turned to me and said, "Don't you feel it? There seems to be something clandestine about this meeting—something that reeks of intrigue. Maybe it's the way you look."

That jolted me. "How do I look?"

"Now you're looking offended and stuffy. I meant that you're rather a dark and mysterious type. That scar might have come from a knife. Your eyes are wary."

"Maybe it is intrigue, Miss Severence, but I—"

"Call me Conny like that hulking O'Dell, the mad Irishman, does. Surely if he can you have the right. What shall I call you?"

"Howard or Garry. Take your choice."

"Garry it is. Now, Garry, my lad, what do you want?"

I turned so that I faced her. We were sitting side by side on a cushioned bench that ran along the wall. I looked hard into her eyes and said, "Who drowned Captain Christoff?"

It was a change from the technique I had used before. I had given O'Dell too much time to adjust, to prepare himself. If there was any guilty knowledge in her, I wanted to blast it out.

112

She looked back into my eyes. I had the impression that there was a lack of focus. They looked very slightly crossed. I remembered a trick from grade school days. If you wish to stare another person down, don't look into their eyes. Look, instead, at the bridge of their nose. I realized that she was doing just that. Her eyes didn't waver. There was no expression in them. I glanced down at her fingertips on the edge of the table. She had clear polish on her nails. She was holding the table just tightly enough to make whitish semicircles near the ends of her nails. As I glanced down she relaxed the pressure and the blood flowed back, turning them pink again. She laughed, a low musical note as phony as a singing commercial.

"Why are you laughing, Conny? What amuses you?"

"You do, Garry. You've sold yourself a plot for the flicks. True friend seeks inside story of chum's disgrace. You're trying to turn a clumsy bounder's sticky death into straight Edgar Wallace."

"You just made a mistake, my dear." She looked at me blankly. "How did you know that he was a friend of mine? How did you know that I wasn't investigating it in an official capacity?" Again I glanced down at her hand. The whiteness was back. She put her hand in her lap.

Again she laughed. "Don't be so dull, Garry! I know official investigators. They have hundreds of beastly little forms and a wretched stub of a pencil which they keep licking. They start by asking you your name even when they already know it."

"Not good enough. O'Dell must have phoned you. Why?"

The boy brought her drink. She picked it up without a tremor and sipped it. "Really, you know, I should tell you to buzz off. You're being rude. I'm not a complicated type. I went on a boat trip with a drunken American officer, and he fell off the boat. I was very sorry about it, but it happened a long time ago. If you can consent to change the subject and stop acting so grim, I'll forgive you and you can buy me another drink. Otherwise, it was most pleasant meeting you, Garry."

I shrugged. I couldn't make her talk. But for the first time I felt the inner sense of excitement. The trail was warmer. She did know something. But she was clever. I had to make the next move. I grinned as warmly as I could. "I'm sorry, Conny.

Maybe I've got a fixation on this thing. Dan was my friend—maybe he was too good a friend. Maybe you shouldn't get so close to another person. Forgive the melodrama, will you?"

"Drink on that," she demanded. We clinked the glasses together, and she looked into my eyes as we drank. For all her slim coolness and composure, I could see something primal behind her eyes, a latent viciousness that was coiled like a sleeping cat.

We had another half hour before she had to leave to get ready for a dinner date. She made the time pleasant with small talk about the Colombo social group. I asked her about the January Club.

She curled her lip a bit. "Not the cream, Garry. There're much finer clubs in the city. A very mixed group at the January. Whites and Burghers and Eurasians and a few Singhalese. High stakes bridge and sloppy tennis. They spice the food too much. Why do you ask?"

"O'Dell said that you and he and Christoff were there before you went down to the harbor. I wondered about the place."

"Oh, yes. I'd met the captain at a party. He happened to be at the January. O'Dell and I had been playing a set partners game against another city bridge team there. As I remember, we won, and the ride was to celebrate the victory."

I walked with her into the lobby, and she gave me her hand just before she got into the elevator. It was very warm and moist. I walked out onto the street, realizing that I liked her and disliked her. She was desirable in a faintly unclean way. I found a public bench in a shaded spot. I sat and thought. As far as the investigation was concerned, I was through. There was nothing else I could do, and yet I was more certain of something odd about Dan's death than ever before. I knew that there'd be no point in talking to O'Dell again. I had sensed his cleverness. Constance wouldn't tell me anything further. I realized that unless I could stir up trouble for either or both of them, I had best leave the island. I wanted proof. I wanted to clear Dan officially, somehow, and I didn't know how it could be done. I felt dumb, stubborn, and bitter.

I was standing in my cool shower, still preoccupied with devising a plan of action, when I remembered her opening conversation about intrigue. Intrigue might be the answer. I toweled myself and walked out to the desk in my room. There was some hotel stationery in the drawer. I took a razor and cut out two small pieces a couple of inches square. I was careful to avoid the watermark. I sat down at the desk with a pencil stub. On the first one I wrote in block letters, YOU GAVE HIM TOO MUCH INFORMATION. On the second one, in smaller, back-hand printing, I wrote, HE KNOWS TOO MUCH. WHAT DID YOU TELL HIM?

I dressed quickly and took a rickshaw back to the Princess. It was growing dark rapidly. The sun had just finished its abrupt drop into the Western sea. I told the boy to stand and wait about fifty yards from the entrance to the Princess. I hoped that she hadn't left, and that her date hadn't planned dinner at her hotel. The lights flashed on over the hotel entrance. It was nearly a half hour before she came out. I recognized her slim tallness and her pale hair. The rickshaw coolie was smart. He grinned at me when I gave him his instructions and followed along a discreet distance behind her rickshaw. I suddenly realized that I had had stupid luck. If she had taken a taxi, I would have been lost. The night was quiet. The bare feet of the coolie slapped on the streets that were still warm from the sun. He ran easily, his shoulder muscles moving under the brown skin with the movement of the poles.

The trip lasted nearly fifteen minutes. Her rickshaw stopped on the Galle Road in front of a brightly lighted bungalow. I thought at first that it was a private home and that my plan would be spoiled. Then I saw the sign, China Sea Inn. There were numerous cars parked closely in the small lot beside the bungalow. I paid off my boy and walked carefully up the sidewalk. She was nowhere in sight. I knew that I was taking a risk in going up on the porch, as she might be just inside the door. I walked slowly up the steps and looked into a wide window. There were dozens of small tables in a large room. Only a few of the tables were unoccupied. Music blared from loudspeakers set high in the walls.

I stood in the door and looked quickly around. I couldn't see her. Off to the left were stairs. A small sign hung over the stairs announcing additional space upstairs. That was disturbing. The place was too small and too brightly lighted. If the upstairs was one large room like the downstairs, I realized that she would surely see me the second I reached the top. I had to take the chance. If she did see me, it would have to be an accidental meeting and my plan could wait. I fingered the slip of paper in my jacket pocket—the one for her. I crossed my fingers and walked up the stairs. To my relief, I came out in a small hall. Apparently, little dining rooms opened off the hall on both sides. Waiters scurried along the hall carrying steaming trays of food.

I located her. She was sitting alone at the table for two just inside the door of the first room. By luck, she was looking at the menu when I saw her. I hurried across the hall and found a table in the opposite room. She couldn't see me, but by leaning forward I could see her shoulder and the left side of her face. I had a good view of the empty chair across from her without having to lean forward.

A waiter came over to me and I ordered bean sprouts, bitter squash, and chicken with sweet and sour sauce. I had a plan for getting the note to her. It would depend a great deal on luck and timing. I saw her order. Again I crossed my fingers. Then she pushed her chair back and got up. She went out into the hall and I ducked far back into my corner. She passed my door and walked down the hall. I pulled a silver rupee out of my pocket and rolled it across into the next room, following behind it. It stopped under another table. I excused myself and fumbled for it. I dropped it on the floor and kicked it as I reached for it. It slid under her table. I put my hand near her plate as I reached for it. I walked back across into my own room. As I had placed my hand on the table, I had slid the note under the edge of her plate. I sat down and waited. She returned in a few minutes. Shortly after that, her food arrived, and so did mine. She didn't notice the note. I realized that I had probably pushed it too far under her plate.

I glanced in at her table and nearly dropped my fork in surprise. There was a man with her. He had slipped in without my noticing it. I had half expected it to be O'Dell. This was a stranger. He was a small man with thinning black hair plastered firmly across an oval skull. His face was the color of

116

very weak tea with too much cream. His eyes were imbedded in small pads of flesh. He talked to her, and he used his hands too much and with too much grace. The shoulders on his white linen suit were heavily padded.

I tried to eat without taking my eyes off him except when I could anticipate his glancing up. He seemed to do most of the talking. I couldn't hear a word. When I leaned forward, I could see her head nodding. It was as though he were giving instructions. I wondered how I could find out his name. I realized that I might have been unintelligent about the way I had handled it. If I hadn't seen her, then possibly I could have dared to sit near enough to her to overhear portions of the conversation. Then I remembered that talking to her had given me my first feeling of true confidence that there was more to Dan's death than had been reported.

She was finished before I was. I watched her lay down her fork, and I waited for the waiter to pick up her plate. When he did, I saw her hands pick up the note and unfold it. She had been holding it down near the table. Suddenly she lifted it closer to her eyes. Her hands looked tense. She was reading YOU GAVE HIM TOO MUCH INFORMATION. She must have said something to the man with her. I saw his black marble eyes widen, and he snatched the note. He read it and crumpled it slowly in his fragile hand. He stared at her in the same way that a man might stare at a disfigured corpse. He pushed back his chair and stood up. He didn't speak to her. He tossed some crumpled rupee notes onto the table and left. As he turned down the hall I heard her call, "Guy!" Her voice had a frightened note in it. He didn't stop.

In a few moments she got up and left. I had a glimpse of her face as she turned into the hall. She was chewing her underlip.

I was sitting in her hotel lobby when she came in. I stood up, and she stopped. She didn't look pleased to see me.

"Hi, Conny. Thought I'd have to wait longer than this. Short date?"

"What do you want?"

"No hidden motives this time. Just a normal male impulse.

117

You're the only gal I know in this town, and I want to make a date."

She brushed by me and I caught her arm. She flung my hand off and spun around. Her eyes looked small. "Don't touch me! Don't talk to me! I don't even want to be seen with you." She turned and nearly ran toward the elevator. That was her second slip.

I walked over to the desk. There was a chocolate-colored smooth-shaven Pancho Villa standing behind it. I took a ten-rupee note out of my pocket and stood in front of him, folding it into a small square.

"Miss Severence has many admirers?" I said.

"A great many, master."

"Could a jealous American learn their names?"

"There are a great many."

I took another ten-rupee note out of my pocket and started to fold it around the first one. "I am only interested in one, a small man whom she calls Guy. A man with black hair which he is losing."

"Possibly, master, you speak of a man called Guy Wend, who owns a small rubber plantation a dozen miles south of Colombo. I know little else about him."

I slid the small fold of money across to him. His hand flicked at it and it was gone. "If Miss Severence should learn from you that I asked this question, I will break several bones in your face. That is a sincere promise." He smiled and bowed. I left.

He didn't get up when I walked into my room. He sat in the chair by the windows and smiled at me. He wore wrinkled whites with scores of faint stains down the front. He wore a small spade beard that looked as rigid as gray steel wire. His face was wide and red and shiny with sweat. His smiling red rosebud of a mouth looked silly above the bold beard. His eyes weren't silly. They were light blue, frigid, unwinking.

"Who the hell are you?" I asked him.

"Van Hosen. I wanted to see you. Forgive the liberty. I

bribed the boy to let me in." His voice was high and sharp, with a faint accent.

"What do you want?"

"Just casual conversation, Mr. Garry. Nothing important. I write for the local papers. Features. You could call this an interview. I like to talk to visitors on the island. Get their impressions. Use them in my articles."

I sat on the edge of the bed. I tried to keep all expression off my face. He might be what he claimed to be. He might be connected with O'Dell, Severence, and Wend. "Go ahead, but make it quick. I'm tired."

"What are you doing on the island, Mr. Garry?"

"Tourist."

"How do you like it?"

"Beautiful."

"Haven't you anything to add to that?"

"Nothing."

He pulled at the spade beard. He stared at my bad hand. I covered it with the other. "Mr. Garry, we usually get more information than that. The tourist talk about the glamour, the air of mystery that seems to be a carryover from the days of the conquerors. You know, Ceylon was taken from the Veddas by the Singhalese. It has been ruled by the Portuguese, the Dutch, and now the English. Polynesians and Macronesians came here across thousands of miles of ocean in outrigger canoes. A Moslem pirate with an Abyssinian garrison held Colombo at one time. Intrigue and revolt and conquest. Plot and counterplot. Assassinations and assignations. Can't you feel it in the air?"

"Can't say that I do."

"Then, Mr. Garry, you're an exception. You see, many of our visitors are carried by this strange feeling. They see bogies behind every bush. They imagine plots where none exist. We think them a little silly, yet in a way we're proud of our heritage. You can consider this as a word of warning. The evil-faced man who glowers at you in a café isn't plotting to steal your money or take your life. He's probably wondering whether he can sell you a used automobile."

"I don't think about plots. Maybe I'm not imaginative."

He grunted as he pulled himself to his feet. Standing, he was much less impressive. His legs were too short for his long torso. He looked tired and old and more than a little shabby. I held the door for him.

"No story here for me, then. Sorry to have bothered you, Mr. Garry."

I shut the door and paced back and forth across the room. It was all too pat. A discreet warning. Tourists were a commonplace. No need to interview them. It was the same warning that O'Dell and Constance had given me—only it was more direct. The trail was growing too warm. Suppose I found out too much. They hadn't hesitated to kill Dan. It was the first time that I was absolutely positive that he had been killed. I stopped pacing and went to the desk.

I scribbled a note to the American consul:

Dear Sir:
I have instructed you to open this in case I meet with an accident. In April 1945, Captain Daniel Christoff, U.S. Army, was drowned in the waters outside Colombo Harbor. The official investigation censured Captain Christoff. I am trying to find out how he was killed and why. If anything happens to me, the following local people will be implicated in some way—Miss Constance Severence, Mr. Clarence O'Dell, Mr. Guy Wend (?), and a man who poses as a reporter and calls himself Van Hosen. He wears a small spade beard. This should give you enough to start on. Trace the connection between the above-listed people. Find their motivation.

I signed it and sealed it.

I took it to the consul's office in the morning. I had half expected them to make a fuss, to become official and difficult. They were very calm about the whole matter. I walked into a hotel near the office. Of all the people I had seen, Constance seemed to be the most vulnerable. It was time to make another date with her. I phoned Naval Headquarters and asked for her extension. A male voice answered and said, "Miss Severence didn't report for work this morning." He hung up before I could ask any more questions. I took a rickshaw to her hotel.

I walked down the narrow lobby and stopped in front of the desk. Pancho Villa smiled at me, the broad welcoming smile of the perfect host.

"What is Miss Severence's room number?"

He rubbed his hands together and smiled more broadly. "It is regretted, master, that you won't be able to speak with the lady."

"She's given instructions about me?"

"Not that, master. The lady has had a misfortune."

"What do you mean?"

"Possibly, master, if you go through that door at the end of the lobby and turn to the right, you will find her in front of the bathhouses. She drowned this morning while taking an early swim. The police are even now examining her."

I stared at him. He didn't stop smiling. Maybe it was confusion that made him smile. He giggled. I turned and walked to the door he had indicated.

I turned right into the glare of sunshine on a white tile walk. Fifty feet ahead were the bathhouses. The wide white beach was at my left as I walked. The blue water rolled up into long ragged white crests that thudded against the sand with constant soft thunder. I saw a group ahead and quickened my step.

She was on her back on the hot tile in front of the bathhouses. Two Singhalese in police uniform stood staring down at her. A big man with a long white face was scribbling in a notebook. A slender British officer knelt on the white square of his pocket handkerchief and looked at her closely.

The pale blue bathing suit revealed the magnificent body that her dress had concealed. Long golden limbs and flowing curves. Her lips were swollen, bluish, protruding. Her eyes were wide. There was a thin green string of seaweed across her forehead. Part of it rested on her eyeball. Her shoulders were scraped. As I looked at her, her skin seemed more bluish. I noticed that the two police were soaked up to the knees. I guessed that they had stood in the surf to recover her body.

The one with the long white face looked at me. "A friend?"

"An acquaintance. How did it happen?"

"Caught by the undertow. The hotel doesn't recommend

121

swimming here at this time of year. Very foolish except for exceptional swimmers. She wasn't."

The slim British officer stood up and picked up his handkerchief. He used it to flick nonexistent dust off his spotless uniform. He carefully wiped his hands on it and then started to put it back in his pocket. On an impulse, he stooped over and spread it over her rigid face. The tall man kept writing. The officer stepped over to me and said, "Too bad. Conny was a pleasant type."

"Oh, you knew her?"

"Quite. Breaks me up a bit. Let's get a peg up at the hotel bar."

I agreed gladly. They had removed the weak link in the chain. They had destroyed my starting point. Of that I had no doubt.

I liked the looks of the officer, except for the fact that he was a bit too pretty. A very fair man, with even bronze tan, regular delicate features, and eyelashes that any girl would have envied. I saw the minute wrinkles at the corners of his eyes and around his mouth and knew that he was older than he had at first appeared. I guessed his age at about thirty-three.

As we walked together up the walk, I stuck my hand out to him and said, "Howard Garry. I'm a tourist."

"Right. Peter Kaymark here."

We went into the bar, and I followed his lead in ordering a gin and tonic. We took them and carried them over to a table near a window. He sighed, as he sat down, and drank half of his drink in one long gulp.

"How'd you know Conny, Mr. Garry?"

"Oh, she knew a friend of mine that was stationed here during the war. A Captain Dan Christoff. You probably never heard of him."

"Yes. I remember him. Chap who was drowned. Big stink about that here. Conny complained for weeks."

I went over to the bar and brought back the second round. We drank it, and Lieutenant Kaymark became a bit flushed. We sat in silence. I was thinking those thoughts that every man has when he sees the body of an attractive woman. What a waste!

After half of the third round was gone, he looked up. "I guess I shouldn't feel so badly about it. She'll be off my list now. One less person to watch. Bloody Intelligence unit always loads you up with too many suspected agents."

"You're in Intelligence?"

"Five years of it out here. I suppose that if I'd told you that during wartime, they could have shot me for it. But now I'm so bloody sick of it, I wish they'd transfer me out of it. It's too much of a piece of cake. Nothing to do. Dull."

I thought it over. A man with the perfect qualifications. And he'd dropped into my lap. It was too good an opportunity to miss. I leaned forward and put my elbows on the table and lowered my voice. "How would you like to have it a lot less dull, lieutenant?"

He shrugged and smiled. "Of course, I'd like it." He looked amused.

"Suppose I tell you that I think Captain Christoff was murdered? Suppose I tell you that I believe that Conny was murdered? Suppose the fact that she was a suspected agent ties in with it all?"

"Bit thick, what?" He grinned at me as if I was a case to be pitied.

"Don't smirk at me, lieutenant." I started with the interviews with the crew members. I gave him the entire story. I didn't spare any details, and I tried to repeat the conversations as near word for word as I could remember. He sat there, indolent but interested, until I told of my interview with Constance Severence. Then he sat forward, alert and excited. His excitement grew as I told of the China Sea Inn, Guy Wend, and the note. When I finished telling him about the visit from Van Hosen, he leaned back and sighed.

"That tears it, Garry. It's perfect. Van Hosen is on my list. Originally from Java. Got out somehow after the Japs moved in. Mysterious circumstances. Claimed to have escaped. He does odd-job journalism around the city. Wend is also on my list. Nasty type. Slippery. Always mixed up in radical island politics. A rebel. I'm surprised about O'Dell. Never figured him for that sort of thing. It ties in with Conny beautifully."

"Then you think I'm right, Peter? You think it's possible

that Dan Christoff got mixed up in some kind of intrigue or spy stuff, learned too much, and was killed?"

He twirled his glass and looked judicious. "I'm certain that you're right, Garry. You've gone about as far as you can go. Let me take it over from here. We'll work as a team."

I was delighted. It was the first backing I had received. I was no longer fighting alone and in the dark. "Where do we start?"

"At the January Club. They don't open until noon. I've got some reports to make out on the Severence woman. Suppose I meet you at the club at twelve thirty for lunch. I'm a member there. I had to join. Too many of my suspects flocked around there during the war."

As we left the hotel, he stopped by a full-length mirror in the hall and made a dozen minor adjustments to his uniform, tugging at the sleeves, straightening insignia, pulling down his blouse. He pulled a small brush and comb out of his side pocket. He brushed his uniform and then carefully combed his hair. He stepped back and took a last look at himself. He smiled at himself. And then we walked out and each took rickshaws in opposite directions.

I arrived at the January Club before Kaymark did. It was a low building with orange-yellow plaster walls and a red tile roof. It was set back from the road behind a screen of thick shrubs and flowering trees. As I walked up the steps, I could see a double row of tennis courts at the side. I estimated that there were twenty courts. A few of them were already in use.

A smiling native in a white uniform met me at the door and directed me to a small cool room to wait for Lieutenant Kaymark. On the small table were copies of the London *Times* and the *New York Times*. The latest copy of the *New York Times* was only nine days old. I was halfway through the front page when I looked up and saw Kaymark smiling down at me.

We went into the pleasant sunny dining room and ordered drinks at the table. I looked over the sprinkling of members at the other tables. I started when I saw the man named Guy eating alone in a corner. I jerked my head in his direction, and

124

Peter looked around. He looked back at me and nodded. "The desk clerk was right, Garry. That's Wend."

The other faces were unfamiliar. After the excellent curry lunch we walked back to the cardroom. Two bridge games had started. As we walked in, an old man with a leathery face looked up from his cards and said, "Ho, Peter! Hear about Conny?"

"Saw her. Unhealthy business, this getting drowned, you know."

"Good a way as any, they tell me." He grinned and turned back to his cards. His partner had been glaring at him as he talked. We stood and watched the play for a time. I've always enjoyed bridge without knowing too much about the finer points of bidding. The table where Peter's friend was sitting was playing slow, careful bridge. I glanced around at the other table. I saw into the hand of a Singhalese who sat with his back to me and noticed with a start that his cards were unsorted. A heart was played and he, with hearts scattered through his hand, played the king of clubs. The opponents picked up the trick. The man's partner saw me staring and muttered something. The hand was lowered so that I couldn't see it, and in a few seconds they all threw their hands in. On the next deal, the man with his back to me sorted his cards properly. I watched for a few minutes. The play was normal. I motioned to Peter, and he followed me out into the main lounge. No one was within earshot.

"Peter, have you ever paid much attention to the game in there?"

"How do you mean? I can afford to watch, but I can't afford to play. Stakes are a rupee a hundred. Roughly thirty cents in your money. If you lose by two hundred points, which would be a very low score, that's sixty of your dollars."

"I don't mean that. I mean have you ever seen anything odd about the way they play bridge?"

"No."

I explained what I had seen. "Suppose this was the nucleus of a group of agents. Imagine the efficiency of it. A man has two thousand rupees to pay off. He has instructions to give. They memorize a simple code. There's twenty-six letters in the alphabet and thirteen cards in a suit. Any red ace is A, and any black ace is B. Any red deuce is C, and any black deuce is D. Any red trey is E, and so on. It would come out even and be easy to remember. They deal new hands until the boy with the message can spell it out. At the end of the game, they fake the score so that he has to pay off. No danger of being overheard. No suspicion."

"How about the casual person looking in on the game?"

"They were probably a hell of a lot more careful during the war, when they could get hung or shot for it, than they are now. Even if what I saw was out of line, how can I prove anything?"

"You know, Garry, that's pretty shrewd. Never thought of it." He dabbed at his upper lip with a clean handkerchief. "Could arrange somehow to get a peephole in the ceiling. Keep a record of the play and break the code. Hard to do that without tipping off the servants, who will tip off the people playing."

"Why don't you pull in one of the servants on some excuse and work him over?"

"That's been done, but it isn't good. My superior, Colonel Rith-Lee, doesn't like it. He says that it shows our hand. Besides, they never talk. They're too terrified. All we can threaten them with is imprisonment. These other people can promise to strip off their hide, a quarter inch at a time. More impressive."

We talked in the lounge for nearly a half hour. He couldn't think of any constructive plan. I had a few, but he showed me just how they were impractical. He stated that I hadn't given him sufficient basis on which Van Hosen, Wend, and O'Dell could be picked up.

Finally I said, "Let me try one thing. It hadn't ought to hurt you."

"What's that?"

"I've got some extra money, money that ought to look big to a servant. I'll give the boy at the front desk a note to come and see me in the Galle Face on a matter that will mean money to him. If he comes, maybe I can offer him enough so that he'll make a statement and then quit his job and leave town. Of course, he may know nothing worth buying, but it's worth taking a chance." He agreed. I went to a desk in the lounge and wrote my note. As we left, I shoved it into the brown palm of the boy on the door.

We stood out in the street. I'd written the boy to come after he was off duty, no matter how late. "Want me to come along and help you question him?" Peter asked.

"No, thanks. You've got a lot of official scruples. I may have to rough him up a little to encourage him. It might get you in trouble. You just sit tight, and I'll come to you tomorrow morning to tell you what I've learned."

We parted, and I went back to the Galle Face to begin the long wait. I began to expect him at one o'clock. He hadn't arrived by three. I pinned a note to the outside of the door which read *Knock loudly*. I went to bed.

When I awoke the sun was bright on the ocean. The note on my door was undisturbed. I figured that he had been too scared to come see me. We'd have to dream up another approach, try another employee. Only we'd have to be more careful, because he might possibly have tipped off the proper people concerning what we were attempting to do.

I rang for the room boy, Fernando. I wanted to order breakfast in the room before taking my shower. He came in and his round face was grave, his eyes wide and bright. He made a little bow and said, "Much trouble in hotel, Garry master."

"Trouble?"

He licked his lips and glowed with the pleasure of having information to impart. "Boy killed with knife in front of hotel last night, master. Maybe one o'clock, maybe two o'clock." He slashed his chubby forefinger across his throat and made a gurgling noise.

I tried to act bored. "Police take him away already?"

"No, master. Police very modern. Have camera. Waiting for sun to come and then taking pictures. Man still out on grass near side of hotel."

I didn't order breakfast and I skipped the shower. I pulled my clothes on and hurried down to the lobby. Once in the lobby I walked slowly across to the front door. Off to one side were a hundred curious people standing in a wide circle, looking at something on the ground. They looked as though they had been standing a long time. Knowing the oriental indifference to death, I suspected that they were staring at something fairly juicy.

I pressed through the crowd and found that I was right on both counts. It was the boy to whom I had given the note. His throat had been slashed with such vicious strength that the cords and muscles had been parted all the way back to the spinal column. Without the support of the neck muscles, the shock of falling after the blow must have broken the neck. His head was strained back at right angles to the body, exposing the severed jugular. The grass was stained black red in a circle around his head, a circle of about the same circumference as a bushel basket. His lips were drawn back from his teeth.

I shoved my way back out of the circle. They had been too quick, too clever. I knew that there would be no point in trying to bribe another one. They had licked me again. Every time I thought of an opening, of a chance to get information, they stepped in first with a block that stopped me in my tracks.

I had poor coffee in the hotel and then went back up to my room and phoned Peter Kaymark at the number he had given me. A clerk told me that he wasn't in and they didn't know when to expect him. I tried three more times before noon, with the same result. At noon I had a small lunch sent up, and, after finishing it, I took a rickshaw to the January Club.

There was a new boy on the door. I looked at him carefully but could detect no change of expression when he admitted me, and I asked to see Lieutenant Kaymark or Mr. O'Dell, if either of them were in the club.

He showed me back to a small curtained room off the main lounge, a different room than I had waited in before. He told me that he would attempt to locate either of the two gentlemen and plug them in on the phone which stood on a small table in the room if they didn't happen to be in the club. I thanked him and he left. The small room was hot and airless. It smelled of mold and dust.

I sat on the edge of a worn chair which faced the curtains. For some reason, I felt uneasy. I didn't have long to wait. The room was poorly lighted. Suddenly figures burst through the curtains at me, moving so quickly that I received only a confused impression of several burly Singhalese. They fell on me and the chair went over backwards. I tried to kick at their heads, but one of them dropped heavily across my knees. I swung my right fist in a short arc and heard one of them grunt as it landed. I tried to buck and spin out of it, but they were too quick and too heavy. They rolled me over roughly and yanked my hands around behind me. Something rough and hard tightened over my wrists and drew them together. I started to shout as I felt the same substance around my ankles. They rolled me over, and as I opened my mouth to shout again, one of them crammed a thick cloth between my teeth. They tied another length of rope around my head to keep me from shoving the gag out with my tongue.

Two of them picked me up and the third peered cautiously through the curtains. Then he motioned to the others and they yanked me up off the floor and hurried out with me. One held me by the shoulder, the other by the knees.

Out in the brighter light of the lounge, I could see that they were all large men. They wore bright plaid sarongs, which had been tucked up to leave their legs free. They were naked from the waist up.

They hurried down the length of the lounge with me, and up a flight of narrow stairs. They bumped my head painfully when they rounded a corner of the stairs. They hurried down a dingy hall and opened the door of a small room. They dropped me heavily onto my face and cut the ropes on my neck, wrists, and ankles. The last one was backing out of the door as I jumped to my feet. The door slammed, and there was the sharp efficient click of a lock. I was alone in a bare room, about ten by ten, with one small barred window and not a scrap of furniture. I looked out the window, down into an enclosed court. I listened. I was so far from the road that I couldn't hear the sound of traffic. There was no sound from the club. I sat by the door with my back against the wall.

I should have felt alarmed, at least disturbed. I didn't. It was direct action, the first concrete thing that had happened. All the rest was supposition. Whatever happened, I would learn something. The gloves were off; the knife was out.

I waited an hour before I heard a sound at the door. When the lock clicked, I jumped up. My ankle hurt from where they had tightened the rope across the scar that hid the silver plate.

The door opened and O'Dell walked in, closely followed by one of the men who had carried me up the stairs. O'Dell grinned and the native shut the door and stood leaning against it, his arms folded.

"We meet again, Mr. Garry. Let me commend your persistence. You've been stubborn, but not particularly intelligent. We won't keep you long. Just a little favor you can do us." I didn't answer. He reached into his white jacket pocket and brought out a piece of Galle Face Hotel stationery. He handed it to me and I took it. It was blank. "I see you have a pen there, Garry. I'm sorry there's no table in this guest room. Just sit down there on the floor and write a note to the American consul authorizing them to turn over to the bearer the envelope you left there. One of the men on our payroll is a clerk there. He told me of the envelope."

He stood, fat, smiling, and confident. He wore a white jacket, shorts, and high white wool socks. He acted like a man soliciting subscriptions for the Chamber of Commerce.

"And suppose that I don't. Suppose I say that when you have the envelope I'll be drowned or run over or have some other kind of accident."

"My dear boy, I'm not underrating you. Of course you'll have an accident, but I guarantee that you'll die easily. It will inconvenience us if we have to force you to sign. You may be familiar with the water cure? We suspend you by your heels and fill your belly with water from a stirrup pump, under pressure. When you're close to bursting, we stop pumping. Then a couple of husky men beat on your abdomen with broom handles. The odd thing about it is that people generally stay conscious. Then you'll write the note."

For the first time, I felt the chill gnawing of fear. I'm no dauntless character. I hate to be hurt. Pain frightens me. Pain in any form. He didn't seem ill at ease or feel that he was speaking melodrama. He was as factual as a man describing with gusto how he had played the seventeenth hole.

"Give me a little time to think. An hour." I lifted my hands a bit and made them shake. He glanced down, and I saw him smile as he saw the quiver.

"We can do that, Garry. And don't feel too badly. This thing is bigger than you or me. You almost interfered with the New Co-Prosperity Sphere for Southeast Asia, if that's any consolation. You and that weakling woman and that blabbering servant. And Christoff too, if that's any help."

He turned around and the native opened the door for him. Then, to my disappointment, the native closed the door again, remaining on the inside. Once again I heard the lock click.

I walked over to the far side of the small room and stared at the heavy brown chest of the man. He was a brute. I remembered the rough hands slapping my clothes, feeling for the outlines of a weapon which I didn't have. I had to trick him in some way. The barred window offered the only possible escape. I stood near it and tried to think. I knew that my precious minutes were fading away.

I made my actions furtive. I reached a hand cautiously into my inside jacket pocket. I didn't look at the man. Out of the corner of my eye I saw him move slightly. I brought my hand out of the jacket pocket with my fingers bunched as though I was holding something small like a pill. I popped the imaginary pill into my mouth and then fell back against the wall, clutching my throat. I slid down the wall as he started toward me, making a horrid bubbling noise in my throat. I rolled my eyes up and held my breath, stiffening my body. He hurried over and leaned over me, his eyes wide in his coarse face. I knew that in a matter of seconds he would turn and hammer on the door. With every ounce of power in my left leg, I kicked up hard against his poised jaw. The force of the kick numbed my toes. It lifted him off his feet and he went over backwards, his head thumping on the floor. I scrambled onto him and hit him twice before I realized that it was unnecessary. He was completely out, the heavy bone of his jaw crushed near the point of his chin.

I hurriedly inspected the window. The bars were about a half inch in diameter and about five inches apart. There were five of them set vertically across the window. The ends were imbedded in a wooden sill, but it looked as though they went on through the wooden sill and into the concrete. I braced my feet on the wall and yanked at one with all the power of my back. It gave a little, but not enough. I examined it from the side and saw that I'd bent the bar slightly. Untempered metal, possibly wrought iron. That gave me the idea I needed. I took off my heavy leather belt and fastened it so that it enclosed three of the bars. I needed something sturdy to use as a lever. There was no furniture in the room to break up. The only thing I could think of to use was my shoe. I wear a twelve A, and I like heavy soles. I slipped one off and inserted it into the belt. Then, with one hand on the heel and the other on the toe, I twisted it around, tightening it like a tourniquet. At first there was no result. The shoe merely became harder to turn. Then I noticed that the bar on the right seemed to be bending. I twisted harder. It bent over until it nearly touched the bar next to it. Then, with a splintering of wood, it pulled free from the frame on the bottom. Bending it had shortened its effective length, so that it had pulled out of the concrete until only the wood was holding it. I grabbed the bottom and pulled up. It pulled free at the top. The hole that it left looked big enough to slip through, but I couldn't take a chance on getting stuck. By using the free bar as a lever, I bent the bars on either side of the orifice. I was lucky that the bars were the usual Colombo burglar insurance, rather than a special set for the purposes of the group that I had run into.

I slid through feet first and then grabbed the bars and let myself down until I was hanging full length against the side of the building. I nudged myself away from the rough plaster with my knee and let go. I dropped onto the ground so hard that I slammed my chin against my own knee.

I didn't waste time looking around. I hobbled toward the high wall. It was at a level with the top of my head and made with broken glass set into the cement on top of it. I tore off my jacket and threw it over the glass. Then I caught the edge and drew myself up. I missed the extra leverage of the fingers I had lost. The glass bit through the jacket and into the flesh of my hands. I dropped over the wall and snatched the jacket. In front of me was a wide field with a house on the far side of it. To the right across another small field was the familiar road. I ran toward it as fast as I could. My bad ankle seemed to be getting more painful by the second.

I pulled the jacket on and hurried away from the club. I stood on the corner until an idling rickshaw coolie sauntered along. He speeded up when I shouted. A few seconds later he was running with me toward the Galle Face Hotel. I sat on the black leather seat, breathing heavily and inspecting the cuts on my hands. I made the promise that Mr. O'Dell would be paid back in the same coin with exorbitant interest.

My jacket was ragged and my hands were bloody when I walked through the lobby of the hotel. I went on up to my room and phoned Kaymark. After I told him two sentences, he told me that he'd come over immediately. I bandaged my hands clumsily and had the boy get me a deep basin of cold water in which I could soak my ankle.

Peter arrived in five minutes. After I finished the story, he sat, looking shaken, and said, "We'll have to get back over there, Garry. Right away."

"How about picking up a bunch of your people? I can charge them with enough to sew them up for years."

He shook his head. "Not necessary. You don't realize how the British Army rates out here. They wouldn't dare try anything with me. Besides, I have this." He slid the butt of a heavy automatic partway out of his tunic pocket and then let it drop back. "Any time you feel well enough to go...."

We were in a taxi headed for the January Club within a matter of minutes. As we pulled up in front, he said, "Now let me handle it. Don't talk."

We walked in, and again the boy was expressionless. Peter asked for O'Dell and was told that he could be found in the cocktail room. Peter walked ahead and I limped after him. I hadn't seen the cocktail room before. It was in the rear of the building, beyond the dining room. It opened out into the garden. O'Dell was sitting hunched at a table near the open doors. He looked up with a wry smile when we walked in.

There were three extra chairs at his table. We were far enough from the bar so that low voices couldn't be heard by the bartender.

"You're off games, O'Dell," Peter said as we sat down.

"Just a little joke, Peter. Afraid this American beggar might take it too seriously."

"It's more than that. You're going to have to do a lot of talking. You're all tied together. You and Van Hosen, Conny, Wend. Conny's death and the death of the boy who used to be on the door. It's all got to be explained."

"Not by me, son. I'm just a bystander. Don't know a thing."

I interrupted. "One thing you should have known, O'Dell, is that I'm too stubborn to talk, no matter what you tried to do. You should have seen that."

O'Dell looked at Peter, his mouth sullen. "Then what's the bloody use of bringing—" I was looking at him. I saw his eyes widen. I turned toward Peter just as the heavy automatic banged. The noise of the shot was deafening in the still room. There was a crash of glassware from the direction of the bar.

I looked back at O'Dell. The slug had caught him flush in the center of his upper lip, turning his mouth into a bloody hole. I could see bits of his shattered teeth. He seemed to clutch the edge of the table for a second, then his eyes seemed to look far beyond us. He bent slowly over to the left and his huge body thumped onto the floor, overturning both his chair and the table. We got up. Peter looked older and very tired.

He turned to me and saw the question in my eyes. "Couldn't take a chance, Garry. Saw him tighten up and knew he was going to try something." I recalled the immense size and vitality of the man. Once under way, he would have been hard to stop. When the table had gone over, O'Dell's drink had crashed to the floor. The spattering liquid had spotted Peter's trousers. He slid the automatic back into the side pocket of his tunic and took out his handkerchief. He bent over and carefully blotted the spots. Attracted by the noise of the shot, half a dozen servants had hurried into the cocktail lounge. They stood ten feet away and gazed with wide eyes at the dead hulk of the retired planter.

The head boy stepped forward and said, "Kaymark master wishes me to call the police?"

"No, Ratmani. I'll do it." He turned to me. "Better stay by the body while I use the telephone. The boys might take his money if we both stayed away long enough."

I upended the fallen chair as he strolled out. I pulled it over to one side and sat where I could see the corpse without having to turn my head. The room was very still. The man was dead, and yet there were small movements from the corpse—the crackle of starched whites as the body settled, the rumble of gases in the abdomen. Fresh corpses will sometimes give the impression of life, but after a few minutes they seem to settle more flatly against the floor, they take on that distinctive "sack of wheat" look which is unmistakable. Then they become substances instead of persons. A few dollars' worth of chemicals that the clothes no longer fit. One by one the other servants backed out until only the head boy and the bartender were left. I ordered a double scotch. I felt uneasy. How many deaths? Christoff, Constance, the doorboy, O'Dell. It began to look as though there would be no one left to give me the proof of Christoff's innocence. Wend and Van Hosen and the men who had been playing bridge.

Kaymark, the familiar man with the long white face, and three uniformed policemen came in as I was watching the door.

Peter was in the middle of a sentence. "... and I'll turn my report in to my colonel. He'll authorize a true copy to be sent to you. Purely a technicality, covered by our existing operating regulations. You understand."

They stood by the body of O'Dell. I stood up. The white-faced man rubbed his chin. He turned to me. "And you were also sitting at the table? Can you give me a report?"

Peter interrupted. "Just a minute, Saxon. Let me send his in with mine with a copy to you later. Army business, you know."

Saxon sighed. "Nothing else to do, I guess. You and your friend can go any time, lieutenant."

"Wait a minute there," I interrupted. "How about a charge of abduction or something? How about those other men that—"

"Hold it, Garry," Peter demanded, his voice loud and sharp. "We'll take care of that also."

Saxon raised his thin black eyebrows. "Suppose you let me know about it now, Mr. Garry."

"You don't have to answer him, Garry," Peter said quietly.

135

I looked from one to the other. Peter had a faint smile hidden around the corners of his mouth.

"I'd better follow the lieutenant's advice. I'll put it in the report." Again the police official sighed. I looked back as we walked out and saw him stooping over the body.

As soon as we were far enough away, Peter said plaintively, "Damn it, Garry, you don't want those beggars in on it. They'd foul it up for you. You'd never find out the truth once they got their heavy hands on it."

I stopped walking and fished out a cigarette. He paused and waited for me. "Look, Peter. While you were phoning I was sitting in there thinking. I've got enough now so that I'm convinced in my own mind that Dan wasn't out of line. And I think I've got enough to convince his wife and his people. What more do I need? Maybe I ought to give the whole thing up and go back to the States. Come on over to my hotel and let's talk it over."

He agreed, but added, "We'll have to make it short. I've got to get that report in."

I didn't have much to say to him as we rode back to the Galle Face in the taxi. I was too busy with my own plans and problems.

We went up to my room, and I dug a bottle of brandy out of the suitcase. There were two glasses in the bathroom. I made two strong drinks and handed him one. I sat on the bed and he sat in the chair, his back to the windows, his elbows almost touching the high bureau.

"You've thought over what I said, Peter."

"Yes, but I thought you wanted to stay around and prove that Christoff wasn't to blame. I thought you wanted it to go on the records."

"I did, but what are the odds? I'm more certain, yes, but what proof have I got? How do I know I'm going to get any more proof? How do I know I won't be killed in the process myself? That crack O'Dell made about a Co-Prosperity Sphere sort of got me. I'm tangling with something big. It's like an iceberg—I've only seen the little part that's out of water."

He sipped his drink and looked thoughtful. I marveled again at the long curled lashes. At last he said, "Maybe you're right. At least I could carry on here, and once we break it up, I could arrange to have Christoff cleared officially. I'm sure we'll break it up in time, whatever it is."

"Let me show you something, Peter. It's a letter that Dan's wife got from the U.S. colonel out here. It's what you've got to counteract."

I got up and walked over to the bureau. He had to move his arm to give me room. I fumbled in the top drawer and cursed about not being able to find it. I looked in the bureau mirror and waited until I could see his head tilt back as he drained the last of the drink. I spun and chopped down hard with my right fist, swinging it like a hammer. It had to be good. It was. It hit him flush on the side of the jaw. My follow-through knocked the empty glass across the room. He was stunned but not completely out. I dropped my right fist and swung it up in an uppercut that straightened him out in the chair. He sagged back into it, completely limp.

I ran over to the door and locked it. Then I stripped the cover off my bed and took a sheet. I ripped it down the middle, the long way. Then I yanked him off the chair and tossed him on the floor, half in and half out of the bathroom. There was a transom over the high bathroom door. I tied one end of the half sheet firmly around his wrist and then lifted him up so that I could throw the other end over the transom. I caught it and pulled down with all my weight. It lifted him until his toes barely touched the floor. I knotted the sheet. Then I did the same with the other wrist. His head sagged forward.

Then I had to wait for him to regain consciousness. I had hit him a little harder than I had intended. I grew impatient. Finally I drew a glass of water and threw it into his face. He tried to lift his head. The second glass brought him around.

He stared at me, and then he craned his neck and looked up at the knots and the transom. He looked back at me, his eyes wide and startled. "Now look here, Garry, this better not be some kind of a joke."

"It isn't a joke. It's the first smart thing I've done on this island."

He smiled. He looked tender and forgiving. "I say, old man, this heat here is pretty grim. Now be a good chap and cut me down. This arrangement hurts my wrists. We'll go see a doctor, right now."

"You're clever, Kaymark, but I can add two and two. You've made a few slips, you know."

"Come on now, this is silly. Cut me down and I'll forgive you the whole thing."

"Wait a minute, Peter. You like mirrors, so you can watch that pretty face of yours. I think you ought to get a look at it now."

I grabbed the heavy bureau and twisted it around so that it stood about eight feet away from him. I tilted the mirror until it was at the right angle. Then I walked forward and slugged him. I hit him high on the cheekbone, turning my fist as it hit so that I could be certain of splitting the skin.

Then I stepped back and waved at the mirror. "Take a look, Pretty Boy."

His eyes widened and then narrowed. "That was cheap, Garry."

"Sure! Cut-rate Garry. Cheap and practical. The working man's thug. Now comes a little something that I happened to think of back in the January Club. I tell you this little something and, if you act dumb about it, I tap you again, in a new spot. Then I tell you something else. You understand?"

"I understand what you mean, but it's senseless!"

"Maybe to you. You haven't heard all. I'll do work on that pretty face that no plastic surgery'll ever fix. I'll tell you when I come to the last point. If you don't start talking then, I put my heart into one dilly that ought to spread your nose wide enough to touch the doorframes. Okay?"

"Please cut me down." His composure was gone. His voice was getting high and thin. I knew that it wasn't helping him any to be able to see the quick swelling of the spot on the cheek where I had nailed him.

"Now for point number one. Remember when I told you that I thought Constance had been drowned by someone? Your normal reaction would have been to go back out and check the body again to look for any signs of violence. You didn't."

"That's absurd. I'd already checked the body."

"But you claimed that you checked it thinking that it was an accidental drowning. Where'd you like the next one, sonny?" I didn't give him a chance to answer. It made me feel faintly sick to hit a man who couldn't hit back, but it had to be done. I swung hard and hit the other cheek. I made a better cut across the cheekbone. It began to bleed immediately. He tried to shake his head to clear it. but the sheets held his upper arms too tightly against his ears.

"Point number two is minor. If you don't work with the police, how did you know Conny had drowned? Who'd inform you? Why would you be out there if swimming isn't recommended this time of year? You popped up too quick. Ready to talk a little?"

"This is mad, Garry. Stop it now before you go too far."

I had to mark him up badly and save the delicate nose for last. I planted a short choppy right on the corner of his mouth. It smacked hard enough to swing him back a little. He shut his eyes and groaned.

"The next pernt, dearie, is the charming way you decided that all my plans concerning the January Club were no good. Even I could see that the smart thing to do would be to gather up all those jokers and sweat something out of them."

"But you can't handle these people that way. They never talk. Damn you, stop all this, you're cutting me."

"Sure, I'm cutting you. And sure it's a bloody shame it is, me fine bhoy."

I slammed another one into his mouth. I felt teeth give under my knuckles and the blood spurted across the back of my hand. I saw him glance beyond me into the mirror. He was twisted around the eyes like a small boy trying not to cry.

"The next point, Peter. Who knew about my bribing the boy at the door? Only you. Certainly that boy looked too smart to let anybody else know. And he got it the same night. Very very peculiar."

"Wait!" he screamed. "They must have found out some other way. They had to find out some other way."

I ignored him. It made me ill, but it had to be done. I hit him hard over the right eye, hard enough to split the cartilage.

I had to plan on his being too inexperienced to know that the marks I was making would be gone in a few months, leaving possibly a few tiny white scars.

"Another point. I don't think that the American consulate employs any local help until their honesty and loyalty has been pretty well checked. O'Dell said that an employee of the consulate tipped him off about my note. Nuts! I told you about it, and you told O'Dell. Talking yet?"

He surprised me. He pulled himself up a little straighter and looked squarely into my eyes. His face was as firm as it could be in its mangled condition. A moment before I had thought he was going to crack. I leaned on the next one a little more. The meaty smack of my fist against his face was loud in the room. It jolted his head back. When he straightened up, the other eyebrow was streaming.

"Another little fact. I was watching O'Dell. He wasn't going to try anything. He was completely relaxed. You gave it to him because he was going to say too much. He never stood a chance. Cold-blooded murder, and not the first one."

His eyes widened as I pulled my fist back. He was too busy being brave to do any talking. I grinned as I let it go. I smacked it into the least damaged portion of his mouth.

"Another point. You didn't want me to talk to the police. That Saxon looks smart. Maybe, if he got enough dope, he might see through you."

Again on the mouth. He started to curse me. He cursed through swelling battered lips that distorted his words. I stood back and let him finish. His voice got hoarse and indistinct and finally faded away completely. The blood was dripping onto his tunic.

"Also, chum, when I brought up the point of my leaving this place and going back to the States, you didn't do much discouraging. You wanted me to go. You put up no argument at all. Just gave me a song and dance about cleaning it up later. And look, I have one more point coming up, a conclusive point, old boy. We are now ready for the master stroke, the slam on the schnoz. Take a peek in the mirror. Take a look at that nose."

He looked. The pointed delicate nose stood out in the midst

of the carnage, shining like that good deed in a naughty world. I saw his face quiver as he looked and realized what would happen when I hit it. He was trying to brace himself.

I needed more psychology. I didn't have any conclusive point. I'd made my last point. So I smacked my lips loudly and wound up like a bush league pitcher. "You don't know how much I'm enjoying this, Pete. Guess I'm a sadist. Maybe I better take a couple of swings at it to make sure I get it hammered down nice and flat."

That got him. He came apart at the seams. Every ounce of guts ran out of him and he sobbed as he talked. "No, Garry! No! I'll tell you about it. All of it. Cut me down."

"Not till you get through talking. I'm aching for a shot at that nose."

"Van Hosen. He's in charge. Subversive group. Money from Japs in Java. Gold and jewels they took from the Dutch. War's over, but Van Hosen ordered to establish Jap-type sphere of influence down here. I've been working for him for three years. I'm perfect cover for them. Can direct suspicion away from them. Van Hosen in charge. O'Dell used to be second, but he's resented Van Hosen for a long time. I had replaced O'Dell. O'Dell was the one who gave instructions to kill Christoff. Christoff stumbled on card code by accident one night. He came to British headquarters to report it as something suspicious. By luck, he came to me. The January Club has been the base."

"How about that boat ride. Quick!"

"I asked Christoff to work with our headquarters in trapping these people. O'Dell's orders. Introduced him to Conny and O'Dell and told him later that they were suspected agents. Told him that we had information that they wanted to get over to India. Asked him to invite them out on the boat and pretend to be drunk and see if they'd ask him to take them across to India. Short trip. Told him that I'd give him a letter later that would cover him in case of any criticism. I told him not to tell anyone else of the plan. He did as I asked him, and at the first opportunity, O'Dell shoved him over the side."

"Why'd you shoot O'Dell?"

"Orders. I reported to Van Hosen that you couldn't be pur-

chased or intimidated. You blocked us when you sent the letter
to the consulate. If you hadn't done that, you'd be dead now.
O'Dell thought he could torture you to write a letter to get the
sealed note back. I knew you'd never write such a letter. Van
Hosen told O'Dell not to chance it. O'Dell disobeyed orders,
and I had to cover it all up. I thought I had."

"Why is this organization so ruthless, anyway?"

"Thousands of weapons and hundreds of thousands of rounds
of ammunition have been stolen and hidden in the hills. We
will lead the revolt of the Ceylonese against England. We were
to get millions, and Van Hosen was going to get us estates in
the interior of Java after it was over."

"Why was the doorboy killed? Did he know anything?"

"Not a thing. He was killed to discourage you from trying
any of the others."

"Who killed him?"

"Wend. That's his job."

"Who killed Constance?"

"Wend again. Sent her a message to swim out to his small
boat early in the morning. She did, and she was held under
long enough to drown her without leaving a mark."

"Was it necessary?"

"Yes. She was weak. She was a danger, particularly with
you around. You frightened her. You sent her a note somehow,
and she thought it was from Van Hosen. She didn't know his
writing."

"Where does this Van Hosen live?"

"Right here. Two floors above you."

"How did you get in on this?"

"I was in the Shanghai Police Department before the war.
I was the only boy taken on locally. The rest were out from
England. Boys of good family. I'm a quarter Japanese. I never
let them know. My grandfather was in the Japanese army. So
was my mother's father. I was loyal until Van Hosen came
here. He had the information about me. I realized that if my
superiors ever found out, I'd be through. Why should I have
loyalty for a country that would throw me out for an accident
of blood? Do I look like a Japanese?"

His voice was proud. He forgot for a moment and glanced

at the mirror. He groaned and hung his head. "Cut me down," he said weakly.

"Not right now, Kaymark. I leave you right here while I go and get your colonel. Rith-Lee, wasn't it? I'll bring him along, and you can tell all this to him."

I looked back at him just as I closed the door. He was too tired to continue bracing his toes against the floor. He slumped and hung with his entire weight on his wrists, his chin hanging against his chest. His blond hair was mussed and rumpled.

British Intelligence was located in a high gray bungalow set back behind a lawn banked with flowers. The creaking taxi took me up the semicircular drive and stopped in front of steep steps. I told the driver to wait for me in the small parking lot adjoining the building.

There is a character in British newspapers called Colonel Blimp. He's a round man, a big man, with a bold bald head and a gray mustache which is one part grandeur and one part pathos. He wears shooting clothes and stout shorts, with a feather in the side of his gray wool socks. He blusters and belches and wheezes. He's supposed to typify the "old boys."

The enlisted man announced me to the colonel as coming on a matter of the utmost importance. He told me to go right in.

The colonel sat behind a massive desk in a room that was high, wide, and rugless. He was Colonel Blimp in person. He wheezed, coughed, belched, and waved me into a chair with a plump hand, tanned by years in the East.

"American, eh? What is it? Speak up!"

"It's about Lieutenant Peter Kaymark. He—"

"Kaymark's assigned to this staff. What about him?"

"I wanted to tell you—"

"For heaven's sake, man. Get to the point!"

I stood up and leaned over his desk. I shouted down into his bright red face, "Shut up and listen for one minute, and I'll tell you. Stop being so damn official."

I sank slowly down into my chair again while he mumbled something about bloody rude Americans.

"I'm telling you that Kaymark's a traitor. He's part Jap.

He's been taking money from a Dutchman named Van Hosen for three years. He just killed a planter named O'Dell. Come with me and listen to him tell it to you."

"That's nonsense, man. Known the rascal for years. He's not a Jap. The heat's got you. Have some water. Go fan yourself."

"Look, will you come with me or do I go and get a very smart apple on the local police force named Saxon? How would you like that, you overstuffed bottleneck?"

"Young man, if you were on this staff, I'd have you shot for that."

"If I was on your staff, you wouldn't have lived this long. Are you coming? I've got a taxi waiting. Just over to the Galle Face. Take you an hour maybe for the whole thing."

He coughed again and cocked his eye at the ceiling. Then he fingered a paperweight. Then he picked up his hat and stick and said, "Move along, then! Let's get done with it!"

The taxi driver popped out and opened the door for Colonel Rith-Lee. He hadn't done that much for me. Privilege of the ruling class. I tried to tell him the story on the short ride to the hotel. He made derisive noises deep in his throat and moved a little farther away from me in furtive alarm.

We walked down the hall, and I pulled out my key. He tapped his leg impatiently with his stick while I unlocked the door. I let him go in first. He walked through the room until he could see Kaymark. Then he stopped so abruptly that I bumped into him. I stepped to the side to where I could also see the lieutenant.

My first thought was that he had lost an amazing amount of blood from the few cuts I had given him. The front of his tunic was drenched. He hung limply from his wrists, a gaudy motionless form. The colonel stepped forward and stooped over to where he could peer up into Kaymark's face. He lifted his stick and nudged gently at the lieutenant's forehead. The head tilted back a little. When he released the pressure, the head sagged forward again.

"Dead. Throat cut. Why'd you do it, man?"

"Me? When I left him he was okay. Somebody must have sneaked in here, but I don't know how."

He glared at me, and there was disgust and alarm in his narrow eyes. "All the room keys're alike. Fit all the doors. No good. You did it. Better come along with me."

I had been moving gradually toward the body. I jumped forward and clawed at the right-hand tunic pocket. The automatic was there. It stuck in the edge of the pocket. Before I could yank it free I felt a cold sharp object against the back of my neck.

"Step aside, man. Slowly now, or I'll punch a hole in the back of your neck. Ought to do it anyway." I let go of the gun and stepped to the side. He kept the sharp point against the back of my neck.

Finally he said, "Turn around, man." He had recovered the automatic. He aimed it at my middle with his left hand. He held the hollow shell of the stick he carried in his left hand also; he fitted the slim blade of the long sword back into the stick. It chunked into place, and he gave the handle a half turn. During all this, he didn't take his eyes off of me.

"You and I, we'll go back to the bungalow. Damned nuisance. International murder. Have to get your government people in on it. Try it in the civil courts, I guess. Open-and-shut case. Nothing to it."

Again they had used death to trump my ace. This time it looked like the end. I had a story to tell but it would have been easier to tell it to a deaf man than to the colonel. He stood in front of me and motioned me toward the door with the automatic. I didn't move.

"Move along there. Don't want to shoot you where you stand. You have to make out statements. Save me the trouble."

"Colonel, will you tell me one thing? Why on earth would I kill Kaymark and then go and drag you here to look at the body?"

"Not much sense in it. Never imagined you American chaps had much sense. All gangsters and crooners. Move along now." I could see why Kaymark had had such an easy time covering up the activities of the group which used the January Club as a headquarters. Again I didn't move.

"Wait a minute. Suppose I take you to a man who knows who killed Kaymark. In fact, maybe he did it himself."

"More nonsense."

I had to get out of it. I knew that if they put me in a cell, I'd never be able to prove a thing. My story would sound like the purest fabrication. I didn't want to deal with this man. I wanted Saxon, the tall man with the lean white face. He had appeared to be intelligent.

I needed a way to bluff the stupid, fast-moving colonel. I placed my right hand near the front of my white coat. I remembered that one of the large buttons was getting loose. With a minimum of motion, I found it and twisted it off. I started to move back toward the door to the hall. It was darker near the door. He followed along, staying a good six feet from me. I shifted the button in my hand until I was holding it the same way a small boy holds a marble that he is going to shoot. I flicked the button toward Kaymark's body. At the same moment I glanced in that direction, my eyes widened. The colonel heard the small clatter on the bare floor. He took one hasty glance over his shoulder. Before he could glance back, my shoulder hit him low in the stomach. He went over backwards with a great gasp, the gun sliding across the rug. I rolled to my feet and snatched the stick out of his other hand. His face was a pale green color underneath the heavy tan. It was startling. Any fight or objection was completely gone. He was too concerned about his stomach.

I sat on the edge of the bed while he stared at the ceiling and gasped. Finally he sat up, moaning. "Sit over in that chair, Colonel Rith-Lee." He wavered as he got to his feet. He stumbled over and fell into the chair.

"Unfair tactics. Took advantage of me. Ever heard of fair play?"

"Sure. Fair play while you railroad me off into some jail. You just sit tight while I make a little phone call."

It took three or four minutes to get my party. When I did I said, "Saxon? This is Howard Garry. Met you over at the January Club today. Can you come over to my room right away? Good. I'm at the Galle Face. Three ten. There's another body here."

146

I hung up. His sane tired voice had sounded good. While Saxon was on his way over, I gave the colonel his instructions. Not a word. Not a murmur, or I'd stick my shoulder in his stomach a little harder than last time. That seemed to impress him. He folded his hands across his middle and I'd swear that he took a short nap, awakening finally when there was a sharp knock on the door.

I covered the colonel as I backed to the door. I opened it. Saxon stood there with two of the chocolate policemen behind him. I stood aside and he walked in. I pointed to the body and he walked over toward it. As he passed me, he spun quickly. I felt a sharp pain in my wrist and fingers, and the automatic was gone. He didn't look at me as he handed it to one of the two policemen.

The colonel jumped up and said, "Arrest this man. Immediately. He killed Kaymark. He attacked me. Quickly!"

Saxon paused on his way toward the body. He looked at the colonel. "I'm most sorry, sir, but Mr. Garry telephoned me to come over. I'll listen to his story first. I beg of you to sit down and remain quiet until I ask you for information."

He took a long look at the hanging corpse. He pulled out the same notebook and scribbled a few notes with great care. He posted one of his men against the room door. At last he turned to me and said, "Your story, Mr. Garry? Please run through it quickly. I can question you about the details later."

I told him the story. I made it short and to the point. I admitted that I had tied Kaymark up and worked him over, and I denied having killed him. I stressed the story Kaymark had told. Then I mentioned the colonel's reaction.

The colonel started to sputter, but Saxon held up his hand imperiously and the sputtering ceased.

Saxon sat on the edge of my bed and fingered his long jaw. "This, Mr. Garry, is a jurisdictional matter. Supposedly, all such things are handled by Colonel Rith-Lee's bureau. However, I feel that this is a time when I can afford to step in. I'm doing it because I believe you. If you have lied to me, this interference may cost me a great deal of local prestige. I know that I am going to make an enemy out of the colonel. I have a plan which I won't bother to explain to you. You will be here to see it in operation." He turned to the nearest policeman and issued some terse instructions in Singhalese. The man hurried to the bathroom door. He pulled out a knife and cut one of Kaymark's hands free. The arm drooped heavily. Then he put his hand against the lieutenant's shoulder and cut the other bond. As he slashed it through, he pushed the body toward the bathroom. The corpse thudded onto the tile floor. The man pulled it farther into the bathroom. Then, with a damp towel, he rubbed up the spots of blood on the hardwood floor of the main room. He threw the towel into the bathroom and closed the door.

Saxon picked up the phone. "Mr. Van Hosen's room, please. Oh, he's in the bar? Connect me with the bar, please." He waited a few moments. "Mr. Van Hosen? This is Leslie Saxon of the Central Police Bureau. I'm in room three ten. Could you arrange to come up here for a few moments? Thank you."

He hung up and turned to me. "When Van Hosen is here, I don't want either of you to say a word. Let me talk without interruption." He gave some more instructions in Singhalese and one of the policemen hurried out of the room.

We all remained quiet. The colonel appeared to sleep again. I fumbled with a cigarette. Saxon sat as motionless and grave as a statue.

The policeman opened the door at the first tap. Van Hosen blinked as he saw the group, and then he smiled. He stepped in timidly, his hat in his hand, a mild and meager man.

"Sit down, please, Mr. Van Hosen. Over here on the bed will be excellent. I have a few questions to ask you which will—" At that point the phone rang. Saxon picked it up and held his hand over the mouthpiece. "Pardon me a moment, I was expecting a call." He removed his hand and spoke into the phone. "Saxon here. Oh, yes, Mr. Wend. You got my message."

I happened to be looking at Van Hosen. His mouth twitched a bit when Saxon mentioned the name Wend.

"I have rather a strange story here, Mr. Wend. Very strange. You know a man named Van Hosen? . . . Slightly, eh. Well, Mr. Van Hosen wishes us to supply him with private transportation away from Ceylon. In return he has given us certain

148

information. I have here a list of some sort of uprising. There is also a list of places where arms are supposed to be hidden, and some kind of an inventory. A great deal of equipment. . . . I agree with you, Mr. Wend, it does sound fantastic.

"Also, he claims that you and he and a Mr. O'Dell, who died this afternoon, a Lieutenant Kaymark, who died within the hour, and a Miss Severence, who died recently, were the nucleus of some sort of weird organization planning a revolution in Ceylon.

"He claims to have come from Java during the war as a Japanese agent. . . . What was that? What has it got to do with you? He states in this report of his, which I have in writing, that you killed Miss Severence, the doorboy of the January Club, and also Lieutenant Kaymark. He accuses Mr. O'Dell of having killed an American officer some time ago."

He stopped talking and listened. I watched Van Hosen. The man was trying hard to keep all expression off his face. His hands were held rigidly against his thighs. The rosebud lips seemed much paler than they had been when he had first visited me.

Then Saxon spoke again into the phone. "Then you believe that the man is ill? You know nothing of such plots and murders? Suppose you stop in at the Bureau at your earliest convenience and give me your story about Van Hosen in person. What was that? . . . No, we have nothing to hold him on until we've made a detailed check of these reports of his. . . . Certainly. Thank you very much, Mr. Wend." He hung up the receiver gently and turned to Van Hosen. Saxon wore a small and very confident smile.

"What kind of a farce is this, Saxon?" Van Hosen demanded.

Saxon shrugged. "Checkmate, my friend. You do play chess, don't you? Good. I believe that all the things which I told your employee, Wend, are correct. Assuming that is so, I'm perfectly willing to let you go. If it is correct, you well know that he'll kill you before you can explain, and I don't believe death comes easy in your group for those who inform. You have one small opening, but a very obvious one. You can give me the information which I told Wend you had already given. Then I can guarantee you police protection. If my basic assumption

149

is wrong, you can stand and walk briskly out, smiling at my stupidity as you go."

Van Hosen stood up and, with careful dignity, smoothed out his rumpled jacket. He stroked the small beard and stared at Saxon. "My good man, you must certainly be mad. All you people are mad."

"You have the privilege of thinking us anything you please. We can't alter your opinions. Only your life. I remember seeing a man once who informed on the patriots in the Burmese underground. He was a man of your build, Van Hosen. They bound a tight white sash around his naked belly and staked him out, back down, in the sun. The sash was very thin. Under the sash they placed several of those hard-shelled beetles that you find at night in the jungle. They hate the light. When the sun strikes them, they dig down into the jungle floor, dig deeply. That man didn't die pleasantly, Mr. Van Hosen."

"A story to frighten children."

"You are free to leave."

Van Hosen walked to the door. He placed his hand on the knob and opened it. Then he turned back and looked at Saxon. He licked his lips. "Suppose that I contend that you have endangered my life by telling lies to Wend. Suppose he is not well balanced. Shouldn't I have the protection of the police?"

"I told you that I have nothing on which to hold you. I refuse to hold you."

"Then imagine the absurd eventuality that these lies that you told were true. Suppose that I could provide you with the lists and the proof you demand. Suppose I were a criminal. What guarantees could you give such a man for turning over the information?"

"None whatsoever, except the one already stated. The protection of the Bureau from the revenge of your fellows."

Again he turned toward the door. He asked a last question, his voice hoarse. "Where was Wend phoning from?"

"The January Club. He knew that you were here with me. That is about five minutes distant by taxi. You have talked for five minutes."

I held my breath as Van Hosen stood with his hand on the doorknob. The phone rang again. Saxon picked it up. "Saxon here. . . . Oh, Mr. Wend again. . . . Yes, he's just leaving. You wish to talk to him? . . . You wouldn't? . . . I understand. You want him to go back to the club with you? I'll tell him that you are waiting downstairs."

He hung up. Van Hosen walked away from the door. He held his knees stiff like a man who is hurt and weak. His face was twisted. He walked over to Saxon, and his voice broke as he said, "You monster! Look what you've done to me! It's all true and he knows that it's true. I can't leave this room. He'll kill me before I can tell him. Maybe he'll kill me when you try to take me away from here. Get more men! Get me strong guards!"

"If it's true, Van Hosen, why shouldn't I force you to go? Why shouldn't I save Ceylon the expense of your trial?"

Van Hosen clutched the arm of Saxon's chair. "I'll give you what you want. I'll give you the lists. I'll tell you of everything, of the hidden supplies, of the men who will lead the people. How O'Dell killed the American who suspected us. How I came here with information from Tokyo about Kaymark's ancestors. How Wend drowned the girl and cut Kaymark's throat. We came in here together to see that fool." He pointed at me. "We found Kaymark tied up. He swore that he hadn't talked, but we knew how much he valued his pretty face. He hadn't been badly hurt. We couldn't chance it. Wend cut his throat— slowly. It wasn't pretty to watch."

Saxon pushed his hands off the arm of the chair. "Be quiet while I write." Van Hosen sat on the bed and trembled while Saxon printed in block letters on one of the sheets in his notebook. There was no sound in the room except for Van Hosen's hoarse breathing and scratching of the pencil.

"Now I'll read this to you before you sign. It says: I, Van Hosen, confess that I operated as a Japanese agent in Ceylon during the war. I have arranged to smuggle arms and ammunition into Ceylon which is now stored at secret points which I will name. I will also name the leaders of the people in a planned revolution. My principal assistants were Clarence O'Dell, Guy Wend, Constance Severence, and Peter Kaymark. I ordered O'Dell to kill an American officer named Daniel Christoff. He did so, under circumstances planned to make

Christoff subject to censure. I ordered Wend to drown Miss Severence. He did so. I saw Wend cut Kaymark's throat."

He handed the notebook to Van Hosen. He scribbled his name hurriedly and handed it back. Saxon took it over to Colonel Rith-Lee. The bulky man signed as a witness. So did I and so did Saxon.

"That should stand up until we can arrange a more detailed confession, Van Hosen. Now, every police officer enjoys telling of his own cleverness. What made you assume that I had Wend on the phone? I instructed one of my own men to call this room, and then to call back five minutes after I hung up. Your imagination betrayed you, Van Hosen."

The little man gave Saxon one wild look and then leaped at him, his arms stretched forward as though to grasp Saxon's throat. The tall man flapped one hand indolently at Van Hosen's face. It hit with a sound like the crack of a pistol. It knocked Van Hosen back onto the bed. The native picked Van Hosen off the bed and shook him. The little man relaxed. He stood looking down at the floor, his shoulders sagging and the brave beard in disarray.

Colonel Rith-Lee hauled himself out of his chair and stuck his hand out to Saxon. Saxon took it shyly.

"Don't be too hard on a stupid British officer, Saxon. Imagine I've been pretty blind. Wonder how many other things I've missed." Then he turned to me. "You mean to say, Garry, that you kited all the way over here just to clear up a little criticism of a friend of yours?" I nodded. "Damn foolishness. Glad you did. Stirred up this mess. What do you want me to do, Saxon?"

"Just take over the Intelligence aspects from here, sir. I can handle the straight murder angles. We can take mutual credit for the arrest."

"Very generous. How about you, Garry? Anything I can do for you after you finish making out the long bloody statements for my bureau and Saxon's outfit?"

"Yes, sir. Write an official letter to the War Department, Washington, D.C., that will clear Christoff of any blame. Give me a copy, and give a copy to the consulate. Then I can go back home."

* * *

Two weeks later I stood at the rail of a small freighter as we pulled away from the great wooden wharves of Melbourne Harbor, headed for the Golden Gate. I had the precious letter buried deeply in my jacket pocket. I knew what it was going to be like to tell his people, to tell his wife. I felt a small shiver of anticipation, and I reached my hand into my pocket and touched the edge of the letter. They had let me live, and I had cleared him. I thought of what would be in Dorothy's eyes when I showed her the letter. I wondered if maybe, after she had another year alone, if...I stretched and decided that it wouldn't hurt me any to try walking around the deck a couple of thousand times.

Breathe No More

He looked like a fat child as he walked gingerly down the beach. He winced, sat down, picked a wicked little sand burr from the pink pad of his foot. For a time he sat there, pouting and petulant, his fat tummy and thick shoulders an angry pink from the midafternoon Florida sun. A porpoise, chasing sand sharks, made a lazy arc a hundred yards out. The Gulf was oily and torpid. The fat man wore spectacular swimming trunks. He was semi-bald, with rimless glasses pinched into the bridge of his soft nose. He sat and looked dully at the small waves, tasting again the sense of utter defeat that had been with him these past two days on Grouper Island. Defeat. Everything gone. Not much more time left. How would it be to wade out and start swimming? Swim until there was nothing but exhaustion, strangling, and death.

He shivered in the sun's heat. No.

Slowly he stood up. Sweat trickled down through the gray mat of hair on his chest. He walked back toward the house of his odd host, toward the gleaming-white terraced fortress of the man called Park Falkner.

Twenty feet farther along he angled up across the dry sand. He saw her, bronze, oiled, and gleaming in the sun. She lay on a blanket, her hair wrapped, turban fashion, in a towel, her eyes covered with odd little plastic cups joined together with a nose band. She was in a hollow in the sand, her scanty bathing suit hiding little of her firm, tanned flesh.

The hate for her shuddered up in him, tightening his throat, making him feel weak and trembling. She had done this to him. She had lost everything for him. He knew it was useless, but he had to plead with her again, plead for her silence. He remembered the last time, remembered her evil amusement.

"Laura!" he said softly. "Laura, are you awake?"

She didn't move. He saw the slow rise and fall of her breathing. Asleep. The wish to do her harm came with an almost frightening suddenness. He looked at the big white house three hundred yards away. No sign of movement on any of the terraces. They would be napping after the large lunch, after the cocktails.

He moved close to her. He knew, suddenly and with satisfaction, that he was going to try to kill Laura Hale. But how? There could be no marks on her throat. No bruise of violence. He squatted beside her. Her underlip sagged a bit away from the even white teeth. Her breathing merged with the husky whisper of the sea. A gull wheeled and called hoarsely, startling him. Sandpipers ran and pecked along the sand.

Methodically, as though he were a fat child playing, he began to heap up the dry white sand, removing the shell fragments. He piled it on the edge of the blanket, near her head. Sweat ran from him as he worked. The conical pile grew higher and higher. The widening base of it moved closer to her head. He stopped when it was over two feet high and again he watched the white house. So far he had done nothing. He forced himself to breathe slowly. He held his hands hard against his thighs to steady them.

Laura slept on. The plastic cups over her eyes gave her a look of blindness.

It had to be done quickly. He went over every step. The pile of sand towered over her face. With an awkward, splay-fingered push, he shoved the tiny mountain over and across her face, burying it deep. He followed it over, resting his chest on the pile that covered her face, grabbing her wrists as they flashed up. He held her down as she made her soundless struggle. Surely she knew who was doing this thing to her. Surely she cursed her own stupidity in sleeping out here alone before the ultimate panic just before death came to her. Her hard, slim body arched convulsively and her hips thudded down against the blanket. She writhed and once nearly broke his grip on her

155

wrist. Then her long legs straightened out slowly, moved aimlessly, and were still. He lay there, pressed against the sand that covered her head, feeling an almost sensual excitement. He released her hand. The arm flopped down as though it were boneless. He squatted back and watched her for a moment. Then, with care, he brushed the sand from her face. Grotesquely, the eye cups were still in place. The sand stuck to the lotion she had used. She did not breathe. The white teeth were packed and caked with sand, the nostrils filled.

Filled with a desperate exaltation, he glanced at the house, sleeping in the white sun glare, then took her wrists and dragged her down to the sea. Her feet made two grooves in the wet sand. He dragged her through the surf and into the stiller water. Her weight in the water was as nothing. He yanked the towel from her head, and her long black hair floated out. He tied the towel around his neck. The sand was washed from her dead face. It was unmarked. He worked her out into deeper water, got behind her, and wrapped his thick arms around her, contracting her lungs and then letting them expand, contracting them again. They would fill with seawater. There would be sand in her lungs also. But that would be a normal thing for one who had died in the sea. If they found her.

He floated and looked at the house again. Safe so far. He wound his hand in her black hair and with a determined sidestroke took her on out, pausing to rest from time to time. When he thought he was far enough out, he stopped. He let her go, and she seemed to sink, but the process was so slow that he lost patience. Her face was a few inches below the surface and her eyes, half open, seemed to watch him. He thrust her down, got his feet against her body and pushed her farther. He was gasping with weariness, and the beach suddenly seemed to be an alarming distance away. As he tried to float a wave broke in his face. He coughed and avoided panic. When rested, he began to work his way back to the beach. He scuffed out the marks of her dragging feet, walked up to the blanket. The eye cups lay there. He spread the towel out to dry, picked up the eye cups and then the blanket, to shake it. He shook it once and then it slipped from his fingers. Her bathing cap had been under the blanket. Why hadn't he thought of that? He trembled.

He picked up the blanket again, shook it, put the eye cups on it next to the bottle of sun lotion.

With the cap in his hand, balled tightly, he walked back to the sea. He swam out, but he could not be sure of the place. When he knew that he could not find her, he left the cap in the sea and swam slowly back.

He walked to the showers behind the house and stood under the cold water for a long time. He went up to his room, meeting no one. He stripped, laid a towel across himself, and stared up at the high ceiling.

He cried for a little while and did not know why.

There was a feeling of having lost his identity. As though the act of murder had made him into another person. The old fear was gone, and now there was a new fear. "I am Carl Branneck," he whispered. "Now they can't do anything to me. They can't do anything. Anything. Anything."

He repeated the one word like an incantation until he fell asleep.

Park Falkner was awakened from his nap by the sound of low voices, of a woman's laugh. He stretched like a big lean cat and came silently to his feet. He was tall and hard and fit, a man in his mid-thirties, his naked body marked with a half dozen violent scars. He was sun-darkened to a mahogany shade. A tropical disease had taken, forever, hair, eyebrows, and lashes, but the bald well-shaped head seemed to accentuate the youthfulness of his face. The lack of eyebrows and lashes gave his face an expressionless look, but there was rapacity in the strong beaked nose, both humor and cruelty in the set of the mouth. He stepped into the faded tubular Singhalese sarong, pulled it up, and knotted it at his waist with a practiced motion. Except for the monastic simplicity of his bed, the room was planned for a Sybarite: two massive built-in couches with pillows and handy bookshelves; a fireplace of gray stone that reached up to the black-beamed ceiling; a built-in record player and record library that took up half of one wall, complete with panel control to the amplifiers located all over the house and grounds; an adjoining bath with a special shower stall, large enough for a platoon. The four paintings, in lighted niches, had been done on the property by guest artists. Stimulated by a certain freedom that existed on Falkner's Grouper Island, they were pictures that the rather prominent artists would prefer not to show publicly.

One whole wall of the bedroom was of glass, looking out over a small private terrace and over the sea. Park Falkner padded out across his terrace and looked down to the next one below. It extended farther out than did his own.

The conversation below had ceased. The two wheeled chaise longues were side by side. The little waitress from Winter Haven, Pamela, lay glassy and stunned by the heat of the sun, her lips swollen. Carlos Berreda, his brown and perfect body burnished by the sun, insistently stroked her wrist and the back of her hand. He leaned closer and closer to her lips. Park Falkner went quickly back into his bedroom and returned with the silver-and-mahogany thermos jug. He lifted the cap and upended it over the two below. Slivers of ice sparkled out with the water.

Carlos gave a hoarse and angry shout and Pamela screamed. Park held the empty jug and smiled down at them. They were both standing, their faces upturned. Pamela was pink with embarrassment.

"Have you forgotten?" Park said in Spanish. "Tomorrow in Monterrey you will meet two friends, Carlos. Friends that weigh five hundred kilos apiece and have long horns. This is no time for indoor sports."

The angry look left Carlos's face, and he gave Park a shamefaced grin. *"Muy correcto, jefe.* But the little one is so ... is so ..."

"She's all of eighteen, Señor Wolf."

"What're you saying about me?" Pamela demanded.

"That you're a sweet child, and we want you to come and watch the practice."

They went down to the patio behind the house. Carlos's sword handler brought the capes, laid them out on a long table, and, with weary tread, went over to the corner and came back trundling the practice device, the bull's head and horns mounted at the proper height on a two-wheeled carriage propelled by two long handles.

Carlos grinned at Pamela. "Watch thees, *muñequita*." He snapped the big cape, took his stance, made a slow and perfect and lazy veronica as the horns rolled by. The sweating assistant wheeled the horns and came back from the other direction. Carlos performed a classic gaonera. Pamela sat on the table by the capes and swung her legs.

She frowned. "But it isn't like having a real bull, is it?" she said.

Park laughed, and Carlos flashed the girl a look of hot anger. "Not exactly, *niña*." The sword handler guffawed.

After Carlos went through his repertoire with the big cape, Park Falkner took the muleta and sword and, under Carlos's critical eye, performed a series of natural passes, topping them off with manoletinas to the right and to the left.

"How was it?" Park asked.

Carlos grinned. "The sword hand on the natural passes. Eet ees not quite *correcto*, señor, but eet ees good. You could have been a *torero* had you started when young."

"Let me try!" Pamela said.

Park moved over into the shade. Carlos had to reach around her to show her the correct positions of the hands on the cape. Three more of the houseguests came out to the patio. Taffy Angus, a hard-voiced, silver-haired ex-model, over forty but still exceedingly lovely. Johnny Loomis, the loud, burly, red-faced sports reporter from Chicago, ex-All American, current alcoholic. Steve Townsend, the small, wry, pale man who had arrived in response to Park Falkner's enigmatic wire.

Park pushed a handy button and a few moments later Mick Rogers, wearing his look of chronic disgust on his battered face, appeared in the opposite doorway, which opened into the kitchen. He winked at Park, disappeared, returned almost immediately, pushing a pale blue bar decorated with coral-colored elephants in various poses of abandon. The glasses clinked as he rolled it over into the shade in the opposite corner.

The others moved over toward the bar in response to Mick's nasal chant: "Step right up and get it. Give yourself a package, folks. The cocktail hour has been on for five minutes."

* * *

Taffy stayed next to Park. "What is it this time?" she asked in a low voice.

He clicked open her purse and took out her cigarettes and lighter. "What do you think it is?"

"Damn you, Park! One of these times you're going to go too far. Why can't you just relax and enjoy it?"

"Baby mine, I'd go mad in a month. Don't ask me to give up my hobby."

"Twisting people's lives around is a hell of a hobby, if you ask me. I don't know what you're doing this time, but it has something to do with that horrid puffy little man named Branneck and that unwholesome Laura Hale and that Steve Townsend."

"How sensitive you are to situations, Taffy!" Park said mockingly.

"Sensitive? I saw Branneck when he got his first look at Laura Hale five minutes after he arrived. He changed from a smug little fat man into a nervous wreck. And she looked as though she had just found a million dollars. I'm just not going to come here to this private island of yours any more."

"You'll keep coming, Taffy, every time I ask you. You have a woman's curiosity. And deep down in that rugged old heart of yours, you have a hunch that I'm doing right."

"Are you, Park?"

He shrugged. "Who can tell? I'll be serious for a second or two. Don't be too shocked, lambie. My esteemed ancestors had the golden touch. Even if there were any point in making more money, it would bore me. The company of my Big Rich friends and relatives bores the hell out of me. So I have some clever young men who dig around in disorderly pasts. When they come up barking, carrying a bone, I just mix some human ingredients together and see what happens. A tossed salad of emotions, call it."

"Or dirty laundry."

"Don't scoff. I just make like fate, and certain people get what my grandmother called their comeuppance."

"It always makes me feel ill, Park."

"And—admit it—fascinated, Taffy."

She sighed. "All right. You win. Fascinated. Like looking

at an open wound. But someday one of your salad ingredients is going to kill you."

"One day a *toro* may kill Carlos. The profession gives his life a certain spice. And I'm too old to take up bullfighting."

She gave him a flat, long, brown-eyed stare. "I wouldn't want you dead, Park."

"After this shindig is over, Taffy, can you stay here for a few days when the others have left?"

"Have I ever said no?" She grinned. "Goodness! I blushed. I'd better rush right up and put that in my diary. Say, are you flying Carlos to Mexico in the morning?"

"I can't leave now, the way things are shaping up. I'll have Lew earn his keep by flying Carlos and his man over."

"And the little girl too?"

"No. I don't throw canaries to cats, my love. This evening I'm having Mick drive her back to Winter Haven."

Taffy whispered, "Here it comes!"

Carl Branneck came slowly out onto the patio. He wore pale blue shorts and a white nylon sleeveless shirt. He was lobster red from the sun and his glasses were polished and glittering. His stubby hairy legs quivered fleshily as he walked. He gave Park a meek smile.

"Guess I overslept, eh?"

"Not at all, Mr. Branneck. Festivities are just starting. Step over and tell Mick what you want."

Branneck moved away uncertainly. Taffy said, "By tonight that poor little man is going to be one large blister."

Lew Cherezack, Park's pilot and driver, came in at a trot. He was young and he had the wrinkled, anxious face of a boxer pup. He grinned and said, "Hello, Taff! Why didn't I meet you before the war?"

"Which war?" Taffy asked coldly.

"What's up?" Park asked.

"Well, I see this car boiling out across our causeway, and so I go over to the gate. This large young guy jumps out with a look like he wants to take a punch at me. He tells me he's come after his girl, Laura Hale, and, damn it, he wants to see her right away and no kidding around. He says his name is Thomas O'Day. I got him pacing around out there."

O'Day spun around as Park approached. He glanced at the sarong, and a faint look of contempt appeared on his square, handsome face. "Are you Falkner?"

"It seems possible."

"Okay. I don't know what the hell you told Laura to get her to come down here without a word to me. I traced her as far as the Tampa airport, and today I found out that your driver picked her up there and brought her here. I want an explanation."

"Is she your wife?"

"No. We're engaged."

"I didn't notice any ring."

"Well, almost engaged. And what the hell business is that of yours? I took time off from my job, Falkner, and I can't stand here arguing with you. I want to see Laura and I want to see her right now. Go get her."

"You're annoying the hell out of me, O'Day," Park said mildly.

O'Day tensed and launched a large, determined right fist at Park's face. Park leaned away from it, grabbed the thick wrist with both hands, let himself fall backwards, pulled O'Day with him. He got both bare feet against O'Day's middle and pushed up hard. The imprisoned wrist was like the hub of a wheel, with O'Day's heels traversing the rim. He hit flat on his back on the sand with an impressive thud. Park stood and watched him. O'Day gagged and fought for breath. He sat up and coughed and knuckled his right shoulder. He looked up at Park and glared, then grinned.

"So I had it coming, Mr. Falkner."

"Come on in and have a drink. I'll send somebody after your girl."

He took O'Day in with him, made a group introduction. O'Day asked Mick for a Collins as Park sent Lew to find Laura. O'Day watched Townsend, finally went over and said, "I've got a feeling I've seen you before, Mr. Townsend."

"That could be."

"Are you from Chicago?"

"I've been there," Townsend said and turned away, terminating the conversation.

Pamela was working the cape and Carlos was charging her with the wheeled horns. She was very serious about it, her underlip caught behind her upper teeth, a frown of concentration on her brow.

"A second Conchita Cintrón!" Carlos called as she made a fairly acceptable veronica. Johnny Loomis, his tongue already thickened, began a braying discourse on the art of the matador.

Lew appeared and caught Park's eye. He left. Park caught him outside. Lew looked upset. "Park, she isn't in her room and I'll be damned if she's on the island. Come on. I want to show you something."

The two men stood and looked down at the blanket. The sun was far enough down so that their shadows across the sand were very long.

Park sighed heavily. "I don't like the way it looks. Break out the Lambertson lungs and be quick about it. Tide's on the change."

"How about O'Day?"

"If he can swim, fix him up. It'll give him something to do."

The sun rested on the rim of the horizon, a hot rivet sinking into the steel plate of the sea. The angle made visibility bad. Park Falkner was forty feet down, the pressure painful against his earplugs, the lead weights tight around him in the canvas belt. It was a shadow world. He saw the dim shape of a sand shark stirring the loose sand as it sped away. A sting ray, nearly a yard in diameter, drifted lazily, its tail grooving the bottom. The oxygen mixture from the back tank hissed and bubbled. He swam with a froglike motion of his legs, using a wide breaststroke.

The last faint visibility was gone. He jettisoned some of the lead and rose slowly to the surface. The sun was gone and the dusk was gray-blue. He pulled out the earplugs and heard Mick's shout. Mick was far down the beach. He squinted. Mick and Lew and Townsend were standing by something on the sand. O'Day was running toward them. Park shoved the face mask up onto his forehead and went toward the shore in a long, powerful, eight-beat crawl.

163

He walked over and looked down at her. She was as blue as the early dusk.

Mick said in a half whisper, "The crabs got her a little on the arm but that's all."

"Wrap her in a blanket and take her over to the old icehouse. Lew, you phone it in. Take O'Day with you."

O'Day stood and looked down at Laura's body. He didn't move. Lew Cherezack tugged at his arm. Park stepped over and slapped O'Day across the face. The big man turned without a word and went back toward the house with long strides.

Mrs. Mick Rogers had laid out a buffet supper, but no one had eaten much. The certificate stating accidental death by drowning had been signed. Mrs. Rogers had packed Laura Hale's suitcase and placed it in the station wagon. The undertaker had said, over the phone, that he couldn't pick up the body until midnight.

Johnny Loomis had passed out and Mick had put him to bed, just before leaving for Winter Haven with a subdued and depressed Pamela. Carlos had complained bitterly about the death, saying that it was bad luck before tomorrow's corrida. He had gone nervously to bed after the arrangements had been made for Lew to fly him and his helper to Monterrey at dawn. Park Falkner sat on the lowest terrace facing the sea. Taffy was in the next chair. Townsend, Branneck, and O'Day were at the other end of the terrace. A subdued light shone on the small self-service bar. O'Day, with an almost monotonous regularity, stepped over and mixed himself a Scotch and water. It seemed not to affect him.

The other three were far enough away so that Park and Taffy could talk without being overheard.

"Satisfied?" Taffy asked in a low tone.

"Please shut up."

"What was she, twenty-seven? Twenty-eight? Think of the wasted years, Park. Having fun with your tossed salad?"

"I didn't figure it this way, Taffy. Believe me."

"Suppose you tell me how you figured it."

"Not yet. Later. I have to think."

"I've been thinking. The little gal was vain, you know. Careful of her looks. You know what seawater will do to a woman's hair, don't you?"

"Keep going."

"I know she had a bathing cap. She didn't wear it. So she drowned by accident on purpose. Suicide. That's a woman's logic speaking, Park."

"I noticed the same thing, but I didn't arrive at the same answer."

"What...do...you...mean?" Taffy demanded, each word spaced.

"You wouldn't know unless I told you the whole story. And I don't want to do that yet."

Branneck stood up and yawned. "Night, all. Don't know if I can sleep with this burn, but I'm sure going to try." The others murmured good night, and he went into the house.

O'Day said thickly but carefully, "I haven't asked you, Falkner. Can I stay until...they take her?"

"Stay the night. That'll be better. I've had a room fixed for you. Go up to the second floor. Second door on the left. Mick took your bag up out of your car before he left."

"I don't want to impose on—"

"Don't talk rot. Go to bed. You'll find a sleeping pill on the nightstand. Take it."

Only Taffy, Townsend, and Park Falkner were left. After O'Day had gone, Townsend said dryly, "This is quite a production. Lights, camera, action."

"Stick around for the floor show," Taffy said, her tone bitter.

"I can hardly wait. Good night, folks," Townsend said. He left the terrace.

Taffy stood up and walked over toward the railing. She wore a white Mexican off-the-shoulder blouse. Her slim midriff was bare, her hand-blocked skirt long and full. She was outlined against the meager moonlight, her silver hair falling an unfashionable length to her shoulder blades. In the night light she looked no more than twenty. In the hardest light she looked almost thirty.

Park went to her. "We've known each other a long time, Taff. Do you want to help me? It won't be...pleasant."

She shrugged. "When you ask me like that . . ."

"Go on up to your room and get one of your swimsuits. Meet me by the garages."

She came toward him through the night. He took her wrist, and together they went into the icehouse. When the door was shut behind them, he turned on the powerful flashlight, directed it at the blanket-wrapped body on the table. Taffy shuddered.

"I want to show you something, Taff. Be a brave girl."

He uncovered the head, held the flashlight close, and thumbed up an eyelid. "See?" he said. "A ring of small hemorrhages against the white of the eye. Something was pressed hard there."

"I—I don't understand."

"I found it right after they examined her. Both eyes are the same. Other than that, and the sea damage, there's not a mark on her."

"Wouldn't contact lenses do that?" Taffy asked.

"They might, if they didn't fit properly, or if they had been inserted clumsily. But I don't think she wore them. She was grateful to me for having her come down here. She . . . attempted to show her gratitude. The offer was refused, but in the process of refusing it, I had a good close look at her eyes. I'd say no. I have another answer."

"But what?"

He took the plastic cups out and held them in the flashlight glow.

Taffy gasped. "No, Park. Someone would have had to—"

"Exactly. Pressed them down quite hard on the eyes. No point in it unless the pressure also served some other purpose. Smothering her. Evidently she was smothered while in the sun, while on her back. Maybe she was sleeping. The smotherer dragged her into the sea, forgetting the cap or ignoring it."

"Did he use a towel to do it?"

"I wouldn't think so. A little air would get through. She'd struggle longer and the plastic cups would have slipped and made other marks. And I don't think a pillow was used. Look."

He curled back her upper lip. Up above the ridge of the gum was a fine dark line of damp sand.

"No," Taffy said in a whisper. "No."

166

"It wouldn't be hard to do. Taffy, maybe I won't ask you to do what I originally planned."

She straightened up. "Try me."

"I want that swimsuit. She'll have to be dressed in yours. You go on along. Leave your suit here. I'll change it."

Taffy said tonelessly, "Go on outside, Park." She pushed him gently.

Outside he lit a cigarette, cupped his hands around the glow. The luminous dial of his wristwatch told him that it was after eleven. The sea sighed as though with some vast, half forgotten regret. The stars were cool and withdrawn. He rubbed the cigarette out with his toe. She came out into the darkness and silently leaned her forehead against his shoulder. He held her for a moment, and then they walked back to the house together. He took the damp swimsuit from her. When the door shut he went up the stairs to his own room. He sat in the darkness and thought of Laura Hale, of the way the hard core of her showed beneath the blue of her eyes. Mick came back after driving Pamela home, and later he heard another car, heard Mick speak to a stranger. Soon the strange car drove back across the causeway, the motor noise lost in the sound of the sea.

Mick knocked and came in. "Sitting in the dark, hey? They took her off with 'em. I delivered Pamela. She thinks Carlos is coming back to see her after he fights."

"He might. Go get Branneck. Don't let him give you an argument or make any noise. Get him up here."

The lights were on and Park was sitting cross-legged on his bed when Mick Rogers shoved Branneck through the door. Branneck's pajamas were yellow and white vertical stripes. His eyes were puffy. He sputtered with indignation.

"I demand to know why—"

"Shut up," said Park. He smiled amiably at Branneck. "Sit down."

Branneck remained standing. "I want to know why your man—"

"Because seven years and three months ago, in a very beautiful and very complicated variation of the old badger game, a wealthy Chicago citizen named Myron C. Cauldfeldt was bled white to the tune of two hundred and twenty-five thousand

167

dollars. He was in no position to complain to the police until he was visited by the girl in the case. She explained to him that her partner, or one of her partners, had run out with the entire take. She was angry. She went with Cauldfeldt to the police and made a confession. In view of her age—twenty— she was given a suspended sentence and put on probation. The man who had run out with the take disappeared completely. Now am I making any sense?" He paused, waiting.

Branneck gave a blind man's look toward the chair. He stumbled over and sat down. He breathed hard through his open mouth.

Park Falkner stood up. "Some day, Branneck," he said lightly, "you ought to do some research into the lives of people who run out with large bundles of dough. They hide in shabby little rooms and slowly confidence comes back. A year passes. Two. They slowly come out of cover and take up the threads of a new life. Sometimes they are able to almost forget the source of their money."

Branneck had slowly gained control. He said, "I haven't the faintest idea what you're talking about, Falkner. It wasn't true, was it, what you said about wanting to buy some of my properties? That was just to get me to come down here."

Mick leaned against the closed door, cleaning his fingernails with a broken match. He gave Branneck a look of disgust.

"Let's review, Branneck. Or should I call you Roger Krindall?" Park said.

"My name is Branneck," the man said huskily.

"Okay. Branneck, then. You are a respected citizen of Biloxi. You arrived there about six years ago and made yourself agreeable. You did some smart dealing in shore properties. My investigator estimates that you're worth a few million. You belong to the proper clubs. Two years ago you married a widow of good social standing. Your stepdaughter is now sixteen. You are respected. A nice life, isn't it?"

"What are you trying to say?"

"You came here thinking that I was a customer for the Coast Drive Motel that you just finished building. Selling it would be a nice stroke of business. I might be willing to buy it. I'll give you ten thousand for it."

Branneck jumped up, his face greenish pale under the fresh burn. "Ten thousand! Are you crazy? I've got two hundred thousand in it and a mortgage of three hundred and twenty thousand outstanding!"

"He won't sell, Park," Mick said.

"No imagination, I guess, Mick."

Branneck stared hard at Park and then at Mick. "I see what you're getting at. Very nice little scheme. Now I can figure how you got a layout like this. Well, you're wrong. Dead wrong. If I was all chump you could have made it stick. But I'll take my chances on what you can do to me. You've got me mixed up with somebody named Krindall. You can't prove a damn thing. And if you start to spread one little rumor in Biloxi you'll get slapped in the face with a slander suit so fast your head'll swim. I'm going back to bed, and I'm pulling out of here first thing in the morning."

He strode toward the door. Mick glanced at Park for instructions and then stepped aside. Branneck slammed the door.

"He knows Cauldfeldt is dead," Park said. "And I think he knows that too much time has passed for the Chicago police to do anything to him, even if they could get hold of Laura Hale for a positive identification. I had him going for a minute, but he made a nice recovery."

"So it blows up in our face?" Mick asked.

"I wouldn't say so. He killed Laura Hale."

The match slipped out of Mick's fingers. He bent and picked it up. "Give me some warning next time, Park. That's a jolt."

Park began to pace back and forth. "Yes, he killed her, and he got his chance because I was stupid. And so was she. Neither of us figured him as having the nerve for that kind of violence. She was a tramp all the way through. She thought I had arranged it so we could bleed Branneck, alias Krindall, and split the proceeds. Finding out that I had other plans was going to be a shock to her—but he fixed it so that she was spared that particular shock. He took his chance, and he got away with it. Now I'm sorry I had to bring him in. He's been warned. And he'll fight. But we can't let him leave in the morning. Got any ideas?"

Mick grinned. The flattened nose and Neanderthal brows

gave him the look of an amiable ape. "This won't be good for his nerves, boss, but I could sort of arrange it so he could over-hear that the coroner has suspicions and is waiting for somebody to make a run for it."

"Good!" Park said. "Then he'll have to make an excuse to stay and that'll give me time to work out an idea."

The roar of the amphibian taking off from the protected basin in the lee of the island awoke Park the next morning. Carlos was being carted away to his rendezvous with the black beast from La Punta. At three o'clock, when it was four in Monterrey, he would pick up, on short wave, the report of the corrida. Park pulled on his trunks and went out onto the terrace. The dawn sun behind the house sent the tall shadow of the structure an impossible distance out across the gray morning sea. He stood and was filled with a sudden and surprising revulsion against the shoddy affair of Branneck and Laura Hale. Better to give it all up. Better to give himself to the sea and the sun, music and Taffy. Let the easy life drift by.

But he knew and remembered the times he had tried the lethargic life. The restlessness had grown in him, shortening his temper, fraying the nerve ends—and then he would read over a report from one of the investigators. "A psychiatrist shot in his office here last year. Three suspects, but not enough on any of them to bring it to trial. Think you could get all three down there for a short course in suspicion." And then the excitement would begin. Maybe Taffy was right. Playing God. Playing the part of fate and destiny. The cornered man is the dangerous man. The cornered woman has an unparalleled vi-ciousness.

He saw a figure far up the beach, recognized Taffy's hair color. She was a quarter mile from the house, an aqua robe belted around her, walking slowly, bending now and then to pick up something. Shells, probably. He saw her turn around and stare back toward the house. She could not see him in the heavy shadows. She slipped off the robe, dropped it on the sand, and went quickly down into the surf.

Park grinned. In spite of Taffy Angus's modeling career, in spite of her very objective view of the world, she had more than her share of modesty. She would be furious if she knew that he had watched her morning swim au naturel. He glanced at the sixteen-power scope mounted on the corner of the terrace railing and decided that it wouldn't be cricket. The perfect gag, of course, would be a camera with a telescopic lens, with a few large glossy prints to . . .

He snapped his fingers. A very fine idea. One of the best.

At three o'clock in the afternoon, Mick was ten miles down the mainland beach. He was hot, sticky, and annoyed.

"Why do you have to be giving me arguments?" he demanded of the fat middle-aged tourist and the bronzed dark-haired girl.

The tourist looked angry. "Damn it! All I said was that if you stand so far away from us with that camera, you're going to get a bunch of nothing. We'll be a couple of dots on that negative."

Mick said heavily, "Mister, I know what I'm doing. I don't want your faces to show. This is an illustration for a story in a confession magazine."

The girl adjusted the suit that had belonged to Laura Hale. "This doesn't fit so good, Mr. Rogers," she said.

Mick sighed. "This time I want to get the blanket in too. I'm going back up on that knoll. Now get it right. We got the marks in the sand across the beach where you dragged her. I want you, mister, to be hip deep in that surf and dragging her by the hair. Don't look around. Girlie, you take yourself a deep breath and play dead."

"We're too far away from the camera," the man said sullenly.

Mick gave him a long, hard look. The man grunted and turned away.

"Come on, sister," he said.

Mick arrived back at Grouper Island at six with the dozen prints. He found Park, O'Day, and Taffy on the lower terrace. Park stood up at once and they went upstairs.

"He still here?" Mick asked.

"Jittery but still around."

"How did Carlos do?"

"Too nervous. They threw cushions at him during the first bull. The second bull gave him a slit in the thigh. He's okay. Now let's see what you've got."

Park studied the pictures one by one. He laid three aside. "It's between these three. Nice job, Mick. The beach matches up pretty good. The girl seems a little small, but that man, from the back, is a dead ringer for Branneck. We can't use the ones with the blanket showing, because we can't be sure whether or not Branneck shook the sand off it before or after he took her into the water. And we don't know how he took her out. He could have dragged her by the wrists, hair, or ankles, or even carried her. But I'd bet on wrists or hair. Now let's see. These two here. The surf blanks it out so he could be holding her either way. We'll have to take a chance on her being on her back. Did you have enough money with you?"

"Plenty. Twenty apiece to the man and the girl and a ten-buck fee to get 'em developed fast. Am I going to be in on this?"

"It looks that way. Taffy drove Loomis over to Tampa this noon. She ought to be back within the hour. Townsend and O'Day are taking a swim. Branneck is tanking up at the terrace bar, and your good wife is fixing some food. Lew radioed that he'll be back by seven. You could bring him on up now . . . no. This'll be better. I've shot my bolt. I'll be in my room. Send Taffy up as soon as she gets back."

Taffy sat hunched on the hassock, the picture in her hand. Park finished the story. She said, "Once three of us had an apartment in New York. That was a long, long time ago. We had mice. One of the girls, Mary Alice, bought a mousetrap, a wire thing like a cage. Trouble was, it didn't kill the mouse. The idea was to catch one and drown him. I remember that first mouse. We got him, and he sat up on his hind legs and begged. He was a nasty little item and I drew the short straw and took him into the bathroom, but I couldn't do it. We finally got the janitor to do it for us. Then we bought another kind of trap."

"Laura was taking a nice peaceful sunbath."

"I know, Park. I know. Don't worry, I'll do it."

"We'll have the tape recorder on, and for good measure I'll be in your closet holding a gun on him."

Branneck came into Taffy's room and shut the door gently. His smile was very close to a leer. He said, "I've been watching you, Miss Angus. You don't belong here with this crowd of sharpies."

"I thought that we should get a little better acquainted, Mr. Branneck."

"Nothing would suit me better, believe me."

"I suppose, as an important businessman, Mr. Branneck, you have a hobby?"

"Eh? No, I don't have time for anything like that. Got to keep moving to stay ahead, you know. Say, I'm going to open my new motel in three weeks. Why don't you take a run over to Biloxi and be my guest? Be the first customer in one of the best suites. What do you say?"

"What would your wife say?"

"Hell, we can use you to take some publicity shots."

"I'm not as photogenic as I used to be, Mr. Branneck."

"Call me Carl. Anyway, I can tell the wife you're there for some photographs."

"That's my hobby, Carl. Photographs. I suppose it came from standing in front of so many cameras."

"Yeah? How about giving me a picture of you? Got any . . . good ones? You know what I mean."

"I've got one of you, Mr. Branneck. Nobody has seen it but me. I developed it myself. Of course, it isn't too good of you."

Branneck beamed. "Say, isn't that something! A picture of me!"

She walked slowly over and took it from the dresser drawer and walked back to him, holding it so that he couldn't see it. Her lips felt stiff as she smiled.

"I'll give you a quick look at it. Here!" She thrust it out. His eyes bulged. As he reached for it, she snatched it back. "This is only a print, Carl."

"You . . . you . . ."

"I used a fine grain. You'd be amazed at how dead she looks when you use a glass on the print."

Branneck clenched his fists and studied his pink knuckles. He spoke without looking up. "You're smart, Taffy. I knew that right away. A smart girl. Smart girls don't get too greedy. They stay reasonable. They don't ask for too much."

"Isn't murder worth quite a lot?"

"Damn it, don't raise your voice like that!"

"Don't tell me I used the wrong word." Her tone was mocking.

"Okay. The word was right. I killed her because she wasn't smart, because she wasn't going to take a cut and shut up. She wanted the whole works. You can call that a warning."

"Don't scare me to death, Carl. Did she die easily?"

"You saw her. It didn't take long. It was too easy. What do you want for the negative?"

"Oh, I'm keeping the negative. I put it in a safety-deposit box in a Tampa bank today, along with a little note explaining what it is. I opened an account there, too. I think you ought to fatten it up for me. Say fifty thousand?"

"Say twenty."

"Thirty-five."

"Thirty-two thousand five hundred. And not another damn dime."

"A deal, Carl."

He stood up slowly and wearily, but the moment he was balanced on the balls of his feet he moved with the deceptive speed of most fat men. His hard-swinging hand hit her over the ear and she slammed back against the closet door, shutting it. He stood with the recaptured photograph in his hand. He gave her an evil smile.

"For this, honey, you don't even get thirty-two cents. I thought something was wrong with it. If it was me and Laura, there'd be a towel tied around my neck. Very clever stuff, but no damn good."

Taffy, realizing that the closet couldn't be opened from the inside, reached casually for the knob. Branneck, alert as any animal, tensed.

"Get away from that door!"

She twisted the knob. Park started to force his way out as Branneck hit the outside of the door, slamming it shut again. He caught Taffy when she was still four steps from the room door. He held her with her back to him. A small keen point dug into her flesh, and she gasped with the unexpected pain.

"Now walk out. Keep smiling and keep talking. This is only a pocketknife, but I keep it like a razor and I can do a job on that body beautiful before you can take two steps."

Park put his back against the back wall of the closet and braced both feet against the door. His muscles popped and cracked. There was a thin splintering sound, and then the door tore open so quickly that he fell heavily to the closet floor. There was an alarm bell in Taffy's room. He pushed it, raced to the side terrace in time to see Mick run out from the kitchens, a carbine in his hand, looking back over his shoulder. The causeway was blocked. Taffy appeared on the sand strip, Branneck a pace behind her, the sunset glinting on the small blade in his hand. Taffy stopped. He kept her in front of him and backed slowly out of sight.

Park cursed softly and raced from the terrace across the house. With a rifle he might have managed it. But the .38 didn't have a high enough degree of accuracy. Branneck pushed Taffy roughly down onto the cabin floor of the small twenty-one-foot cabin cruiser. As he ran to the bow to free the rope, Park risked a shot. Branneck flinched and scrambled aboard. The marine engine roared into life and Branneck swung it around in the small basin, crouching behind the wheel as he piloted it down the narrow mouth, dangerously close to the causeway where Mick stood. Mick leveled the carbine but did not dare risk a shot. The cruiser sped out in a wide curve in the quiet water between the island and the mainland.

Park gave a shout as Taffy jumped up and went over the side in a long, slanting dive. The cruiser swung back and Branneck stood at the rail, the light glinting blood red on the polished metal of the gaff. Park's fingernails bit into his palm. Branneck raced to the wheel, adjusted the path of the cruiser, and hurried back to the rail. Taffy turned in the water. Branneck lunged for her with the gaff. Even at that distance, Park saw

175

her hand reach up and grasp the shaft above the cruel hook. Branneck tottered for a moment, his arms waving wildly. Park heard his hoarse cry as he went overboard. Two heads bobbed in the water in the wake of the cruiser. Taffy's arms began to lift in her rhythmic, powerful crawl. Branneck turned and began to plow toward the mainland.

Park ran down and out the back of the house, across the patio to meet Taffy. Mick already had one of the cars started. He spun the tires as he yanked it around to head over the causeway and cut Branneck off.

The cruiser, with no hand at the wheel, came about in a wide curve. Park watched it. He saw what would happen. It swept on—and Taffy was the only swimmer. Mick stopped the car and backed off the causeway and parked it again. The cruiser continued on, missed the far shore, swung back, and grounded itself at the very end of Grouper Island.

Park went down into the water over his ankles. Taffy came out, the powder-blue dress molded to every curve. She shivered against him.

"He—he's swimming to the mainland."

"He was. Not any more. The *Nancy* swung back and took care of that little detail."

"He tried to gaff me," she whispered.

"Come on. I'll get you a drink."

As they walked up to the house, she smiled up at him. Her smile was weak. "The next time you get me to help in any of your little games..."

"Branneck had a capacity for pulling off the unexpected."

"What will you do?"

"Accidental death. That widow he married may be a nice gal."

O'Day had left to accompany the girl's body back to Chicago. Park sat on his private terrace, with Taffy sharing the extra-wide chaise longue.

Townsend came out and said, "Not that I want to be a boor, people, but it is nearly midnight and I've got to mark this case off my books and get back to work."

"Sorry it didn't work out," Park said.

"Better luck on the next one. 'Night."

He left and Taffy asked, "Who was that man?"

"Internal Revenue. He helped my investigator get a line on Branneck. You see, when Branneck was calling himself by his right name—Krindall—he forgot to declare the money he squeezed out of Cauldfeldt as income. Branneck didn't know it, but all we were going to do was get satisfactory proof that he was Krindall. Penalties, back taxes, and interest would have added up to six hundred thousand."

"But Branneck had his own answer."

After the house was silent, Park Falkner took the woman's bathing suit, the dozen pictures, the permanent tape off the recorder and put them neatly and gently into a steel file box in the cabinet behind his bookshelves. Once the sticker with the date had been applied to the end of the box, it looked like all the others.

Falkner slept like a tired child.

From Some
Hidden Grave

Park Falkner took a deep breath, exhaled half of it, squeezed the trigger slowly. The rifle spat, a sound as vicious as an angry wasp. Far out across the dancing blue water of the Gulf the glint of the can jerked, disappeared.

"Enough," he said. He stood the rifle in the corner of the private terrace that opened off his bedroom, the highest terrace of the vast gleaming-white fortress that dominated the two-mile sandspit called Grouper Island, and sometimes Falkner Island.

He stretched and yawned. He was a tall, spare, rock-hard man in his mid-thirties. A tropical disease had eliminated, forever, hair, eyebrows, lashes. His eyes were a startling pale shade against the sun-glossed mahogany of skin. There was a touch of cruelty in the beaked nose and set of the mouth, and humor as well. He wore a faded Singhalese sarong, knotted at the waist.

"I should think it is enough," Taffy Angus said, in her hoarse gamin voice.

She stood on her hands, her heels against the wall of the house, her white hair hanging in fluid lines to the terrace tiles. She wore a bandanna as a halter, and the jeans, salt-faded to powder blue, were hacked off raggedly at knee length. The position brought a flush under her tan.

"Does that make you a junior leaguer?" Falkner asked.

"Don't be nasty, darling," she said. She dropped onto hands

and toes, came gracefully up onto her feet. "I'm an old, old gal, as you well know, and a daily handstand has therapeutic values."

Falkner looked at her admiringly. "Bless you! You're my favorite neighbor. When I forget you're forty-two I feel like a cradle snatcher."

"In my prime, I came a little after the Gibson Girl, Park. But just to change the subject, how about those people who are coming?"

Park looked at his watch. "The cocktail hour approacheth. Go prettify thyself, wench."

She bowed low. "Sire!" she breathed. Her lips thinned a little. "Park, just for the record—couldn't we drop the Mussolini edict about living dangerously and grow fat and happy in the sunshine on your money? These people you ask here . . ."

They had walked to the hallway door. He opened it and gently shoved her through.

"Okay, okay." She sighed. "I never opened my fool mouth."

Falkner shut the door. His smile faded. Taffy knew as well as he did what had happened those times he had tried stagnation. He had grown restless, irritable. There was no point in trying to add to the fund, which was more than he could possibly spend in his lifetime. The company of the equally affluent brought a sickening boredom. And so life had to be spiced by the house parties. An amateur cop or a god of vengeance. Take your choice. Flip a coin. When there's guilt in the air it can be scented, as an animal scents the odor of fear. He looked along the beach to the spot where one of his houseguests, Carl Branneck, had killed Laura Hale. For a moment there was revulsion in him, and he wanted to call his newest house party off. Then he remembered the report from the New York agency and his interest began to quicken.

He crossed the big room to the built-in record player. He pondered. Atonal stuff would probably help tension along better than anything traditional. He selected two hours of Milhaud, Schönberg, and Antheil, stacked them on the spindle, cut in the amplifiers of the sea-level terrace, where they would have cocktails, and the amplifiers in the east garden, and then adjusted the volume down for background.

The only thing in the big room not suitable to a practicing Sybarite was the hard, narrow cot on which he slept. There were deep couches, a massive gray stone fireplace, paintings of a certain freedom in deep niches, softly lighted.

He untied the sarong, dropped it, stepped out of it. The shower stall was big enough to hold a seven-handed poker game. The dressing room adjoined the bath. As he was toweling himself he heard the descending roar of the amphib. That would be Lew Cherezack flying in the ladies, right on schedule.

He selected a gray casual shirt, trousers of a deeper shade of gray. As he walked from the dressing room into the bedroom he heard Lew's knock at the door.

Lew came in, his boxer pup's face slyly wrinkled. He turned with an expansive gesture. "Look what I got!"

A blonde and a brunette. Both tall and grave, with knowing eyes, sweet, wise mouths. "The blonde," Lew said, "is Georgie Wane. Blackie is called June Luce. Say hello to the boss, girls."

"How do you do, Mr. Falkner," they said gravely, almost in unison."

"Nice to see you. You know what the job is?"

Georgie, the blonde, turned spokesman. "If the job includes anything over and above what Mr. Empiro stated, Mr. Falkner, the deal is off. I want that understood."

Park grinned. "I left out a few details, but nothing either of you will balk at. Four young men are coming to visit me. They should be along any minute now. You are each being paid two hundred dollars a day. I want you to be as charming as possible to my guests, and I insist that they be kept in ignorance of the fact that I'm paying you. Now here's the additional instruction. There are two of you and four young men. Both of you are lovely enough to have learned how to handle men. I want them played off against each other. I want their beautiful friendship split up in any way you can manage it. Each night, at twelve, you go off duty, as far as I am concerned. Lew will show you your rooms right now. The doors lock. You have the freedom of the place. We're well equipped for amusement here. Tennis, badminton, swimming—in the Gulf and in the pool. There is only one restriction. I do not want either of you to leave the island until, in my opinion, the job is done."

"Fair enough," June Luce said. "But who are we supposed to be?"

Park grinned. "Call yourselves nieces of mine. That ought to spice their imaginations a little."

When Lew took them out, Falkner went down two flights to the kitchens. Mrs. Mick Rogers, cook and wife of the battered ex-pug who was Park's man of all work, smiled at him. Francie, the doughy little maid, was at one of the worktables finishing the construction of a tray of canapés.

"Set for the deluge, Mrs. Mick?" Falkner asked.

"What's eight people, counting yourself? A nothing. Practice, yet."

Just then Mick drove in across the private causeway from the mainland with the station wagon. Park walked out the side door of the smaller kitchen and across to the parking space. Mick slid neatly to a stop.

The first one got out, looked hesitantly at Falkner. "I—I'm Bill Hewett. Are you the host?"

Hewett was tall, frail, gangly. Physically he seemed barely out of his adolescence, but his pale-blue eyes were knowing and there was a downward sardonic twist about his wide mouth.

"Glad to see you, Hewett. Let me see. You're the copywriter, aren't you?"

"Right. With Lanteen, Soran and Howliss. I write deathless prose for TV commercials. And this is Prine Smith, our newspaperman."

Prine was dark, stocky, muscular, with a square strong jaw and an aggressive handshake. He said, "We're pretty much in the dark about all this, Falkner, and—"

Park smiled. "Let's talk about it over cocktails."

Hewett broke in. "And this is the actor in the group. Guy Darana."

Guy was tall, with a superb body, classic profile, brown, tightly curled hair. But there was a vacant docility about his expression, an aimless childlike amiability in his eyes.

"Howya," he said softly in the richest of baritones.

The fourth and last was a wiry redhead with pointed features, a jittery hyperthyroid manner. "You hear that?" he said. "The actor in the group, he calls Darana. What about me? What about Stacey Brian? I make with the voice on the radio. Character parts. I work at it. All that hunk has to do is revolve slowly to give them a look at both sides of the profile."

"Radio is a dying medium," Darana said languidly.

Falkner sensed that it was an old argument. He shook hands with Stacey Brian. Mick Rogers was taking the luggage from the tailgate.

"We'll take our own stuff up. Don't bother," Hewett said.

"Mick, you show them their rooms," Park said. "As soon as you all freshen up, find your way down to that front terrace. You can see it from here."

Falkner went back up to his room, started the music, went back down to the front terrace. Mick had already changed to white jacket, and he was putting the small terrace bar in order.

"Jittery as hell," Mick said. "All of them. And seven thousand questions. I didn't know nothing."

"Make the drinks heavy for the boys, Mick. And light for our two new women."

"Festivities about to begin?" Taffy said, close behind him. Park turned. She wore a white blouse pulled down off her deeply tanned shoulders. The gay skirt swung as she walked. A hammered-silver Aztec bracelet looked impossibly heavy on her slim wrist. Her white hair was a purer form of silver, heavy, thick, molten, alive.

"Jezebel," he whispered. "Lilith! Krithna of the purple seas."

"Don't mind me," Mick said.

"This," said Taffy, "is what you get for inviting little girls who could be my daughters. I have to keep up my morale."

There was no more time for talk then because Stacey Brian came out onto the terrace. The sun was slipping toward the blue Gulf. The others came, were introduced. Mick was chanting, "Step up and name it and I can make it. They go down like honey and then kick you behind the ear." Taffy sat on the wall and looked smug. She made Georgie and June look awkward and young, and she made the others look. She winked solemnly at Park Falkner.

Conversation was general, polite, aimless. Georgie Wane had inconspicuously drifted to the side of Guy Darana. He looked at her with mild, sleepy approval.

June Luce said in a silky soft voice, "Miss Angus, I must tell you. My mother took me to see you in *Time for Play*—oh, ages ago! I think I was six at the time. That was before you became such a successful model, wasn't it?"

Park concealed his grin by taking a drink. June looked with rapt interest at Taffy. Taffy looked puzzled. She said, "My goodness! Now I know I'm ancient! I've just forgotten how to make kitty-talk. Why, if you'd said anything like that to me five years ago I'd have thought of some nasty-nice way to call attention to the way you're letting yourself get—" She stopped. "Oh, I mustn't be rude. I'm sorry." She beamed at June.

June's eyes narrowed. "What's wrong with me?"

"Nothing, sister," Mick said. "You're a nice dish. You just ain't bright. You challenged the champ. Now shut up, or she'll make you so mad you'll be sick to your stomach and she'll just sit here grinning at you."

Taffy pouted. "He never lets me have any fun."

Prine Smith walked scowling over to Park, planted his feet, his stocky legs spread, his square hand holding the cocktail glass. "Look!" he said. "I don't go for cat-and-mouse games. Maybe I'm not properly civilized. So you're a big enough shot to get strings pulled to get us all off at the same time. So you play on curiosity in a smart enough way to get us all down here, expenses paid. You're out after laughs, Falkner. Let's blow away the smoke screen and talk sense for a minute."

"Glad to," Park said. "I guess I'm just a nosy type. I like mysteries. Nine months ago the four of you lived in a big apartment in the Village, two blocks from Sheridan Square. You've split up now, but that was the status quo. Hewett had a girl friend, lovely from all reports, named Lisa Mann. On a hot afternoon, June fourth to be exact, Lisa Mann, using a key that Hewett had given her, let herself into the apartment. A girl named Alicia French happened to see her. Alicia lived in the next apartment down the hall. All four of you were able to prove that you were out that afternoon. The first one to get back to the apartment was Guy Darana. He returned a little after eleven that night. No one has seen Lisa Mann since. Apparently she never returned to her own apartment. There was an investigation. Her parents are well-to-do. I asked you four down here because things like that intrigue me. I hope that during your stay here one of you will, directly or indirectly, admit to his guilt in the death of Miss Mann. Does that blow away the smoke, Smith?"

Prine Smith stared at him. "Are you crazy?"

Hewett said softly, "I know she's dead. I know it. She would have come back."

"Young girls disappear every day," Stacey Brian said. "That she happened to come to our place was coincidental."

June and Georgie listened with great intentness, their mouths open a bit.

"Are you serious, Falkner?" Prine Smith asked, still scowling. "Do you actually think that just by having us down here you can break open a case that the metropolitan police haven't been able to unravel?"

Park shrugged. "It might work that way."

"I don't get it. If one of us should be guilty, which is silly even to think of, wouldn't you have given him warning by now?"

"Of course."

Prine Smith sighed. "Okay. Have your fun. It's your money, and I guess you know what you want to do with it. Me, I'm going to relax and enjoy myself."

"That's what you're all supposed to do," Park said amiably.

Hewett had been drinking steadily and with purpose. He said, "Her eyes were tilted a little, and the black lashes were so long they were absurd. She came up to my shoulder, and when she laughed she laughed deep in her throat."

"Knock it off," the redheaded Stacey Brian said sharply. "Drop it, Bill."

"Sure," Bill Hewett said. "Sure."

The dusk was upon them, and the music was a wry dirge. Taffy's face was shadowed. A gull swung by, tilting in the wind, laughing with disdain. The soft waves were the tired breath of the water. Death whispered in the thin jacaranda leaves.

Hewett laughed with excessive harshness. "Sure," he said again. "Forget her. We're all nice clean young men, we four. Our best friends don't have to tell us, because we've bought

the right products. We have built-in value, four-way virtue.
Remember the brand name. Go to your nearest crematory and
ask for our product. That's a joke, son. But forget little dead
girls because little dead girls have nothing in common with
these four upright, sterling, time-tested young men of market-
proven value. You can't write a commercial about a dead girl.
The product will never sell."

"Shut up, Bill," Guy said.

June hugged her elbows, though the dusk was warm. Mick's
face, behind the bar, was carved of dark stone. Over on the
mainland a diesel train bellowed, a distant creature of swamps
and prehistory.

"You people can eat any time," Mrs. Mick said.

Taffy lay on her face in the sun by the pool. Falkner sat cross-
legged beside her, rubbing the oil into the long clean lines of
her back.

"Mmmmm," she said, with sleepy appreciation.

June came to the edge of the pool, her dark hair plastered
wet to her head. She hung on and said, "Hello, people."

"How goes the war of the sexes?" Falkner asked.

June pursed her lips. "Georgie has attracted the big handsome hunk, Guy Darana, and also Mr. Muscles, the newspaper
guy. I am left with the agile little redhead, who can sling passes
from any off-balance position. Hewett is not interested."

"How is Georgie doing?"

"Reasonable. Guy and Prine Smith are now on the beach
showing off."

"Back to the battle, June," Park directed. "Take Stacey
Brian down there and see if you can confuse things."

June swam away. Taffy yawned. "Legs," she said.

Park moved down a bit, filled his palm with oil. Taffy sat
up suddenly.

"No, dearie. I think I do this myself," she said. She took
the bottle from him. "An aged creature like me has to be well
smeared with this glop or the wrinkles pop out like wasteland
erosion." As she worked she looked over at him. "Falkner, my

man, this little house party makes me feel physically ill. Why don't you break it up?"

"Just when everybody's having so much fun?"

"Fun! They've all got the jumps."

"Sure they have. Right from the beginning each of them, the three un-guilty ones, whoever they might be, have had a dirty little suspicion. They were trying to forget it. Now I've reawakened the whole thing. They're drinking too much and laughing too loudly, and they're all wound up like a three dollar watch. We just wait and see."

Her brown eyes were suddenly very level, very grave. "But you usually add another ingredient, Park."

"This time, too. Maybe tonight."

"Do you really think one of them killed that girl?"

"I do."

"But why?" Taffy wailed.

"Why do people kill people? Love, money, position, hate, envy, passion, jealousy. Lots of reasons."

"Please be careful, Park. Don't let anything happen to you."

"Am I that valuable?"

"With you gone, what would I do for laughs?"

He leaned his hand tenderly against her bare shoulders and pushed her into the pool.

He had gone apart from the others, and now he sat on the sand with his hands locked around his knees and he thought of the small thin sound she had made as he struck her and how he had caught her as she fell and listened, hearing the pulse thud in his ears, the hard rasp of his own breathing. She had felt so heavy as he had carried her quickly to where he had planned. She was really a small girl. There was no blood.

Again the dusk, and the music and the cocktails. And Mick behind the bar and Taffy in pale green and all of them suntanned by the long hot day, tingling from the showers, ravenous, bright-eyed.

"I don't want to be a bore, Park," Prine Smith said, "but what are you accomplishing?"

186

Falkner shrugged. "Nothing, I guess. Maybe we ought to talk. That is, if nobody objects."

"Talk," Bill Hewett said tonelessly.

"Objectivity," Park said, "is often easier at a distance. The police concentrated on the apartment. That, I feel, was a mistake. The fact that the body has not appeared indicated to me that it was a crime carefully planned. Too carefully planned to assume that the murderer would select a city apartment as the scene of the crime and hope to get away with it, to walk out with the body. She was seen going into the apartment. She was not seen coming out. The apartment had a phone. All four of you were able to prove that you could not possibly have gotten back to the apartment before eleven. But you couldn't prove, had you been asked to do so, that Lisa Mann had not come to you. She could have been summoned by phone to the place where she was murdered and where the body was disposed of so successfully."

"Just how do you dispose of a body successfully?" Prine Smith asked.

"Fire, the sea, chemicals. But, best of all, legally. Death certificate and a funeral."

Something deep inside him laughed. The forest floor had been thick with loam under the needles. He had scraped away the needles, and the edge of the new spade had bitten deeply, easily. The hole was not long enough for her, and so he put her in it curled on her side, her knees against her chest. Later, after he had patted the earth down, replaced the needles of the pines, he burned the new shovel handle and the old coveralls. He kicked the hot shovel blade over into the brush. No trace. None.

"Why would anyone kill her?" Hewett asked. "Why? She was my girl. There wasn't any question of that. What good would she do anyone dead?"

"Sometimes a man kills," Falkner said, "for the very simple reason that the act of killing gives him pleasure."

"It would be nice to meet him," Hewett said. "Nice." He looked hard, first at Guy, then Prine Smith, then Stacey Brian.

187

"Off it!" Prine said harshly. "We were over that. You know we aren't capable of anything like that."

Hewett continued to stare and there was a trace of madness in his eyes. Slowly it faded. He walked over to the bar. Mick filled his glass.

"Hell," said Stacey, "Lisa may be wandering around right now. Amnesia. You can't tell about things like that."

"Sure," Hewett said. "Sure. It could be that." He didn't speak as though he believed it.

On the way to dinner Georgie Wane took Park aside. "The money," she said, "is nice. I like it. You've got a nice place here. But how about this, uncle? One of these boys maybe clobbered a girl. It leads one to think. Maybe it's a habit yet."

"Not a habit. Not quite that. Call it a tendency."

"I thought maybe you could tell by looking at hands. I've been looking. No dice, uncle. I would say Hewett didn't. Beyond that I cannot go. Shouldn't a murderer look like a murderer?"

"I knew one once who could have been your twin, Georgie."

"I can see how she got in the killing mood," Georgie said.

At three in the morning Falkner awoke at the sound of the first tap on his door. He came completely awake in a fraction of a second. He pulled his robe on as he went to the door. It was Taffy.

She looked small, young, wan in the lamplight. "You can't sleep either, eh?" she said.

"What's got you down, Taff?" he asked. "Come on in."

They walked out onto the terrace. The wind was directly out of the west. It had sea fragrance.

She said, "You hear about something like this. I mean it's a problem like filling in a nine-letter blank beginning with G meaning a South African herb. Then you meet the people and it's something else again. Gee, they're nice kids. I don't want it to be one of them."

He put his arm around her. "Old Taff, the world mother. She loves everybody. Maybe I'm wrong this time. The agency checked it out pretty carefully, though. Lisa Mann was one of those rare people who make no enemies. No one profited by her death. She was exceptionally striking. Emotions can get wound up pretty tightly."

"If one of them did it," she said softly, "I wonder if he is sleeping right now. I don't see how he could be, knowing that all this is supposed to make him give himself away. I've been watching them so carefully. It's not Hewett, of course. Darana seems like a big sleepy animal. But he did come alive when he did that part out of his last play for us. Stacey Brian is an awful nice little guy. Prine Smith is a little quarrelsome, but you sense a certain amount of integrity in him. I can't see him murdering anybody. Park, you must be wrong. You must!"

"The tension is building, Taff. You can feel it."

She moved out of his arm. "And you love it, don't you? It's bread and wine to you. Park, there's a faint streak of evil in you."

"Man is a predatory animal," he said happily.

She sighed. "Too late to change you now. I should have adopted you when you were a baby."

"Foster mother at the age of seven?"

"I matured early."

He lay rigid in the darkness, remembering, remembering. It was Lisa's fault. No one could get around that. He had told her he loved her. He had told her this affair with Hewett had to stop at once. But she laughed, even when he told her she would be very sorry if she continued to torture him this way. He cried, and she laughed again and again. Sin must be punished, whenever it is found. There is no wrong in that, and this great clown, Falkner, can do nothing because there will never be any clue. He knew from the way Hewett acted that Lisa had never told him about the scene.

When Falkner came down, Taffy, Georgie, Guy, and Stacey Brian were breakfasting on the patio, shielded from the brisk morning wind. He heard them laughing before he saw them. They made room for him. He had touched his bell a few minutes before coming down. Mrs. Mick brought him his breakfast tray.

Georgie said, "I was telling them about home in Scranton

when I had a crush on a guy who drove a hearse. We didn't have any place to be alone, so we used to go and neck in the room where they stored the coffins. Well this one time Joey heard the boss coming back unexpected, so what does he do but pop me in a box and shut the lid and then make like he's taking an inventory. My God, I was petrified. It's dusty. I sneeze. The boss says, 'Whassat?' He opens the lid and says, 'Girl, you ain't dead!' Joey, the dope, says, 'Her aunt died. She was looking for a box.' Next time I see Joey, he's driving a bread truck. Terrible kind of breakfast talk, isn't it? But on this house party maybe it isn't so far out of line after all."

"You say you and this Joey had a place where you could be alone," Guy Darana said. "That isn't a question. I'm just thinking out loud."

"Stop making like a detective," Stacey Brian said.

"He's working on our little problem," Taffy said. "Can't you see the look of the hunter?"

"What kind of a detective you want?" Stacey Brian said. "A Jimmy Stewart type? Like this? Wal, I guess all you . . . uh . . . nice people need a . . . uh . . . little detectin' done around here. Or how about an Edward G. Robinson? Like so. Listen to me, sugar. You got to lay it right on the line, see? You're not talking to no small-town copper, see? This is the big time, sugar. See?"

They laughed and applauded. The imitations had been uncannily accurate. Hewett came onto the patio, and the look of of him quenched the high spirits. His eyes appeared to have receded back into his head. His mouth was a thin, bitter line.

"Good morning, all," he said. "Fun and games?"

"You look rocky, honey," Georgie said.

He smiled coldly. "Bad dreams. Copywriter's dreams. I could see Lisa with her eyes bulging and hands around her throat, but I couldn't tell whose hands."

"Ugh!" Georgie said.

"By the way, Bill," Park said, "I'm assuming that you would like to find out whether or not one of your friends killed her. I'm assuming you'll help by answering questions. Did you and Lisa have a place where you used to go to be alone?"

"It's not any of your business," Hewett snapped.

190

"Blunt and to the point."

"We did have. A farmhouse so broken down you couldn't go into it. Just the foundation where the barn had been. But you could drive in there and not be seen from the road. She used to pack lunches, and we'd picnic there."

"Did you ever go separately?"

"Sure. We'd meet there. She had a car. You know that already. It was in the newspapers. They found the car five days later in a big parking lot on West Forty-first Street. Nobody could say who'd driven it in there. Maybe she did. I used to take a bus out to Alden Village and walk to the farm."

"Did you tell the police that?" Park asked.

"Why should I? She never went there except when we went together, or when we were going to meet there."

"Her body might be there, Hewett. She could have been decoyed there."

"How do you mean?"

"A faked message from you. It wouldn't be hard. Any of your apartment mates could get their hands on your handwriting."

Bill Hewett looked down at his plate. Suddenly he looked no longer young, as though he had donned the mask he would wear in middle age. "I went back once. Alone. It was like visiting some damnable cemetery. The wind whined. She could be there, all right."

"I'll wire the New York police. Tell me the name of the farm or how to direct them to it."

"About a mile and a half north of the village on the left of a curve. Route Eight. They call it the Harmon place."

He sent the wire after breakfast. At eleven thirty they were all out by the pool. Park was nursing a purpling bruise high on his cheek where Mick Rogers had tagged him heavily during the usual morning workout. Mick hummed as he made drinks. He seemed well pleased with himself.

"Gotta remember to keep that left hand higher, boss," he said, grinning.

Taffy swam effortless lengths of the pool, her brown arms

191

lifting slowly from the pale-green water. Stacey Brian, in deference to his redheaded lack of skin pigmentation, was the only one in the shade. Stocky Prine Smith was whispering to June Luce. He was propped up on his elbows. She lay on her back with plastic linked cups on her eyes to protect them from the sun glare. From time to time she giggled in a throaty way. Stacey glared over at them. Georgie Wane was trying to teach big Guy Darana how to make a racing turn against the end of the pool.

From the amplifier came muted music, old jazz piano by Errol Garner and Mary Lou Williams and Art Tatum. The last record, one by Garner, had played twice. Park thought of sending Mick up to reverse the stack, but suddenly an idea came to him. He went up himself, walking slowly, planning it in detail. It was based on the sensitive mike he had hooked into the set. Once, when it had been left turned on quite inadvertently, during a party, one couple who had sneaked away from the crowd came back to find that every word, every sound, had blared out above the noise of the music. He had had the mike installed to simplify some of the problems of running the household.

He reversed the stack of records, waited for the music to start, clicked on the mike at the point of a loud remembered chord in the music, hoping that it wouldn't be heard. He picked the table mike up gingerly and carried it away from the set. He set it on the bedside table, picked up the phone, and dialed the number of the hotel. Before anyone could answer, he pushed the receiver down with his fingers.

"Give me Mr. Norris's room, please. Four-twelve, I think it is. . . . Hello, Lieutenant Norris? This is Falkner. I guess your trip hasn't been a waste after all. . . . Yes, I think I know who our man is. . . . Right. He'll crack under the strain, and we'll have something definite to go on. . . . Yes, I'll call you just as soon as—"

The door burst open and Mick came running in, panting from the run up the stairs. "Hey, the mike's on! Every word is coming over the—"

Park reached out quickly and clicked the mike off.

He grinned. "Thanks, Mick." He hung up the phone.

Mick's eyes widened with comprehension. "So! A fake, is it?"

"Did you hear what I said?"

"No. I started running when I heard you dial."

Park repeated the conversation. "What do you think?" he asked.

Mick scrubbed his heavy jaw with his knuckles. "It ought to make the guy pretty uneasy. I can't figure which one it could be. Maybe it isn't any one of the three."

"I'm placing my bet that it is one of them."

They went back down. The atmosphere had changed. Hewett was the color of watery milk under his two-day tan. He stood with his fists clenched, staring at his friends, one by one. June had sat up, moved a bit away from Prine Smith. Taffy stood near the diving tower, toweling herself. Georgie sat alone on the edge of the pool, her feet in the water. Guy Darana stood behind her, his eyes slitted against the sunlight, looking half asleep. Stacey Brian looked at Hewett and said, "Easy, boy. Easy."

"I'm terribly sorry that happened," Park said. "It shouldn't have happened. Like a fool I forgot the mike was on. I'm afraid I've forewarned the man who killed Lisa Mann."

Hewett walked over to Park. "Who is it?" he said. "Tell me who it is."

"Not quite yet, Bill," Park said soothingly.

"Tell me, damn you!"

"I don't think I'm wrong, but there's always that chance. I'm not ready to tell you. You're in no emotional condition to handle yourself properly if I should tell you."

Hewett threw his fist full at Falkner's face with an almost girlish ineptitude. Park caught the fist in the palm of his hand and squeezed down on it. Hewett's mouth changed with the impact of the sudden pain.

"Don't try that again," Park said.

Hewett yanked his hand free, turned without a word, and walked across to the house.

Everyone started to make bright, shallow conversation to cover the awkwardness. Taffy came over to Park and lowered her voice so that only he could hear her. "Dirty pool, friend," she said. "Very dirty pool."

"I don't understand, Taff."

"The music suddenly got louder and then faded back again. The mike stands near the set. You should have carried it over to the phone before turning it on."

"You know, you'd be a very difficult type to be married to."

"I don't think I can quite class that as a proposal. You and your mythical lieutenants!"

He grinned with a flash of white teeth against the deep brown of his face. "That's where I got you, Taff. There is a Lieutenant Norris, and he is registered at the hotel, and he is from New York. But he's on an extradition case. If I can't give him something to get his teeth into by tomorrow night, he has to start back with his man."

He fell silent, and the talk around him was meaningless. It had to be a clever trap. There was nothing Falkner could know. Nothing. But the man was clever. It took cleverness to locate a body sixteen hundred miles away, a body that had been searched for by experts. They might not find it. Probably they would. He hadn't risked going back to see if the dirt had settled. The laboratories would go to work on the body. He had carried the body a short distance. Could some microscopic bit of evidence have been left?

Dusk broke up the badminton doubles. The last set had been Guy Darana and June Luce against Georgie and Stacey Brian. Everyone had played in their swimsuits. Brian's wiry quickness had made up for Darana's advantage in height. Georgie was nursing a swollen underlip which, in some strange fashion, she had managed to club with her own racket.

All four were winded. Mick had wheeled the rolling bar out onto the edge of the court, plugging in the ice compartment at the outlet near the tennis court floodlights.

"Sometimes," Stacey said, "it's good to become bushed. When the infantry reluctantly let me go, I swore I'd never get physically tired again for the rest of my life. Here I am, running around in the sun and beating on a cork with feathers sticking out of it."

"Infantry!" Darana said with heavy disgust. "Why didn't you pick yourself a branch?"

"Don't tell me what you were, Guy," Georgie said. "Let me guess. A fly boy. A hot pilot. A tired hat and nine rows of ribbons."

"Not a hot pilot," Guy said. "I pushed tired old transports and tankers around Asia. I was too big to fit into a fighter with any comfort. But old Prine here had the real deal. Warm food, good bed. All the luxuries. Of course they sank a couple ships under him, but the Navy was it."

"How about Bill?" June asked. "What was he?"

"G-Two. Hell, I wish he'd come down out of his room and stop sulking."

Taffy giggled. "You know what our jolly host did for his country."

"Whatever it was, I bet it was a job smarter than the one Stace picked," Guy said.

Before she could reply, Hewett came walking out of the gray darkness. "Sorry I blew my top," he murmured.

"Quite all right," Park said.

"You see," Hewett continued, "if I lose my head I won't get my cracks at whoever killed Lisa. I've got to stay calm. I have it all figured out. As soon as you know for sure, you'll tell that lieutenant. But maybe I can find out for sure before you do, Falkner. And if I do, he might not stand trial, whoever he is. I'm beginning to get an idea."

Stacey Brian stood up and shivered. "That wind's getting cooler. Or have I got a chill just because there's a murderer in the house? Goodbye, you people. I'm off for a shower."

The group slowly split up until only Prine Smith and Park Falkner were left. Mick wheeled the bar inside. Prine Smith's face was in shadow.

He said, "I can almost see your point. A dilettante in crime. Give you a purpose in life, maybe." His tone was speculative. "But human beings aren't puppets, Falkner. They take over the strings. They make up their own lines. I've done some

195

checking. You've had considerable violence here on your Grouper Island. Do you sleep well at night?"

"Like a baby."

"I've been in the newspaper game longer than you'd think to look at me. I can smell violence in the air. Something is going to bust open here."

"It's possible."

"What precautions are you taking?"

"I think that would be pretty valuable information to someone."

"Don't be a fool! You can't possibly suspect me."

Falkner was surprised at the trace of anger in his own voice. "Don't try to judge me or my methods, Smith. Don't set yourself up as an arbiter of my moral codes or lack of same. A girl died. There's the justification."

In the darkness he could sense Prine Smith's grin as he stood up. "Glad to know you sometimes doubt yourself, Falkner. Maybe I like you better."

· He went off to the house. Falkner stayed a few minutes more.

Sometimes there is safety in inaction, he thought. And sometimes it is wise to move quickly. He locked the door, opened the toilet-article kit, took out the small bottle of white powder. It was cool against his palm. They said that later the lips smelled of almonds. He wondered.

Bill Hewett looked full into the eyes of his friend. The others were by the beach fire. Hewett knew that he had drunk too much. Falkner's room wavered dizzily. He struggled for soberness. He said thickly, "You said you could tell me who killed Lisa."

"I can."

"What's that you've got, a recorder? What have you been doing here? It seems to be a funny place to meet, the host's room."

"Yes, this is a recorder. I got here first. I made a tape on his machine."

"You mean you say on the tape who killed her?" Hewett asked.

"That's right. Here. Have a drink. Then we'll listen to it. Together."

"Can't you just tell me?" Hewett asked plaintively. He tilted the glass high, drained it.

"Now I can tell you. I'll turn the tape on. Like this."

"Who is it? Who killed her?"

"You did, Hewett. You killed her. Can't you remember?"

"What kind of a damn fool joke is this?"

His friend went quickly toward the door, opened it, glanced out into the hall. He turned. "Goodbye, Bill. Give my regards to Lisa. My very best regards. I think you might live another ten seconds—after that drink I gave you."

The door shut softly. Hewett stared at the empty glass. It slipped from his hands to the rug, bounced, didn't break. He put both hands to his throat and turned dizzily. The moon was bright on the small private terrace. He saw a brown arm, almost black in the moonlight, reach over the terrace wall, saw a man pull himself up quickly.

Hewett fell to his knees.

They were all near the fire, the ember glow reddening their faces. Mick was telling them how the lights went out in Round Five during his bout with John Henry Lewis.

Park came close to them. Mick looked over and stopped talking.

"What is it?" Taffy asked quickly.

"I've just told Norris to come over. The local police will be here, too. Our little house party is over, I'm afraid."

Georgie Wane looked around the circle. "Where's Bill?" she demanded.

"Bill is in my room. He's very dead, and not at all pretty. Poison."

He heard the hard intake of breath. Taffy said, "Oh, no!"

"Before he did it he left his confession. I think you might like to hear it. Mick, go on up and play the tape that's on the recorder right now. Pipe it onto the front terrace. We'll walk over there to listen."

Mick went across the sand and into the darkness. They stood up slowly, full of the embarrassed gravity with which any group meets the death of one of their number. Taffy came next to Park in the darkness as they walked, her fingers chill on his wrist.

"No, Park. I can't . . . believe it."

They stood on the front terrace, close to the sea. The amplifier made a scratching sound. The voice that came was thin, taut with emotion. There was no need for the voice to identify itself.

"I can't pretend any more. She said she was through with me. She told me she was fed up with neurotics. I had her meet me at the farm. Falkner trapped me about that. I took a shovel and coveralls. I came up behind her, struck her with the flat of the shovel blade. I carried her fifty feet into the woodlot and buried her there. I burned the shovel handle and the coveralls. I drove her car back and put it in the busiest lot I could find and tore up the check. I couldn't face the thought of her going to someone else, someone else's arms around her and lips on hers. I'm not sorry. Not sorry at all . . ."

There was a dry, rasping sound of needle on empty grooves and then silence as Mick lifted the arm.

"Crazy," June Luce said softly. "Plain crazy. Gee, the poor guy."

Sirens shrilled through the distant night, coming closer. Park said quickly, "Go on into the front living room, all of you. They'll take the body out and then Norris will probably want to talk to you. I see no reason why it might not be simple routine."

It was a full forty-five minutes after the cars had swung across the private causeway and parked that Lieutenant Norris came into the front living room. He was a tall, stooped, sick-looking man, with a face that showed the lean fragility of the bone structure underneath. He wore an incongruous dark suit and his eyes were remote, disinterested.

"Let's get it over," he said. "You're Smith? No? Oh, Darana. And you're Brian. Okay, I got you all straight now. I

198

guess. I can question you all at once. Did Hewett seem depressed since you've been here?"

Several people said yes at the same moment.

Georgie said, "The guy was pretty antisocial. I thought it was because his gal had disappeared. I've been wrong before."

"Now," said Norris, "about this beach party tonight. Anybody see him leave?"

There was silence. Park said, "The sea was warm. About half the group were swimming from time to time. You couldn't really keep track of any individual. I guess that at one time or another every one of us wandered off. I found Hewett, as I told you, when I went up to my room to change to dry clothes. It was getting just a little chilly."

Prine Smith crossed his arms. "Let's drop this patty-cake routine, shall we?"

Norris stared coldly at him. "What's on your mind?"

"Hewett was drinking too much. That record sounds too sober to me. And I knew Hewett inside and out. I say nuts to this suicide angle. Lisa was his gal and she meant every look she gave him. I'm the only one outside of Bill and Lisa that knew the wedding date was set. I thought Falkner's idea was a bust for a time, but I've felt the tension growing here. And now I think I know the angle." He spun and took two steps toward Stacey Brian. "Come on, kid. Make imitations for the people. Show 'em how you can be Jimmy Stewart, or Edward G. Robinson—or Bill Hewett. Maybe you were Bill Hewett over the phone when you got Lisa to go out there to that farm. Bill never killed himself. He had more guts than anyone you know. For my money, Stacey, you got him up there to Falkner's room, made the record yourself, and slipped him a drink with the stuff in it."

Stacey Brian turned as white as a human being can turn. He came out of the chair like a coiled spring suddenly released. His fist spatted off Prine Smith's mouth before Smith could lift his arms. Park leaped in and grabbed Brian from behind. He struggled and then gave it up.

"Will you be good?" Park asked.

Stacey Brian nodded. Park released him.

Stacey said in a level monotone, "Any guy who can think

199

up that kind of an angle probably did it himself. He was on the make for Lisa ever since the first time Bill brought her around. We all knew that. We didn't tell the cops because we didn't think he was a guy to kill anybody. Sure I make imitations. But if any of you think I did a thing like that, you can all go to hell in a basket."

Norris drawled, "You guys can slap each other around until you're tired. It doesn't make no nevermind to me. I got my case solved, and I like the solution. Hewett smeared his gal and covered it nice. I got the dope today they found the body just like he said in the tape."

"But, damn it, man," Prine said, "can't you see that Brian could put that on the tape and make it sound just like Hewett?"

Stacey said, "Smith, I don't want to ever see you or talk to you or hear your name again as long as I live. I'm going back to New York just as fast as I can get there, and I'm packing my stuff and moving out of that apartment we got two months ago."

"Good!" Smith said.

"You sound like a couple of babies," Guy Darana said.

"He's a slick one, he is," Prine said. "He even did his imitations here for us, because he knew that if he didn't do them somebody would wonder why he'd given up his pet party trick."

Norris sighed. "I'm tired. You people are trying to foul up my case. Sleep on it, will you? Nobody leaves the island. I'll be back in the morning. They've taken the body to town." He looked around with a sudden, surprising, wry amusement. "Have fun," he said. He turned and left the room.

Guy whispered to Georgie and then said to the room at large, "We're taking a walk. The air is fresh out there."

"Be back in half an hour," Park said. "We'll all meet at the enclosed patio at the rear of the house. I think that by then we'll be able to talk calmly and iron out this trouble."

"Never!" Stacey Brian said calmly.

"But you'll give it a try."

"If it'll amuse you. It's your party."

Park walked off the terrace out into the night and sat in the sand, his back against the concrete seawall. He heard a sound and looked up over his right shoulder. Taffy stood with her elbows on the wall, her head bent, her thick white hair falling toward him, a sheen in the pale moonlight behind her.

"He's right, you know: Smith," she said. There was utter sadness in her voice.

"Don't fret, Taff."

"The poor lost man. Poor Bill. This is a night for losing things. We're lost too, you know."

"How do you mean that?"

"I could go along with your plans before this happened, Park. I told myself you were doing good. But I really didn't believe it. Now a boy is dead. And boys stay dead a long time. It's been nice."

He found her hand. "Trust me."

"I want to. But I can't. Not any more. Because this thing that happened is wrong. Norris is a fool. You're being a fool too."

"I don't want to lose you, Taff."

"But you did. When Bill died you lost me."

"Old Taff. The world mother, the open warm heart for lost dogs and children."

"Don't make bright talk. Just kiss me and say goodbye like a little man."

"You can't go now."

"I'll stay until morning, but this is a good time for goodbye."

When he came in with Taff they were all in the enclosed patio. The wall lights were on, the bulbs of that odd orange that repels insects.

"Post mortem," June Luce said. "A post mortem by my generous uncle who pays me two hundred a day to grace his lovely home." She laughed. There was liquor in her laugh.

"Please shut up, dear," Georgie said.

"Well," Park said, "it all seems to be over. And I, for one, am satisfied with Norris's conclusion."

"I'm happy for you," Prine Smith said. "You're easily satisfied."

Guy Darana stood with his big arm around Georgie's slim waist. He rubbed his chin against her sleek golden head.

Taffy wore the look of a lost child. Mick, by the corner bar, was glum.

"He didn't die easy," Park said. "It was quick, but from the look of his face there wasn't anything easy about it."

"Is this discussion necessary?" June asked. "Even at my wage scale there's a limit."

"I'm switching to bourbon, Mick," Stacey said.

June glanced beyond Falkner to the stone arch that led out into the side garden. She made a sound. It was not a scream. It was harsh and long and came from the deepest part of her lungs.

Park moved to one side.

Guy Darana had his arm around Georgie Wane's waist. With one heave of his shoulder he flung her to the side. She spun, tripped, and fell hard.

Bill Hewett, ghastly pale in the archway, his mouth twisting so that lips were pale worms entwining, said, "I left some unfinished business behind, I think."

Prine Smith stood without a movement, with no expression at all on his face. Stacey Brian stood with the glass in his hand. His hand shut and the glass made a brittle sound. A clot of blood dropped and spattered on the stone.

Guy Darana stood with his hands flattened against the wall behind him.

"No," he whispered. "No!"

His big pale hand flickered in the light, disappeared, reappeared with the glint of metal. Bill Hewett took a slow step toward Guy. The gun spoke, a slapping, stick-breaking sound, metallic in the enclosed patio. He fired point-blank at Bill Hewett. He fired six times. The hammer clicked three more times. The gun dropped onto the stone. Hewett took another slow step toward Darana, grinning now, grinning in a ghastly fashion.

Darana's big, handsome face lost its human look. The features seemed to grow loose and fluid. Knee bones thudded against the stone. It was as though he were at prayer, worshiping some new and inhuman god. His lips moved and he

202

made sounds, muted little growlings and gobblings that were zoo sounds.

Norris came in from the garden as though walking into a drugstore for a pack of cigarettes. "Okay," he said, "print that. It ought to do it. On your feet, Darana."

Guy looked up at him and said, the words pasted stickily together, "There's nothing you can do to me because it is part of me to avenge and destroy. There is sin and weakness in the world. Weakness and sin. They have to be punished. I'm an instrument of death. The garden and the word. The time is now. All the rich orchard time of turning, and no man is known who can unbend the others." He glared around at them, then slipped down onto his haunches and began idly patting the stone with the palm of his hand, cooing softly, crooning to himself.

"Ain't it the way," Norris said with disgust. "You go to all this trouble and what do you get? He flips just as you grab him. Well, maybe we piled it on a little strong. Help me, you guys. If he's violent he'll be tough to handle."

But Guy Darana let himself be led out placidly. He looked vacantly at Georgie on the way out. She put the back of her hand to her lips, and her eyes were wide and terrified.

They gathered in Falkner's room. It was two in the morning. The fireplace fire drove back the night chill.

Georgie's burned knee and elbow had been bandaged. She had lost almost all her casual flippancy.

"What can you believe about people?" Prine Smith asked. "I had Darana pretty well evaluated in my own mind. A big handsome hunk with more of a spark of acting talent than he was willing to admit. I had him pegged to go a long way. Hollywood had nibbled once, but he didn't like the offer. How do you figure it, Park?"

Falkner shrugged. "Women came running to him. He must have alternated between thinking he was a minor god and feeling a strong sense of guilt, probably the result of a strict childhood home life. Guilt can do odd things. He must have been on the edge when he made a play for Lisa. She turned him down. That was something new. He brooded over it. The one woman he wanted he couldn't have, and Hewett's happiness with her was like a blow in the face. He was an actor. He could do tricks with that voice of his. We'll never know for sure, probably, but I think he phoned her pretending to be you, Bill. I guess you can fill out the rest of the details. He justified himself by saying to himself that he was punishing her for a sin."

Park turned to Prine again.

"Our precautions were very simple. Lew and Mick took turns going through your rooms, deactivating anything that looked lethal. Lew was the one who found the gun while Guy was swimming. He reloaded with frangible blanks that look like the McCoy. Mick found the unlabeled bottle. He emptied it on a hunch, washed it, refilled it in the kitchen. While we swam at night, Lew was out beyond the breaker line in the *Nancy* watching with night glasses to see that nothing funny happened. I saw Darana talk to Bill and then leave in the direction of the house. In a little while Bill followed along. I followed him. When I saw him go into my room I went down onto the terrace below mine and climbed up. Guy left the room as I came over the wall. Poor Bill thought he'd really been poisoned. When I convinced him that he hadn't, he was willing to play ball with us. I called Norris and explained it to him. We needed a little more on Darana than Bill's naked word. Well . . . we got it."

Hewett said, "It's over now, I guess. I knew all along she must be dead. But because I didn't know who or how, I couldn't relax. Now I can start rebuilding."

"Can you use any help?" June asked, smiling.

Hewett grinned. "I'll consider it."

The group broke up. Park promised transportation after breakfast. Taffy and Georgie Wane lingered behind. Georgie gave Taffy a quick look and then she smiled at Park, saying, "Here I am, wounded. Look, does a girl get a chance to stay here for a few days? Recuperation, we could call it, and it won't cost you. Only what I can eat."

Park looked expressionlessly at Taffy. "Why, I suppose that it would be—"

Taffy gave Georgie the warmest smile in her book. "Darling, Mr. Falkner intends to give you a little bonus to take care of that scraped knee and elbow. I really think it would be best for all concerned if you went with the others."

Georgie shrugged. "Sorry, boss. I didn't see any signs on him. 'Night, all."

Taffy shut the door firmly. She turned, her hands on her hips. "If you think for one minute I'd let you keep that—that female here after the others go . . ."

Park gave her a look of outraged innocence. "But you told me we were through!"

"Well, we aren't. Any arguments?"

He didn't give her an argument. He was too busy.

A Time for Dying

The swimming pool, under the moon, was like black ink in a white stone tray. Beyond the fringe of trees, blatant and gaudy, were the lights of Los Angeles, that painted lady of the Pacific.

Up on the night hill, by the pool, it was a time of silence, of quiet voices and a blessed peace. Jimmy Hake, that round and comical man of television, that owl-faced, elfin, blundering character in whom every man saw a part of his own image, reclined on the wheeled redwood chaise and watched the way the faint light from both the moon and the house windows made mysterious the features of his beloved.

Jimmy Hake needed all his acting talents to keep his voice and manner relaxed. Murder makes the breath short, makes the palms sweat, the voice tremble, the neck muscles bind.

Murder is something that had been two years a-growing. Murder is the answer to a question that couldn't otherwise be answered.

It was a Sunday night. Tomorrow the final rehearsal, and then the network program itself at eight, live because the network and the sponsor thought a live show would be a good hype, a good kickoff for the series. Jimmy Hake, presented live by the makers of Shynaline Products, the cosmetics that bring out the natural beauty of your skin. Available at all fine department stores. . . .

Going back to a series was a gamble, after two seasons of guest shots, talk shows with Merv and Johnny, one motion picture that grossed medium okay, three well-paid beer commercials. But his instinct told him this series would work. The character was perfect. The scripts were great. They had five good shows in the can, so they could follow up the live opener on the agreed weekly schedule.

Three people by Jimmy Hake's pool: Jimmy, Bob Morrit, his head writer—and Anna, wife of Bob. In the early part of the evening they had gone over the script for the last time. In the morning Bob would get the right number of copies made and then, at rehearsal, last-minute changes would be made in all copies.

Bob Morrit was saying, ". . . and we'll have the thing pinned down tightly enough so we can stay right in the same groove. Character established. Type of incident. Just switch the cast around from time to time."

Jimmy knew that Bob had been largely responsible for the program pattern that had made him a success. Sure, Bob was clever, but what did he know about how to make a million bucks the hard way? That start, thirty years ago, eighteen and already a baggy-pants specialist in the burlesque circuit. Coffee money for years and years. Small clubs. Rough. Rough all the way.

Then one day you hit the top and what have you got? Weariness that feels like you have putty instead of marrow in your bones. High blood pressure. Shortness of breath. Dyspnea, to be exact. Technically you are forty-eight, but you feel seventy-eight.

Oh, that jolly, jolly Jimmy Hake! That comic fellow!

You have everything except the one thing in the world that you want. Anna.

Funny, sort of. There were always lots of women. Eager to help you spend the bankroll. Laughing women. Tender women. Bitter women.

Not one like Anna.

He watched her. He had watched her for three years. A deep, strong, calm, incredibly beautiful woman. Safe harbor for the rest of his years. Straight and true. And loyal to Bob Morrit. Married to Bob Morrit. All bound up in Bob Morrit. And time for Jimmy Hake only as a friend. A good friend.

When Jimmy Hake remembered the times he had tried to

tell her how he felt about her, he flushed. She had handled him so easily. "Please, Jimmy."

Just that. A tone of voice. The tone of voice said two things. It said, "If you persist, I will go away." It also said, "You are nice." But Jimmy didn't feel nice.

Silver-blond hair and sea-gray eyes and a face that would be beautiful at sixty. That sort of a face. You could tell by the line of temple and jaw, the set of the eyes.

You get to the top and have everything you ever wanted. Except Anna. And the need for her makes everything else worthless, tasteless.

There is no way out. No answer. There can be no deviation in her loyalty—except if there is no longer anyone to whom she could be loyal.

And like the simplest equation written on a school blackboard, the answer becomes . . . murder.

In amusement parks there are small, silvery, streamlined boxes in which one sits and is strapped in. They hang at the end of a long bar. The silver cockpit goes around and around in a vertical circle. Jimmy Hake felt as though he had a very tiny such apparatus in his heart. It went around endlessly. Strapped in the seat, holding the crossbar in brittle fingers, sat a miniature skeleton. The shape of the skull was like that of lean, serious Bob Morrit.

During the two years that he had thought of murder, he had thought of many ways. Many methods. To murder and go free. Conviction would make the murder pointless.

At night Jimmy Hake would awaken, cold sweat oily on his body, his fists tightly clenehed. Then, in the silence of the night, he would think of Bob Morrit.

Not of Anna. Of Bob and of death.

Ten months before, without the faintest idea of how he would use it, he had acquired, in Rio, a small amount of curare. Vegetable-base poison. Instant paralysis of the lungs. A few words whispered to a ragged guide. A large bill. A small tin aspirin box pressed into his hand. Inside, a grayish sticky substance.

He knew there was no way it could be traced.

He realized that Bob had just asked him something.

208

"What was that?"

Bob laughed. "It is getting late. I was asking you if you didn't think this no-good wife of mine could be of more help in the programs."

"How?"

"He's got the idea," Anna said wryly, "that I ought to listen to the programs. Isn't listening to you two chew up the script enough?"

"You're a good girl," Bob said, "and we both love you, but you're no darn help to us. You don't even laugh any more at the script."

"I used to laugh to make you feel good."

"If you listened," Jimmy Hake said, "you could tell us what sounded flat to you. You are our most unforgiving public."

She sighed. "I always forget until after the program is over. Life is so full of a number of things. Besides, I hate the commercials and I hate the opening patter before you get into the meat of the script."

"Then tune in late," Bob said.

She yawned. "All right, you guys. Tomorrow at eight ten I will be your ardent listener. I will sit home and laugh like mad."

She stood up, clean and straight in the faint light. She said, "Bob, darling, you are such a collector of gadgets. Why don't you find a gadget that will get me home and into bed at night without any effort on my part."

"I'll look for one like that," he said.

As Jimmy Hake stood up, she said, "Jimmy, what a life I lead! In the car, lighted cigarettes pop out at you. In the apartment the windows open and shut at regular hours. Things go off and on. Civilization, they call it."

"It makes life easier," Bob said firmly.

Jimmy Hake was suddenly anxious for them to go. He was afraid of the conversation. He was afraid of the turn it might take. Because murder had already been consummated, at least as far as he was concerned.

But Morrit was standing there by the pool, talking, his arm around Anna's waist. And yet he was dead. It was queer. His life was over. Finished.

Anna would be broken up over it, of course. She would weep. But there would be the handy and familiar shoulder of Jimmy Hake on which to weep. Then it would be only fitting that the two people who were the closest to poor Bob should themselves be married. He would make her happy. Far happier than Bob had made her. Of that he was sure. And that was, in part, his rationalization.

He stood in the drive, and the headlights of Bob's car swept across him. He waved, shouted good night, and watched the taillights diminish and suddenly disappear as they rounded the curve.

Suddenly sweating, he hurried back to the bathhouse near the pool. He clicked on the inside lights and stood for a moment, conscious of the fact that these next few minutes might mean life or death.

It was the men's side of the bathhouse. The two shower stalls were on the left, the lockers on the right.

Bob Morrit had been in the shower when he had done it. He had been prepared. He had timed Bob in the shower a dozen times and found that four minutes was the minimum time he would have. While Bob had splashed and sung tonelessly, he had pulled open Bob's locker. Bob's favorite gadget, the trick Swiss silent alarm watch, was on the shelf. It was a clever thing, actually. It was a wristwatch. Once the alarm was set, a blunt brass plunger jabbed out of a small hole on the wrist surface of the watch at the proper time.

When it was new, Jimmy Hake had borrowed it once. It was remarkably effective. The pressure of the little plunger was sudden, strong, and startling.

With fumbling fingers he had set the alarm for the moment while Bob was in the shower. The little plunger clicked out. With a triangular file, he carefully and quickly sharpened the little plunger. Then he smeared the tip with the sticky gray curare, forced it back into the recess, and turned the alarm off.

Closing the locker door quietly, he had placed the file and the aspirin tin in the bottom of his own locker. When Bob came out of the shower a minute or so later, Jimmy Hake was out by the pool talking with the fair Anna.

All evidence had to be removed. Three items. The little tin

box, the file, and the minute brass filings. He had filed the brass while holding the watch inside his own locker. In the harsh light he saw the tiny yellow glints of brass.

Locating the tin box, he opened it and carefully brushed the filings into it, snapped it shut. He was sweating as he undressed, pulled on his swimming trunks. The servants would see nothing odd in a midnight swim.

The file and box clutched in his hand, he pulled himself under the water by means of the metal ladder at the corner of the pool. His groping fingers found the drain, unscrewed the mesh cover. He dropped the file and box down, replaced the cover.

With slow strokes he made two lengths of the pool, climbed out, and, incredibly weary, walked back to the bathhouse.

Bob Morrit walked about with death on his wrist. It was as though he wore a coral snake coiled there. Sooner or later, Bob would set the alarm to remind himself of an appointment. When the alarm went off, the blood would carry the poison to his brain and Bob would be dead a minute or two after he stopped being able to breathe.

And there would be no basis on which to try the famous Jimmy Hake. Opportunity, yes. Motive, no. Would a comedian kill his head writer? Of course not. And, of course, there was a good possibility that the cause of death wouldn't be diagnosed.

As he went up to his bedroom, he fully expected not to be able to sleep. He put water and sleeping tablets on his bedside table. But moments after his head touched the pillow, he dropped off into a sleep that was like death.

Last-minute script changes were made by Jimmy Hake. Because such changes were usually to fit the show into the schedule, there was no need for Bob to attend. He seldom did. When Jimmy Hake got to the studio just before rehearsal, he picked up the dozen copies that Bob had arranged for.

The rehearsal was like a program in a dream. Jimmy Hake could hear his own words without understanding what he was saying. It was hard to keep from looking at the doorway through which they would come to tell him Bob was dead. In his heart the little carnival toy went around and around, the body of Bob Morrit strapped to the infinitesimal seat.

The band music seemed much too loud, the voices of the supporting characters much too shrill. He wanted to hold his plump hands over his ears and run from the studio. But somehow he got through it. Some mechanical part of his mind ordered the script changes, made the pencil corrections on his copy. The program finished exactly sixty-five seconds before the allotted half hour. Sixty seconds for the closing commercial, and five more seconds for Jimmy Hake to sign off in his unforgettable manner.

Close of rehearsal allowed the cast a half hour to get coffee before returning to the studio to get set for the actual broadcast. Jimmy Hake had coffee downstairs with the guest star. He knew that he was making the right comments, smiling in the right places. But he didn't know how he was managing to do it so unconsciously.

At any moment he expected to get word that Bob Morrit was dead.

The elevator took them back up to the twelfth floor, and he walked with the guest star to the stage. He looked up and saw Bob Morrit standing, talking with the band leader. Somehow Jimmy Hake kept smiling, kept walking. Not dead yet. Not dead yet, but soon.

He forced himself to go over, grin at Bob and say, "Not many changes in the script, boy."

"Good. About ready to roll?"

"Just about." He glanced up at the big clock. The studio audience was hurrying in, struggling for seats. Jimmy Hake turned and gave them his famous smile, a wave of his hand.

He looked back just in time to see Bob Morrit pull up his cuff, glance at a bare wrist, and then grin. "Habit, thy name is Morrit."

Jimmy Hake's voice sounded hoarse. "Where—what happened to your watch?"

"That fine absentminded wife of mine. I set the alarm for ten after and strapped it on her so she wouldn't miss the show this time. Hey, you better get on the ball and start warming up the studio audience, Jimmy."

Jimmy Hake walked with leaden steps toward the front of the stage. A routine done so many times. Automatic. He did not know what he was saying. But he could hear their laughter, see their open mouths. The smile muscles of his cheeks were tight.

Everything was lost. Anna instead of Bob. Anna instead of Bob. Anna will die.

He looked back over his shoulder. Three minutes to eight. Thirteen minutes for Anna to live.

They gave him a signal. One minute to eight. Eleven minutes before Anna died. What could he do about it? Leave the studio? He couldn't get to Bob's apartment in fifteen minutes. How could he explain, even if he could get there in time?

". . . that man with no future, a sad past, and no presence— Jimmy Hake!"

He shook his head. The printed idiot boards wavered so he could not read them. On the air. On camera. Twenty million viewers.

He licked dry lips. Ad lib it, Jimmy. You can't read what it says and you can't remember.

"I'm trying to get up the courage to read the jokes my writers made up for me." They laughed. That was a good sign. He realized he was throwing the timing off. But still he couldn't read the words. He glanced over to the side. Bob's face was white. He was biting his lips. The rest of the cast had odd expressions.

Suddenly it was unbearable that Anna should die. She had eight minutes to live. No. Seven minutes.

He looked directly into the red-lighted camera. His voice was thin and tight. "A matter of life and death. To anyone in the Foster Apartments on Wilshire. Go to apartment Six-B right away and take a gold watch from the wrist of Mrs. Robert Morrit. A matter of life and death—"

His throat tightened up and no more words would come.

It had been the only answer. The only way to save Anna from death. They would have nothing on him. He could quit. Go away. Retire. Nobody would prosecute.

The studio seemed to swing around him as though he were standing in the center of a garish phonograph record.

Suddenly he was in a corridor. Bob Morrit had him by the lapels and was shaking him. Bob's lips were drawn back from his teeth and his eyes were wild.

"What were you trying to say, Hake? What is this all about? Answer me, you rubber-nose comic! You fat little fake! What about Anna?"

Jimmy Hake fought for self-control. He was alone with Bob for a moment. "I had to do it. I—fixed the watch so it would kill you. I wanted Anna. I'm—I'm quitting the business."

Bob slowly dropped his hands to his sides, and his eyes went dead. His voice was as dead as his eyes. "So you fixed everything up."

"Yes, Bob," Jimmy Hake said eagerly. "I must have been crazy. I—I couldn't let her die."

"Do you know what time it is?"

"No. Why?"

"It's twelve after eight, Jimmy. Twelve after."

Bob walked heavily away from him, turned, and said, "You better start running, Jimmy. You acted funny. As soon as you said Foster Apartments, the control booth took you off the air."

Jimmy Hake stood alone in the corridor.

His wide lips were still spread in the automatic, lovable smile that had made him famous.

Wearing the same smile, he walked toward the window at the end of the corridor.

He walked with the comic, jerky little shuffle he had learned thirty years before.

Noose for a Tigress

The gooks were coming through the rice. I could see it moving, and there was no wind. I cursed Beldan, out at point, and I couldn't move. A heavy automatic weapon started a slow cadence. *Chaw-pah, chaw-pah, chaw-pah!*

I did the only thing I could do: I woke up, slick with sweat. Panting. The automatic weapon was the beat of steel wheels on the rail joints. Beldan was long dead. Maybe I was dead too. A bedroom, they called it. A moving coffin on wheels. Aluminum and stainless steel, boring a roaring hole in the afternoon.

I looked out. Flatland, a lot of horizon. A gray, baked ranch moved by in forgotten grandeur. I lay there, feeling rested in spite of the violent end of my nap, and scratched my naked chest while I conjured up a vision of bourbon in the lounge car. Taller than tall. Colder than cold.

I washed my face in my private little sink, put on some of the nice new San Francisco civilian clothes, and admired myself. Oh, you hollow-eyed veteran, you! Same face that I'd taken to Nam. Smug and bland. I looked like a prosperous young account executive from a New York agency. Which I had been, they tell me. But it didn't seem right that I should look like that now.

Funny thing. The Marines get stuffy about whether or not you have toes. They said, "Captain Pell, you have lost your toes in the service of your country. You are obviously no good any more. No toes. Goodbye, and muchisimas gracias."

The shoes were tricky. When you walk, your toes bend and

215

give you a little spring. When you don't have toes, they put the spring in the shoe. A steel one. So I went springing down to the lounge car, bourbon-minded.

Marj, my ex-wife, was sitting on the left as I entered. Hanneman, her dignified beefy lawyer, sat cozily beside her.

Marj opened her sweet, moist, musky lips. "You dirty stinking welcher," she said melodiously.

I smiled. "Enjoying the choo-choo ride?"

Hanneman smiled stiffly. "Sit down, please," he said. "I'm still sure we can make some arrangement."

He'd been saying that ever since we all got on the train. I sat down and waited. You know. Eager expression. Avid. Boy listening to smart gentleman.

"You can't talk to that," Marj said to him.

"Please, my dear," he said, patting her hand. "Please."

So I said, "Gosh, Mr. Hanneman, I don't know why she's so sore. I'm the one who should be sore. She tricked me into standing still for the divorce, and then she nibbled the judge into giving her fifty percent of all my future earnings. Now she's mad because I went off fighting the Communists and all she could collect was half my base pay."

"You dirty stinking welcher," Marj said, wetting her slightly redundant lip line.

"See?" I said. "See, Mr. Hanneman? Now she's sore because I'm not going back to work. She wants me in there knocking off my seventy-five thousand like before. She's like a fight manager, trying to put a poor tired pug back in the ring. I'm a crippled veteran. They're giving me a very small amount of disability money for the rest of my life. That isn't earnings, so she can't have half of it. With what I've saved, I'm going to build a shack in the tropics and lie on my back for the rest of my life. Can't a man retire, Mr. Hanneman?"

He looked at me as though he smelled something bad.

"Mr. Pell, Mrs. Pell considers your offer to be unsatisfactory."

I had offered ten thousand cash for a cancellation of the alimony agreement. This was a poker game we were playing. They were bucking aces backed.

"What does she want?"

"We feel certain you could manage to scrape up thirty thousand, Mr. Pell."

I yawned. I made it a nice big juicy yawn. "I guess it's ten thousand or nothing. I'm retiring. No more work for Simon Pell."

Marj worked her fingernails like a cat. "If I take the ten, you'll go right back to your job, damn you!"

"And if you don't take it, I'm through working. Why should I work just so you can get half? You were a dope. You should have taken a property settlement instead of that silly fifty-percent business, Marj. You're over a barrel and you know it."

"We can't force him to work, Marjorie," Charles Hanneman said.

Marj switched tactics. She leaned across Hanneman's beefy thighs and laid her moist eyes and cream of raspberry lips against my little gray soul. "You're making things so dreadfully difficult, Sim, darling."

"Gosh," I said, "I thought you were having fun. A nice train ride like this. You and the majestic Mr. Hanneman. It gives you such a cozy excuse, you know."

She chopped to my face with those claws. I got a coat sleeve in the way, and she broke one nail back to the quick.

Charles Hanneman said floridly, "I don't care for those implications, Pell."

I swallowed the remains of the bourbon and waved for more. I said, "And you, sir, should smarten up. Missy, here, is a playmate for men, not boys. She walks in an aura of dangling scalps. She's a gun-notcher. She's a pelt-stretcher. Why don't you trot home to the wife and kiddies, Mr. Hanneman? Your wife probably senses the phoniness of your excuse for this trip anyway."

He rose to his full height, towering red-faced. He clenched his fists. "Stand up, sir!"

I smiled at him. He made the mistake of reaching with both hands for my new lapels. I put a hoof in his midriff and snapped my knee straight. The Hanneman bulk moved backward toward the waiter bringing my drink. In the narrow space, the waiter did a pass with the tray that would have pleased a matador.

He watched Hanneman bounce off the doorframe and land on hands and knees on the rug. Then he served my drink with a special flourish and a white-toothed grin.

Hanneman grunted and stood up and clamped both hands over his kidneys. He wore the expression of someone listening for something. It had happened so quickly that the other people in the lounge car looked at the poor man who had tripped and fallen. Up the line, a perfect hood type in a sharp suit with the face of a depraved weasel watched alertly. Too alertly. As though he knew too much of the score.

Hanneman crouched behind a facade of upright dignity. "I shall not stoop to your level, Pell," he said. He turned and strode off.

Marj stood up. She wears clothes that pretty up the merchandise, though the merchandise is such that it would make a flour sack blush. She gave a flaunt and twitch of her hips that melted ice in the drinks all down the line.

"You dirty little monster," she said in that musical sand-throated gargle.

She tilted off on her mission of mercy to soothe the back-wrenched ego. I glanced up the lounge. The hood type's nose was back in his scratch sheet. Up the line was an empty seat by a cornflower blonde. The petaled eyes drifted across my face with a sensation like butterfly wings. She looked like the kind who wants to talk baby talk and is smart enough not to.

I trotted up and sat beside her. She smelled the grandma's garden.

I breathed deeply and said, "Hah!"

The blue eyes were sly. "What's with the 'Hah'?"

"It's a substitute. I get tired of an opening wedge about weather, or how slow the trains are, or do you live in California. Hence the Hah."

"Hah to you too. Now where are we?"

"Launched on my favorite hobby. Hacking at attractive females."

"Hack away, MacDuff. You'll just dull your little hatchet. The girl is armor-plated. I'll angle you for a free dinner and then pat you on the head. I never get tight and I'm not im-

218

pulsive, and I've got four brothers, every one of them over six feet."

"Round one coming up. I just got back from Nam. I haven't talked with a girl like you for many long months. My name is Simon Pell."

"I just got back from Hawaii, and you've *never* talked to a girl like me, and my name is Skipper Moran. End of round one."

"You must have read Thurber. The war between the sexes."

"Nope. Just another Sweet Briar graduate. Fencing Three is a compulsory course."

Then we laughed and began to get on well. So I drank two more than enough; and then we ate, and then we drank some more; and then, as promised, she patted me on the head and went off to bed, leaving my tentative kiss planted firmly in midair.

I trudged back to my little bedroom, whupped for the nonce. Marj was waiting outside my door. "Please may I come in, Sim? I have to talk to you."

Her underlip was out like a candy shelf and her eyes looked like a stoked furnace.

I opened the door and waved her in. Courtly. Controlled. She had changed clothes. Where do they get that line about a "simple print dress"? Maybe the print was simple, but the dress was pretty complex. It had to be complex. It had a job to do. It had to fit like the hide of a speckled trout, play give-and-take with varied sinuosities, and still manage to make the package look like a lady.

She sat on the little padded shelf seat that folds down out of the wall beside the closed door. I sat on the unmade bed. She looked at me until smoke drifted out of my ears.

"We had something, Sim. Where did we lose it? How did we lose it?"

"Our pockets were picked, maybe?"

"Be serious, Sim. I'm serious. I'm dreadfully serious. You stopped loving me, Sim."

"I've always hated crowds, honey. I got out when it started to look as if I was going to have to stand in line."

"Don't be cruel, Sim. Don't throw that up to me. I'm weak.

I know I'm weak. I don't know how I could have done that to you."

"You're weak like the Kremlin."

"I know why you say such dreadful things to me, Sim," she said softly. "It's because I hurt you so dreadfully. You're striking back."

I smiled at her. "When they flew me to Japan, there was a nurse there. A little bitty thing with a face like a hopfrog and a figure like a milepost. She smelled of anesthetic and walked so heavy she kept shaking the bed. I would rather spend five minutes with her than ten lifetimes with you, darling."

She shut her eyes and her lips went taut. I guessed she was mentally counting to ten. She got it under control and stood up dramatically, spreading wide her arms. The simple little print cooperated nicely. She said, "Do I mean nothing to you, Sim?"

She moved closer to me, she and her perfume. I knew her, knew exactly how she looked in shadow or sunlight or under a two-hundred-watt bulb.

"Aren't you getting a little hippy, Marj?" I asked her solemnly.

She pivoted and tried to spoon out my right eye with her thumbnail. I stood up and hammered her twice with the heel of my hand. Her eyes went blank and her knees wobbled. She sat down hard. Panting. And then she started to cry.

"Okay," I said. "Now that we've had our little drama, get to the point."

She looked at me. Now she was herself. Chrome steel and broken glass. "I've got to have money. Quickly."

"How much and what for?"

"Thirty thousand dollars. I pay it or go to prison. I did something silly."

"What did you do?"

"I met a man. I thought he was nice. He sent me to Juarez, and a Mexican gave me a package to bring back. He wouldn't give it to me until I signed a receipt. I took the package back to the man, and he gave me five thousand dollars. They picked him up twenty minutes later.

"A month ago another man contacted me. He has the receipt

I signed. He wants thirty thousand dollars for it. If I don't give him the money, he'll turn it over to the authorities and put them on me. I didn't sign my right name. But the handwriting is mine, and the cops have my description. I told him he had to wait until you came back, when I could get the money from you."

"What was in the package?"

"I don't know."

"Don't try to kid me, Marj."

"All right. It was heroin."

"And you knew it in advance, before you went after the package."

"No, I didn't.'

"Keep lying, baby, and I won't even give you the right time."

"All right—so I knew what it was! But it meant five thousand dollars. That stinking allotment from you didn't even buy cigarettes."

"Anybody that gets messed up in a filthy business like that deserves to go to prison, Marj."

She started to cry again. She covered her face and sobbed incoherently. "Work in prison laundry . . . starchy foods . . . come out when I'm an old woman. . . ."

"Where does Hanneman fit?"

"He's nothing. He's just on the string. I can brush him any time." She said it calmly, the tears gone.

"Why do you expect me to give you the money?"

"Because it is all your fault, Sim. If you hadn't gone running off like a fool, I would have had enough money so I wouldn't have gotten in a jam. Now you've got to get me out of it. You've got to!"

I pitied her. It wasn't her fault she had been born this way. Marj grew up without the very essential knowledge of what is right and what is wrong.

"How much time have you got?"

"A week from today. He won't give me any more time."

"What am I supposed to get out of it?"

"I'll do anything you want me to do. Anything, Sim."

"There's nothing you can do for me, Marj. When you cured

221

me, you cured me for good. I really loved you. Seems funny as hell, now."

"I wish I were back with you, Sim."

"My friends miss you too."

"Now you're being cruel again. Please don't be cruel, Sim. Give me the money. You have it. I know you have it."

I sat and thought of all the times she had lied to me, her eyes bland and sweet and her mouth like an angel's. Turnabout was fair play.

"I guess I've been kidding you along, Marj," I said. "When I was ordered to active duty I liquidated my securities and put the whole works into irrevocable annuities. I couldn't touch it if I wanted to."

She looked at me. I saw her face change. First, incredulity. Then horrified belief. Then a fear that ripped through her like a rusty bayonet.

She stood up and reached blindly for the door. I said, "Let me know if they give you enough cigarettes while you're doing time. I can afford that for old time's sake."

Marj went out and shut the door softly behind her. I looked at the door a long time. You think of some way to take revenge, and then you get your chance, and it leaves an evil taste in your mouth. I'd been a patsy for her, and now the situation was reversed. The saddle was strapped to her back now. And I had sharp spurs. Let her tremble. Let her eat dirt. Let her come out of the pokey with all the hopes and juices and muscled sheen dried up forever.

Serves her right, I said. But I knew that I couldn't do it. I knew I was going to give her the money. Kiss it goodbye. I don't know why I thought I owed her anything. On the other hand, maybe it was a good deal. In one year I'd make it back, once I got out from under that fifty-percent agreement.

Anyway, I could let her sweat it out until we arrived in New York. That would be time enough. I undressed and turned out the light and shoved the shade up. Starlight was bright, and I lay in the rattle-sway of the train, cradled in the night roar of wind and steel wheels. I like trains. I had told her I wouldn't talk to her anywhere else.

* * *

I fumbled up out of sleep and snarled at the door. I wrapped myself in the sheet and, without turning the light back on, pushed the latch over. She came in with the recognizable perfume floating around her and shoved something toward me. "Take this, Sim."

When awakening, I'm not at my best. I'm dull. I've got a reaction time like somebody in a morgue drawer. So I took it. It was sticky.

She shut the door with herself on the inside. I clamped the sheet with my arm, got the light on, and stared stupidly at what I was holding: a big fat switch knife with a six-inch blade. A blade that looked as though it had spent all day on the farm, butchering pigs.

I opened my hand. The knife fell out. I looked stupidly at the blood on my hand. And then I looked at Marj. She was the color of a skid-row handkerchief. Her eyes were holes in the side of the world, leading nowhere. She wore a blue something-or-other hung over her shoulders. Underneath the blue was black. Black lace and shiny black satin. She had blood on her hand, too. She was breathing fast and hard, putting considerable strain on the black lace.

I looked at the knife and then at her. "Who the hell did you kill?"

Her words were like moths trying to get out of a lampshade. "I didn't kill anybody. Charles was in my compartment. I went down to the women's room. When I came back, he was dead. I've got to get him out of there!"

"Complain to the conductor."

"Hell with you, Sim. Now you're in it too. You help me, or I say you came in and stabbed him. Jealous. Ex-husband. I'll swear it on the stand, on a million Bibles. I'll never change my story."

"Who did it?"

"I don't know who did it. Or why. I just know he's there and he's too heavy to lift."

"So you came and gave me the knife. How sweet of you, darling!"

"I couldn't take a chance on your saying no, Sim. Get him back in his place. Then we can put the knife back in him and get the blood off us."

"Otherwise?"

"They'll try to hang it on me, Sim. And I'll tell them I saw you do it."

It was nice and tight. A comfy fit. It was like a size fifteen collar on a size sixteen neck. A rope collar.

"You're in the next car, aren't you? Anybody see you come in here?"

There was triumph in her eyes. "I knew you'd help me. Nobody saw me."

She scouted the corridor while I pulled on pants and a shirt and shoved my feet into the trick shoes. I wished very much that I hadn't socked him in view of the whole lounge car. We went to her compartment in the far end of the next car toward the engine.

Charles Hanneman was exceedingly dead. He knelt beside the bed, chest and face flat against it, hands all tangled up in the blankets. The hole, like a wet coin slot, was on the left side of his back, just below the shoulder blade. Blood had run down his white shirt into the waistband of his trousers. Not much blood. I had recently seen some very messy bodies. This one had all its parts and did not bother me. And it didn't seem to bother Marj.

"I'd hate to think you did this, Marj," I said.

"I didn't, if that makes any difference to you."

"Where's his place?"

"The second bedroom down the aisle."

Hanneman's suit coat was there. I worked his putty arms into the sleeves, rolled him onto his back onto the floor, and buttoned the coat in front.

"How do you want to do this?" she asked.

"I can manage him alone. Take a quick look and see if his bedroom is okay. Then come back and make like a guide."

I pulled him into a sitting position, then hoisted him up onto the edge of the bed and held him so he wouldn't topple over. His fat flesh jounced peacefully in the vibration of the train.

She came back and nodded. I pulled his arms over my

shoulders, held his wrists down in front of me. Then I stood up, leaning forward like a man carrying a trunk.

I staggered like a nine-day drunk. I was carrying the horrid results of too much pastry and too many mashed potatoes. The motion of the train didn't help a bit. By the time I rolled him off onto his own bed, my eyes were out on the end of stalks and I was puffing like an also-ran at Santa Anita.

She tried to hand me the knife.

"Uh-uh," I said. "You take that into the women's room, and if you're real bright you'll find some way to drop it out onto the tracks."

Hanneman's wallet had fallen out of his pants pocket. Marj sat on her heels on the floor and opened it. She looked at the sheaf of Uncle Sugar's IOUs and her eyes shone like a bride's.

"This will make it look like robbery," she said.

"Odd, isn't it? Let me see the wallet."

She gave it to me, without currency. The card case was quite full. It was very interesting. Charles Hanneman, Attorney at Law. And some others, equally crisp, equally new. C. Arthur Hineman, M.D.; Charles A. Hand, Bursar, Powelton College; C. Andrew Hanson, Broker.

"What do you know!" I whispered.

"What's that? What's so interesting?" she said, breathing down my neck.

"Never you mind. Pop will take care of this."

She used the blue thing to wipe the door, inside and outside. The coast was clear and we parted. I disposed of the wallet and cards in the manner I had suggested to her. I went back and sat on my bed and thought about obese, florid confidence men.

When she tapped on my door, I let her in without turning on the light. She came into my arms, trembling and whimpering. I held her and made comforting sounds. Pore little girl. Pore tired little girl. She was nice to hold. Her lips came up tentatively, then enthusiastically. I broke the clinch with the heel of my hand against her pretty chin. She blundered around in the little bedroom, grumbling and kicking anything handy, and then left in a tizzy.

As soon as she had gone, I put the light on and started

225

hunting. It didn't take long. It was under the bed where she'd tossed it, covering the sound with her pretended anger. I reached under and pulled the knife out and presently sent it to join the wallet.

Skipper Moran gave me a pretty smile that meant, Join me for breakfast. She said aloud, "Does your little head still burn where I patted it, Simon?"

"Burned all night. Throbbed like a toothache. All I could do was lie there and pant."

"You lie as good as you pant, Mr. Pell."

"We're in Chicago in another hour or so. Are you going all the way through to New York? Can we get on the same train?"

She smiled. "Poor throbbing boy." I made another inventory of the face. Sweet stubborn chin. Flower-petal eyes. "Why are you staring?"

"It's just pleasant to look at a woman with a certain amount of decency in her face. You've a good face, Skipper. It has been around, and it has gotten wisdom instead of toughness."

She looked at me oddly. "That's quite nice. That you should think so. Trying to disarm me, Simon?"

"That's a splendid idea."

She grinned. "You're too soon out of the hospital for the big leagues, rookie."

Something was wrong. I didn't catch on until the second strip of bacon. "I didn't mention any hospital, Skipper. I mentioned Vietnam, nothing more. What kind of spy are you?"

She looked upset. Prettily confused. "You must have said something about it, Simon."

"I was careful not to, Skipper. A sympathy pitch is not my style. And another thing. That empty chair in the lounge car was almost too opportune. There are never empty chairs by lovely blondes. And I did get the eye. Oh, very subtly, but I got it."

She laughed. A good try, only faintly strained. "Oh, Simon! You've got to stop reading novels. I'm a gal on a train. I'm heading for New York."

A neat brisk young man with a neat, close shave and an eye like the accounts receivable ledger came down the diner, looked through me, and put his lips practically against my gal's little pink bunny ear.

She had been looking at me. She started looking through me. She got up, remembered her manners, gave me a smile about three millimeters long, and departed.

When I had gotten tired of toying with my third cup of coffee and half decided it was time to pack, she came back. She sat down and ordered coffee.

She balanced me on the razor's edge of her eyes and said, "Your ex-wife's friend was knifed during the night. Know anything about it?"

"I never knew Dick Tracy was such a master of disguise."

"Don't clown, Simon. I'm talking off the record and out of order and against instructions. So don't clown. What do you know about it?"

I forked a groove in the tablecloth and admired it for a moment. I heard her coffee being brought. I heard her tear the paper off the sugar.

"My ex enlisted me last night. The corpus undelectable was in her boudoir. It was either pull an assist or try to talk myself out of an eyewitness report. So I moved junior back to his own room."

"You just made a very intelligent decision, Mr. Pell."

"Moving the body, or telling you?"

"Moving the body was almost unforgivably stupid. I suppose you told her you wouldn't give her the money."

"If I kept a diary, I'd swear you'd been peeking."

"Why do you feel such a compulsion to be flip?"

"Counter question. Who are you?"

"A working girl. Working."

"You don't know what a shock this is to me. I thought it was my good looks and sparkling personality that intrigued you."

"When, as a matter of fact, it was the criminal tendencies of your ex-wife. Marjorie has been a cooperative little morsel, Mr. Pell. Without knowing it, of course. We've had the net over her ever since Juarez, hoping for leads."

"Hmmmm. A junior G girl."

"No. A clerk-stenographer CAF-ten filling in because our

little club is a bit shorthanded. The man who came and spoke to me is phoning ahead. I'm afraid we're going to have to take her into custody now."

"Do you think she killed Hanneman?"

"Oh, no. Hanneman was hired to ride herd on her and protect the investment. She must have told him you turned her down. My guess is that he tried to tell the others and they thought he was pulling a fast one. The knife work is typical of—some others we've found."

"Hanneman had her convinced that he was a trustworthy legal eagle."

She smiled sweetly. "No one is as gullible as a cheap crook, Simon."

"Then you can just pick up the guy who did it, eh? No fuss. No problem."

She snapped her fingers. "Sure. Just like that. All we've got to do is pick him or her out of a hundred and ninety-three passengers."

"Maybe I've spotted him for you. The slick-looking punk in the sharp suit in the lounge car."

"Mr. Delehanty is one of us, Simon. Sorry."

"Nice guess, Pell. Try again. Some sweet little old lady, maybe?"

"I said others. We know of one of them. And we also know he didn't have the opportunity to kill Hanneman. So there are two of them. That was our tip. Two aboard. Plus Hanneman and Mrs. Pell. These people are canny. They don't contact each other. Not where it can be observed."

I frowned. It didn't seem to fit just right. "Look, maybe I'm stupid. But I thought, according to the comic books I read, that there was big dough in this importing dope for the twitch and glitter trade. So why the uproar over a lousy thirty thousand?"

"Thirty thousand, plus a willing tool, Simon. First they'd take the thirty thousand, and then they'd show her one of the photostats of that receipt she signed. And then they'd send her down to join the Mexican end of the organization. They have a spot all planned for her, we think. Using her obvious charms on gullible tourists to get them to take stuff across the border. She would do it well."

"And enjoy the work," I said flatly.

"She did hurt you, didn't she?"

"A long time ago, Skipper. Just the scar itches sometimes." I frowned again. "Say, don't they organize the smuggling better than that?"

"My dear Mr. Pell. The very best man you can get is some banker from Toledo with shining face, balding head, and sterling reputation."

"Marj could collect that type like postage stamps."

"She's still got a little too much spirit for them. They planned to break her down, flatten her out good, and then put her to work after they had taken her for as much money as they could get."

"Lovely people."

"I've seen what they've done. I've seen fifteen-year-old children who open their wrists with a pin and use an eyedropper to squirt in the dreams. I hate the peddlers, Simon. I hate their guts!"

"Look. I better pack. Not much time left."

"You'll have plenty of time, Simon. Everybody on this train is going to have a long personal interview and show credentials. All of them are going to be hopping mad except one. And he's going to be scared and desperate."

They ran the Amtrak train over onto a siding that hadn't been used since Casey Jones took his header. It was in a wilderness of tracks, out near a jungle of derelict boxcars and rusting steam locomotives. Chicago came equipped with its usual strong wind. The train stopped and the men were already spotted. Spaced out. A perimeter guard with shotguns and riot guns through the crooks of their arms. Neat young men who leaned against the wind while their topcoats flapped.

A puffy little man with protruding glass-blue eyes collared me in the aisle. "Friend, this is an outrage," he wheezed.

"What's the trouble?"

"Haven't you heard? Look where we are. Out in the middle

229

of nowhere! Some bum was knifed on the train. Busybody cops have taken over one of the cars up front. We got to go up there, one at a time, and let them question us. Me, I got a meeting to go to."

The little man stamped on down the aisle, grunting and wheezing with indignation.

An official came through. "Kindly remain in your own car until called."

I looked out my window for a while. They were handling it pretty well. Every few minutes one person or a couple would head across the tracks, windblown Elizas crossing the ice, heading toward civilization.

I wondered about Marj and decided to pay a little social call. I went into her car and tapped on her door.

"Yes?" a stentorian female voice said.

I pushed the door open. An iron-gray slab-faced matron with eyes like roller bearings stared at me. She had three parallel scratches down her cheek. Marj sat on the bed. I forgot about the planted knife, about her greedy amorality. She was a child who now stood outside life's candy store, nose flattened wistfully against the glass, looking in at the goodies she could no longer afford.

They'd put handcuffs on her. The sleeve of her dress was ripped and her cheek was puffed, turning blue. She looked at me and said in a soft voice, "Thanks so much, Sim. Thanks for turning me in."

There was no hope of explaining to her. She had gone too far away. She wouldn't hear anything I said.

"Out," the matron said.

Out I went, feeling exactly as though, hat in hand, I had tiptoed into sickly flower scent to view a waxen face on the casket pillow. I felt soul-sick and emptied.

As I walked back, I told myself I was a big boy now. I shaved and everything. I'd even snuck up on a gook tunnel and dropped a present inside that went boom. So this was just a tramp I happened to marry once. Lots of people marry tramps. Lots of tramps marry people. The silken wench was no longer a part of my life. It would be easy to forget her. Just as easy as leaving your head in the hatbox along with your hat.

I went into the men's room and sat on the leather bench and exchanged cool stares with a salesman type inhabiting same bench, lipping an evil cigar butt.

"Hell of a note," he said.

"Yeah," said I.

He got up and slapped himself vigorously in the belly, belched largely, and left, dropping the butt into a shallow spittoon, where it hissed softly like a dying balloon.

I got up and aimlessly tried the john door. Locked, of course. I had me a drink of ice water. I wondered if the lounge car was in a fluid state. I wandered back toward it.

A conductor in a dark blue shiny suit said, "Stay in your own car, mister." He had bright red cheeks and frosty blue eyes and a shelf of yellow teeth that pushed his upper lip out of the way.

"Got the time?" I asked him.

He looked at his wristwatch. "Nearly eleven, mister."

I clumped back to the men's room. I stood and looked out the top of the window, the unglazed part. The staunch young men were still leaning against the wind. I wondered how they'd work out as replacements in Vietnam. Replacements are so shocked at having the countryside loaded with eager little brown men who desire earnestly to shoot them dead that they obligingly freeze and get shot. The ones who scramble fast enough to avoid this unhappy fate six or seven times thus become what the newspapers call "combat-hardened veterans."

The unobliging conductor appeared from somewhere on my right, spoke to one of the young law enforcers, and plodded across the tracks toward the distant station, shiny shoulders hunched against the fingers of the wind.

In due course they got to me. They said, "Okay, Pell. Sit over there." I sat. They were thorough with the ones who came after me. Name, occupation, residence, identification, any personal letters, please. Reason for the trip. All recorded neatly.

A hefty man with a tombstone face who seemed to be in charge said, with considerable satisfaction, "Okay. That's one ninety-two. He's on the train, boys. Go get him, and be careful."

Skipper moved over and sat across from me. "He was afraid to try to bluff his way through. We've got him now, Simon."

It took thirty minutes. The boys came back. They looked as if the old farmer had just rock-salted them out of the orchard.

"He's gone, chief."

Tomb-face stood up. "Gone! How?"

"Maybe he dropped off the train before it got here, chief."

"Impossible! You know that as well as I do. Did you look everywhere?"

"Even the ladies' rooms," the thinnest one said with a pretty blush. "One part of them is locked, of course. The train people locked them as we were coming in."

"Maybe he picked the lock on one of them. Where's that conductor? Get his keys."

"He went over to the station. He'll be back."

"Get keys someplace, dammit!"

"Yes sir, chief."

Skipper said, "If they don't find him that way, the only answer is that he brought his invisible coat along." She tried to smile, but there wasn't much heart in it. "We wanted to get this one. Our tipster told us he was very high in the organization."

I stared at her. I said, too loudly, "He did bring his invisible coat, honey."

Tomb-face glared at me. "Shut up, you."

I looked at him steadily. "Friend, maybe you've gotten too accustomed to talking to the lower classes. You use that tone of voice on me again, and I'll slap a little courtesy into you."

"When we want suggestions, Pell, we'll—"

"Ask me, because I happen to have one. Something has been nibbling away at the back of my mind. Now I know what it is. If you want to hear it, suppose you tell me that you'll take it as easy as you can on Mrs. Pell."

"That isn't my decision to make, Pell."

"Then kindly go to hell. Every minute you stall, your friend is getting further away from here."

That got him. He probably had superiors riding him. He licked his lips and looked almost human.

"I'll see what I can do," he said uneasily.

"Okay. Did you ever ask a conductor what time it is? He pulls out a big gold turnip and tells you it is three and a half minutes to eleven. I ask a conductor the time. He looked at a wristwatch and said it was almost eleven. And then I saw him walk right through your cute little cordon out there. Who looks twice at a conductor's face? I can even tell you where the real conductor is. Knocked out, or dead, and locked in one of the johns with his own keys."

"I don't suppose you'd know what he looked like?" Tomb-face asked, but gently this time.

"I've got a vague idea. Five nine or ten. Hundred and sixty pounds. Gray hair, possibly bald on top. Bright red cheeks, high cheekbones, very cold little blue eyes. Big yellow teeth that stick out, making him look like Barney the Beaver. A lot of black hair on the backs of his hands. A gold ring, I think. Deep voice. Some holes in the side of his neck where he'd been lanced once upon a time. The right side of the neck."

"I didn't see him on the trip," Skipper said.

"You'll probably find a porter that brought his meals to his compartment or bedroom."

Tomb-face roared out of the car and lit running, bellowing, waving his arms.

"You surprise me, Simon," Skipper said. "That was a nice job of identification."

"It doesn't surprise me as much as it would have a year ago. I've just had a lot of training in observation, Skipper."

They found the conductor with a mild concussion. He had opened a john door and a citizen had yanked him in by the front of his conductor suit and thumped his head against the wall. In there with the conductor was a nice gray expensive suit with the pockets emptied and the label ripped out of it. In a bedroom they found a brown bag, topcoat, felt hat. The hat had been purchased in Los Angeles, the bag in Seattle, and the laundry marks on the shirts were traced to a San Francisco hotel.

Skipper kept me informed. I had to remain in Chicago. I was the guy who could make a positive identification, when and if they picked up our boy. Evidently Barney the Beaver had walked through the station and into a bottomless pit. The man they had been able to grab on the train was small fry, and he was not inclined to be talkative.

Yes, Skipper kept me informed. She let me hold her hand in the movies. The petaled eyes stared at me over the rims of cocktail glasses. Her stride was long beside me as we walked dark streets. She let me kiss her, and, unlike Marj, it wasn't a tigress reaction. It was more like a kitten when you start to cuddle and then it takes a surprisingly sharp slash at you. We traded life histories, exchanged likes and dislikes, discovered a song that was "our song," and all the rest of it. You can't dress it up. It is common, ordinary, everyday falling in love. To the people involved it feels like it had never happened before to anyone in just that way.

Marj's charms had been startlingly self-evident. But Skipper had a knack of creeping up on you. She would happen, by accident, to turn just so or stand in a certain way, and *whoomp*!— there would be a line so breathtakingly lovely, so full of a soft and lingering promise, that it could make a bill collector weep.

Over 3 A.M. coffee in a bean wagon, I told her she better marry me. She was lifting her cup and it stopped in midair, wavered, and floated back down to the saucer. Her lips were the shape of your first game of post office.

"This is so sudden. Give me time to think it over. . . . Okay, I've thought it over. Yes, Simon."

The ham-handed counterman propped his chin on his fists and looked dreamy. "So lovely," he purred. "Such a beautiful emotion, love."

Coffee was on the house. Wedding present number one.

For three days I went around patting children on the head. Some of the hard-bitten Chicago tykes spat through a curled lip and said, "Go pat ya own head, ya creep."

My phone rang beside my hotel bed in the middle of the night. "Simon, darling. I'm down in the lobby."

"Check in with the house dick and come up."

I had time to ice-water my face and belt myself into a robe and jam the ugly toeless foot stubs into the trick shoes before she came through the door I had opened for her.

I kissed her. "Aha! You are now in my powah, fair maid," I said.

234

She didn't smile. "Simon, I had to come and tell you this. I had to be the one to tell you. Dear Simon. I've been so jealous of her, of what she had of you and what she took away from you. Now I'm so ashamed."

I stared at her, at tears she ignored. "You talking about Marj?"

"Get yourself a drink, Simon, and sit down."

I obeyed orders. I slugged myself with a dollop of bourbon. I had the feeling I wasn't going to like this.

I didn't like it at all. Mrs. Pell, in the middle of the night, had taken her baggy gray prison dress and had ripped it into strips, woven the strips into a makeshift rope, fashioned a slipknot. Then she had soaked the rope so that the knot would slide tight. There being nothing in the cell she could hang herself to, she had merely put the noose around her neck, tied the free end to a bar of the cell door, then thrown herself backward. Apparently she had tried to change her mind later. She had clawed and torn her throat in the area of the wet knot, but it had buried itself too deeply.

I got up and walked to the windows, looking out, seeing nothing. I was remembering things. The position in which she always slept. Curled up, childish, seemingly innocent. Her passion for lizard shoes. Sound of her laughter. Her warm lips.

Though I had thought myself cured of her, some part of me died while I stood and looked out the windows at the sleeping city.

Incongruously, I remembered two marine sergeants who had hated each other with bloody fervor. Twice they had gone after each other with knives. No name was too foul to call the other. Fate had trapped them in the same outfit and kept them there. And then I had seen one of them by a swing bridge over a jungle river, crying like a child, vocalizing his sobs, staring at the mortar-smashed body of the other.

Skipper came up to me and put her hand on my shoulder. "Do you want me to stay for a while, Simon?"

"No, thanks. I'll be okay in the morning. Thanks for telling me right away, Skip."

"I love you, Simon. Remember that."

235

"You're my girl. That woman was a stranger. Someone I happened to know once upon a time."

I smiled at her, but I guess the smile wasn't too convincing. Maybe the ache and sense of loss was showing. Her tears had stopped and her smile was measured, precise, careful.

"Good night, Simon."

I walked her to the door and opened it. Barney the Beaver slid in, kicked the door shut, and slid along the wall. His gun was aimed in exactly the right place to keep me from moving—right where Skipper's high round hip curved into her slender waist.

"You're the bright boy," he said huskily.

"You're looking a little shopworn," I said. "Lost weight, haven't you? Where have you been hiding? In the zoo with the rest of the beavers?"

"Pick the girl up. Go on. Pick her up."

I did so. One arm under her knees, one arm under her shoulders, my left hand under her armpit where I could feel, against my fingers, the delicate rib cage, the hard *ka-thud* of her heart. It was a cute idea. She couldn't do anything and neither could I. Unless I wanted to rush him, using her as a shield.

"What are the plans?" I said.

"With you gone, Pell, they haven't got anything that will stand up in court. They can inconvenience the hell out of me, but they can't prove anything for keeps."

"Sounds logical. Gets you out of one jam and into another."

It is distinctly a lot of Shinola about guys fresh from combat sneering at a feeble little thing like a Police Positive with a two-inch barrel. I did not feel confident that I could catch those slugs in my teeth and spit them back at him. I felt that they would make large holes in me and those holes would hurt like hell, and I wanted no part of them.

His face was more yellow than I remembered it. He still looked, though, as if he should be wearing a conductor suit. He chomped his underlip with those horse teeth.

He appeared to be thinking.

Skipper looked at him for a long time, then turned her face toward my chest. Her arm was around my shoulders. I didn't blame her for looking away. A truly evil man is never pretty, particularly when he is busy contemplating evil. He gave a little shrug that meant he had made up his mind.

"Now do just like I tell you, and it won't hurt either of you a bit."

"What are we going to have, a suicide pact?"

He sucked the big teeth. It sounded like a Ubangi kiss. "Out the window hand in hand," he said. "Lover's leap. But you'll be sleeping while you drop, kids."

Skipper took a deep breath and began to tremble more violently. She wasn't at all brave. Me, I showed no reaction at all, if you don't count the sweat that was running down into my socks.

"Set her down," he said. I did. "Now come here, girl. Circle around so I can keep an eye on smart boy. That's a girl. Now turn around. Easy."

As soon as her back was to him, he reached out with his free hand and grabbed her wrist, twisted it up between her shoulder blades. Her small whimper was quickly stifled. I saw her face turn gray.

"Now, smart boy, sit down at that desk and write. Move!"

Any hesitation I felt was immediately canceled out by her slightly shriller sound of pain. She didn't break down. She didn't cry. She stood and took it and shut her teeth hard on the pain of it.

Chess is a lovely game. The opponent starts making a series of forcing moves. You make the predicted answering move each time. And you wait and you hope to find a hole in the attack.

"Write what I say. 'To whom it may concern. We are taking the only way out. We have no regrets.' Got that?"

The hotel nib scratched along the stationery.

"Sign it," he said.

I signed it. My own death certificate.

"Now don't move. Put your hands flat on that table and don't move a muscle."

My chance. I put my hands flat on the table. My ears went to work for me. I could hear the grass growing in a park three blocks away. I could hear city traffic in Cleveland. And with my hands braced, I heard the soft scuff of shoe leather on the rug. I heard the fabric of his sleeve scrape against the fabric of the side of his coat as he lifted his arm.

I shoved myself back toward him, hard. With all the strength I could put into my arms and legs, I shot back at him. And shot back into the direct path of some damn fool who was driving through the hotel room with a tractor-trailer combo. He ran me down and smashed my head like a stomped pumpkin.

I was nine fathoms deep in a warm tank of oil, dirty oil that would raise hell with your ring job. I was swirled gently, end for end, in the depths of the oil tank. And then I stopped whirling and began to float slowly toward the surface, face down. Surface tension held me under, then let me up with a popping sound. Now I rested my cheek on top of the surface of the oil. And under my cheek the texture changed. From oil to hotel rug. The truck had run over my head with tire chains on.

I have a notoriously hard skull. In my school we used to have butting contests. Simon the Goat, they called me. Flushed with victory, I let a girl named Hortense tap me one day with the flat of a hatchet. She used both hands. I was punchy for three weeks but otherwise undamaged.

I had come recently from a place where, if you are knocked down, you do not sit up until reasonably certain that what you intend to sit on has not been shot off in the excitement.

Shoes whispered on the rug. Hard fingers got hold of my ear and twisted it. My head was lifted off the floor by the ear. When the fingers let go, I let my head bounce on the rug. I looked through the lashes of the eye closest to the rug. A large shoe was three inches from my nose. It went away. Beyond it I saw my girl. Not all of her. Just the pleasant curvature of her back as she lay face down on the floor. Her back moved just enough so that I could tell she was breathing.

And suddenly she was hauled out of sight. The window was over that way. I took a look. Barney the Beaver was dragging her to the window. I didn't want my girl dropped out the window. My room was on the fourteenth floor. Barney had said we were going out hand in hand, not one at a time. Drop one first and somebody is going to look up in time to see the

238

second party get thrust out. But it was hell to keep my head down and wonder if he'd changed his plans.

His feet came over again. He hoisted my ankles and dragged me over to the window, face down. I let my head roll to the side. Warmth touched my hand. Warmth under the girl's clothes. The window slip up. Nice and wide open. Probably the Beaver planned to put us face down over the wide sill, side by side, then upsy-daisy with our heels.

Thoughts and conjectures were roaring through my mind like trains heading through a tunnel. And before the sound of the opening window had completely ceased, it occured to me that the most natural thing for any man to do when planning to drop a heavy package out a window is to take a look down and make certain that there is nothing in the way of the drop.

I counted up to the square root of minus three and came up fast.

Maybe some character comes to rescue the girl on horseback, waving the lance like crazy. And some other joker bares his manly fists and whips the seven villains while she looks on, her eyes glowing with girlish pride. Me, I merely put each hand firmly against the two hemispherical sections where his shabby pants were the tightest and gave a nervous shove. I think I also gave a nervous giggle. I didn't feel heroic. I even felt it was a dirty trick.

He went out like the fat clown who always gets pushed into the swimming pool. His legs scissored through the open window without even brushing the sides.

He must have taken a big gulp of that cold night air as he went out. Because the whistling scream started immediately, and he screamed all the way down through the night, like one of those whistling skyrockets they used to shoot off on the fourth of July.

When the scream stopped, I looked out cautiously, gagged weakly, and sat on the floor.

My girl had blood in her hair. I pulled her head into my lap. I kissed her lips, nose, cheeks, forehead, and eyelids. I tried to pick her up, but she had gotten too heavy for me. I looked at her, and Marj was something that had happened to another guy in another country in another generation. I knew that Skip would be very glad to know that this had happened to me, and I would tell her as soon as possible.

I struggled up with her and wavered over to the bed. There was a knock at the door. I opened it.

A chesty somebody beefed his way in and said, "You got some kind of fight going on in here, fellow?" As he asked the question, he was staring at Skipper.

My lovely sat up. Great girl. Bust her one on the head and she wakes up looking like a mattress ad.

"That is no woman, sir, that is—"

"Don't give me no smart talk, bud."

A siren moaned in the distance, drawing nearer. I said, "Excuse me, sir, but I'm afraid we dropped something out that window a few moments ago. It landed down by the streetlight."

"Bud, there's an ordinance against dropping stuff out hotel windows. If it was hotel property, you got to make it good."

My cornflower blonde had begun to comprehend. Her eyes looked faintly sick, but at the same time awfully glad.

The beef trust waddled over and stuck his head and shoulders out the window. He stiffened, and his wet lips made flapping sounds in the night. I paused behind him and looked, with a tinge of regret I must admit, at the general area where his pants were the tightest.

I put my hands firmly in my pockets. You've got to watch a thing like that. It can turn into a compulsion neurosis.

My lovely lassoed me with her big shining eyes, and I didn't hear a yammering word the beef trust said, even though he was jumping clean off the floor every time he took a breath.

Murder in Mind

She was a plump blonde, and she lay dead in the trail on her back. There were streaks of drying mud on the right sleeve of her pale yellow sweater. There was more mud on her freckled right arm. Death had flattened her body to the ground. Her tweed skirt was pushed up halfway between knee and hip. Her heels rested in the mud and her brown sandals toed in.

The black trees, stripped naked by autumn, stood high around her, and the chill wind off the lake hurried the dry brown leaves across the trail. A leaf had stuck to her hair over the right temple, where the hair was sticky with new blood.

I would have guessed that when she was alive she was pretty and vivacious. Her lids were half closed, showing a semicircle of glazed bright blue.

Her husband, Ralph Bennison, or more accurately, her widower, had phoned Burt Stanleyson from the nearby village of Hoffwalker. Burt and I had climbed into the white County Police sedan and driven to Hoffwalker, where Bennison had been waiting in his car.

He had stopped on the state road opposite that part of Lake Odega where summer camps are clustered along the lakeshore.

We had followed him down the trail to the lakeshore, seeing ahead of us the spot of color against the brown earth—her yellow sweater.

I leaned against a tree and Ralph Bennison sat on a rotting log, his face hidden in his hands. Burt Stanleyson stood beside the body of Mrs. Bennison, staring down at it, while he chewed a kitchen match.

241

I couldn't help noticing the differences between my friend Burt and Ralph Bennison. They were both big men. Burt wore a wrinkled gray suit and still managed to look as if he belonged in the woods. Perhaps it was the way he moved and the weather wrinkles that lined his brown face.

Bennison wore a red-and-black wool shirt with matching breeches and high shoes. But his face was white and he moved quickly and nervously. He had the city label on him, all the way from his big shiny fingernails to the bright new leather of his knife sheath.

Suddenly Bennison lifted his blotched face out of his hands and said in a tight voice, "Why are you standing around staring at her? Why aren't you across the lake trying to find out who fired the shot?"

Burt gave him a steady look and then knelt beside the dead woman. He fingered the hair around the wound, dislodging the crisp leaf. I could see the hole in her head, neat and round. Burt reached down and gently pulled the tweed skirt down to cover her knees. He stood up again and poked with his toe at the mud caked on the sides of her brown shoe. He sighed. The wind swirled a dancing funnel of leaves down the trail.

If it happened in the summer, there would have been a crowd of summer folks standing around. But in November the camps are empty except for a few hunters, and they were still out in the woods after their deer.

Bennison stood up and glared at Burt, then scuffed the hard ground with the toe of his spotless high shoes.

"Look here," he said. "Alice and I were walking down the trail with the lake at our right. She was ahead of me. The trail is muddy and uneven, and I was watching my feet, like I told you. Out of the corner of my eye, I saw her fall on her face. I jumped toward her, thinking that she had tripped. As I jumped, I heard a distant noise like a shot. I rolled her over and held her head in my arms. I saw she was dead, and realized that she had been killed by a stray shot. Then I came after you. Why aren't you after those people across the lake?"

Burt said patiently, "Mr. Bennison, there are two dozen hunters in there. It's four o'clock now. We couldn't round 'em up before dark, and most of them will be cutting back to the other road and driving out of the woods. They'd deny firing high toward the lake. We'd have to take their guns away from them and fire a sample slug from each one. Then we'd have to dig the slug out of your wife's brain and send the slugs down to a comparison microscope. It would be a colossal job. We'll just give it a lot of publicity and hope that some man's conscience will punish him."

"The bullet sort of came down on her, didn't it, Burt?" I asked.

"That's right, Joe. Thirty-caliber. From better than a half mile, or it would have gone right through her."

He turned to Bennison and asked a blunt question. "Did you folks come up here to do some hunting?"

Bennison sat down again on the log. He didn't seem angry any more. "Yeah. We rented the Tyler camp for a week. I was going to do the hunting."

"Where's your gun?"

"Back in the camp."

"Have a gun for her?"

"I told you I was doing the hunting."

"I was just wondering. I notice she's got a little bruise under her right eye as if a gun stock had slapped against her face."

Burt pulled the sweater away from the rounded white right shoulder. There was a purplish bruise there too. He covered the shoulder again.

"She did some target practice with my gun," Bennison said. "She bruised easily."

I couldn't figure what Burt was driving at. He's never been one to ask useless questions. He's too lazy. It was obvious to me that the shot had come from a greater distance than a man can aim.

"What's your business?" Burt asked.

"Well . . . nothing at the moment. I used to be in the investment business."

"Married a gal with money, hey?"

"Look here, Stanleyson, I resent this questioning. What's that got to do with finding out which one of the hunters across the lake shot her?"

"Then she did have money?"

243

"Suppose she did? We both had money."

Burt sighed again and turned away from the body. He walked toward the lakeshore and then looked back. A big tree grew close to the rocks along the shore. He squinted up at the tree. Then he ambled down the bank, squatted on a big rock, and stared moodily at the water. Bennison shrugged helplessly and looked at me.

Burt came back up the bank and said, "Let's go back to the spot where you did this target practicing. Behind the Tyler camp, wasn't it?"

Bennison stood up, and we all walked back down the lakeshore trail. Once Burt stopped and looked back at the dead woman and said, "Guess there's no need to move her just yet."

They had been firing at tin cans propped against a high bank behind the camp. Burt grunted and squatted and picked up a dozen or so of the gleaming brass cartridge cases. He examined them carelessly and stuffed them into his pocket.

Bennison seemed to have gotten tired of trying to figure out what the big man in the wrinkled gray suit was trying to do. He leaned against the cabin and stared out across the lake.

"You only brought this one gun of yours up here?" Burt asked.

"That's right," Bennison said in a flat tone.

"Mind if I look around the camp?"

"Go ahead."

We walked in and Burt picked up the Remington rifle that stood in a corner of the front room. He glanced at it and put it back. Next he went under the camp to the workshop that old Tyler used to use before he died two years ago. Bennison seemed to be getting more irritable.

Burt glanced at the top of the work bench near the vise. He took the kitchen match out of his mouth, scratched it on the underside of the bench, and then ran the flame back and forth, an eighth of an inch above the surface of the bench.

At last he grunted and turned to Bennison, who was leaning against the wall, his arms folded.

"Well, mister," Burt said slowly, "I guess we'd better drag the lake beyond that tree and get the other rifle."

I stood with my mouth open as Bennison whirled and leaped

244

through the doorway. Burt was right behind him. It took me a couple of seconds to wake up. I ran after the two of them. Outside, I saw that Bennison was running at full tilt up the trail toward the road. Burt had grabbed the Remington out of the corner. He leveled it, drew a deep breath, then squeezed the trigger.

The flat explosion of the shot echoed through the clearing. Bennison fell and rolled through the dry leaves. When we reached him, he was clawing with his fingers at his shattered leg, and his face was the face of a madman. He was trying to curse Burt, but only guttural sounds issued from his throat. . . .

After the details had been cleaned up, the dead girl's relatives notified, and Bennison put in the hospital, I sat in Burt's office, drinking bourbon with him and waiting for him to tell me in his own way.

"You see, Joe," he said, "I never would have tumbled to how Bennison did it, if he'd acted right. Maybe you didn't see it, but he was out of character. Any guy who loves his wife shows it in more than one way—even if she has died suddenly and violently. If he was on the level he would have yanked that skirt down himself. No fellow who loves his wife wants a couple of strangers seeing too much of her, even if she's dead. Also, he didn't object when we walked off and left her dead in the mud there. A normal guy would have wanted her moved and covered up."

"But was that enough?"

"No, but that started me noticing things. Things like her shoes being caked with mud and his being clean. Why would he clean his shoes? That started me thinking some more."

"What were you doing down by the water?"

"Looking for a little of that rainbow color that always shows up when you put a little oil in some water. Even one drop will do it—like when you toss a rifle in the lake. I found a little of it close to the rocks. Remember the wind was from the lake.

"You see, he went down the trail first, climbed the tree with the rifle, shot down into her head, and threw the gun out into the lake. He wiped the mud off his shoes so he wouldn't leave mud on the tree when he climbed it. The trunk was fat enough to hide him from her."

"But why did he throw away the gun?"

"Because it could easily be proved that the slug in her skull had come from it. I figured he'd have to do that, so I guessed there were two guns to start with. The oil convinced me I was on the right track, and when I picked up those cartridge cases and found that on some of them, the firing pin hit flush on the rim, and on others the pin hit just a hair inside, I knew I was getting warm."

"But Burt, it still doesn't make sense. If he did like you said, that slug would have gone through her head and dug itself six feet down into that mud."

"Joe, use your brains. How would you cut down muzzle velocity of a bullet so you'd lower the penetration?"

I thought it over as I sipped my drink. When it all came to me, I spilled a little bourbon on my pants.

He grinned as I said, "I get it. Bennison used the vise and took some of the charge out of the bullet shell. You figured it out and guessed that he might have spilled a little powder doing it. The match flame burned little grains of the powder that had dropped on the bench. He wedged the slug back in the case over the reduced charge and then shot her from the tree so it would look as if the slug had traveled in a high arch from across the lake!"

"You keep on getting so smart, Joe," Burt said, "and I'll be able to quit and turn over this thankless job to you. Bennison was sick of her and he wanted her dough. He brought her up here to kill her with the method all worked out. The biggest thing he forgot is that a fellow can't think of his wife who has just been killed as a dead body—unless he got used to thinking of her that way."

We sat for a couple of minutes and thought about Bennison. Then Burt sighed and said, "Just think. Middle of November and I ain't had a chance to get my deer yet this season."

Check Out at Dawn

At five minutes of five the disc jockey topped off his program with a recording by the All Stars. Barney Bigard's clarinet was sweet and strong, to the counterpoint noodling of Earl "Fatha" Hines. He kept the car radio tuned so low that the rhythm was a whisper, the tune like a memory in the mind. As the piece ended he turned off the radio, cupped his hands around the lighter from the dashboard as he lit another cigarette.

When it was finished he eased the car door open and stood out in the crisp, pre-dawn air, the wet spring-smell of the woods. Four months of waiting and watching. The tiredness was deep in him, and the boredom. A leaden-muscled, sag-nerved tiredness.

Behind the house three hundred feet away, the roosters screamed brassy defiance at distant hen runs, and lonesome through the dregs of night came the far-off sigh and pant of a train.

Barry Raymes leaned against the side of the government sedan, sensing, for the hundredth time, his own unreality—neatly dressed, as the Bureau demanded, the regulation Special making its familiar bulge, the regulation hammer on the regulation empty chamber, the entire picture anachronistic in the threat of dawn, in the sleepy peace of the Georgia countryside. In the war there had been the long time on the ship, so long that things that happened before faded away, and the future was immeasurably distant. This was not unlike that time on the ship. At eight Sturdevant would relieve him, to be relieved in turn at four in the afternoon by French, who would carry on until midnight, when once again Barry Raymes, with the thermos of coffee, the bundle of sandwiches from the hotel, would begin the vigil that had begun to seem pointless. But no agent of two years' seniority can hope to point out to the Special Agent in Charge that the assignment, in his measured opinion, is of no value. Patience is a quality more precious than gold to the Bureau. A man without patience does not last long.

'And so there has to be reconciliation to the night after night, the hundred and twenty-six nights thus spent, and the possible hundred and twenty-six yet to come. Even though each night added another cumulative factor to the deathly weariness. Weariness came from recurrent alertness, the adrenaline that came hard and fast into the blood whenever a car seemed to slow on the highway. Or there would be an unidentifiable sound that made necessary a cautious patrol of the grounds with the Bureau variation of the wartime infrared snooperscope.

All because the Bureau was gambling that Craik Lopat would return to see the girl he had intended to marry. . . .

As dawn paled the eastern sky, the kitchen lights went on, slanting yellow-orange oblongs out onto the packed dirt of the dooryard, and he could see her, tall, as she moved about in the kitchen, putting the coffee on before going back to her bedroom to exchange the robe for the cotton dress and sweater that she usually wore. The sweater was a heavy maroon cardigan, too large for her, and he suspected that it had belonged to Lopat. Somehow, this past month, when he thought of Marra Allen wearing Lopat's sweater, an ugly anger thickened within him. He recognized the potential danger of his attitude and sought to recover his original indifference, but without any particular success.

In the night watch you could think of taking this Marra Allen, with her ignorance and her superstitions and her unlettered tongue, and becoming Pygmalion, because there was no denying that her slim loveliness was more than just an attribute of youth. The bone structure was good, and she would take beauty to her grave. And French told of the innate fastidiousness, the kitchen shades drawn, the water heated each night in the big tub in a countryside where Saturday baths were a mark of eccentricity.

And also, in the long night, you could think of her breathing softly in sleep on her bed and think of how her warm breath would come from lips parted just a bit, probably, and the golden hair spread over the pillow. She was three hundred feet away, and one night you quite calmly stepped over to the birch which was white in the starlight and clubbed it hard with your clenched fist, later sucking the swollen knuckles, but cured for the moment.

Barry Raymes had always been a quick and competent— though shy—man, with a wide dark line in his mind separating right from wrong. The frequency with which his thoughts and his dreams turned to Marra Allen disturbed him because he sensed wrongness in a Bureau agent's involving himself personally with any female in any case, no matter what intrinsic worth said female seemed to possess.

Sturdevant and French both made the usual, the expected, jokes about the midnight-to-eight trick, and the obvious advantages pertaining to the hour, and in the beginning he had laughed in the expected way and hinted broadly of the mythical delights of such an assignment, but of late he had felt the flush on the back of his neck, and laughter had not been as easy.

When she returned to the kitchen the dawn light was brighter, paling the artificial light from the kitchen. She opened the kitchen door and looked over toward the small side road where his car was hidden in the heavy brush. The light behind her outlined her, and the morning wind caught at the hem of the cotton dress.

He had long since decided that there was no compromise of Bureau directives involved. The SAC—Special Agent in Charge—had made it quite clear that it would be impossible to carry out the assignment without tipping off the girl. And so his conscience had been made easy. And it had become a morning custom.

He came across the dooryard, taking out the Special when he was forty feet from her. She stepped aside as usual, saying, "Morning, mister," that look of amusement on her face as though he were a small boy playing some absurd variation of cops-and-robbers.

He went through the house as he had been taught in the School. It did not take long. Four rooms, like small boxes, on one floor. Bedroom, sitting room, storeroom, and kitchen.

When he came back into the kitchen she had put the coffee cups on the table, taking, as usual, the one without the handle.

Without turning, she said, "Find any crooks in my house?" She stood at the wood stove, turning the eggs.

"Not today."

"Gives me a funny feeling, kinda, mister. You don't trust me much, do you?"

"Of course I trust you, Marra. I just have to follow orders."

"Sure," she said, her tone weary. He sat down in his usual place, his back to the wall. She brought over the two plates of eggs, the thick-cut bacon, taking, as usual, the chipped plate for herself.

They ate in silence, and, as on every morning, she lowered her face almost to the plate for each forkful. In another woman it would have amused and partially revolted him. In Marra it seemed oddly pathetic. It seemed as though a girl of breeding sat there, intent, for some strange reason, on playing this part that had been given her. And in the depths of her gray-blue eyes he saw the deadness, a nothingness, as though a part of her had been dead—for four months.

They finished breakfast, and he found the fifty-cent piece in his pocket. He slipped it under the edge of the plate, without her seeing him do it. They had never spoken of the fee he had arbitrarily selected as proper for the morning breakfast, and he knew that she would not take the plate away until he left.

"When you people goin' ta give up?" she asked.

"When we get Lopat."

"He hid good, eh?"

"He hid very good. Maybe we'll find him. Maybe he'll come back to be found."

She took one of his cigarettes. She sighed. "For me, mister, it might just as well be jail. When Craik was around I got to go jukin' once in a while. Now none of the boys'll ask me.

Solly, or Tad, or Jesse or any of 'em. They know there'll be you G's taggin' along."

"Are you in love with Craik Lopat?"

"Love is a big word, mister. Craik's always good for laughs. Big husky guy with a mean eye on him. Like a—well, like one of them mountain cats. Mean. Big white teeth. See him work out once on one of them Turner boys from Patton Ridge. Gouged an eye out of him in about three seconds."

"Did he get into trouble just out of meanness, do you think, Marra?"

She frowned, took her time answering. "I can't say. He always wanted a big shiny car and money in his pocket. He got fired off the gas station, and they wouldn't take him back in the mill again because of the trouble last time. I guess he was sore at the mill and that's why he done it."

Barry Raymes, thinking aloud, said, "And he had beginner's luck, all right. If they'd gotten the safe closed . . . if it hadn't been payday . . . if that guard hadn't lost his nerve . . . lots of ifs. He got thirty-five thousand, in small bills and change, and drove off in the plant manager's car to boot and took that payroll clerk with him. That's how we come into the picture."

"Because of the state line?"

"He rolled the clerk out into the brush in Alabama, remember, and shot him through the stomach. The clerk didn't die easy, Marra."

"He was always wild-like," she said softly. "Even when he was just a kid."

"You were going to marry him," he said accusingly.

"Oh, I know what you mean. He'd have given me a bad time, that's for sure. Other women and getting likkered up and maybe slamming me around. He done that once, you know." She laughed, almost fondly. "Gee, did I have a fat eye on me!"

"After what's happened," he asked, "if you had a chance to go with him, would you?"

She regarded him steadily. "Mister, I couldn't rightly say."

"You would, wouldn't you?"

"I might."

He wanted to hurt her. He pushed his chair back and stood up. He said, "You'll find the half buck under the plate."

She flushed. "That's all right."

Anger didn't fade entirely until he was back at the car. And then he was ashamed for speaking of the money, knowing that it would make a difference between them.

Sturdevant showed up a little before eight, and Barry Raymes drove back to the small city eight miles away and went to bed.

He was up at five, had another breakfast, and went to a movie. At eleven he finished his lunch, picked up the sandwiches and coffee, and went out and relieved a bored and sleepy Paul French.

The long night hours went by without incident. She did not come to the kitchen door. He waited longer than usual and then went over.

"I want to search the house," he said harshly.

She stepped aside without a word. As before, the house was empty.

He went back into the kitchen and said, "I could use some breakfast, Marra."

"I can sell you coffee, eggs, and bacon for a half a buck, if you want it."

"I—I'm sorry I acted like I did yesterday, Marra."

She looked directly at him. "You was ugly."

"I had a reason."

"What reason?"

"You said you might go away with—with him. Marra, I don't know what's happened to me, but . . ."

She moved a half step closer to him and, with dignity, lifted her face to look directly up into his eyes. He felt the warmth of her breath against his chin. As he bent to kiss her, her hands fastened with hard force around his arms above the elbows. His reactions were delayed. He twisted away, reaching for the revolver.

"I wouldn't try that," a man said softly. The army Colt in his hand was aimed at Barry's belt buckle. "You did right well, Marra, and I thank you for it. Back real slow against the wall next to the stove there, mister. Hands way up. That's right. Go git me some cloth, Marra, a wad of it."

Craik Lopat wore an expensive-looking suit, but the knees were stained with dirt and one button was missing from the suit coat. He wore no tie, and his white shirt was open at the collar. He was thick in the shoulder, slim and flat in the belly and hips. Black eyebrows met over the bridge of his nose, and the mouth was heavy with cruelty and sensuousness.

"A cop," he said, "trying to love up my woman! They musta got you outa the bottom of the barrel, sonny. I been here for two days, layin' up in the hills until I figured out your hours. When you looked around, I was outside the bedroom window. And it'll be nearly two hours before the next one shows up. You couldn't find me before, and you won't find the two of us either. I got a good car stashed over beyond the grove."

Marra came back into the kitchen with a wad of sheeting.

"You want me to tear it into strips, Craik?" she asked.

"No. Give it here. I got to wad it around the end of this here forty-five because it makes too damn much noise. You want to see me shoot him, you kin stand over there, 'f you want. Sonny gets it low down in the gut. He woulda got it in the head except for what I seen him trying to do to you."

Barry Raymes felt the sweat run down his ribs. His mouth was dry and he was dizzy. Some of it was genuine fear. More of it was anger and frustration that he should have been taken in so easily. He looked at Marra. Her face was pale, and she moistened her lips.

"Right—right here in the kitchen?" she asked weakly.

"You got no more use for this little old shack, honey. You don't like it, go on in the next room."

"They'll never give up if you kill me, Lopat. Never," Barry said. He despised the tremble that came into his voice.

"They got no pictures of me, sonny, and no prints. I got a nice new name and a lot of good neighbors in a place you'll never find. I told 'em all I was going back to pick up my wife." He wrapped the barrel in the sheeting. "Brace yourself, sonny."

"Craik," she said. "Wait a minute. Let me get my stuff together afore you kill him. It'll make some noise, and I don't want to have to run for it without my things."

"I'm going to buy you new stuff, honey."

"After we get married?"

Craik Lopat frowned. "If we get time to make out the papers, honey. You'll get the new stuff anyway."

"I'll hurry. Don't shoot him yet. I want to see it, Craik. I never did see a man get hisself killed yet."

She smiled, quite merrily.

"Make it fast, baby," Craik growled.

She hurried out of the room. Craik stood, whistling tonelessly, the muzzle, shrouded in sheeting, steady as a boulder. Barry made his plans. They hadn't taken the revolver. That was an oversight. He'd watch Craik's eyes. They might flick over to the girl when she came back into the kitchen. At that moment he'd throw himself to the left, snatching the revolver as he fell, hoping to get in at least one shot.

He heard Marra's quick footsteps. She appeared in the bedroom door. She lifted the shotgun, and the full blast at short range caught Craik Lopat in the back of his thick, tanned neck. The big man stumbled one step forward, his head nearly severed from his body, and fell heavily, full length, the .45 spinning out of his dead hand, his face smashing against the worn floorboards.

Barry Raymes bent stupidly and picked up the .45. Marra Allen knelt beside the body, picked up the dead hand, sat back on her heels, and crooned—a low, sad tone that was without tears.

"You were going to go with him."

"He was changed, mister. Changed. He was like a dog I see once in town, with suds on his mouth and his eyes crazy."

"Was it because he was going to kill me?" he asked softly.

She turned her head slowly and looked at the wall against which Barry had been standing. Her voice sounded far away. "You see that blue color, don't you? Last year I wanted to fix the place up. He bought the paint and painted it. I got those little red things. Funny little things. You wet the paper and then they slide right off onto the wall. He thought they were pretty. And we were going to live here, you know."

She still held the lifeless hand. He saw the expensive band of the watch, the black hair curling harshly on the back of the hand, between the knuckles of the fingers.

"That's where he was going to kill me, against that wall."

"It didn't mean anything to him, mister. It didn't mean a damn thing to him."

He shifted his weight uneasily and said, with mock joviality, "Well, no matter why you felt you had to do it, I want you to know that I really feel..."

She wasn't listening. She had started that toneless crooning again, and he suddenly realized that it was the sound many women make when they wish to soothe infants, wish to send them off to sleep.

He walked out the open kitchen door, then turned, saying, "Did you say something?"

"I just said, mister, that it'll scrub off the floorboards. It sure would have messed up that wall."

He walked through the dooryard and across the vegetable patch, careful not to step in the freshly planted rows. The night mist was drying on the hood and top of the black government sedan. When the sending set warmed up, he lifted the hand mike off the prongs, knowing as he did so that not only had Craik Lopat died but also a girl who had existed almost entirely in his mind, and said, "Raymes reporting, Raymes reporting in."

"Go ahead, Raymes."

He licked his lips and planned how he would phrase it.

She Cannot Die

He was working in the far corner of the yard, sorting the jumbled shipment of aluminum sheet which had arrived in the morning, working hard and fast because the November wind was cold. He caught a glimpse of movement out of the corner of his eye and straightened up, saw Stella Galloway hurrying across the yard toward him, picking her way around the sorted piles. He saw her smile, saw the papers in her hand, and felt the familiar embarrassment as he realized that she could have sent one of the men out with the orders but preferred to come herself.

As protection against the chill wind, she had slung her gray coat around her shoulders. He smiled at her, anxious to see her, knowing that somehow she had become a necessary part of this new life.

The wind diluted the flat, smashing noise of the shot. As she hurried toward him, something drove her ahead as though she had been hit with a club. Falling, she half turned, landed heavily on a pile of jagged copper scrap, rebounded, lay still on the damp packed earth of the yard. The wind took the papers from her hand and whipped them away.

Jud Brock stood stupidly, unable to move. He looked at the office building seventy feet away. A window was flung up and one of the male clerks looked out, openmouthed. Jud ran to her. Her cheek was against the earth, and a dark red stain spread in the fabric of the gray coat. Her eyes were open, and there was an odd frown of surprise on her face. The saliva ran from her half-open mouth and her trim left leg twitched, in that muscular spasm that happens sometimes as sleep comes.

He ripped his canvas work glove off, dug blunt fingers into her wrist, and felt the weak fluttering. A girl ran from the side door of the office, paused, and looked uncertainly toward him as he knelt beside Stella.

"Ambulance! Doctor!" he yelled, his voice oddly shrill in his ears. The girl turned and darted back into the office.

Jud took the coat gently from her shoulders, took his knife out with fumbling haste, and slit the white blouse from the nape of her neck to the waist. He tore it across the shoulders and peeled it tenderly away from her white back. Her right shoulder was oddly misshapen, the thick blood oozing freely from a large-caliber hole in the bluish-white skin. He wadded a piece of the white blouse, jammed it against the hole in her back, and held it there with the palm of his left hand, the fingers of his right hand seeking the faint, irregular pulse, his ears straining for the distant sound of a siren. . . .

When the ambulance backed into the yard, he could still feel the pulse, but it was much weaker. The numb eyes had rolled so that only the whites were visible, and her face had a greenish-blue pallor.

They taped a wad of gauze against the hole in her back, lifted her gently onto the stretcher, and slid her into the back of the ambulance. He noticed with annoyance that a lock of her hair had fallen across her face and knew that she wouldn't like that and felt an absurd desire to run to her, to smooth her hair back with his fingers.

As the ambulance drove away he suddenly became conscious of the babble of voices, of questions, saw that almost the entire working force was gathered around him, the women hugging themselves against the chill wind, the eyes of the men bright and excited. He noticed that even the heavy thudding of the big baler had stopped, noticed that Karkoff, the operator, was standing with the others.

Walter Brasher, owner and manager of the Brasher Scrap Metal Company, Incorporated, was prancing through the group, saying, "Come on, now. It's all over. Back to work. Come on, now. All of you." Brasher was a stocky little man with a shining bald head and a pitted face on which the features were gathered in a muddy little clump.

He continually roared and made fierce noises, but every employee knew that inside he was soft and weak and had never fired an employee. He always asked someone else to break the bad news.

Karkoff spat, turned, and walked back toward the shop, back toward the baler which took the loose jangling heaps of scrap and turned them into small, neat, heavy bales. The girls turned and, walking with short steps, their shoulders hunched from the cold, hurried back to the warmth of the office.

Walter Brasher scowled up into Jud Brock's face. "What happened to her?" he demanded. "What happened to Miss Galloway?"

"She was shot in the back with maybe a forty-five. Something heavy. She was coming out with orders for me."

Brasher turned pale under the mud color of his skin. "Why? Why should somebody shoot one of my girls?"

Jud looked down at the man with quick irritation. "How the hell should I know? The cops are probably on the way."

"You get back to work."

Jud saw the gray coat, half on the ground, half on the pile of copper scrap. He bent and picked it up, looked at the small hole in the fabric. He held the coat and said to Brasher, "No, I don't want to work. After the cops talk to me, I'm going to the hospital."

Brasher frowned, turned on his heel, and walked with an attempt at dignity back toward the office. Jud followed him slowly, fancying that in the coat he held in his hand he could still detect the faint warmth of her body.

He hurried and caught Brasher at the door. He said, "Make sure that no one has left since it happened. Don't let anybody leave."

Brasher didn't answer. Jud climbed the stairs to the main office, walked across to a group of girls who stood by the window, looking down at the yard where Stella had fallen. Jane Tarrance, a vivid dark girl with a wide, mobile mouth, Stella's roommate, turned quickly and said, "She was shot, wasn't she?"

"Yes," he said, heavily, hearing the others gasp. He held the coat out. Jane took it quickly, her mouth twisted as she saw the bloodstain. She folded it, folded the stain inside.

At that moment Boris Howe, the accountant, a slow man with a wrestler's body and the lean, myopic face of an introvert, walked over to him and said, "Uh . . . Brock, Mr. Brasher said for me to tell you that after the cops are through, you draw your pay and get out."

Jud ignored him. He turned and looked toward Brasher's glassed-in office, saw the gleaming top of Brasher's bald head. He brushed by Howe, walked to the door of the office, opened it, and stood in front of Brasher's desk until the man glanced up.

Brasher scowled, but his voice quavered as he said, "Well?"

Brock sat down, pulled out a cigarette, and lit it. "I got your message, Brasher."

The voice was shrill. "To you I am Mr. Brasher!"

"You knew when you hired me that I had been a cop."

"Certainly I knew it. And I knew that you had the shakes so bad that you could only work a little."

"I'm over that now. I've gotten all I need out of this place. I'm ready to quit."

"I fired you, Brock," the plump little man said with surprising firmness.

"No, you did not. You're about to change your mind. I'm staying on here until I find out why that girl was shot and who did it."

"That is police business. You're through here. You refused a direct order."

"She's my friend. It's my business too. I want to stay on the payroll at a dollar a week until I find out why she was shot. I want the run of the place, and I want all employees told that I can ask any questions I wish to ask. You can call me the company cop if you want, but I'm staying."

"You're not staying."

Brock reached quickly across the desk and grabbed Brasher's wrist. His wrists and arms were like iron from the eight months of handling scrap. He clamped down on the wrist, and Brasher squealed. "Maybe you don't understand me, Mr.

259

Brasher," Brock said heavily. "Unless you change your mind, I will find a chance to catch you on the street. When I do, I promise you that I will break both your fat arms like sticks."

He released Brasher's arm suddenly. With the pressure gone, Brasher's chair rolled a few feet away from his desk.

Brock said softly, "And when I find out, I'll leave here."

Brasher smiled with his lips alone, said heartily, "I didn't know you felt so strongly about it, Brock. I . . . I'll be glad to have your help."

Brock looked woodenly at him for several seconds, turned, and left the office. He stopped just outside the door as he saw Detective Lieutenant John Maclaren and Sergeant Joe Horowitz reach the top of the front stairs and look curiously around the office. John Maclaren saw Brock first, nudged Horowitz, and said something in a low tone. They both came toward him, grinning unpleasantly.

"Hello, John," Brock said.

Maclaren turned to Horowitz. "Since when does a lush get to call a police officer by his first name?"

"Maybe it's a new custom, Johnny," Horowitz said. "Maybe it says he can on the back of his union card."

The girls were back at their desks and they smiled with bright curiosity at the police, making no attempt to work. Maclaren glanced at them and then turned back to Brock. "We got it a girl was shot here. Accident?"

"Intentional. It looked to me like it might be a fatal wound. Maybe you better alert Homicide to keep a check on her condition."

"Horowitz," Johnny Maclaren said, "listen to the guy give orders!" He turned to Brock. "Just where do you fit?" he said in a flat tone.

Brock heard Brasher come out of his office, knew that he was a few feet behind him. He said loudly, "I'm representing the company in the investigation." He turned around. "Isn't that right, Mr. Brasher?"

Brasher coughed and licked his lips. He gave one startled glance at Brock's eyes and said, "Yes. Yes, that's right. I'm the manager here. Mr. Brock is handling it for us."

Maclaren glanced at Brock's dirty coveralls, at his reinforced shoes, sneered, and said, "You ought to dress your key personnel a little better, Brasher. Let me use your phone." Without waiting for an answer he went into Brasher's office, called the hospital, and asked for a report. When he got it, he called headquarters, got hold of Captain Davis of Homicide, and said, "A girl was shot in the back at Brasher Scrap Metal twenty minutes ago. The intern says she's in bad shape. Maybe you want one of your people to cover this with me just in case. . . . Okay, I'll brief him when he gets here."

He walked around the desk and sat in Brasher's chair. He flapped a hand at Brasher. "Shut the door on your way out."

Brock leaned on the wall near the window. Horowitz sat on the edge of Brasher's desk.

Because of Brock's background, little time was wasted. In ten minutes, Maclaren knew that because of the danger of theft there were only two ways in and out of the grounds, the main entrance and the truck gate. There was a guard at the truck gate and a receptionist at the lower hall at the main entrance. The fence around the property was a nine-foot hurricane fence with three strands of barbed wire at the top. No one had left the area since the shooting.

The property was roughly square, with the office building running along one side at right angles to the road. The shop was in the back, parallel to the road, forming an L with the office building. The truck gate was at the other end of the front and was wide enough to include the spur track. A magnet crane was located near the loading platform. The entire center of the area was filled with mounds of scrap, some over twenty feet high.

Throughout the questioning both Horowitz and Maclaren treated Brock with amused contempt. Brock ground his fingers into the palms of his hands and managed to keep all expression off his heavy-boned face.

Cantrelle of Homicide arrived just as Maclaren had started to question Brock about the girl. Maclaren stopped and briefed Cantrelle on the information so far and then continued with Brock.

"How well did you know this Miss Stella Galloway?"

"I've been out with her several times."

261

"Girl friend, eh?"

"Not exactly. A friend. She roomed with Jane Tarrance, that dark girl in the far corner of the office. Miss Galloway was a quiet girl, well-educated. She left here and worked for three years in Washington, D.C. She came back to Louisavale and got her job here a month later. She had been here over a year when I started work. She . . . she took an interest in me. Her parents are dead. She has a married brother in California and a married sister in Toronto. She has a very small income from her father's estate. I don't know of any enemies, or any reason why she should be shot." Jud Brock had managed to keep his voice low, his tone calm and unhurried.

Cantrelle snickered. "You have bad luck with your women, don't you, Brock?"

Brock started across the office toward Cantrelle, his chin lowered on his chest, his fists clenched. Maclaren grabbed Brock's shoulder and spun him around. "Try anything funny, Brock, and I'll gun-whip you."

Brock stood perfectly still and tried to force the anger to run out of his big, raw-boned body. At last he shrugged and stepped back against the wall, the anger still with him but changed to a small hot glow deep inside of him.

It was bad because they all knew about it. They all knew the story of Jud Brock. He had put in six years with the Louisavale police, going on the force directly from college. He had advanced rapidly, had been transferred to Homicide, where he worked under Captain Davis. He was looked on as one of the bright young men in the department. Since Louisavale was a city of two hundred thousand, he could plan on merit promotions to the point where he would make a good living and have a responsible position. He was popular and he liked his work and he was good at it.

During his sixth year on the force he became engaged to Caree Ames. She was a slender, enchanting blonde, the only daughter of the city manager.

They were engaged for just two months before they were married. She seemed pleasantly but curiously anxious to be married, as though it would be some sort of haven for her.

Five weeks after the wedding and three weeks after they

had returned from their Bermuda honeymoon, he came home to their new suburban house to find that a man with whom Caree had been intimate before he had ever met her had broken into the house, shot her twice in the skull, and then shot himself. She was dead. The man was still breathing. She had died almost within reach of the telephone. The man lived in a coma for five days before he too died.

He could not get that kitchen scene out of his mind, the two of them on the vinyl pattern he and Caree had selected, both face down in the pattern of a grotesque T, the still-breathing man lying across her dead legs.

Later he found out that quite a few people had known of her affair with the man who killed her. Her father had been anxious for her to be married. The man was demonstrably unstable, potentially dangerous.

For two months after the funeral he had continued his duties, walking through each day like a mechanical man. He had found he could not forget that scene; it was inextricably mixed somehow with some of the bloodier episodes which had happened during his years of police duty before he had met Caree.

During those two months, all the reality of the world around him took place dimly behind the shining screen of memory, and at last he had discovered that alcohol would dim the memories. At first he had been suspended for a month and had managed to get himself in shape to go back to duty at the end of the month. The second suspension was for six months.

After a long period of forgetfulness, he had walked into headquarters, his broken shoes flapping on his feet, his gray face dirty and whiskered, and found out that his suspension had been up for over three weeks and that he had been suspended indefinitely.

The period after that was impossible to remember. There were vague memories of a ward and of people strapping him down while he fought to get away from the incredibly slimy things that were creeping across the floor toward his bed.

One morning he had stopped and looked at the reflection of himself in the plate glass of a store window. He had frowned at it for a long time, trying to see in the watery eyes and hollow cheeks of the reflection something familiar—something of Judson Brock. There were coins in his pocket, and he waited until the bars opened. He bought a beer and held the first swallow in his mouth, looking across and seeing in the mirror of the back bar the same face that had looked back at him from the store window. Then he had spewed the beer onto the floor, turned, and left.

He had scrubbed his body with harsh yellow soap at the mission and put on the suit and shoes from the Salvation Army. There was no money in the bank. The house had been sold, the money spent.

Two days later, in spite of his weakness, Brasher had hired him, sensing that here was a man whose spirit was so far gone that he would accept without question the long hours and the small pay.

He had gone to work in the yard, learning dully what was expected of him. The heavy sheets and plates cut into his soft flesh through the canvas gloves, and he could work for only an hour at a time before weakness hit him.

Brasher had given him an advance, and with it he rented a cheap room and bought food his stomach could retain.

At the end of a month his eyes were clearer and the moments of weakness came less often. During the second month he began to fill out, and with a thick, stubborn pride in the strength that had come back to him, he punished his body, working at high tempo so that at the end of the day he could fall exhausted into bed, into dreamless sleep.

For a time one of the office men brought his orders into the yard, copies of the material shipped in and the manner in which it should be sorted. Gradually he became conscious of the fact that it was a girl who came out with the orders, and that each time she came she smiled at him and that he liked the way she walked and smiled.

No longer could he completely exhaust his body with the day's work, and in order to fill his evenings, to keep from remembering, he went to dull movies, sat in his room, and read books, fighting against the face of Caree that threatened to come between his eyes and the printed page.

One night he grew tired of fighting, and when the face came before his eyes he saw that it wasn't the face of Caree, but the face of the girl who brought the orders out to him as he worked in the yard.

The next day he asked her clumsily to have dinner with him, and to his relief she acted neither coy nor haughty. She accepted with pleasure, and later, as they sat over coffee and she told him about herself, he realized that at last he had begun to heal.

He found out that she knew all about him from one of the girls in the office whose brother worked in Identification at headquarters. He had tried to tell her one night, and she had stopped him and said that she knew about it and it was probably better if he didn't talk about it until some day when it would be easier.

She became a habit, and more than a habit. She became as necessary to him as warmth and food and shelter. And yet he was awkward and uncertain with her. He felt as though somehow, in the past, his soul had been dug out of him with a hasty spoon and the bits and fragments of it left inside him were too few to offer to anyone.

And, as he was gradually coming back to life, as each night he managed to be more cheerful, less strained, she walked out of the doorway and moments later the wind plucked the orders out of her limp hand, danced them over the piles of scrap, and plastered them flat against the wire mesh of the fence.

Brock said, "I was standing in this exact spot. Here is the sheet that I had picked up when I saw her coming. I was going to carry it over and lay it on that pile over there, but when I saw her coming, I put it down and waited. John, you're standing exactly where she was when the slug hit her. She came toward me, her head tilted back with the force of the blow, her right side turning half toward me. She landed on her side on that pile of copper scrap and bounced off. She lay with her cheek against the dirt, her face turned away from the scrap pile."

"How was she facing when it hit her?"

"I couldn't be sure. You see, with the junk about here, she didn't come on a straight line but sort of picked her way through on a zigzag. If I had to guess, I'd say that she was heading almost directly at me, turned maybe a little to her left."

Maclaren took off his soft felt hat and scratched his thinning hair. He looked back at the direction from which the slug, and Stella Galloway, had come. He said, "What happened to your head, Jud? That shot was fired either from the back end of the office building, the far end of the shop, or from behind one of the piles of scrap. If you'd been on your toes . . ."

Brock managed a tight grin. "Since when does a police officer get to call a lush by his first name?"

Maclaren looked angry for a moment and then sighed. "The hell with scrapping, Brock. Did the shot seem far away?"

"Somewhere between maybe sixty and a hundred feet from me. Not much farther. You can't hit anything with a forty-five much farther than that. I figure that because she was between me and the pistol, or whatever it was, if it had been much over a hundred feet, I'd have seen her lurch before I heard the shot. As it was, the two things happened at the same instant."

Horowitz said softly, "That makes sense." He drifted over to Maclaren and whispered in his ear.

Maclaren stared at Brock for a few moments. He said, "Any chance that somebody was gunning for you and hit the young lady by mistake?"

It was a new thought. Brock said, "Could be, but somehow I don't think so. I haven't made any enemies lately, and if somebody wanted to knock me off for old stuff, they could have had me while I was . . . on the town."

"Maybe somebody didn't like the girl being friendly with you and wanted to knock you off and hit her instead. She mention any ex-boyfriend?"

"Told me of a few locals who had made passes. One guy works here that she used to know. Fellow named Hodge Oliver."

"Where was he when Galloway was shot?"

"You'll have to get the stories on that. I haven't had a chance to check on anybody."

Maclaren walked close to him and looked full into his eyes. "Okay, Brock," he said gently. "I don't know your angle, but Brasher says you represent the company in this so we'll deal with you, even if I don't like it. Just get one thing clear in your mind. When you were on the force you liked to bang off on angles of your own. Don't try it this time. Don't get in our way, and do just what we ask you to do. Understand?"

"You need me for anything right now?" Brock asked.

Maclaren shook his head. Brock went to his locker, changed into street clothes, and took a taxi to the hospital.

The intern said, "Galloway? Doing very nicely. Very nicely."

"Don't give me customer talk, friend, I represent the company, private investigation. I asked you how she is."

The intern shrugged. "She's all chopped to hell inside. The slug hit flat against her shoulder blade and smashed it. The lead split into two hunks. One went up through the top of her right lung and stopped just under the skin. The other hunk sliced down through her lung and belly, perforated her intestines twice, and came out just above the left hip. A hunk of the shoulder blade was driven over against her spinal cord, and we don't know what damage that did. She just came out of the operating room ten minutes ago. We gave her two transfusions, and she'll probably need another. Providing there's no spinal injury, she's in bad enough shock so that she's got maybe one chance in ten of lasting through the next twelve hours. There's a cop in her room with her just in case she comes out of it. I just gave a full report of her condition to Police Headquarters."

"Did she recover consciousness in the ambulance or before the anesthetic?"

"No. You want to look at her?"

"Sure."

The elderly patrolman who sat next to the bed with a notebook and pencil in his hand and a bored look on his face changed the look to quick recognition and then distaste when Jud Brock walked in.

"Relax, Jones," Brock said. "I just want a look at her."

He stood by the bed and looked down. There was a faint trace of color in her greenish cheeks, but she was breathing shallowly, rapidly. Her eyes were shut and seemed to have sunk farther back into her head. The nostrils looked pinched, and her hair had turned brittle and dead. Her lips were dry. She breathed rapidly through her mouth, and he could see the tip of her tongue protruding slightly beyond the even lower teeth.

As he looked down at her, he wondered if the slug had been

meant for him, and he knew suddenly that he would soon be face to face with whoever had fired the shot. Whether Stella Galloway lived or died, he would stand face to face with someone, and with the new strength that corded his arms and shoulders he would smash that face with a fist like a rock.

Jones had been watching him. The elderly patrolman said, "You look good, Brock. You off the bottle?"

Brock transferred the anger that burned him. "What's it to you?"

"Nothing, boy. Nothing at all."

Stella Galloway's lower jaw dropped and she began to breathe more hoarsely. Jones glanced at her and hitched his chair closer. "Miss Galloway! Stella!" he said insistently.

She didn't answer. Brock turned and left the room.

At five they let the ones go who had been searched and interviewed. Captain Davis, acting on the report from the hospital, had assigned more men, and, while Brock had been over at the hospital, Inspector Durea had looked in for a few minutes.

The investigation had narrowed to three angles. One: Where had each person been when the shot was fired? Two: What had happened to the weapon? Three: Had the shot been fired at Galloway or Brock—and why?

At six only Brasher, the watchman, and Brock were left of the working force. Everyone else had been interviewed and dismissed with a warning to stay in town. Brock saw that Maclaren was weary, but he felt no weariness himself. He felt no hunger. He stood, solid and impassive, and listened to Maclaren, Horowitz, Cantrelle, and the others discuss the case, and he knew that, as for himself, he could keep going for an unknown period before exhaustion finally beat his strong body.

The trucks arrived with the floodlights, and the watchman let them into the yard. Lights were thrown across the piles of scrap, and everybody except Brasher and the watchman began to hunt for the pistol. Two men with a metal detector were left back in the office building, covering all the desks and closets and other possible hiding places.

Brock marked off the piles in which the assailant would have had no chance to hide the weapon. Horowitz looked at the other piles of scrap and groaned. "Give me a nice simple needle-and-haystack proposition any day."

Brock searched along beside Horowitz and found out that of the working force of sixty-three there were fourteen who could not substantiate their location at the time the shot was fired. Eliminating the possibility that two or more had been in on it, they were left with fourteen suspects. Among those were Walter Brasher, Karkoff, Jane Tarrance, Hodge Oliver, and Pennworthy, the guard. The other nine included the receptionist in the lower front hallway; a stenographer named Nudens, who claimed she was in the women's room; the operator of the indoor crane in the baling shop, who claimed he was out for a smoke; Brasher's office boy, who couldn't remember where he was; Boris Howe, the accountant, who said he was at the water fountain on the stair landing; two laborers in the back end of the yard near the loading platform; and two men who were off-loading aluminum scrap from a railroad car.

At ten o'clock a new batch of men reported, and many of the searchers went off duty. Maclaren sent Horowitz home for some sleep and looked as if he could use some himself.

At three in the morning there were no places left to search. The piles of scrap in which the gun could have been hidden were dismantled and restacked in new locations, piece by piece. The men stood around and inspected their bruised hands and wrists, felt gingerly of the small of their backs.

Brasher had gone home at midnight. Maclaren sent the rest of the men home except for one at the front door. The harsh lights were on in Brasher's office. Maclaren, his face pale and lined, sat behind Brasher's desk and drew red pencil marks on a small scale floor plan of the plant. Brock sat woodenly in one of the straight chairs, staring at the far wall.

Maclaren finished marking the plan and shoved it over to Brock. Brock said, "You sure you're asking me for my opinion, John?"

"I've got no time to fight with you, Jud. We were good friends once."

"That's right. Until I was down and out. We were swell friends."

Maclaren smiled at him. "Sure, kid. And one night I found

you on Water Street in the gutter, and I took you home and got you cleaned up. You were still in bed when I went on duty in the morning. You got up, dressed, and left with my three shotguns. I had to pay eighty-eight dollars to get them out of hock. The next time you took the electric clock and the wife's solid silver. Two hundred it cost the second time. I couldn't afford it, kid."

Brock waited a full thirty seconds, his face changing slowly. "I can't even remember it, John. I'm sorry. I'll pay back that money. I've got it in savings. I'm sorry."

"Forget it. Look at the floor plan here. It shows the yard, shop and all. See the fourteen red circles? Those are where the ones say they were who can't account for where they were at the time of the shot. The X shows where she fell, and the great big circle shows where somebody had to be to shoot her— whether they were aiming at you or not. Now look. This floor plan shows how it would have been impossible for Jane Tarrance, the guard, the receptionist, the girl in the can, Boris Howe, or the two guys unloading the aluminum to have gone over into the area from which the shot was fired. They would have been seen going and coming.

"That leaves us seven. Brasher and his office boy, Hodge Oliver, Karkoff, the two guys in the yard, and the crane operator."

"You can take off Karkoff. The baler didn't stop until long after the shot was fired. It won't work without an operator."

"Good work! On my own hook I'm taking out the office boy. That kid is too dopey to know which end of a gun to hold onto. Now we're down to five: Brasher, Hodge Oliver, Lavery the crane operator, and the two guys in the yard. Let me see: Howard Barnes and Duke Schortz. Brasher, Oliver, Lavery, Barnes, or Schortz. Of course if more than one was in on it, we're way out of line and we'll have to start all over. Now we need the gun and the motive."

"Could the gun have been tossed over the fence out into the weeds to be picked up later?"

"I thought of that and made a thorough check. Superman couldn't have thrown it any farther than we looked."

"Then it's still on the place?"

270

"Unless either my boys or the matrons missed any spots on the people big enough to hide a forty-five. And my money says they didn't."

"How about the gun being tossed out of one of the front windows into a moving vehicle?"

Maclaren thought it over. "Boy, that booze didn't soften your head any. I'll have to consider that as a possibility."

"Another thing, John. That slug split up when it went in. It had to have some encouragement. My guess is that somebody sliced it good before they loaded it. That means they wanted whoever they hit to stay dead, right?"

"Go on."

"Okay, then. You put a deep notch in a forty-five slug and you spoil the ballistics. I figure that a guy who would know enough to notch it would know about it shortening his effective range. The slug hit her in the back while she was still forty feet from me. The odds are that he couldn't have hit me with anything but an unmarked slug. That means it was aimed at her, not me, and you can look for motives for her death, not for mine."

Maclaren chewed his lip. "Pretty damn slim, Jud, but we'll go along. We'll check into her before we check you."

"How about Hodge Oliver? As far as I know he's the only guy who knew her in the past."

"I don't think so, Jud. He's a clean-looking kid with a good record. He worked in Washington too. At the Pentagon. He says that he knew Galloway as one of the girls who worked in a nearby office. She was a stenographer for a while, and then she was in charge of the filing of blueprints and specifications. He was upset about her being shot. You could see that. He doesn't owe any dough, he's got a steady gal, and he got a raise two weeks ago. I got all this from him and from others. Of course, I'll check it, but I've got a hunch it'll all be true."

"Personally I don't think Brasher's got the guts to shoot anybody."

"Don't low-rate those nasty little soft guys who can only talk big. Force them into a corner and you can't tell what they'll do. I could see from the way he acted that you moved in on him in this investigation. In a way, I don't blame you. After

271

all, she was knocked off on her way to see you." Brock felt quick alarm and a feeling of loss at the easy way Maclaren made the assumption that Stella was already dead. "Suppose that this Brasher made a pass at Galloway and she pushed him off in a way that hurt his pride and then, when he saw her falling for you, he couldn't take it. After all, the woman who turned him down getting chummy with . . . well, with unskilled labor. Did you notice anything about him, any way he might have looked at Galloway in the past?"

Brock stared down at his clenched knuckles. "John, I've been in a fog for a long time. I haven't paid much attention to what has been going on around me."

"Sure, kid. I see what you mean. But you're out of the fog now?"

"Way out. Brasher's line is plugged open on the switchboard, John. I'm going to see about Stella. Mind if I use your name?"

After Brock had identified himself as Lieutenant Maclaren, the night intern came on the phone and said, "Condition unchanged, sir. She's had two more plasma transfusions, but she's losing fluids so fast that she'll be due for another one soon." Brock thanked him and hung up, told Maclaren the score.

"You tired, Jud?" Maclaren asked.

"Not yet."

"Here's Hodge Oliver's address. An apartment on Quenton Street. I've got to follow the book or they'll yank my badge. Maybe you could . . ."

"Kick him around and see if anything drops out?"

"Something like that. But you're on your own. I'm going over and have another talk with Brasher."

Hodge Oliver's eyes were puffed with sleep. He blinked in the hall light and said, "Oh, it's you, Brock. What do you want?"

Brock pushed in, found the switch, clicked the lights on, and closed the door.

Oliver said, "Now wait a minute! Can't you—"

Brock planted a big palm against Oliver's chest and sent him sprawling across the living room couch. Oliver braced

272

himself on his elbows and stared at Brock. "I'm going to toss you out of here," he said quietly. He was lean and rangy, with brush-cut blond hair, a strong-looking neck, and knobby knuckles.

He came off the bed fast, charging in. Brock caught a wild right in the palm of his left hand and blocked a left hook with his elbow. As Oliver planted a second right high on Brock's cheek, he was caught right on the point of the chin with a gentle right. It made a noise as though a clod of wet mud had been thrown against a brick wall. Brock caught him and laid him gently on the couch.

Oliver's papers were in the second drawer of his bureau. Not much to go on. A file of personal letters. An address book listing people in Washington, Louisavale, and Detroit—plus a few other people scattered across the country. On the bureau was a large picture of a very lovely girl with blond hair. She looked something like Caree had once looked. . . . Brock, realizing that, was surprised to find how little pain there was in the thought—as though Caree had been married to someone else, a different Judson Brock. A younger, softer Judson Brock.

He pulled a chair up beside the couch. A few minutes later Oliver opened his eyes wide and groaned. He tried to sit up. Brock reached out a hand and pushed him back down. "Take it easy, boy," he said.

Oliver felt of his chin and gave Brock a twisted grin. "What did you hit me with, a city bus?"

"I was afraid you'd be sore. As you know, I'm handling the company end of the investigation of Miss Galloway's injury. She will probably die without regaining consciousness. You knew her in Washington. What's the angle? Anything you can say to give us a reason?"

Oliver hoisted himself up and reached for his cigarettes on the coffee table. He gave Brock one, and Brock lit the two of them. "Look, Brock. I just knew her in Washington. She happened to be in the same section, that's all. Ordnance procurement. I had lunch with her a few times, and a few times we went to the cola bar in the Pentagon in the middle of the afternoon. She was very nice in a quiet way, very tidy and polite. She seemed to know her job well. That's all I know about her. I've got a girl of my own, man. That's her picture over there."

"Did you know her friends in Washington?"

"I saw her with the women she worked with, of course. And I remember seeing her once at a hotel. She was dancing with someone, but I haven't any memory of what he looked like. I remember thinking he was too short for her, and that's all."

Brock leaned back in the chair, shook his head, and sighed. "Sorry I had to pop you, Oliver."

He shrugged and smiled. "I didn't give you much choice. No hard feelings."

Brock stared at the far wall of the room for a few moments, and then at the glowing end of the cigarette he held. "Where are you from, Oliver?"

"Detroit, originally. Before I tried the civil service job, I had a two-bit position working in the mechanical drawing department of one of the independent auto-parts makers."

"You've got family there?"

"Sure, but I don't want to go back. They try to run my life. My mother is a very domineering woman. I've been around some, and I like the looks of it here. It suits me. I'm not sorry I stayed. I wouldn't have met Alice if I hadn't found a job here."

"Like your work?"

"Well enough. The money is medium okay. Enough to get married on, at least. Hey, maybe I shouldn't ask. You sound like a man with education. I've wondered about you off and on. What are you doing out in that yard as a common laborer handling all that heavy scrap?"

Brock didn't smile. "You might call it a health course."

"Oh."

Brock stood up. "Go on back to sleep, boy. You'll have a little mark on that chin in the morning."

Brock was sitting in Brasher's office when the puffy little man walked in that morning. He marched up to Brock and said, "A fine thing! A very fine thing! You force me to put you in charge of the company end of the investigation, and then you let that Maclaren hoodlum get me out of bed at three

274

thirty in the morning to ask a lot of insane questions leading to nothing. The kids woke up. My wife got a headache. You aren't worth the dollar a week you asked for."

Brock saw Maclaren when he came in. Brock said, "No dice on Oliver; how about Brasher?"

"I think he's clean. I got to Lavery last night, too. Rather, at five this morning. I think that angle is okay too. I found out that this Karkoff had told Lavery to knock off and grab himself a smoke. The way it works, the crane that Lavery runs gets ahead of the baler once in a while, and then Karkoff gives him the sign to climb down and go out in the end of the shop to the can where he can smoke. If Lavery was the one, it would mean that he'd have to depend on Karkoff giving him the sign at just the right time for him to slip out, plug the girl, and get back. It's too thin. I saw Karkoff and he backed the guy up. By the way, this Karkoff has a record. Yeah. Did a year back in 1973. Grand theft auto. Been straight ever since—he says. You sure that baler was working all the time?"

"It makes a hell of a racket. It stopped after she was down and I had my fingers on her pulse. You have to have a guy on it to keep it running."

By noon they had worked on Barnes and Schortz for an hour apiece and gotten nowhere. Brasher complained that they were slowing down operations and wasting time. At noon, Brock took Jane Tarrance down to the lunch wagon down the street.

He could see that she had been crying, and she told him that she had phoned the hospital just before noon and they had said there was no change in Miss Galloway's condition.

"Jane, you lived with her, roomed with her. Have you got any hunches? Did she act differently the last few days?"

Jane sipped her coffee. "I . . . I think so. She was dressing last Tuesday night. You were coming to pick her up, remember? She was looking in her mirror, and I looked at her and she seemed to be miles away. I asked her if it was an old boyfriend and she said no. She said that there was something she was going to try to remember, and that if it didn't come back, she was going to phone an old friend of hers and he'd help her remember. I tried to tease it out of her, but she just

275

smiled sort of mysteriously and said that I could sit back and watch the fireworks. Those are the words she used."

Brock stirred his coffee, said, "You realize, of course, that if she had told you, you'd now know the reason why she was shot."

Jane's eyes went wide. "You think so?"

"Elimination. It is the only clue to motive that we have. Therefore, it must be the clue. Did she make the phone call she talked about?"

"No. The next night she came back from the date with you. She was happy as a lark. She woke me up and told me that she had remembered that little thing she was thinking of on Tuesday night, but that before she jumped she'd have to make certain that she wasn't being tangled up in a coincidence that would just make her look silly."

"Jane, please try to remember her exact words on each occasion. Tell me what you said too, and I'll write them down. They may be the answer."

Back at the plant he met Maclaren, who said that he was going home and get some sleep and the hell with it. Maclaren said that it didn't look like it could be any one of the five and yet he felt it had to be. He said that he'd feel clearer in the head if he got some sleep, and he advised Brock to do the same. Brock felt the weariness in his back and legs, and his eyes felt as though there was grit in them, but he knew that he could keep going. He knew that if he went back to his bed it would be impossible to sleep.

He didn't tell Maclaren about the conversation with Jane. He had cautioned Jane to be silent, knowing that sooner or later Maclaren or one of his men would come around to her. The information he had was too vague to go on. He took the notebook out of his pocket and stood by the water cooler, reading the conversation.

Oliver came down the stairs, grinned at him, and said, "Did you hear the peeling I just got?"

"No, I didn't."

"Well, this whole mess has got little Walter into a foul humor, and he's been taking it out on me. I am no longer his

276

fair-haired boy. Now I'm a dope who wasted forty thousand bucks of the firm's money."

Hodge Oliver leaned over the fountain and drank. As he straightened up, wiped the back of his hand across his mouth, Brock said, "I don't get it."

"Heck, Brock, I talked myself into this job on the basis of some mechanical engineering background. You see, the old idea was that Brasher bid on miscellaneous mixed scrap, performed the sorting and baling, if necessary, with cheap labor, and then resold the clean scrap for enough to cover his costs and make himself a profit. I sold him on the idea that I could go around and buy junk equipment whenever I could find a good price and felt certain that, with the dismantling of it, we could get our dough back plus a profit. He sent me around to auctions and sales, and now he doesn't like the last forty thousand I spent. I was working on the stuff at the time Stella was shot."

"What is the stuff?"

"Oh, two thousand gimmicks that were Vietnam surplus. I got 'em for twenty bucks apiece. Sort of a computing gadget. They're all out in the back end of the shop. I'm certain that I can rig them around some way so that we can unload them at a profit, but now little Walter thinks I'm nuts and he's sorry he ever got off the straight, semifabricated, and unfabricated scrap business."

Once again Brock stood by her bed and looked down at the face, darkening with the shadow of death. He stood, large and brooding, looking at her dry lips, at the painful slightness of her under the hospital blankets—and for a long time he thought.

From the lower corridor of the hospital, he phoned Maclaren, who was back on duty. Maclaren objected at first, but at last he listened to Brock's plan.

Brock went back to the plant and went into Brasher's office, managing to smile. "The doctors just told me that Miss Galloway will be okay. She'll be able to talk tomorrow."

He also told Jane and Karkoff and Oliver and the switchboard girl and the guard and the office boy. Every one of them looked pleased. Everyone told him that it was swell, that Galloway was a good kid.

Horowitz and Maclaren sat in Brasher's office and the overhead light shone out across the shadowy expanse of desks, across the hooded typewriters. Brock stepped over to the desk and reached for Maclaren's cigarettes. He missed the pack, staggered slightly, and got it with his second grasp. Maclaren looked up at him suddenly. "When have you slept, Jud?"

"Not for quite a while."

"Go to bed. We'll take care of this."

"I couldn't sleep if I did, John. I'm okay."

"All we can do is wait," Horowitz said.

"Have we got good men on Galloway?" Brock asked. Neither of the two seemed to notice the use of the word "we." Somehow Brock had gained acceptance.

"The best," Horowitz said. "Plus good guys on each of the others. The only one we don't have to fret about is Oliver. He's over in the shop working on something. I guess he fouled up and he's trying to redeem himself with the boss."

The minutes passed in silent monotony while the three men smoked and glanced at the phone. Maclaren sent a man out for coffee and more cigarettes.

Maclaren snatched the phone when it rang. "Yeah? What! Sure. Grab him. Don't lose him. Bring him right back here. Thanks." He hung up.

He looked puzzled. He said, "For the hell of it, just to play safe, I stuck guys at the bus station, railroad station, and on the two bridges. I figured that if any of the tails slipped up, we'd have a second line of defense. Walker, over on the Anders Avenue Bridge, has picked up Karkoff in his jalopy headed out of town. He's bringing him over. Hell, we didn't even have a tail on that boy. According to the noise of that baler, he couldn't have done it."

Brock felt a lot of his weariness disappear, felt the muscles bunch along his thick arms as he clenched his hard hands. This was a start. Maybe this was it.

Karkoff slouched in the straight chair and said, "I tell you, you guys are on the wrong track. Sure, I got a record. That was a hell of a long time ago and I've been straight ever since. But that don't do me no good when it comes to a thing like this. I figured that if you guys couldn't find out who did it, you'd pin it on me somehow. I was skipping out of town, sure. But I don't know anything about it."

Brock stepped over to the chair, clubbed Karkoff in the side of the head with a clenched fist, picked him up off the floor, and jammed him back into the chair.

Karkoff shook the mist out of his eyes and said, "That stuff won't do you no good, pal. I got nothing to tell you."

Brock glanced at Maclaren. Maclaren shook his head slowly. Horowitz was kneeling on the floor, going through Karkoff's luggage. He straightened up. "Nothing here, John. A mess of tools and wire and clothes. One hundred bucks in a tin box along with some pictures of some lush women."

"You guys going to book me?" Karkoff said.

"Sure. Maybe we haven't got anything to go on, but we'll find something," Maclaren said with a tight smile.

"Okay. I don't mind. But there's no sense in carting all this stuff of mine down to your game rooms. Let me drop it off at my room and pick out some clothes when you take me down."

Something restless stirred in the back of Brock's mind. Something wasn't right. Why should Karkoff be concerned about such a trivial thing? It didn't make good sense. The man was too casual. He glanced at Maclaren. Apparently John felt nothing wrong. Neither did Horowitz. Brock wondered if the lack of sleep was harming his mental processes.

He stepped over the tin suitcase and looked down. Wrenches, a battered micrometer. Some spools of fine, white wire. This was the stuff that Karkoff wanted to leave in his room.

Suddenly a lot of things made sense. He felt the quick thud of his pulse. He went over it again in his mind. It still checked. Maclaren said sharply, "What is it, Jud? I've seen you look like this before."

Brock said, "I can't tell you...yet. Play along with me, John. Just a little while. Hold Karkoff here. I want to go down into the shop."

He heard the scream of boards ripped loose as he stepped

into the shop. Oliver was prying open a small case. Against the far wall was a pile of empty cases. Oliver, a smudge on his cheek, grinned up at Brock. "A little night work, Brock. Got to get all this stuff uncrated so we can see what we've got. If I don't unload it soon, Brasher is going to take the forty thousand out of my pay."

Just beyond Oliver was a bulging burlap sack. Brock kicked it. "What have you got here?"

"Oh, some damn wire that's fastened to each unit. No good to me. Thought I might as well peel it off as I uncrated the stuff."

Brock grinned. "Don't work too hard, Oliver." He walked back to the office. He didn't answer Maclaren's questioning look. He picked up the phone, dialed the operator, and asked to speak to the President of the Stoeffer Corporation of Birmingham, Alabama. The operator said she'd call back. He hung up.

Horowitz said, "Have you gone nuts? Alabama! What goes on?"

"Leave him alone," Maclaren said. "Take a look at Karkoff."

The man had slouched further in his chair and his face was white, his lips compressed.

A Mr. Stoeffer got on the line and Brock asked him a few questions. Stoeffer said, "I'm afraid that I don't have the detailed knowledge to answer that question. My production head was a man named James Beeson. He's no longer with me, but he's still here in town. Try phoning him."

Beeson came on the line in a few minutes and Brock heard him yawn into the phone. Brock snapped him out of it by saying, "This is police business, Mr. Beeson. You worked for the Stoeffer Corporation on government contract W-one-eighteen—ORD-three-two-five-five?"

"I guess so, but I can't remember them by number. What sort of an item was it?"

"Computer, M-eighteen. Do you remember it?"

"Yeah, I remember it, but what's the tieup with police business?"

"How big a contract was it?"

280

"Two thousand units at a price of eighteen hundred a unit. Three million six hundred thousand. That was what they called an experimental quantity. They were for the Artillery Section of the Office of the Chief of Ordnance. You can tell that by the ORD in the contract number. We made those . . . let me see, now . . . about four years ago. Then we found out that some other device had made them obsolete anyway."

"Suppose somebody managed to buy the whole lot at twenty bucks a copy?"

Beeson laughed. "I don't know what the hell they'd do with them. Maybe they've got a—" He stopped, and Brock, his heart pounding, heard the man gasp. Beeson's voice was shrill. "Hey! Wait a minute. Our unit price was only eight hundred bucks, and the reason it became eighteen hundred was when we found out that the damn specifications called for a lot of platinum wire for each one. About a thousand bucks' worth, if I remember rightly."

Brock thanked him, hung up, and stooped over the metal suitcase. He picked out the reels of white wire and put them on the desk in front of Maclaren. "This stuff is platinum," he said.

As Maclaren picked up one of the reels, Karkoff jumped for the doorway. It was unexpected. Horowitz made a grab for him that missed and then yanked the Positive from his hip holster. There was no point in shooting. Karkoff had disappeared into the shadows. He thumped down the side stairs.

As the three of them, hearing Karkoff clatter against a pile of scrap, spread out and followed him across the yard, the light in the shop went out suddenly.

Brock realized he was without a gun. He fumbled in the darkness and found a two-foot length of one-inch bar stock. It fitted his hand snugly.

Their eyes were getting used to the darkness. The glow of the city against the low-hanging clouds faintly illuminated the yard. Following Maclaren, Brock drifted out to the side, hurrying around the far end of the shop. A dark figure was struggling against the fence, drawing himself up. Maclaren aimed carefully and fired. The figure screamed like a woman and dropped heavily to the ground. A dark shape ran back into the shop.

Horowitz took the main entrance and Brock and Maclaren covered the back door through which the figure had run.

"Where are the lights?" Maclaren whispered.

"I think there's a set just inside the door on the left. Let me try."

"Okay. But stand back when they go on. He might have a gun."

His fingers found the switch, and the sudden glare of light threw the shop into sharp illumination. The massive baler, hydraulic plungers silent, stretched squat and powerful along one side of the shop. The crane hook dangled without motion.

Maclaren bellowed, "Come on out!"

Gun ready, Maclaren walked into the shop. Brock saw Horowitz standing framed in the main door, his gun in his hand.

The shop seemed to be empty. The three of them stood stupidly. Brock caught a glimpse of movement high overhead, hissed, "Up there! On the catwalk!"

A shadowy figure ran quickly along the catwalk to a skylight. Brock knew then what the plan was. Smash through the skylight and run down the sloping roof. From the edge of the high roof, an active man could jump the fence.

Horowitz fired, but the figure didn't stop. There was a smash and tinkle of breaking glass. As Maclaren fired, Brock turned and ran out the back door, along the side of the building. He heard the pound of running steps on the roof.

He drew back the heavy bar in his hand. The figure appeared and seemed to hesitate, balanced on the very edge of the roof. With all his strength, Brock threw the bar, leading the figure outlined against the glow in the sky by a few feet.

There was a thud as the figure jumped into midair. A hoarse cry. It fell against the barbed wire, clawed for a moment, and then dropped inside the fence. There was a small bubbling noise, and then silence.

Maclaren squatted beside the body of Hodge Oliver and lit a match. Brock looked down.

"Hitting him in midair like that put him off balance, I guess,"

Maclaren said calmly. "Or maybe he wouldn't have made it anyway. That barbed wire caught him right in the throat and ripped it wide open. He was probably dead ten seconds after he hit the ground."

Captain Davis, lean, gray, and quiet, shoved the pack of cigarettes across the desk to Jud Brock. Horowitz sat by the window. Maclaren leaned against the closed door, his face relaxed.

"Better tell me the whole thing from the beginning, Brock," Davis said.

"I got onto it because a lot of little things all of a sudden added up. She was shot by one of the people we narrowed it down to. Oliver was working in the rear end of the shop. He could go outside and shoot her and go back in in seconds. Her roommate said that Stella was trying to remember something long ago and far away. That pointed to Washington. Oliver was in Washington. But the disposal of the gun had me licked. Also the motive. Oliver came and told me his private difficulties with Brasher. Oliver was a gambler. He was afraid I might have overheard the argument, and he wanted to kill off my suspicions by telling me himself. He was too eager. Also he was too nice about it when I slapped him around in his room.

"Stella was shot with a forty five. He wanted the girl dead. He notched the slug to make certain of it, knowing that if he missed a vital spot when he fired, the slug would spread and smash her all to hell inside. The problem began to shape itself up. The motive had some connection with Washington.

"I pulled the cornball play, the old gimmick about her recovering, and Maclaren covered all the angles. Karkoff started to run. We grabbed him. I knew that he couldn't have done it, but he must have started to run because he had helped somehow. I remember his baler. It looked as though maybe Karkoff had been paid off for not noticing when Oliver came back into the shop and tossed the gun into the scrap that Karkoff was baling. That tied in with Karkoff's telling Lavery to go get a smoke. He couldn't chance having Lavery, up on the crane, see Oliver toss the gun into the scrap, see Karkoff compress the batch of scrap into a neat little bundle with the gun in the middle.

"Even if it had happened that way, I couldn't see how Karkoff had been paid off for his help. It didn't make sense. Then Karkoff wanted to drop his stuff off at his room. That indicated that maybe Horowitz hadn't seen something of value in the stuff.

"As I looked down at the suitcase, a lot of things popped into place in my mind. Both Oliver and Stella Galloway worked in a procurement section. Oliver had told me that he had bought some war-surplus stuff that Brasher couldn't see any value in. Maybe that war surplus was the angle.

"I went out into the shop and got the contract number and company name off the cases. Oliver was out there working. I realized that he was out there because he had heard that on the next day Stella would be able to talk and she would point the finger right at him. It didn't make sense to have Oliver opening all of the cases. Hell, if the things were all alike, he could just unpack one. He was filling a bag with wire. Karkoff had wire in his suitcase. I went back and phoned the company who made the stuff and found out that Oliver was stripping a thousand bucks' worth of platinum wire off each one. I guess he intended to get as much as he could and try to clear out of town at dawn before Stella could pop off about him.

"Karkoff heard the phone call and knew that was the end of the road because he was carrying five thousand bucks' worth of the wire in his suitcase. He made a break, tipped off Oliver, and they tried to go over the fence. Maclaren smashed Karkoff's knee, and Oliver killed himself when he jumped short and hit the barbed wire."

Captain Davis sat in thoughtful silence for a time and then said, nodding, "I can see how it was. A civil servant in military procurement, a man with some mechanical and electronic engineering background, discovered that these computer gadgets with two millions' worth of platinum wire in them had become surplus. Maybe Miss Galloway happened to mention it to Oliver, in an ironic way. It would intrigue anyone, that much platinum in an obsolete device. Oliver quit and found work with a scrap company which could bid on the devices, because he didn't have the forty thousand. It was his rotten luck that he picked a scrap outfit in the city of Louisavale, Miss Galloway's home town. Maybe she said nice things about our city. His terrible luck was compounded when she came back and went to work at the same place.

"He must have prayed she would never remember what had probably been a very casual conversation over coffee, after Brasher made such a loud stink over the waste of forty thousand dollars. But she did. She must have confronted him, then foolishly gave him time to think it over. He knew that she brought your orders out into the yard, Brock. He bribed Karkoff, shot her, and tossed the weapon into the baler. He must have felt pretty safe. In the vast, confusing picture of military procurement, he must have thought that his motive would be hidden." He paused. "Two million dollars is a great deal of money, gentlemen."

Brock stood up, stubbed out his cigarette. The weariness was fogging his brain and he knew that at last he could sleep. "Do you need me for anything?" he asked.

Davis looked at Maclaren and then at Horowitz. Both men nodded briefly. "Yes, Jud. We need you for something. We need you to walk a beat for six months or a year. At the end of that time, if you're still in line, we need you back in here."

Brock couldn't answer. His mouth was dry and his eyes stung. He said, hoarsely, "Thanks," turned, and left the small room.

The intern said, "We can't tell yet, Mr. Brock. She's done well lasting until now. Respiration is a little deeper, but . . ."

With one hand, Brock smoothed the dry, dead hair back from her damp forehead. Her eyelids fluttered and opened, and she stared up at the ceiling, unseeing.

He leaned close to her and said thickly, "Don't go away! I need you."

She turned her head the barest fraction of an inch, and he caught the flicker of recognition in her eyes before they closed once more.

He got up and slid the chair back. The intern said, "That's

what they need. They need to be given the will to fight. I hope she heard you."

"She heard me."

The intern said wistfully, "She must have been a lovely girl."

Brock looked at him, staring heavily. "Just for the hell of it, son, let's say that she *is* a lovely girl."

The intern stood outside the door to the private room and watched Judson Brock walk down the corridor toward the exit. Something of almost frightening intensity had looked out of the big man's eyes when he had spoken. The intern noticed that he walked with a step of infinite, dogged weariness.

As Brock stepped out into the dawn, the intern turned and looked back into the room. He said softly, "Something tells me, lady, that you better get well. I don't want to have to face that guy if you don't."

Dead on the Pin

My name is Joe Desmon, and I'm manager of the Wonderland Bowling Alleys on the turnpike three miles out of town. I've held the job ever since I got back from Vietnam. The hours are long, but I'm not kicking. I've got a little stashed away and I'm getting the experience, and someday I'm going to have my own layout and hire some stupid guy to keep the crazy hours I keep.

The town needs more alleys, and so the leagues are stacked. The way it is now, they've got me working twenty-six hours a day during the season. All the time I'm yapping at the waitresses or calming down some clown full of beer or ducking the big looping passes made by the members of the Industrial Girls' League. That in addition to paying all the bills, keeping track of the cash, running the snacks and beer business, seeing that the equipment stays in shape, renting shoes, and giving lessons.

So it seemed like almost too much to expect when one day about three months ago this little guy showed up and asked if I could hire him to do jobs around the place. Said his name was Johnson. He was edging close to fifty, with the top of his head up to about my chin. He was the sort of little man you would push out of your way, but not if you looked close. There were hard, blunt bones in his face and a pair of pale-blue expressionless eyes and a tight slit for a mouth. He had a thick look through the shoulders, and his arms hung almost down to his knees, with big square wrists.

He was well dressed, and I figured he'd be out of my salary

range. I asked him how much he had to make and he said, "Whatever you can give me, kid."

"How about seventy-five a week, and I'm not kid. I'm Mr. Desmon."

"That'll be fine, Mr. Desmon. Just dandy."

"For that dough you brush down the alleys whenever they're clear, mop the floors, empty the ashtrays, check the equipment, and scrub the restrooms. And anything else I can think up."

He said mildly, "I'd like a chance to bowl a little, too."

I took a quick look at his right thumb. It had that swollen, bent-back look of a man who has done a lot of it. But I didn't see any calluses. His hands looked pink and soft.

I wasn't behind and it was a slack hour. I said, "How about a quick one?"

I had my own ball and shoes behind the counter. He picked a pair of shoes out of the rental rack and spent at least five long minutes finding a ball to suit him.

With my double and spare in the first three frames and his two splits and a miss, I felt pretty arrogant. When I got my strike in the fourth, it made my fill on the third frame a fat 69 to his 27. I started to get bored, but in his fourth frame, his ball ducked into the pocket for one of the prettiest cleanest strikes I have ever seen. His ball had been curving in too fast before that, giving him those thin Brooklyn hits.

And so while I got spare, strike, spare, he got three more of those boomers, where all the pins jumped into the pit in unison.

He looked at me and said, "Mr. Desmon, do you fire people you can't beat?"

"What do you think I am? No. And I'm not beat yet."

"Just asking, ki—Mr. Desmon."

So he kept chucking them in there, and in the end he had put eight strikes in a row together, and he wiped me out, 235 to 202.

So I said, "Okay. And I think you could keep right on wiping me out. You're not fired."

He grinned for the first time. It came and went so quickly I almost missed it. He wanted to know if he could practice a little when his work was done. I told him to be my guest.

I kept an eye on him. He did his work and got along well enough with the rest of my people. He got along by staying out of the way. After the first month I began to throw some lessons his way, giving him a cut. He had perfect style, laying the ball down so smoothly it wouldn't have dented the top of a custard pie. He could pick up the flaws and point them out and demonstrate how to cure them. He eased the pressure on me, but I never did really get to know the man.

When he bowled, it was either alone or with me, just before we closed the joint in the small hours. I began to keep a pocket score on him.

As he was leaving one night I said, "Hey, Johnson. Wait a minute."

He turned around. "What?"

"In the last ten games you've rolled, you've averaged two-twenty-one."

"So?"

"So I'd like to wangle you a spot on one of the pro leagues. You're as steady as a rock. How about it? I know an outfit that could use a new anchor man."

He walked slowly back toward me. For one funny moment he was the boss and I was a stooge working for him. He said, "Drop the idea, Desmon. I don't like it."

"But why? I should think it would please you."

"Just say that I don't like to bowl with people. Maybe I blow up under pressure. Put it any way you want, but don't go talking up my game. Understand?"

I almost said, Yes, sir.

He walked off into the night. I shrugged and went back to the books.

All of that should have been a tip-off. I should have gotten wise, maybe, the night Billy Carr came in. Billy has the sort of reputation that makes me wish I had the nerve to tell him not to come back. He's young and tall and sleek, somehow like a big cat. He had two of his boys with him. He's considered locally to be a pretty heavy stud. Anyway, the three of them came in, got shoes, shucked off their coats, and changed shoes down at the semicircular bench, ready to do some bowling.

Johnson was walking down the alley pushing the wide brush, wearing the lamb's wool mitts over his shoes.

I was too far away to stop it. Billy Carr grabbed a ball off the rack and rolled it down at Johnson. Johnson heard it coming. He looked around and sidestepped it, but it hit the brush and knocked it out of his hands.

He turned and walked slowly back up the middle of the alley toward where Billy stood laughing.

Between laughs, Billy said, "Did I scare you, pop?"

"You scared me plenty," Johnson said mildly. He grabbed the front of Billy's shirt and tossed him into the rack. Billy tumbled over it and landed on his shoulders. One of the hired boys reached for a sap as he moved in on Johnson. Johnson caught his wrist, ripped the sap out of his hand, and belted him flush across the mouth with it. The hired boy sat down and began to spit out teeth.

The other hired boy was reaching. "I wouldn't!" Johnson said in a low voice. And the boy didn't.

Their sole remaining gesture of defiance was to throw the shoes at me as they went out.

I said to Johnson, "That wasn't smart. They might give you a bad time outside."

He gave me a look of surprise. "Those three? Grow up, ki—Mr. Desmon."

They didn't bother Johnson, and they didn't come back.

Last week I woke up and there was a man sitting on a chair beside my bed. I shut my eyes hard, and when I opened them again he was still there.

"Good morning, Joe," he said.

"How did you get in here? What do you want? Is this a gag?"

He handed me a picture. A double picture. Full face and profile. With numbers. "Know this man?"

"Johnson. He works for me."

"Not exactly Johnson. Dan Brankel is a better name. Wanted in five western states for armed robbery and murder. Rumored to be a one-time associate and business partner of Al Nussbaum. Did some work with the King gang. That was a long time ago. He skipped the country with a fat bankroll. He's been where we couldn't touch him. By we, I mean the FBI. A while back we got a tip that he had moved. Since then we've been waiting for him to show up. We've been checking bowling alleys. That was his passion in the old days. So with your help, Joe . . ."

I was a wreck all day. I tried to charge people for more games than they'd rolled. I cussed out the waitresses, and one of my best ones quit on me. I even broke down and drank some of my own beer during business hours.

While the leagues were on, I was worse. No matter how tightly I held onto the edge of the desk, my hands still shook.

But I couldn't hold the clock back. The diehards finally pulled out, the last of them, at quarter to two. I said to Johnson, "Game tonight?" I barely managed to keep the quiver out of my voice.

He nodded and went to get his ball and shoes. Somehow he'd managed to buy them out of his pay. When he came back, I said, "Back in a minute. Got to check the doors."

Just the two of us were left in the place. I went to the side door, slammed it hard, then opened it silently and put the little wedge in it to hold it open.

The light controls were near my desk. I killed everything except the small light over the desk and the lights on the one alley we would use. My heart was swinging from my tonsils.

Johnson popped his thumb out of the hole on the ball, lined his sights, and swung a sweet ball down the alley. It made a low drone as it rolled. Then it hooked into the pocket, and the pins went down with a single smash.

The rack crashed down and I took my first ball. Even though I had used a lot of chalk, my hands were still greasy with sweat. The ball slipped, hung on the edge all the way down, and plinked off the ten pin.

Johnson said mildly, "Getting the hard one first?"

I laughed too loud and too long and stopped too abruptly. I got eight more on my second ball and Johnson marked the miss.

A nightmare game. I didn't dare turn around. I was afraid I'd see one of the men slipping silently in, and my face would give me away. Johnson was bowling like a machine. I piled up misses and splits, and I even threw one gutter ball. Each ball he rolled was just right. Once in the sixth frame one pin wavered and threatened to stay up, but finally it went down.

We had never talked much while bowling. I had to bite my tongue to keep from babbling to him. It might have made him suspicious.

It didn't hit me between the eyes until he marked up his eighth straight strike. And suddenly I realized, that if he kept on, I might see the first perfect game I have ever seen. It was a little bit easier then to forget the figures silently closing in.

He put in the ninth strike and the tenth. I had a miss on the ninth, for a score to that point of one-twenty-one. Worst game of the past three years.

After the tenth strike he said softly, "You know, this might be it. I never had one of those fat three-hundred games before. I've always wanted one."

"Don't jinx yourself talking about it," I said.

He put the eleventh ball in the pocket for a clean strike. "One more," he said. The ball was trundling back up the rails when I saw the little flurry of movement down near the pin setter. That was my signal.

I said, as nonchalantly as I could, "Wait a second. Got to get cigarettes."

As I turned and walked up the stairs he took his ball off the rack, walked slowly back, and chalked his fingers, pulling the towel through them.

I ran the last few steps to the desk, wiped my hand across the light panel, turning on every light in the place.

They had crept up in the darkness. They were in a half circle around him. He looked very small and old and tired standing down there.

"Okay, Dan," one of them said. "End of the line. All out. Put the ball down slowly and lie on the floor, your arms spread."

A dozen weapons were pointed at him.

In a weary voice he said, "You win. Let me heave this last ball down the alley."

Before he could get an answer, he moved over and turned to face the pins. From the angle where I stood, higher than the others, I saw his left hand flick from his belt up to his mouth. He swallowed something.

He stood for a long second, then started his stride. Halfway to the foul line his smooth stride wavered. The ball thumped hard, bounced, and he went down on his face across the foul line.

He was a dead man when he hit the floor. Even I knew that. I dimly heard the hoarse shout of anger and disappointment.

But I had my eyes on the ball. It rolled with pathetic slowness. It wavered in toward the head pin, hit the head pin on the left side. The pins toppled slowly, all but the six pin. It stood without a waver. A pin rolled slowly across the alley, nudged the rebel, and tumbled it off into the pit.

As though I was walking in my sleep, I went back down the stairs, took the black crayon, marked in the last strike, and drew the 300, making the zeros fat and bold.

I knew he was a crook. I knew he was cruel and lawless. They told me about the way he shot the Nevada bank clerk in the stomach. But I also know that he was a homesick guy who came back to the only thing he liked to do and scrubbed out lavatories for the privilege of doing it.

Maybe there's something wrong with me.

Because I don't think I'm ever going to like the game as much as I used to.

A Trap for the Careless

This James Garver drove out to Sharan Point with his problem on the afternoon of the fifth day of badminton, all set to lay it in Shay Pritchard's lap. The court was set up in the lower garden about fifty feet from the pool. I saw Krimbow coming slowly down the steps, favoring his rheumatism, his mouth set in the perpetual lemon-taste, the sun gleaming on his bristling white Prussian haircut.

It was my serve and I was at the point where the bat weighed forty-nine pounds, my mouth was full of cotton, and the pain in my side felt as though it had always been there.

I held onto the bird and Shay glared at me. "Come on, Robby!"

There are a few Shay Pritchards in every generation. They are seldom happy. The fates give them a triple portion of energy, a restless mind, an enormous capacity for boredom, a measure of personal charm, and a hint of savagery. Three years ago I went to Sharan Point to write Shay up for a national magazine. By now the editors have written me off. I've wanted to leave a dozen times. But somehow . . .

Physically he is a big slope-shouldered character with a round, guileless face, baby-blue eyes, curly blond hair, and a shade more weight below the belt than above it. Dressed in his best he looks like an overgrown kid being sent off to a church social. Stripped down, his thighs are like beer kegs, and restless slabs of muscle crawl on his shoulders and arms with every movement. Through some alchemy of personality he can look one moment like a bashful farm boy on his first date, and seconds later like a demon avenger, a conscienceless tool of doom.

I have seen him kill. And I have seen women look at him.

Either I hate him or he is a combination best friend and employer. Someday I will have to make up my mind.

Shay Pritchard: fullback, Rhodes scholar, infantryman, sculptor. Man of colossal hungers, of gargantuan appetites— with the instincts of a crook, and of a cop.

A sweet son of a bitch

Krimbow spat with precision into a circular flower bed and said, "He's one of those people keeps cracking his knuckles."

Shay sighed. "Who, Krimbow?"

"Drives an eight-year-old sedan and wears a ten-year-old suit and says he's got to see you. Says that a Lieutenant Ryan sent him out here."

"Ryan knows I don't work for love."

"I told this fella the usual fee for just talking to you, Shay, and unless he's got the inside of that roll packed with ones, it ought to be enough for two–three new cars. Calls himself James P. Garver."

At the mention of the roll the annoyed expression slid off Shay's round face. He beamed. "Help all those who can pay," he said. "Where'd you put him?"

"I was going to leave him in the hall, until I saw he was loaded, and then I moved him into the small study."

"Go tell him to wait fifteen minutes," Shay said.

Krimbow went back up toward the house. "Ryan is missing persons," I said.

When we went into the small study, James P. Garver jumped up, smiled nervously. He was a weedy little man close to fifty with a farmer's cross-hatched neck and hands thickened and permanently curved into the shape for grasping tool handles. He had a dried, unmemorable face, colorless gray eyes, rusty hair, and an air of tension. His teeth were cheap, glassy and too even.

He looked at me, licked his lips, and said, "Mr. Pritchard, I—"

"Sit down, please," Shay said in irritation. "I'm Pritchard. This is Mr. Moran, my assistant."

Garver bobbed his head in acknowledgment, sat down on the edge of one of the deep leather chairs, and rested his hard hands on his thighs.

Shay strolled over to the cabinet. "Drink?" he asked.

"I don't much, but right now . . ."

With the glasses distributed, Shay perched one massive hip on the corner of the desk, towering over Garver, and said, "My man told you that for three hundred dollars I'll listen to you. If I want to take on the problem I'll state a fee commensurate with the difficulties involved. That fee will not include expenses, and I cannot, of course, guarantee results. Then it will be your decision to tell me whether or not to go ahead."

"Lieutenant Ryan seemed to think—"

"Forgive me, Garver, but I can't think of anything I'm less interested in than the opinions of Lieutenant Ryan. State your problem."

"Well, it's about Allie, Mr. Pritchard. It's only Thursday, but it seems like she's been gone for longer than just since Tuesday afternoon. She's my wife. I've been just about crazy. I went to a cattle auction in Randolph on Tuesday and when I came back she just wasn't there. I've got a picture of her here. . . ."

It was an eight-by-ten glossy print, and he had folded it once lengthwise and shoved it into the inside breast pocket of his suit. He handed it over to Shay almost reverently.

Shay had a look on his face of pronounced disinterest. The farmer's wife had grown weary of the farm. He looked at the picture. His eyes narrowed and he sucked at his lower lip. He handed it to me.

It was a professional job by a man who knew how. She was reclining on some sort of chaise longue, and the picture was of head, throat, and shoulders, stopping just at the verge of becoming too intimate. Eyes too deep and too wise for her age, and a soft, wide mouth that was not wise at all—only willing. The blond hair was spread out around her head. We both stared at Garver.

Suddenly there was something indescribably goaty about him, and his cackling laugh was that of the eternal Pan. "Guess you fellas didn't expect my wife to be a pin-up girl. The rest

296

of her is just as nice as that face, too. Surprised everybody, I did, coming back with her that day. She's only twenty." Then anxiety overcame the sudden wet-lipped look and he said dully, "Can't imagine what happened to her."

"Where did you meet her?"

Surprisingly, Garver flushed. "I haven't told anybody else this, but I guess you ought to know. About six months ago I got a crazy notion to go away by myself. Working too hard, I guess. I went down to Endor City, about a two-hundred-mile drive, and got myself a hotel room. Went to a lot of movies, and then I got tired of the movies and I had a few drinks. Asked the cab driver to take me somewhere where I could have some fun. Drove me way outside Endor City and I didn't like that place, so he brought me back to a place right in town. You'd never find it if you didn't know where to look. They call it Roger's Place. There's friendly girls there that'll talk to you right at the bar. I met Allie there. She was unhappy. She said she was tired of young kids that weren't serious and she said she liked older men. We went to a few other places, I disremember where, and then we went to her place and—well, I guess we kind of forgot ourselves. Anyway, she was a-crying, and a-carrying on and saying she wasn't that kind of girl at all and I could see she wasn't and we got married two days later."

"What was her address there?" Shay interrupted.

"It was a sort of rooming house. Wait a minute. I got it here in my wallet. Oh, here it is. Ten-eighteen Columbine Street. We checked her right out of there. The poor kid didn't have much more than enough to fill one suitcase. I brought her back here. I live over on the River Road and the house isn't much, so I contracted for a new house. We just moved into it ten days ago. No, eleven. We've been pretty happy. Best six months of my life." Again his eyes held the hard glint of Pan.

"What is her full name?"

"Allana Montrose Garver."

"Where from?"

"I don't rightly know. Back East somewhere."

"Relatives?"

"The poor kid is alone in the world. Leastways, she was."

"You have relatives?"

"Neither kith nor kin. There was some second and third cousins, but I don't know where they are. Haven't for twenty years."

Shay poured fresh drinks. Garver covered his glass with the top of his hand and shook his head.

"Now tell me about yourself," Shay asked gently.

Garver sighed and looked into the past, his eyes clouding. "Got married when I was twenty. Mary died a year later when the kid came. The kid died two days after she did. I went back with my pa. When he died I took over the farm. When I began to do better with feed business and the cattle trading, I sold off a lot of the acreage. My partner is Sam Jarone. We've been doing well for the past eight–nine years. He handles the feed business, mostly, and I work out the cattle deals."

"What are you worth?" Shay asked bluntly.

Garver looked startled. "I don't know as I—"

"I must know everything, Garver."

He didn't like it. "Let me see. Real liquid stuff'll go maybe four hundred thousand. About another hundred and fifty thousand tied up so tight it'd take a long time to get it loose."

"A half million, eh?" Shay said dryly.

"I don't think about it that way."

"I hope you don't mind if I do, Mr. Garver."

"Well, I'm pretty careful about not throwing money around."

"Now I must ask you some questions that you might not like. First—did Mrs. Garver know your financial position?"

Garver beamed. "No, she didn't. That's how I knew she fell in love with me for sure. I never did tell her until after we'd been married a month. That was when I changed my will and the insurance over."

"She seemed pleased?"

"Why, she certainly did! Huggin' me and kissin' me for fair."

"How was your money going to go before you changed it over?"

"The estate was going half to the Baptist Church and half to the State College and the Department of Farm Economics, and the insurance to Sam Jarone."

"Much insurance?"

"Eighty-five thousand paid up. It was sort of partnership insurance, but bigger than it had to be. So when I transferred it, I took out forty thousand renewable term, with Sam as beneficiary. That's what he has, with me named to get it in case something happens to him."

"Did Jarone seem annoyed that you got married?"

Garver flushed. "Yes, damn him. He has been giving me a terrible time with all those nasty remarks of his. Way he tells it, I could be a hundred and ten years old marrying a kid of fourteen. Matter of fact, I'm forty-eight. Not too much difference there. Hell, when I'm seventy, Allie'll be forty-two."

"Are you expecting an increase in the family?"

"No, we're not. I've been hoping, but it just hasn't turned out that way yet. Can you find her, Mr. Pritchard?"

"Have you considered the fact that she might not want to be found?" Shay said softly.

"That's a lie! Allie's been happy with me. I'm thinking it's this here amnesia and she wandered off, or else somebody took her off and I haven't gotten a kidnap note yet."

"Ryan is working on it?"

"He put her on the tape today. I tried to pay him to go at it with special handling and he said he couldn't and sent me to you. Will you take it on?"

"The fee will be five thousand dollars. Plus expenses. And another five thousand if it goes over two weeks."

Garver swallowed hard. He stared at Shay. "Say, you didn't even blink when you said five thousand."

"Should I have?"

"It's a lot of money."

"Allana's a lot of girl, Mr. Garver. I'll accept your check."

"I'd have to think about spending that much money so fast."

Shay looked at his watch. "Think about it for two minutes, Mr. Garver. And then you can leave if you decide it's too much money."

Garver muttered, "Five thousand, eh." He brightened. "Say, I'll give you a check for five hundred and three thousand cash. That way you don't have to report it for taxes and the net to you'll be about the same."

Shay stood up slowly. "Mr. Garver, diddling the federal government in that manner smacks of shooting fish in a washtub. It isn't sporting. And your two minutes are up."

Garver scribbled the check, waved it back and forth to dry it. He handed it over. "Now what are you going to do first, Mr. Pritchard?"

"Tell you to go back to your affairs and keep your mouth shut and report anything unusual to me immediately. We may call on you later. You said you are out on the River Road?"

"A quarter of a mile north of Bliss Corners. On the left. My name's on the mailbox."

"Good day, Mr. Garver."

We watched him go down the walk to the side drive, a man following a hypothetical horse across a nonexistent plowed field, his shoulders bowed by plow handles that weren't there. Shay whirled an ice cube in his glass, frowning down at it.

"That was pretty heavy, wasn't it?" I asked.

"For that he-goat? I was charging him for his marital bliss. Spread over six months it doesn't come to much."

"A pretty obvious situation," I said. "She found out he was loaded so she grabbed him. But money doesn't make some things easier. And so she left."

"If you're right, and I hope you are, it's an easy five thousand. But I have a funny hunch about this."

"Jarone?"

He shrugged. "Five after four. We need a woman's opinion. Bets likes martinis and the pool. Tell Krimbow and phone her up, will you, Robby?"

"I know your curious charm, Shay, but Bets won't come within a mile and a half of this place again and you know it."

"A month has passed, Señor Moran. A full and lonely month. I suggest that you play up the forgive-and-forget angle."

After he left the room, I perched my heels on the desk and dialed. After four rings, Bets answered.

"This is Robby, honey. Don't hang up."

Bets is a combination oil and air force widow, a dark angular cutie of twenty-nine who lives five miles up the road with maid, gardener, five-year-old daughter, and a portable typewriter on which she sublimates herself by turning out lurid confessions for money that she does not need. For a time it looked as if she and Shay could make it, but on those two the rough edges just don't rub off.

"Am I supposed to be mad enough to hang up? It just isn't that important."

"At five we're using the old-fashioned glasses for martinis. The water in the pool was changed this morning, and we're both bored and we have nothing lovely to look upon."

"Tell that big clown to go look in a mirror for an hour or so. That ought to make him feel pleased."

"Bets, you hurt me. We live too close, Shay says, for the war to keep going on. Let's all be pals again."

"He's a bastard."

"We both know that, but he's cute sometimes. Like a tame bear. Come wallow in our pool, honey. Shay says to wear the bikini, the yellow one."

"That one's for looking, not swimming." Her voice sounded friendlier.

"We'll share the risk with you. Five-ish?"

She sighed. "I might as well. I've confessed myself into a hell of a corner, and I can't seem to write my way out of it."

We had been out of the pool long enough for it to turn back into a sheet of green glass. Bets lay on the rubberized mattress on the apron of the pool, her almost boyish body a startling tan in the sunset light contrasted with the brave yellow of the skimpy suit. Her cheekbones are high and sharp enough to give her a gaunt look. Her eyes are hawk-hooded and her mouth is a wide, harsh slash. If she could get down three notes lower, she could sing baritone. She has never failed to give me a quickened pulse.

She and Shay had been distinctly cool until he had at last broken the tension by immersing her firmly and deeply. She had come up sputtering behind and had made a fair attempt to sit on his head. Then they were old friends again.

Our martini pitcher is as tall as a hydrant and seems to contain as much fluid. Shay serves too much liquor and drinks too much himself, but he is never out of control and any guest who gets that way is having his last visit at Sharan Point.

Shay had padded off to the house. I was stretched out on the concrete at right angles to the mattress, stealing a bit of it as a rest for the back of my head. Bets's fingers moved moth-light across my forehead, expressing nothing except in their rhythm, and that was more than enough.

"Belay it, woman," I said. "Or I'll have to go leap in the pool."

Shay came back. I sat up. He handed her the picture of Allie.

"Please classify," he said.

Bets held it so that the fading light caught it.

"Hmmm. I'd really have to hear her talk to do a good job. Let me see. Car hop, movie extra, commercial playmate. Hard to tell. But the little gal has been here and there and back again."

"Farmer's wife," Shay said, laughter in his voice.

She sat up with a long, easy motion and stared at him. "Don't tell me! That must be quite a farmer. What well did you drop him into?"

"I didn't. He's a remarkably unattractive little man pushing fifty. His fingernails are dirty and his breath is bad. Nor is his linen spotless."

"Oil under his farm?"

"He has it, but the little girl didn't know it until after she said yes."

"Are you positive of that?"

"Even if he had told her he had money, he was in a situation where she would be likely to think he was lying. So I want a woman's opinion. List the reasons that would cause that little item to marry the farmer, omitting money."

Bets lay back and stared up at the dusk sky. She still held the picture between lean brown fingers.

"That's not so easy, Shay. A girl gets lonely. But not that lonely. Here's one. Masochism. Somebody lets her down hard. She takes her revenge by marrying into an impossible situation. But the gal doesn't look like either the sentimental or the mas-ochistic type. If you want melodrama, sometimes people have

302

to hide. And sometimes you have a person with legal problems. They can inherit only if married. The last item, of course, is a girl who is—shall we be delicate and say infanticipating?—who grabs the first security that comes along. That covers it, Shay. Like any of them?"

"It clarifies my thinking."

"Why do you want to know all this?"

"She left, either alone or aided. The farmer is upset."

"Maybe somebody raided the cookie jar and she'll be home, contrite, tomorrow."

"Could be. Tonight my subconscious will work on it. It does better than I do."

She shivered. "Would somebody please mention getting dressed," she said.

Krimbow had seared the steaks in his own incredible fashion. Bets ate like a female wolf. She phoned and checked on Prim, her little girl, and later I watched her play chess with Shay on the glassed-in terrace.

She played a slashing, vicious game, bringing all her power to bear at every point, ignoring defense to strike out. Shay parried and covered himself well, then moved onto the offensive when her attacks lost momentum.

I was watching their hands on the board. I saw her reach out and pick up a bishop. She held it in midair. It was not a proper piece to move at that point. Her knuckles were white. I looked at her and saw that she was looking into Shay's eyes. Her face was expressionless.

In a flat voice she said, "You never did finish that last figure, did you?"

"The pose wasn't right. That pose wasn't for you. It wasn't worth casting."

"You said you would try another one."

"You said you would never pose again."

I gave my stage yawn and muttered good night as I left the room. No one answered me.

After I was in bed, I knew that they were up in the studio, the harsh lights bright above them, his big, thick-fingered hands molding the clay with surprising delicacy, Bets standing on the

303

raised platform, on the turntable that moved around at the rate of one inch a minute.

It had all started again between them. Over chess.

The roar of her station wagon, the sputter of gravel against the fenders, woke me later. Moonlight was white in the room. I heard a sound and went to the window. Shay Pritchard was swimming up and down the length of the pool, low in the water, his arms lifting slowly. I counted six laps and went back to bed and to sleep.

It was a small ranch-type house, sparkling new. Garver met us at the door, incongruous in those *House Beautiful* surroundings. His eyes were puffed as though he had slept badly. His face lighted up as he recognized us.

"Did you find out something already?"

"No. We want to look around," Shay said.

He showed us the house. In the living room Shay went immediately to the magazine rack. Mixed in with the farm periodicals and cattle journals was an ample collection of glossy-paper true-crime magazines.

"Yours?" Shay asked.

"No, Allie liked those. She'd curl up like a kitten in that big chair over there, of an evening, and sometimes read that stuff until way past midnight. Her eyes'd shine funny-like over some of 'em. When we stayed up late I'd go out and scramble us a few eggs and put on a pot of coffee."

"She didn't like to cook."

"I wouldn't say she doesn't like to. She just can't do it so good. Me, I'm pretty handy around a kitchen from living alone all these years, so I do most of it."

"I'd like a look at her clothes."

Garver led the way back to the two bedrooms. He pointed to a big record player. "Bought her that for a wedding present. She wanted one bad."

Shay looked over the albums. A lot of Cuban rhythms. The rest was rock with a heavy beat.

"She picked all them out," Garver said. "She'd—well, she'd dance to 'em when we were alone. She knew I liked it."

Shay moved over to the dressing table. He stared at the

massive array of bottles, jars, jugs, vials. He picked up a small bottle. "Expensive."

"Fifty bucks an ounce," Garver said proudly. "Smells good."

The big closet covered one whole wall. It had sliding mirror-paneled doors. Once they were open I could catch the woman-scent of her. Shay leafed through the racked clothes like a man reading an out-of-date magazine in a dentist's office.

"Can you tell which of this stuff she had before you met her, Garver?" he asked.

"She threw most of that out. The blue dress there, the long shiny one, she had."

Shay took it off the hanger. He glanced at the label and said, "I'm taking this along."

Garver shrugged. There was a section of built-in drawers. Shay yanked them open, one at a time. Nothing but an array of filmy black panties, yellow ones, pink, powder blue—bras to match. The dressing-table drawers were full of small items. Junk jewelry, a lot of it heavy and barbaric.

"Did she have any good jewels?"

"No. I was going to get her something. She wanted an emerald. I hadn't gotten around to it yet."

"Where did she keep her private papers?"

"She didn't have any. I helped her pack when she left her place. Just clothes and shoes."

"What did she take with her?"

"I don't know. When I left the house in the morning she wasn't up yet. I made her breakfast and took it to her. I can't see as there's anything missing, but I don't rightly remember all the clothes she had. Or even the suitcases she bought. Lieutenant Ryan asked me all that too."

"Toothbrush?"

"That's still hanging right in the bathroom, and her hairbrush and stuff is still in the cabinet. That's why I don't think she took anything except the clothes on her back."

"What did she do all day while you were working?"

"Read and played the radio and her records, or went shopping."

"Did you two have friends?"

"Well, my friends are pretty old, and she was a stranger

here, and she said it would be nice if we were selfish for the first year or so and stayed by ourselves. That suited me okay."

We thanked him and left. Shay had the blue dress over his arm. It was a hard, electric blue in heavy satin. I slid behind the wheel and we went down the road.

Shay saw the old woman sitting, rocking, on the farmhouse porch, shelling peas. "Pull up," he said.

As we walked up to the porch I saw him carefully adjust his clean-cut boyish manner.

"Lovely day, ma'am," he said shyly.

"Seems to be." She had the eyes of a chipmunk. "What can I do for you?"

"I'm Shay Pritchard and this is Robert Moran. We don't want to bother you, Mrs. Carriff."

"Read the name off the mailbox, eh? What's on your mind?"

"I know that a good woman like you wouldn't discuss her neighbors with strangers."

"Depends on which neighbors, Mr. Pritchard."

He grinned boyishly. "Let's say Mrs. James Garver."

Mrs. Carriff braced her feet and stopped rocking. She looked at Shay and then at me. She started rocking again. "She won't be back."

"Why are you so sure of that?"

"Girl like her? Jim Garver was softheaded to marry the likes of that. Her reeking of cheap perfume and wearing no proper undergarments and more coats of paint that Murphy's barn! Young enough to be his granddaughter. She was after his money, but she found out she'd have to wait too long. Jim's sturdy. Lucky for him, she wasn't the kind to help him on his way. It's happened before. No, she just got right sick of living out here where it's quiet and went on back to the city."

"You saw her leaving?"

"No, I didn't. I didn't have to. I know her kind."

"Did she ever have any callers—that is, while Jim was at work."

"Men callers? They could have parked up Garrison's lane and come across lots. Easy enough to stay out of sight that way. She probably had 'em, all right. But the only one I ever saw was that silly Garrison boy. Big, gawky thing. His mother

306

told me he went off his feed after Jim brought that woman home. He must be nineteen now. Used to hang around out on the road and just stare at the house, hoping to see her through a window. But don't let on I talked about him if you go see him. His mother'd be mad as hops I told you anything."

Ted Garrison was working on a yellow tractor. He had the fuel pump dismantled and spread out on newspaper. There was a wide smudge of grease from his cheekbone to his jaw across his wind-burned face. He was tall and wide, and when he moved I saw nothing gawky about him.

"Want something?"

"How well did you know Allie Garver?" Shay asked. His tone was harsh and blunt.

The fuel pump diaphragm slipped out of the boy's fingers and rolled across the newspaper into the dooryard dust. His face paled under the ruddiness.

"Is—is she dead?"

"Why would you think she was dead?"

"You said how well did I know her. Like she was dead."

"She's gone. She could be dead. We don't know."

The color seeped slowly back. The boy's brown eyes hardened. "How well I know her is none of your damn business."

He had shoulders like a horse, and they were tensed under the blue work shirt. I moved out to one side a bit to flank him, just in case.

Shay sneered. "She's the kind to use a punk like you for laughs while Jim was working. Where'd you meet her? In the woods?"

The boy rushed with ponderous rage, swinging a right fist like a stone in the end of a sling. Shay moved to one side, evading the blow, and made what seemed to be a pawing, awkward gesture toward the boy's middle. Ted Garrison whoofed as the wind went out of him. He staggered and went to his knees, fighting for air. He lunged up and went down again, this time onto hands and knees. He shook his head, almost sadly.

"Now, be nice," Shay said.

Ted pushed himself back onto his haunches. His face was

307

twisted. "She isn't that kind. She isn't! She wouldn't even look at me. She was too good for that old buzzard Jim Garver. I don't know how he talked her into marrying him. I wanted to ask her to leave him."

"Did you ever talk to her?"

"Once."

"What about?"

"A letter for her got stuck to one of ours and got into our box. I took it down to her. I said, 'They left this letter in our box by accident. I'm Ted Garrison.' She said, 'Thank you, Ted.' And then she closed the door."

"When was that?"

"Last Monday."

"Did you take a look at the letter?"

"It was from Endor City, and there wasn't any return address on it. It was typed, and the envelope was the kind you buy in the post office—the long kind with the stamp already on it. It wasn't addressed to her very good. It just said, 'Mrs. Garver, Bliss Corners.' At the post office they'd penciled in 'Route Two.' I held it up to the sun, but—" He stopped suddenly.

"But you couldn't read through the envelope, eh?" Shay said. He laughed.

Ted stood up. "She's the—the most wonderful person I ever saw. It makes me mad the way the old hens around here talk about her." He looked hard at Shay. "And if you make another crack about her, I'll come at you again."

I wandered around the house while Shay worked in the studio. The problem of Mrs. Garver seemed to have slipped from his mind.

I was too restless to shut myself in the library and make progress on my book. I swam a bit, even though it was raining. At five he came downstairs, tenderly carrying an object wrapped in burlap sacking.

I followed him into the study and watched him place it on the desk. It was about two and a half feet high. I knew that last night's clay image of Bets had been coated with a trick rubber solution and that, after the solution had hardened, he

308

had cut it through to pull the clay figure out. The rubber, when hardened, served as a mold for the white plaster. The last part of the afternoon had been spent buffing the rough edges from the white plaster. Then, as usual, he would wait a month or so. If, at the end of a month, he still liked it, the plaster would be a pattern for the mold to cast it in metal.

"Unveiling of Bets," he said acidly, unwinding the burlap.

She was taking a half step, and her head was lowered and turned so sharply to one side that the left cheek pressed against the left shoulder. Her arms were rigid at her sides, fingers splayed and pressed hard against her thighs. Viewed from the front the figure expressed shyness and a sense of guilt. I had seen those qualities in Bets, but I hardly considered them dominant.

I frowned. "It doesn't—"

"Doesn't it?" he asked mildly. He turned it around gently, so that the back was toward me. I saw the reason for the odd angle of the head. She was looking back over her shoulder. There was slyness and lust on her face, invitation in the cant of her hip and the arch of her back.

"I'm calling it Hypocrisy," he said. "The two-sided image of shame and desire."

"It's—it's cruel," I said.

"And very like a woman. She'll like it."

"She'll smash it!"

"Robby," he said sadly, "I thought you knew Bets better than that. The last pose failed because I got tangled up with conjectures about her soul. Now we are pretty well agreed that Bets's soul has a twenty-three-inch waist, thirty-two-inch bust, and thirty-one-inch hips." He looked at his watch. "If you can be ready in fifteen minutes, we ought to be in Endor City by nine o'clock for a late dinner."

We arrived at Roger's Place at eleven. A cobblestone alley in the old portion of Endor City, an alley too narrow for a car. Three steps down to a door made of cypress boards, grooved and ancient. At the third step we broke the beam of a photoelectric cell, and the door swung silently open. Nothing could have been more incongruous in that setting.

The ceilings were low and the massive beams were painted Chinese red. The walls were an odd pale aqua, dimly and indirectly lighted. The cypress bar was on the left, a tiny band in the back right corner: marimba, muted trumpet, and bass. The three musicians looked, at first glance, like college boys taking time off. But the crew cuts were dyed, the jackets were sodden in the armpits, and their eyes had been imported from some quiet corner of hell.

Shay took three steps beyond the check girl and planted his feet. He has the knack of imposing himself on the people in a room, of hitting them across the mouth with amused insolence, of showing them, like a black ace flashed quickly, the constant threat of violence.

The thin man who sauntered over wore a Shetland tweed jacket, iron-gray masculine hair. His eyes had the bulging impermanence of droplets of blue spring water spattered on a slick white surface, as though, by shaking his head violently, they would rain to the floor. The eyes flicked across my face, leaving an indescribable sensation of wetness.

"You gentlemen would like to stand at the bar." He murmured it, and it was a statement rather than a question.

I had moved over to where I could see Shay's face. It had a heaviness, a glazed, animal look. "Place was recommended to me. You're Roger."

Without seeming to, he led us over to the bar. "I'm Rogah."

"I'm Smith," Shay said. "John Q. Smith. And my pal— Joseph Q. Brown. Can't have any fun in the old home town. Too close to the flagpole, as they say. You sell any fun here, Rogah?"

"Life is so full of a number of things, Mr. Smith. Fun is spelled many different ways."

"We'll let you write the prescription, Doc Rogah."

He floated away. My eyes were used to the dimness. Smoke drifted on the sour-sweet air, and some of it had the tang of pot. Several couples moved to the slow beat of the music, glazed and somnambulistic. A girl at a table laughed. A man with a full, silky brown beard made quick Gallic gestures and talked in a low tone to a sleepy boy.

Maybe Rogah, maybe the bartender, pushed a concealed

310

button. They came through a curtain in the back left corner, two of them. Graded, no doubt, to the cut of our clothes. Tall and long-legged, with that look of breeding that has gone too far, that has decayed, like collies too long in the muzzle, like continental automobiles, like French perfume bottles, like rapiers so frail that they become toys, not weapons.

Rogah joined them and he walked as they did. "Mr. Smith, may I present Miss Smith? And Miss Brown? Mr. Smith and Mr. Brown." He floated back into the gloom, drifting like something that had become untied under the sea.

Miss Brown's pupils were so vast that they shrunk the iris to a thin frame of blue. Her honey hair was intricately coiffed. The dress was an off-orange that should have been the wrong color for her but wasn't. She moved close to the bar between Shay and me, and the other one was on the other side of Shay, his big shoulders turned so that all I could see of her was the crown of her head, the mist-brown hair, ringleted.

"It's so difficult to meet interesting people," Miss Brown said. The diction was flat, clipped, precise.

"It seemed easy this time. Boston?"

"Dedham. And please call me Lee."

"I'm Robby. And your drink is either Scotch or brandy."

"How perspicacious, Robby. I like men who guess. Earlier in this dull evening it was Scotch, but now it's five star."

I ordered. She tilted her head on one side, and I saw that some of the precision of her speech and the carefulness of her movements was due to a case of being taken drunk. Her shoulder, where she leaned lightly against me, was warm.

She said, "Do you work for Mr. Smith?"

"Don't tell me it's beginning to show, Lee."

"Don't be hurt, Robby. I just felt that relationship in the atmosphere. And I prefer people without that . . . certain ruthlessness that employers have. You're a small boy trying to be as tough as the big boys, aren't you? There—I can see I've hurt your feelings."

"You're odd, aren't you?"

"That," she said briskly, "is a gambit I grow weary of. Dear Lee, you're so intelligent, so charming, so lovely, so obviously well educated. Then the next step is to ask me why I'm doing

311

this. I'll tell you in advance, Robby, before you work your way up to the question. It's because the world is a very, very dull place."

"Since he left?"

The tiny brandy glass lifted slowly, was emptied, and moved just as slowly back down onto the bar. "Darling," she said, "if you get nasty and make me cry, I'll spoil your evening, but good."

A new customer moved in at the bar beyond Shay. He looked around almost shyly, like a small boy who has just finished writing a dirty word on a fence. He took off his glasses and wiped them on a crisp white handkerchief. I ordered another round. When I looked at him again there was a girl with him. He had adopted an uncle's attitude. I heard his jovial laughter. The girl was young and she was neatly and plainly dressed. The man had a comfortable round tummy and a pin-striped business suit, a lodge pin in his lapel.

Shay pulled his girl around so that we stood in a group of four. He said, glancing at his watch, "Robby, the party ought to be in full swing by now, and now that we've got dates, let's go."

His girl pouted. "Don't want to go to any dull parties, Shay."

"Let's not," Lee said.

"Come on, we'll have fun," Shay said.

"Let's stay here," Lee said firmly. "Then later on we'll go over to my apartment and have a more select party. No strangers. Just the four of us."

"No, I insist we go," Shay said.

I caught the look that Lee gave the other girl. The other girl said, "You two looked like fun, but I guess we were wrong. Have a good time at your party, boys."

There must have been another signal I missed. Rogah appeared, as if he had sprouted up out of the floorboards. "All you sweet people shouldn't quarrel," he murmured.

Shay smiled. "I have a strange aversion to going to any place a girl suggests. It so often turns out to be remarkably expensive."

"What are you implying?" Rogah said. He smiled.

312

"Nothing at all. My friend and I are in a strange town. Our guard is up. Is there a law against that?"

Rogah sighed. "I make my share of mistakes. Considering the hour, I think that the girls can go with you to the party you mentioned, but I do think you should pay me the profit I would have made from your drinks and theirs."

"Anything to make both ends meet, eh?" Shay said, smiling with his lips.

"A hundred should cover it."

"That's a fair bit of drinking."

"The glasses have false bottoms, Mr. Smith."

Shay looked at the girls. He shook his head. "Thanks just the same, Rogah. The refreshment is overvalued."

"Why, you cheap—"

"Lee!" Rogah said. It was almost a whisper, but it whistled and snapped like a whip end. She stopped and she was pale around the mouth. Rogah made a small gesture with his hand and they walked off, balancing false dignity like schoolgirls carrying books on their heads for the sake of posture.

"Don't hurry back, gentlemen," Rogah said. He smiled. His teeth were small and quite pointed.

Outside, in the alley, Shay said, "Now we check another piece of the puzzle."

"If you're collecting pieces of a puzzle, friend, you're one up on me."

The cabstand was right around the corner. The flag was up and the driver lounged behind the wheel, the radio turned low.

"We want a cab," Shay said, reaching for the door handle.

"Sorry, Mac. Waiting for a customer."

"Your flag's up."

"So my flag's up. Don't give me an argument, chubby. Go on down the street. There's other cabs."

Shay, to my surprise, walked meekly off. Our sedan was around the corner.

He slid behind the wheel and made no move to start the motor. "The shell in the middle has the pea under it, mister," he said.

"You lose," I said.

"It smelleth to highest heaven, Robby. It stinketh, in fact.

313

Wait here. I want to stir James P. Garver out of his downy nest." He slid out and went off into the darkness. I lit a cigarette. When it was half gone, he was back.

"The address," he said, "is the Henderson Hotel. Neat, clean, efficient. Horse your bag out of the back and check in there. Let the desk clerk know you're on vacation and you want to say whoopee in loud, harsh tones. Give your right name and a fake address."

It was twelve thirty when I registered. The Henderson had an aseptic look. The lobby was the severe inside of a concrete shoebox. I was too tired to give my lines much life when I leaned over the desk and asked the clerk if this was "a pretty good town."

He slid his fingers inside his shirt and scratched himself. "Depends."

"I'm not afraid to spend money."

"That case, you might have yourself a time. Take a look at your room and then come on down to the bar. I'll page you later, Mr. Moran. When I get things set up."

I tipped the bellhop two dollars, to stay in character. After he left I yanked one black hair from my head and wound it around the catch on my suitcase. Then I went downstairs. They gave me time for one drink before the call came. The horse-faced clerk moved in so close he was nearly nibbling on my ear.

"You just go along where the cabbie out the side entrance takes you. Good man. You can trust him." I slipped the clerk a five and went on out.

Three steps from the cab I began to make two and one add up to four. It was the same cab which had been at the end of the alley.

"Hear you want some fun, mister," the cabbie said jovially. I held my breath. He glanced at me but I could see that he didn't recognize me.

"I could do with some."

"There's a place outside of town runs wide open. You ought to like it."

"It's your town. Let's go."

* * *

The music thump shook the silent fields for a hundred yards around. Cars nuzzled up against the clapboard walls like fierce, patient dogs awaiting their masters.

"I'll stick around," he said as I paid him. "No charge. I might pick up a fare going back, and if you don't like it I'll be right here."

The first face I saw when I walked in was the face of Rogah. I stiffened. But the clothes, though of the same order, weren't quite right. And the dimensions were off in a subtle manner. I got it then: Rogah's twin brother. He was busy laughing politely at someone's jokes. I went over to the bar and angled to where I could keep him in the mirror. In a moment a kid in a white jacket, one of the waiters, came in from outside and spoke into the twin's ear. He glanced over at me, then strolled along the booths lining the far wall. A husky citizen with crinkled ears heaved himself out of a booth a bit later and moved in my direction. As smooth as cream.

His voice was slurred and drunken, but his eyes weren't. "I'd say you're a stranger in town, friend."

"That's right."

He lurched against me. I felt the quick cat-light flick of his hands as he made a close and clever check. "Ooops. Sorry, pardner." He belched, lowered his voice. "Lookin' for fun, mister?" I nodded. "You won't find it out here tonight. The joint is dead. Better go back to town. Try Roger's Place."

"Thanks for the tip."

"Don't mention it, friend." He wavered off, but his steps steadied as he neared the booth. The twin was looking into the booth. I saw him get the sign and nod toward the door. The waiter went outside again. I had been looked over, searched, and apparently okayed. I finished my drink, left a quarter tip on the bar, and went back outside. The cab pulled over and the driver opened the door.

"Pretty dead in there tonight, I guess. My mistake. I won't charge you for the haul to the next place. I'm taking you to a sweet little spot called Roger's Place."

He spun out onto the main highway and gunned it toward town. It was beginning to shape up. But I was worried. Roger's

Place would be a bit unhealthy to go back to. A little thinking was in order.

"Roger's Place?" I said slowly. "I've heard that before. Now I remember. A fellow told me about that place."

"Yeah?" he said, caution in his tone.

"I'd forgotten it until now. He told me that if I ever got to this town to go there and ask for a girl called Allana Montrose. He said she hung around there."

"Oh." I detected the relief. "Little blonde?"

"That's what he said."

"She isn't around any more. The word is that she got married." He laughed huskily. "They make good wives, the fella says, those little blondes."

"I'm getting pretty tired. Maybe we'd better wait until to-morrow night."

He slowed down, turned in the seat, and stared back at me. "What's the matter with you? Figure this is a clip operation?"

"Not at all. I said I was tired."

"I know you wise guys. Somebody tried to do you a favor, you figure there's angles on it." He slowed almost to a stop. "I got a notion to bust you one in the chops, Moran."

"You got the name from the desk clerk. I wonder why he told you."

The cab stopped completely. He yanked on the emergency brake. His tone was wheedling. "Look, Mr. Moran, I wouldn't steer you wrong. Be a nice guy and let me take you there for free. If I take you back to the hotel I got to charge you for the trip in. Ten bucks."

"It was only three to go out there."

"It's later now. So you see it would cost you a ten just not to take a look at Roger's Place." His rearview mirror was tilted down. I glanced in it and saw, in the glow of the dashlight, his square hand, the fingers cramped around a lug wrench. I smacked the door handle down with the heel of my hand and dived out. The wrench thudded against the upholstery behind me. I landed on my hands and knees and rolled into the shallow ditch, rolled up onto my feet, and moved back quietly another forty feet before lowering myself into the dry grass.

He stood beside the cab for a long time, staring out into the darkness. Then he jumped behind the wheel and roared toward Endor City. I estimated that we'd gone a half mile. I went back to the first place he'd taken me to—the Club Three—in a fast walk.

Rogah's twin stared hard at me as I strolled in. He moved in beside me at the bar. "Back so soon?" he said softly. His voice was pitched lower than Rogah's.

I nodded. "I was going into town, but I had trouble with the cab driver. He got wise, and I wanted him to take me back to the hotel. He wanted to charge me ten bucks and collect with a lug wrench. So I left him fast."

"Indeed? I can't have my patrons treated that way. Do you have his number?"

"Yes."

"Let me phone the police for you."

"I don't want any trouble."

He stared at me hard. "They'll have a prowl car here in minutes."

"Look," I said. "I would prefer not to talk to any cops. Is that all right with you, or do you want me to type out an outline?"

His eyes hardened a bit. "Oh, I see."

"And if you don't mind, I'll stay right here."

"How hot are you?"

"Like a cucumber. This is the wrong state."

"Then you can stay."

"Thank you so very much."

After a fanfare by the brassy band, the floor show started. It was a dull affair of blue jokes, a raspy emcee, a chorus line with meaty thighs, and a comic juggler—as funny as a case of typhoid. I was glad when it went away. I didn't want to go back to the hotel. And I didn't want to stay in the Club Three. The only other choice was to go for a walk. And that seemed like too much trouble. I stayed.

Beyond the booths was a stairway going up. The entertainers came in from a doorway beyond the bandstand. I wondered what was upstairs.

At five minutes past two, when I had one over the limit, Allana Montrose Garver, in pale yellow slacks and a halter,

317

came down those stairs and slid into the first empty booth, sitting so she could watch the band. Rogah's twin brother, in a crow-flight line, came across the floor and leaned over the booth, his face angry. She leaned forward, and I could see by the shape of her mouth that she was using four-letter words. He tugged on her arm to pull her toward the doorway, and she snatched it free. The crinkly-eared guy moved in and joined the party. He leaned over the booth and she leaned back out of sight. His arm moved quickly and he straightened up. They both stared at her. Once again the twin took her arm. This time she came along without a struggle. There was a red blotch on her jawline, and she staggered as she stood up. They got her onto the stairway and watched her go up.

I went outside as fast as I dared. The upper windows were dark. A light clicked on behind a screen on the third window from the left. Her silhouette crossed between the light and the screen. Her head was bent in dejection, her arms craned back in that odd distortion necessary to untie a halter or unhook a bra. I turned and went back inside.

Shay came in twenty minutes later. He didn't look at me. He had one drink and left. I slid into the car beside him.

"You did good," he said wryly. "A cop is watching for you at the hotel. A little question of deadheading a taxi bill."

"Either that or go to see Rogah or get slugged with a wrench. I liked my way best. How'd you find this place?"

"The taxi man talks fast when you get his arm in the right position. This lovely little city gets warmer and warmer."

"Now," I said, "here's something you didn't expect. Allana Montrose Garver is up there behind the third window from the left. Her light's out now. She came downstairs to watch the fun and games. They urged her to go back up."

He exhaled slowly. "You sure?"

"Positive."

"Then we'd better get her out of there, Robby."

"And then go down and heist some gold from Fort Knox."

"Don't be a defeatist. Anyway, you know the score now."

"Sure. The badger game on a mass-production basis. The well-to-do strangers are screened first at the hotel, then out here. If they pass both inspections, they are funneled to Roger's

Place. There the trained gals take over. With a good screening job they can make a killing on every sucker. The rooms and apartments may be wired for sound. James P. Garver was going to be a routine sucker. They had time to check on him after he registered in and found they had a widower of close to fifty with a half a million bucks. So they put their best talent on him—one Allana Montrose."

"And," he said softly, "it was a change of assignment for her. The blue dress I took comes off in four different ways. She was part of the show here. They had a way to put the pressure on her."

"But what are they planning to do?"

"I have a faint, disturbing idea," he said gently. "And so we go collect Mrs. Garver. If I can park under that window, do you think you could reach the sill?"

"I might. But how do we turn invisible? There's floodlights around here."

"Invisibility is a question of degree."

With the motor barely turning over, he slid the big car ahead. The gravel popped under the tires. He put the car under the window and left the motor running. The lights of the car went out.

"Get out of the car," he said, "and count ten after I go through the door. Then scramble up as fast as you can go. Bust the window if you have to. And get that girl. I have a hunch she'll want to come along. Lower her onto the car top and drop down yourself. Get her in the back on the floor and get behind the wheel and open the other door. Have that motor already turning over and give it one blast on the horn as soon as you've moved it up opposite the door."

He took a last drag on his cigarette, flipped it away, tugged on his belt, and walked to the door. He went inside.

I counted to ten. On the count of nine there was a sound from inside as if a tubful of steel washers and bolts had been thrown through a plate-glass window. The music faltered, lost the beat, and faded off. The window sill came even with my eyes. I broke the window with my elbow and yelled, "Allie Garver! The window! Let's go!"

I found the catch and slid the window up. The shade was

in my way. I tore it off, wiggled through, my stomach across the sill. Her mouth was wide open, and she held the blanket up against the front of her.

"Move!" I said. "We've got about ten seconds!" There was a blue robe on the chair. I threw it at her.

She shrugged into it as I heard the steps pounding up the stairs.

"Unlock the door, Allie!" yelled the voice of Rogah's brother. I unlocked it. It swung inward. He took one step into the room. I jumped full into his chest with both feet. He shot backwards across the narrow hall and down the mouth of the stairway. She was at the window. I swung her up, slid her out feet first, and lowered her by the wrists until her feet touched the car top. She was on the ground by the time I dropped. I felt the metal dent under my heel.

Voices were roaring in anger. She fell full length on the floor as I shoved her into the back. I gunned the motor, yanked the car forward twenty feet until it was opposite the door, reached over, and opened the far door at the same moment as I blew on the horn.

I could see inside. The crinkle-eared gentleman lay on his back on the floor. His mouth looked like a tomato that had fallen on the sidewalk. Shay, his face alight with a vast, animal glee, yanked a man toward him, lifted him by throat and crotch, and hurled him at the others. He staggered as a bottle hit him over the eye, plunged toward the door. They caught him from behind. He ducked forward and threw one of them over his head, turned sideways to avoid a vicious kick in the middle, spun, and punched twice with precision. The last man between him and the door lost heart and stepped aside at the last moment. I had the car thirty feet away before Shay could pull the door shut. He glanced down into the back.

"Nice work, Robby. Nice!"

"Have fun?"

He was breathing heavily. He gingerly touched his forehead. One arm was gone completely from his jacket and his shirt was buttonless. His knuckles were gashed.

"Nothing to clear the head like a good brawl. She was glad to come along, wasn't she?"

"Hurry," Allie said, plaintively. "Please hurry!"

He turned so he could smile at her.

"Why, kitten?"

"They're killing him tonight!"

Shay made the phone calls while I waited in the car with Allie. There was, as I had expected, an unidentified lipstick in the glove compartment. She used the dome light and the rear-vision mirror. She had fallen from the car roof. The right hip of her blue robe was gritty and torn, and her elbow was skinned. She winced as I used the antiseptic in the first-aid kit on it.

Shay came out of the all-night drugstore at a half trot. "Make time, Robby," he said.

As I held the speedometer at ninety and the big car swayed and roared through the night, Allie spoke over the sound of the rush of the wind.

"I've always been a sucker for a pair of dice or a wheel," she said. "I wouldn't have sold my act to Jeff Maydo at Club Three if I'd known it was a bust-out house on the side. I don't know how it happened. They let me keep playing and they took my notes, and all at once I was eleven thousand in hock. That's when things got rough. Jeff's brother, Roger, runs Roger's Place in town, but they work close together. The two of them had what they called a heart-to-heart talk with me. They wanted to put me on the list down at Roger's Place and let me work my way out of the hole with the extra income. I think they knew I'd blow up at that. I'm no prude, but I'm no hooker either. I said no and then Roger, the creepier one, he said that he'd have to have a friend of his operate on my face, just as a lesson to the other deadbeats. I knew he meant it. He said I'd have a hard time getting my new face into any kind of an act except the circus."

"Lovely people," Shay said.

"Oh, the best. We compromised. They said that they'd save me until a prize sucker came along and then, if I did my part, they'd cancel out the debt and give me a five-thousand-dollar bonus. I—I said okay."

"And the sucker turned out to be Jim Garver."

"That's right. Believe me, when I saw him, it wasn't an act when I did my crying at the bar at Roger's Place. Then I took on so many drinks that I don't remember much. Anyway, the next day I got my instructions, and the idea was that I had to marry him. They put the pressure on until I had to say I would. I didn't understand what they wanted to do. They had me in the bag. I married him. You'd never know he had any dough at all. They must have really checked on him, because a month after we were married, I found out about the half million. I used to call Jeff. He'd keep telling me to sit tight, sit tight. So I did. It wasn't bad. I got to like old Jim. He's kind of a sweet guy, and he's a wonderful cook. And I liked it nice and quiet in the country. Then the letter came for me to come in here. I had to leave without anything, and keep anybody from seeing me leave. I guess I managed it all right. I went to the Club Three. It was . . . like a nightmare. I didn't know they were going to kill him until then."

"When did you find out?"

"Yesterday. I guess I haven't got much . . . courage. They made me sign the papers."

"A confession?"

"Sort of. It gives all the details. I can buy it back from them for four hundred thousand dollars, and if I don't they can give it to the cops. They won't be implicated in any way. I haven't any proof against them. I came downstairs tonight hoping I could sneak out and stop it. But they made me go back up again."

"Faster, Robby," Shay said.

We left her with Krimbow and went over to Garver's house. I cut the lights before we came over the last rise. The night was bright enough so that I could see the turnoff to Garver's place. The willows made the shadows heavy. I cut the motor.

A voice at the window said, "Nice and easy, now. Press the palms of your hands against the car roof."

The pencil beam shot through the window. The faint rebound of it picked up the trooper's brass and the gun-muzzle glint.

"Oh, Mr. Pritchard!" the trooper said, recognizing Shay.

"Where's Burns?"

"Right here, Shay," the big trooper captain said softly. "Nothing yet. We've got a net all around the place. The old man's been in bed for hours."

Shay got out on his side. He latched the car door softly. "The tip is good, Ed. The only danger is that when it went wrong on the Endor City end, they might have had a chance to call their man off."

"Jim Garver pays his taxes. He gets protection."

"Have you planted a man in the house?"

"Haven't wanted to take that chance."

Shay was silent. He said, "I've been in there. I know the floor plan. Mind if I work my way close?"

"Better leave it to us, Shay."

An awakened bird made small throaty sounds and subsided. Off in the swamps the peepers shrilled endlessly. Over on the main highway truck motors thrummed. The gray in the east began to be touched with rose. The car, invisible moments before, emerged from the blackness.

I glanced at Shay. He had an odd expression on his face. He had a listening look.

"I'm going to the house," Shay said.

"You gave us the tip, Shay," Burns said with a hint of anger, "but this is my show. When I call it off, which will be soon, you can go take a look."

"Garver has lived alone," Shay said. "He has farmer's habits. The way the house sets, we can see the kitchen windows from here. There's no light on yet. Why?"

"Maybe he was tired."

"And maybe," Shay said, "he's dead tired."

"A mouse couldn't have crept in there since we started covering the place," Burns said impatiently.

"And suppose the mouse was already holed up in there before you circled the place? Or had killed him and gone?"

"I had a trooper phone him and hang up when he answered. The light went on, so he was okay then."

"He should be up by now," Shay insisted.

"Okay, okay," Burns said wearily. "We'll both go take a look."

Nobody stopped me, so I followed along.

The house was as tight as a drum. We circled it. When Burns shined his light into the bedroom window through the screen and began to curse softly and slowly, I looked in.

His bare, gnarled feet hung motionless, six inches from the floor. He wore faded blue-and-white flannel pajamas. The overturned chair was off to his left. The cord was tied to the metal handle of the trap door set into the bedroom ceiling. His thick-knuckled hands hung at his sides, curled as though to grasp a tool. The cheap teeth were clamped into the swollen blue tongue and, all around the dead irises, the muddy whites showed.

Burns kicked a hole in the screen and yanked it out. He started to climb over the sill when Shay yanked him back.

"What the hell are you—"

"If a mouse couldn't sneak in, a mouse couldn't sneak out, either."

Burns stood very still for a moment. "Worth a try," he said.

Twenty minutes later it was broad daylight. When the man broke from cover near the garage, running like a rabbit, Burns drew the .38 special without haste. He held the muzzle high and slowly lowered it, intersecting the line of flight. The sound of the shot was flat in the still morning air. The running man did a complete somersault and rolled to a stop.

"Knee?" Shay asked.

"Hip. It's a safer shot."

He had a sullen, stolid face. He bore the pain without any change of expression.

The doctor worked on him back in the trooper station. Shay, Burns, a few others, and myself stared at him.

"He hasn't got a name," Burns said gently, "and he doesn't know what he was doing on Garver's land."

"The Maydo twins are going to be very unhappy," Shay said. The man's eyes betrayed a sudden surprise, then went blank again. The doctor applied the final strip of tape and stepped back quickly as if he had been touching something dirty.

"We can convince him he ought to talk," Burns said.

"Oh, he'll talk right now," Shay said. "He'll tell us who told him to kill Garver."

"Are you nuts?" the man said hoarsely.

Shay was smoking a cigarette. He nibbled a half moon of thumbnail from his left hand and laid it across the horizontal cigarette, just above the glowing tip. He held it close to the man's face. When the flame touched the nail, it curled and stank.

"Smell that? That's the way a man smells after they kick the switch, friend. He jumps up against the straps three, sometimes four times. A husky kid like you might go for five. It sure makes a terrible stink."

The man on the table swallowed hard.

"Sure," Shay said, almost fondly, "you can keep your mouth shut. You can be a hero. You make your little jumps against the straps and then, before the worms even have a chance to go to work, they'll forget who the hell you were. At least, even when you get life, which you might not get, you get to see sunshine once in a while, a chance to walk around the yard."

The man licked his lips. "You got somebody to write this down?"

Shay and I came out of the restaurant. He climbed into the car as though he had suddenly grown old. The lump on his forehead was an angry purple. He sat woodenly beside me.

"Big callous character," I said.

"Shut up, Robby."

"No, you don't feel these things a bit, do you? A dead old guy and five thousand salted. The five is what counts."

"I told you to shut up!"

"I can't shut up. It's such a shock to me to find out that you become emotionally involved in these shoddy little affairs."

"Why the hell do I keep you around?"

"You mean why do I stay, don't you? Maybe I stay because once every six months I get a look at the vulnerable part of you, Shay, the part that can grieve for strangers. It's the only thing that makes you human. You've got the dough. If you don't want to be hurt, why don't you just sit on your fanny at Sharan Point and add to your collection of statues of the female form. Maybe underneath you're some sort of white knight looking for grails."

He boiled out of the car and raced around the hood. I was out of my side before he could reach the door. The restaurant was a truck stop. They came out fast and stood back to give us room. The right that I blocked numbed my left arm from elbow to fingertips. I put a lot of pent-up irritation into the counter and the shock went all the way down to my heels. It stopped him. His arms sagged, and he shook his head like a great blond bear. In his second rush he got me back against the car. I hurt my knuckles on his head, then opened his mouth with an overhand left while he worked on my middle. He was tearing me apart in the middle. I had to fake out of it, so I sagged. He stepped back. I came up out of the crouch, all my wind gone, and drove ahead behind a straight right. But there wasn't enough left for me to keep my feet. I went down onto my hands and knees at the same moment he dropped onto the gravel. We glared at each other for three seconds, and then he began to grin. In a moment we were laughing at nothing at all.

"Aren't you guys even mad?" a trucker asked in an awed voice.

We were still laughing, idiotically, when I drove between the big stone gateposts of the house at Sharan Point.

The three of us were at the edge of the pool: Shay, Allana, and myself. Shay was face down on the mattress and Allana sat beside me on the edge of the pool, her feet dangling in the water. The wind ruffled the edges of the newspaper, the *Endor City Journal*.

THIRTEEN INDICTED, FOUR ON MURDER CHARGE, IN BLACKMAIL RING ROUNDUP

Allana frowned. "I feel guilty about it all. It doesn't seem right that I not only get off without being charged for anything, but I get all Jim's money."

"You'll have a job getting the insurance," Shay said. "They don't pay off on big policies where there's something strange about it. My guess is that you'll have to bring suit and prove that you were held against your will."

"Maybe I won't even try to collect," Allie said.

Shay propped himself up on one elbow. "Don't be a damn fool! Money won't buy happiness, but it'll make unhappiness a hell of a lot easier to endure. And don't feel guilty. You gave the tip-off that helped in the roundup of the whole dirty crew. God knows how many poor innocents had the pressure put on them and paid and paid and paid. Old Jim just walked into a trap. And it would have been perfect. Young wife leaves. Farmer hangs himself in fit of depression. Young wife returns, full of remorse but loaded with dough. And their hired assassin did such a neat job it would have been next to impossible to prove murder unless he talked."

"I—I've got to live with myself," Allie said. "And right now I don't think much of myself. I'm going away, I guess."

"Worst thing you could do," Shay said firmly. "Stay right in that little house. Face it out. You said you liked the country. Get a woman in to stay with you. The neighbors will never know what really happened, unless you tell them. In a year you'll be a part of the community. Be smart about it. Learn to cook and bake. Take cakes and things around when your neighbors are sick. Cut down on the makeup and don't dress ahead of the fashions, dress just a little bit behind them."

She swirled her feet in the water. "Gee, maybe I could."

"Sure you could," I said.

She giggled. "Allana Montrose! The real name is Alice Mertz. Allie Mertz. Now it's Allie Garver. I'm almost back where I started as far as names go. But not in the money department. There were seven kids. The old man had a candy store in Camden. He made book in the back, and when the horses were rough on the suckers, he'd close up and disappear. He'd come back in a week or two with a bad case of the shakes. Then one time he didn't come back. I was next to the oldest. I quit high school and clerked at the K-Mart. Do you think I can act like a lady, Robby?"

"We'll see that you do."

"A lady," Shay said, "usually has a speaking acquaintance with the arts. We can start right now. Those big windows up there are the windows to my studio. I do figures in clay and cast them myself. If you'd like, we could go up there and I can show you the sort of work I do. Maybe a little later you'd like to pose."

I glared at their backs as they walked toward the house, Allie small and trim beside Shay's hulking build.

I swam two angry lengths and got dressed. They were still in the studio.

It was only three o'clock and only five miles to Bets's house. I walked it.

COPYRIGHT ACKNOWLEDGMENTS

"Dead on the Pin" originally appeared in the Summer 1950 issue of *Mystery Book Magazine*.

"A Trap for the Careless" originally appeared in the March 1950 issue of *Detective Tales*.

ABOUT THE AUTHOR

The author of 20 Travis McGee novels, 600 short stories and nearly 70 books in all, John D. MacDonald is simply one of the world's supreme storytellers. His worldwide best sellers include not only every one of his McGee mysteries, but such blockbusters as *Condominium*.